D0982553

◀▷ALTERNATIVES *is a series under the general editorship of
Eric S. Rabkin, Martin H. Greenberg, and Joseph D. Olander
which has been established to serve the growing critical audience
of science fiction, fantastic fiction, and speculative fiction.*

Other titles from the Eaton Conference are:

Bridges to Science Fiction, edited by George E. Slusser, George R.
Guffey, and Mark Rose, 1980

Bridges to Fantasy, edited by George E. Slusser, Eric S. Rabkin, and
Robert Scholes, 1982

Coordinates: Placing Science Fiction and Fantasy, edited by George
E. Slusser, Eric S. Rabkin, and Robert Scholes, 1983

Shadows of the Magic Lamp: Fantasy and Science Fiction in Film,
edited by George E. Slusser and Eric S. Rabkin, 1985

Hard Science Fiction, edited by George E. Slusser and Eric S.
Rabkin, 1986

Storm Warnings: Science Fiction Confronts the Future, edited by
George E. Slusser, Colin Greenland, and Eric S. Rabkin, 1987

Intersections: Fantasy and Science Fiction, edited by George E.
Slusser and Eric S. Rabkin, 1987

Aliens: The Anthropology of Science Fiction, edited by George E.
Slusser and Eric S. Rabkin, 1987

MINDSCAPES
THE GEOGRAPHIES OF
IMAGINED WORLDS

Edited by
George E. Slusser
and
Eric S. Rabkin

Southern Illinois University Press
Carbondale and Edwardsville

92 91 90 89   4 3 2 1

Library of Congress Cataloging-in-Publication Data

Mindscapes: the geographies of imagined worlds/edited by George E. Slusser
and Eric S. Rabkin.
   p. cm. — (Alternatives)
   Essays presented at the Ninth Annual J. Lloyd Eaton Conference on Science
Fiction and Fantasy Literature held Apr. 10–12, 1987, at the University of
California, Riverside.
   Bibliography: p.
   Includes index.
   ISBN 0-8093-1454-1
   1. Fantastic literature—History and criticism—Congresses.
   2. Science fiction—History and criticism—Congresses.
   3. Geographical myths in literature—Congresses. I. Slusser, George Edgar.
II. Rabkin, Eric S. III. Eaton Conference on Science Fiction and Fantasy
Literature (9th: 1987: University of California, Riverside) IV. Series.
PN3435. M55 1989
809.3'876—dc19   88-18299
                                                        CIP

Contents

Acknowledgments

The essays in this volume represent a selection, chosen by its editors, of those presented at the ninth J. Lloyd Eaton Conference on Science Fiction and Fantasy Literature, held April 10–12, 1987 at the University of California, Riverside. The conference is sponsored by the University Library, the Department of Literatures and Languages, and the College of Humanities and Social Sciences at the University of California, Riverside. The organizers wish to thank University Librarian James Thompson, Dean Henry Snyder, and Donald Daviau, Chair of the Department of Literatures and Languages, for their support. They also wish to thank the following people for their participation: Greg Bear; Paul Alkon; Jean-Marc Lofficier; David Layton; Sheila Finch; and Pascal Ducommun from the Maison d'Ailleurs in Yverdon, Switzerland.

George E. Slusser
Eric S. Rabkin

Introduction:
The Concept of Mindscape

George E. Slusser and Eric S. Rabkin

As if to comment on the idea of mindscape, the speaker in Yeats' "Among School Children" tell us: "Plato thought nature but a spume that plays/Upon a ghostly paradigm of things." Plato in his parable of the cave incriminates the mind's perception of the world. The cave dwellers think they perceive a landscape. At best, however, they only *imagine* it. It is a copy of the world of real essences. And in this sense it is a mindscape, for (as Plato later tells us) the mind, at the higher level of apprehension, needs neither these images nor the material thing but connects directly with the ideal form.

What Yeats implies, though, is that the higher apprehension itself may be endlessly deferred. Natural appearances are a "spume" playing on something equally shadowy—a "ghostly paradigm," not the form but an illustration of that form (*para-deiknymi*—"to show beside"), in other words another mindscape. In the Platonic sense, mindscape is illusion, for the productions of the theater ("seeing place") of the mind, its visual or theoretical landscapes, are ultimately phantasms. In the Yeatsian sense however, the mindscape is not only illusion, but it may be, as illusion, the only reality we can ever know. For if the natural object is a spume, the essential form is equally vaporous. We remain trapped in our mental landscapes because we never cross Plato's divided line and thus can never reach any term—be it "matter," "reality," or "god"—that will allow us to distinguish between illusion and nonillusion. If everything is mindscape then, the concept becomes useless as a means of analysis.

The question arises naturally from our Yeatsian quote: how valid is this idea of mindscape—as spume or paradigm—as the means of

guiding sustained investigation of the role and function of the geographies of imagined worlds, particularly those of fantasy and science
fiction? It is commonly known that these are forms characterized by a
need to create, "build," or otherwise imagine worlds in which individuals or societies, elsewhere or in the future (but always in the not-now),
can act and develop. Every reader knows that building such a world, in
any given text, occupies a great deal of its space and time—so much in
fact that, in many cases, the imaginary world becomes either the
protagonist or antagonist of the tale. But what more do we learn about
the how and why of such world-building by calling its products "mindscapes"? All fictional worlds, to the extent they are "feigned," can be
called mindscapes. The concept, it seems, offers little real help in
making generic distinctions.

But this is precisely the point. The concept of mindscape, by
leading inquiry away from genre issues, frees it to move in areas more
essential to fantasy and science fiction and to contemporary literature
and art in general. Fantasy and science fiction, by being forced into
narrow generic categories, are often separated from issues that they, as
"speculative," world-imagining forms, clearly raise. These forms bring
into acute focus issues that concern all fiction, art, and technology. And
these various issues all address, ultimately, a single fundamental problem: the two realities question that derives, in Western culture, from the
constant need for a relation between mind and some being external to
mind. It is this question that (as Whitehead and others tell us) lies behind
the development of Cartesian investigative science. It is the same
question that impels fantasy and science fiction, as the modern artistic
forms most engaged in "thought experiments," to generate landscapes,
new or extrapolated, that are meant to be realizations of our mental
forms "out there." We witness the mind using its speculative power in
hopes of reaching beyond itself, of turning ghostly paradigms into
solidly realized places—a terrain in which the whole man can act,
interact, and ultimately grow.

Imaginary landscapes proliferate in fantasy and science fiction. But
only by considering these maps and geographies as mindscapes do we
see that this activity—describing and mapping—has been a constant
need of Western art and science from their beginnings. Indeed, the need
to link inner and outer reality, mind and matter, by means of a mindscape
is probably, if we can judge from the inquiries in this volume, a general
human one. For these inquiries range from Hindu myth, early Greek

travel literature, Dante and Pascal, to contemporary neuroscience and structuralism. They engage fantasy and science fiction in a broad, yet at the same time carefully focused, network of comparisons.

The concept of mindscape, in this volume, generates three interactive lines of investigation. (1) It causes examination of its own premises. By asking what underlies and constitutes a mindscape, this group of critics seeks to set theoretical coordinates by which the central relation between mental and nonmental worlds can be defined. (2) It stimulates expanded mapping activity of speculative worlds. These critics are less interested in justifying the idea of mindscape than in using it as a pragmatic device that allows them to posit and thus chart various areas or realms of humankind's projected landscapes; (3) It brings the critic, finally, to examine his or her own methods and goals—theoretical or practical—as mapper of imaginary worlds. For the critic is a creator of imaginary landscapes, in this case mindscapes of mindscapes.

The first set of essays, "Premises," offers a set of questions. Is the mindscape, Poul Anderson asks, a faithful rendering of the natural landscape? Does nature, though it offers both "laws and surprises," ultimately control and shape the boundaries of the fictional mindscape? Or, as Wendy Doniger O'Flaherty suggests, is that same nature finally only organized, hence understood, when it becomes a mindscape, which is here a "mythscape"? But this latter vision, in the context of our debate, poses problems as well. For to O'Flaherty, myth barely "survives" in science fiction; new myths are not being generated, and the forces both of natural entropy and of individual mindscaping appear to erode the cohesive power of the old. Science fiction can, for O'Flaherty, at best look to the past. Yet to Ronald J. Heckelman, however, the basic premise (and structure) of fantasy is the promise. The promise offers a future of mindscapes. These however, as products of the promise, are necessarily double—fulfillment that is always, as promise, deferment of fulfillment. To David Brin, the premise of the science-fiction mindscape is the lie. But again, the process is double. For this must be the "good lie," that which gives fiction its "metaphorical drive" to generate new landscapes (or mythscapes) from that natural world it now names, in interactive fashion, as its corresponding "truth." For Frank McConnell, the premise of the mindscape, the thing that allows people to create them, is the game. The game, by giving rules we agree to abide by, gives us our speculative "playing fields." But these, as O'Flaherty suggests by calling this game myth, can be closed by fiat. George E. Slusser, however, considers these to be seeing fields instead of playing fields. He considers the premise behind the mindscape to be mimesis not poesis. And as means of conveying mindscapes, the science-fiction book, he contends, in both its physical and commercial geography, is an open field.

The second set of essays, "Mapping," presents the variety of realms that, today, serve as the mindscapes of fantasy and science fiction. James Romm discusses fiction that takes us to the edges of our known earth—the distant rather than the other world. Jack G. Voller, on the other hand, considers the use of a whole-earth vision—the Gaia hypothesis—in creating other worlds like Helliconia. Peter Fitting and Michael R. Collings examine the ways in which two ideascapes—utopia and immortality, social and individual perfection—become fictional landscapes. Pascal J. Thomas considers real cities, which as "avenues of power" become mindscapes. Reinhart Lutz looks at the relation between real and mind cities in J. G. Ballard. Joseph D. Miller finally, in his discussion of "neuroscience fiction," looks at the mindscapes of the brain itself—maps of the mapping organ itself.

The final set of essays, "Methods," shows us not the brain but the mind of the critic in the process of mapping itself, examining its own methodological mindscapes. Gary Westfahl shows us how and why we map the science-fiction library, chart its bookscape. Bill Lee contends that, when reading children's literature, we should ask what really happened on Mulberry Street. For by doing so we see how these mindscapes become real landscapes, in the child's mind and in the child's part of our mind. Max P. Belin reveals how, through the device of the "pocket universe," fictional characters can be physically moved in even the most imaginative mindscapes. Williams Lomax treats myth in science fiction not as a premise for mindscapes but as the device that, since the Romantic period, has generated mindscapes and is in a sense their metaphorical "drive." Donald M. Hassler creates a map of the scholar's mind—a Gothic building, or Library of Babel, where a labyrinth of possibilities is "policed" by the rational ability to create mindscapes, models of order.

Ultimately, we have four examples of such policing, short incursions, guided by the concept of mindscape, into the broadest field of literature. Jean-Pierre Barricelli sees Dante's *Paradiso* as the "ultimate mindscape," as meeting the challenge of charting perfection through the imperfect medium of words. Gregory Benford finds that later writers grapple with descriptions of a like mindscape—Pascal's silent, infinite spaces. Gary Kern discovers that revolution, specifically the Russian revolution, offers a mindscape that forces, on the part both of writers and genre critics, constant remappings. David N. Samuelson however, despite initial doubt before the vastness of the science-fiction mindscape, is able to use the concept to construct a typology of subtypes, a map of the genre.

This volume, then, is itself a cartography of mindscapes. For between Barricelli's "ultimate" and Samuelson's science-fiction mindscape, all these investigations are contained and themselves mapped. There is the vertical axis of "transhumanizing" landscapes. The worlds it defines have immediately perceived horizontal limits, as in the eternal geography of the opening lines of *Paradise Lost*. Writers or critics who create mindscapes on this axis do so as a search for meaning—the sacred, "mythic" symbol behind secular, material appearances. They are still (even in works that some call science fiction) justifying the ways of God to man. But what Samuelson and others call science fiction operates not on a Platonic but an Aristotelian axis. Its mindscapes are investigative structures, openly transformational. Here myths do not, as O'Flaherty says, merely "survive." They are generated forms that in turn, and without end, generate other forms. The purpose of the science-fiction mindscape, made clear in the contrastive structure of this volume, is to justify the ways of man, and the human imagination, to God.

Premises

I

Nature: Laws and Surprises
Poul Anderson

I take "mindscapes" to mean imaginary settings—geographies of the mind as used in fiction. As a writer, I would like to discuss the construction of such imaginary settings, with reference, but not exclusive reference, to the role that natural law and scientific discovery play in their making.

I am not a literary critic nor a literary historian. What I can do or have done is make constructs of this kind. I propose to look at imaginative literature from that viewpoint, from the side where the nuts and bolts are. Needless to say, my remarks will be highly personal, and many of my fellow practitioners will probably disagree with some or all of them. Furthermore, for reasons both of time and of ignorance, I will necessarily omit a great deal. If your all-time favorites do not get mentioned, please forgive me.

Let us go straight to the subject. It seems to me that the setting of a story is as important in fiction, any kind of fiction, as it is in real life. There is the social setting, of course, the whole intricate web of human conditions, assumptions, and ways of going about things. Personalities in one kind of society differ in ways that are often very basic from personalities in another kind. But that is a separate large matter.

There is also the physical setting, the geography. Here on Earth, geography has had a powerful, pervasive, often decisive influence on societies. Civilization itself appears to have begun as a set of responses to a set of environmental challenges. Civilizations have had enormously different characters of their own, and much of this appears to be due to environment. For example, Karl A. Wittfogel argued that despotic government originated in the Orient with what he called the hydraulic civilizations, where the work of building and maintaining irrigation systems required organization of mass efforts. A quite similar form of despotism evolved in the Andes, culminating in the empire of the Incas, although there the labor undertaken was of a different kind. Be this as it may, a farmer on arable land and a nomad in the desert not only live differently, they think differently.

There are subtler influences too. For example, being blessed with ample space and resources, Americans developed concepts of individualism and privacy far beyond those of Europe and still more beyond Asia. To this day, from an American viewpoint, they seem lacking, or rudimentary, in Japan. And yet the Japanese have a strong, creative, altogether admirable civilization. It simply is not the same as ours, and much of the difference appears due to the fact that the Japanese have less elbow room than we do.

Environment may work on even deeper levels than this. Oswald Spengler developed a quasi-mystical concept of societies as organisms, each with its unique "soul," its inherent capabilities, drives, limitations, ways of understanding the world. He suggested that these arose from the landscape of the *Urheimat,* the country in which the core society came into being. For instance, the Apollonian Classical society, with its sense of order and boundedness, was born in the narrow valleys of Greece, while Faustian Western society, infinitely ambitious, was born on the great plain and in the great primeval forests of central Europe. This may strike you as pretentious twaddle, and I will agree that it goes far beyond any verifiable facts, but it does have a certain suggestiveness. And in any event, there is little doubt that the settings in which all of us grew up and in which we now live have had much to do with making us the kinds of people we individually are.

Imaginative literature can make this interaction vivid. The author is free to construct radically strange environments, put people there, simplify social factors, and thus show us societies, with the individual persons in them, that are clearly shaped by their settings. An obvious example is the late Frank Herbert's novel *Dune.* He imagined a planet that is one vast desert but nonetheless has been colonized. In the course of generations, human beings there have had to adapt all their institutions and ways of thinking to the harsh conditions around them. One might raise various technical quibbles about the likelihood of this or that feature of Arrakis and its civilization, but there is no disputing that Herbert did a marvelous job of visualizing his world in so much detail that while we are reading *Dune* we are lost in it, utterly convinced.

Apropos desert worlds, here I would like to put in a word on behalf of Edgar Rice Burroughs. He may not have been much when it came to style or characterization, but he knew how to tell a story, and he was also an uncommonly conscientious workman where it came to building his settings. Too many planets in science fiction are lazily made exactly like Earth, except for having neither geography nor history. Burroughs' Mars of the hurtling moons and dead sea bottoms and dying canalside cities has no more to do with astronomy than does Ray Bradbury's Mars. It has serious logical flaws, such as the coexistence of swords and ray guns. But damn it, there is a lot of colorful and coherent stuff to explore on Barsoom! Likewise for Burroughs' Venus and Pellucidar.

I will come back later to the importance of sound construction as the basis for even the highest-flying fantasy. Here let me mention that in science fiction we also have the interesting option of letting our imaginary worlds bring forth intelligent beings of their own, nonhumans. Thereby we can speculate on how not only society but evolution may depend on setting.

As an example, allow me to bring in a novel of my own, *The Man Who Counts*. It is not the greatest thing of its kind ever done—Hal Clement is the unchallenged dean of world builders—but this is a piece of construction that I know from the inside out. We have a planet large but poor in metals, therefore of low density. The result is that gravity at the surface is about the same as on Earth, but the gravitational potential is considerably higher. Therefore, the planet has hung onto more gas than ours has; the atmosphere is a great deal denser. This means that it can support winged, flying creatures more or less the size of a human, hence big enough to have large enough brains for intelligence. In addition, the planet has an axial tilt about like that of Uranus, rotating almost in the plane of its orbit, so that winter means total darkness over an entire hemisphere.

For lack of metals, nowhere on the planet have our flying natives gotten beyond the Stone Age, though some of them have invented some pretty sophisticated things. Even before there was intelligence, their ancestors had to make annual migrations between hemispheres. This conditioned the reproductive pattern and therefore the entire psychology. However, in recent centuries one society among them has partly liberated itself from the requirement by taking to the sea on huge rafts and catamarans. Normally the effort of making the migration works through the glands to release a sexual impulse, so that the migrant majority breed only at one time of year. However, the sailors work hard on their vessels all the time, and therefore are subject to a milder but constant sexual impulse, like humans. You can see how profoundly alien these two kinds of society become to each other, and the potential for conflict between them. Religion, morality, law, custom—everything traces back directly or indirectly to the environment.

Now, of course, the more people advance in technology, the more they make, or even become, their own environment. This is not always for the best. Look at what we are doing to Earth and its biosphere, as well as to ourselves. Not that I want to sound like an ecofreak. Ignorance and conclusion-jumping, not to speak of hysteria, are far too common already. I remember some twenty years ago, following an Apollo mission on television, hearing the commentator solemnly declare that the Moon has no environment.

Having been a farm boy, I harbor no illusions about the so-called simple, natural life. But I do point out that already much of the human race, including those of us here today, spend most of our lives on what amounts to an alien planet. We are surrounded by manmade things, materials and objects and conditions never found in nature.

Science fiction has been looking into this business of man-made and man-modified worlds for a long time. Captain Nemo's *Nautilus* is a classic artificial environment. It also enabled Verne to introduce readers to the wonders and strangeness of the undersea world, long before Cousteau. The spaceship *Enterprise* of "Star Trek" continues this tradition. It was thought out with some care; you can actually buy plans of it. To be sure, I wonder if it has an organizational chart at all. An officer on an aircraft carrier, which is an environment not so unlike that of the *Enterprise,* once told me in some detail how little those entertaining adventures have to do with any real-world naval operations. But never mind.

In a story called "Universe" and its sequel, Robert A. Heinlein did a marvelous job, also in this tradition. Probably many of you know the stories, perhaps under their joint title *Orphans of the Sky.* A giant spaceship, limited to speeds less than that of light, was built to go to Alpha Centauri. Since the voyage would take generations, the interior of the ship must be a self-renewing, fully recycling environment. A mutiny broke out, order collapsed, the survivors degenerated into barbarians and savages. At last nobody even knew they were in a spacecraft. Its interior was their entire universe. They had only dim, mythic traditions about "the Trip," and the more thoughtful among them interpreted these in a mystical or symbolic way. Since the only "gravity" they knew was due to the rotation of the gigantic cylinder they lived in, they also developed some curious notions about the physical nature of things.

Larry Niven's *Ringworld* and its sequel *The Ringworld Engineers* come close to giving us an ultimate artificial environment. You surely recall his astronomically huge annulus spinning around its sun, the inner surface with many times the area of Earth, possessing any number of unique regions and local phenomena. The development of the implications of a concept is one of the very special delights found in science fiction.

To be sure, it also has its special dangers—for the author, at any rate. He or she has thought of the basic idea, worked out the details as logically and thoroughly as possible, described them in a story, and gotten the story into print. Now there it sits, an irresistibly tempting target for anyone who suspects it contains mistakes of either fact or logic. Hal Clement calls this "the game." It is played between author and readers. The author's moves are all made beforehand, with the object of having zero flaws in the construction. (Purely literary quality is something separate.) The fewer scientific nits readers can pick, the higher the author scores.

It is more fun for him or her than it sounds, actually. Learning and argumentation are among the great pleasures of life, after all. This experience can be enlightening, and even profitable. In Niven's case, certain fundamental difficulties with the Ringworld as described were pointed out to him. So he wrote the sequel, mainly to deal with these matters, and it too was a highly successful book.

Heaven knows I have made my own share of blunders. Once I had some characters in a novel waiting out a crisis, meanwhile sipping the best wine in the house, which I specified. Somewhat later I got a letter from a gentleman in France: "Pretty good story, but as for that wine— oh, no, no, monsieur, that was a very bad year for it."

Another time, in a story set in Ice Age Europe, I made mention of a saber-toothed tiger. Another Frenchman, my late friend the paleo-anthropologist François Bordes, told me this was an error. Although sabertooths were still around in America at that time, they were long extinct in Europe. Remarked he: "It seems long-toothed carnivores always survive later in America."

In a lengthy series of stories, all set in the same future universe but covering centuries of time and scores of planets, I have made considerable effort to keep things consistent; but inevitably, on occasion I have heard from some eagle-eyed fan to the effect that something in one story did not jibe with something in another. My standard reply to this has come to be: "Perfect consistency is possible only to God Himself, and a close study of Scripture will show that He doesn't always make it."

But of course, even though we often will fail, the ongoing effort to get things right is of fundamental importance. I really see no excuse for sloppy workmanship. A literary genius of the first rank may, once in a while, erect a splendid edifice on foundations of sand, but literary geniuses of the first rank are few and far between. Frankly, I doubt that any are alive at this moment, in any branch of literature. Whether this is true or not, I do not see that careful construction ever does any harm; and in most cases it makes all the difference.

By this I do not mean that absolute scientific accuracy is a sine qua non of good imaginative literature. For one thing, the scientific picture is always changing. We can still enjoy C. S. Lewis' *Out of the Silent Planet,* for instance, in spite of what our space probes have since told us about Mars. Much of the cosmology in Olaf Stapledon's *The Star Maker* is now obsolete, but his magnificent cosmic vision has lost nothing thereby. Yet I do invite you to note how solidly timbered these works are.

In fact, to name a few other tales, I remember sitting next to Jerry Pournelle at a meeting of the American Association for the Advancement of Science quite a few years ago, when the findings of the Pioneer One mission to Jupiter were first publicly described. Afterward we compared notes and found we had been thinking the same thing. As one revolutionary discovery after another came forth, we had thought: "There goes *Farmer in the Sky.* There goes 'Meeting With Medusa.' There goes 'Desertion.' There goes 'Call Me Joe.' There goes 'Bridge.'" And so on for every memorable story ever written about Jupiter. Regardless, most of them are still remembered, still alive in reprint. Meanwhile, here we have been presented with this whole absolutely wonderful new world to write new stories about.

Besides the mutability of what we knew, or believe we know, there is the fact that often a story requires a nonscientific or counterscientific assumption. Travel faster than light is an obvious example. If ever we find that this is possible after all, we will probably find it within the context of a physics totally different from any that we have any hint of today, a physics in which general relativity is just a special case. The upheaval that that implies is beyond imagination. Nevertheless, when we need to get our hero from star to star in a reasonable time, we go ahead and use "hyperspace" or whatever. This is legitimate enough in itself, provided we respect the body of well-established fact otherwise. Indeed, speculation about the nature and characteristics of, say, hyperspace can form quite an interesting element in the story.

Scientifically preposterous environments are acceptable when really necessary to the author's purpose. Bradbury's Mars comes to mind. Here, though, we border on out-and-out fantasy, about which I would like to say a few words later on.

First I would like to return to planet building. It exemplifies the literary riches to be found in science, riches almost entirely neglected by the so-called mainstream. There are other uses of hard science in science fiction, for instance in creating imaginary biologies, but planet building is closest to our topic of environments. Besides, I have spoken on it and written about it repeatedly in the past, and so can claim to know some aspects of it pretty well. I am by no means alone in this, of course, and can name Greg Bear, Greg Benford, and David Brin, all of them masters of the craft.

This is not the place to repeat myself. I simply want to skim over the subject as a way of showing that when we abide by the findings of science as best we can, we do not constrict ourselves. Rather, we get inspiration, and the tools with which to do a job that inspires and excites readers. I have sometimes called science fiction the tribal bard of science. Like a bard of old singing of the exploits of heroes, science fiction sings of wonders and possibilities revealed to us by our quest for knowledge. This is not the only thing science fiction does, of course, or even what it mostly does, but I do submit that it is something no other literary form ever really gets into.

Let us consider constructing an imaginary planet. First, unless it is wandering free in space, it has a sun. What kind of sun? There is a broad variety of types, not all of them well understood yet. Some are too unstable or otherwise short-lived, some too dim and cold, some too surrounded by lethal radiation, to be plausible hearth fires of life. However, a writer sufficiently imaginative *and* well informed may take this as a challenge, and go on to provide some such star with organisms that look plausible but that are quite alien to anything earthly.

Even with more conservative assumptions, we have to think of just what our sun is like in temperature, color, mass, and so on. Is it a single, a double, a triple star? If it is a multiple, how stable an orbit is a planet likely to have, and of what shape? How does that orbit precess, and otherwise change with time?

From a few assumptions, many consequences flow with mathematical inevitability. For instance, take a star of a given mass. If it is on the main sequence — an astrophysical technicality of great importance — then that mass and the age determine how bright it is, within a fairly narrow range. Set a planet revolving about it at some given mean distance. This immediately determines the length of the year and the irradiation received — in other words, the range of temperatures, the color of light, the basic patterns of climate and weather, and so on for a long list.

The sun is not the only factor in these calculations, of course. The planet itself has a great deal to do with them. Just for openers, its own mass and density tell you about its gravity field, which in turn gives you important clues to what sort of atmosphere and hydrosphere it may have, which in turn begins to give you a little insight into conditions down on the surface.

I have already mentioned rotation, the tilt of the axis, and naturally the rate of spin as crucial factors. They are to at least some degree involved with any satellites the planet may have and now you start getting into things like tides and ocean currents and their effects.

I could go on at great length, but you get the idea. The end product is a set of dry-looking numbers. Few or none of them will get directly into the text of the story. And yet they are vital numbers — nuts and bolts, if you will, but also ribs and foundations, integral to the creation and to whatever sense of reality it may have.

Needless to say, this is the bare beginning. One must go on to geography, life forms, societies, eventually individual characters and their destinies. About these, obviously, there is progressively less and less inevitability, less precision, until in the end we reach those questions of life itself where calculation is impossible and only intuition can take us farther.

Even when it comes to the nuts and bolts, I do not want to get dogmatic. If I have sounded that way, it was mainly in order to save time.

Right down at the elementary level of physics and chemistry, high school stuff, there is an immensity we do not understand. For instance, our ideas about how planets form are still vague and controversial. Lately it has turned out that even if we know all the laws and have all the data, we are often inherently unable to predict how a system will behave. In other words, we do not have to invoke quantum mechanics; we can think entirely in terms of differential equations and Newtonian determinism and still find the course of events unforeseeable in principle. The study of this is known as chaos theory, and I for one consider it to be of fundamental philosophical significance.

Then there are the remaining unknowns in our underlying concepts of the physical universe itself. Earlier I mentioned faster-than-light travel as an impossibility, unless we make such discoveries in the future that we must revise our entire physics. Well, that was another oversimplification. Frank Tipler has shown that a kind of faster-than-light travel, and for that matter a kind of time travel, are logically compatible with general relativity. They still seem to be physically impossible, but perhaps someday we will learn that here and there the conditions are actually met. In any event, this is an enormously exciting development, out of which I got a novel myself. I steal only from the best sources. It illustrates how marvelous, how profoundly meaningful, modern science really is.

By postulating natural phenomena and laws beyond our present-day ken, a number of writers have been enabled to work out some fine, fully conceived, soundly carpentered imaginary environments. Doubtless the foremost creator in this area is Philip José Farmer, who has probably given us more distinct settings than everybody else put together. Just think of the Riverworld stories, with a single river many thousands of miles long, looping all around its planet and running into itself, on whose banks awakens recreated every human being who has ever lived and died. Superscience is allegedly responsible for all this, but we know it is really magical omnipotence and that we are on the boundaries of pure fantasy here. Likewise, Farmer's multitiered "pocket universes," with their own laws of nature to fit the requirements of the story, allow the introduction of actual gods.

This is reminiscent of the grand old Unknown Worlds tradition of fantasy relentlessly and often hilariously following out the logic of its own premises. Thus, in the Harold Shea stories by L. Sprague de Camp and Fletcher Pratt, if there is an infinity of parallel but distinguishable universes, everything one can imagine must exist some-where among them. The hero finds a way to travel to whichever he chooses, but the method does not always work, and even when it does, the place is never quite as he had envisioned it, whether it be the world of Spenser's Faerie Queene or the world of Irish heroic sage. In each of the stories, the plot depends on just these carefully worked out details of the setting.

Before going on to really pure fantasy, I might mention one more extraordinary set of environments generated by what is ostensibly a science-fiction device. The book is *Eye in the Sky*, by the late Philip K. Dick, and the settings, one after another, are the minds of the principal characters. Each comes out as a kind of landscape, special, weird, and yet deeply convincing. C. S. Lewis did something of the kind too, in a short story called "The Shoddy Lands."

But let us continue briefly to pure fantasy. I do not much like that term. It suggests there is some clear-cut boundary with science fiction, which of course there is not. For that matter, I do not think it makes sense to fence off either kind of literature, or any other, from the *soi-disant* mainstream. All fiction is fantasy, in the sense that it deals with unreal people and events. However, we can in a rough fashion mark off those stories that are not obliged in any way to take the facts of science into account. We visualize it, perhaps, as writing that makes more use of the right brain than of the left.

Yet I do not think its settings are any more exempt from the requirments of thought and care than any others. Certainly, to the extent that they use ordinary, nonmagical things, they should make sense. I once wrote an essay on the absurdities that disfigure so much heroic fantasy, such as having the hero swing a fifty-pound broadsword, gallop a horse all day, or go somewhere by sailing ship as steadily as he might if he had a motor. The supernatural element is different, of course. It can be spelled out with complete logic in the Unknown Worlds manner, but it does not have to be. In fact, I would say that except for humorous purposes, it is generally better to leave something mysterious, some questions unanswered and unanswerable. Nevertheless, the author does need to have a good understanding of the magic and the elven folk and the gods and so forth. He or she needs a kind of feel for them, if the reader is to get any.

Turning from generalities to the question of settings, one rather surprising feature appeared to me as soon as I started thinking about this. One would suppose the environments of fantasy are usually more strange, more evocatively set forth, than those of science fiction. But actually, the reverse is the case. Most fantasy stories take place on Earth of the present or the past, or a thinly disguised version of it. In fact, most fantasy characters are rather familiar and prosaic compared to the aliens or the far-future humans of the best science fiction.

Why is this? I suspect the reason is largely what I was discussing earlier, that science fiction draws much of its inspiration from science, from the vast and complex natural world that science reveals, and this always holds far more than the merely human can. As the Psalmist cried a long time ago: "When I consider thy heavens, the work of thy fingers, the moon and the stars, which thou hast ordained; What is man, that thou art mindful of him? and the son of man, that thou visitest him?" (8:3–4). By making an imaginative effort, we can create some wonderful fantasy settings. Such efforts can be cumulative over generations, and this is why nobody has ever bettered the environments of myth and folklore. At least, I do not know of anything that beats the places in the *Odyssey* or those that Sindbad the Sailor visited, nor that entire cosmos the Eddas put in and around the world tree Yggdrasil, nor a number of others. There are some splendid environmental touches in the Chinese classic known as *Journey to the West,* such as a river of quicksand three hundred miles wide, but its authorship is uncertain and it amounts more to a compilation of legends than to an entirely new creation.

It is therefore understandable that modern writers often use ready-made settings with little or no modification. There is our present-day world for a start, and heaven knows, as I remarked earlier, it is quite weird enough. One thinks of H. P. Lovecraft's New England towns or Fritz Leiber's marvelously eerie phantoms rising from the smoke and grime and electricity of great cities.

There used to be remote, unexplored parts of the world, used by such imaginative writers as H. Rider Haggard, but jet aircraft and Earth satellites have taken those away from us. In this connection, I would like to put in a good word for another underrated writer, A. Merritt. His style was no doubt a bit florid, but his lost lands were beautifully visualized and worked out in loving detail.

You can go back into the past in search of a glamorous setting. Consider the current popularity of novels about King Arthur; most of them have a fantasy element. Currently my wife Karen and I are finishing the last volume of a novel that grafts the city Ys of Breton legend onto a late Roman Empire as realistic as a lot of research can make it.

There is also the pseudohistorical setting, in which the world much resembles something like, say, medieval Europe but is not identical. I am not putting down this class. Among other great works, it includes J. R. R. Tolkien's *The Lord of the Rings* and Leiber's tales of Lankhmar.

The author can take over a mythical cosmos and play things out in it. Mark Twain did this in both a witty and touching way for the universe of the Bible, in his stories "Eve's Diary" and "Extract From Captain Stormfield's Visit to Heaven." Later writers have used various pagan mythologies, though some of these have gotten rather overworked.

It is more challenging to create one's own mythology, but also apt to be more rewarding when it does come off. Three cases in point are the Zimiavia books of E. R. Eddison, the Earthsea books of Ursula K. LeGuin, and Tolkien's *The Silmarillion*.

In creating an imaginary world or a new mythology, it helps mightily to have a good ear, a gift for inventing names that are strange and evocative and right. For instance, in Fletcher Pratt's *The Well of the Unicorn,* the battlefield Skogalang sounds as if there just has to be a battle there. In Eddison's *The Worm Ouroboros,* the harshness of the name "Eshgrar Ogo" makes an enemy stronghold seem all the more forbidding. Lord Dunsany was an absolute master of the singing name; —Merimna, Rhistaun, Perdóndaris. So, currently, is Jack Vance— Starbreak Fell, Aerlith, Embelyon, Kaiin.

We are moving on into realms where there is less of the known world and more of the author's sheer imagination. L. Frank Baum's various places in the land of Oz may have their sources, but they are all uniquely his. Still more splendidly themselves are the countries Alice found in *Wonderland* and *Through the Looking-Glass.*

I have mentioned dreamscapes in a science-fiction context. We find a superbly visualized fantasy one in Rudyard Kipling's story "The Brushwood Boy." The trick is much harder to pull off than one might suppose. I once spent a week on quite a short story attempting it, "The Visitor," and still cannot judge the degree of its success or failure.

There is nothing overtly supernatural, but there is everything eerie and dreamlike, in Mervyn Peake's Titus Groan novels. That huge, moldering mansion is as original and unforgettable a setting as I have ever seen.

Dunsany's stories of imaginary realms and of the borderlands of

Faerie are equally haunting, because they are equally well realized. The author *knew* them. By far my favorite Lovecraft story is "The Dream Quest of Unknown Kadath," which is strictly a Dunsany pastiche. Then there are all those lovely little touches elsewhere in Dunsany, like falling off the edge of the world, or opening a manhole, looking down, and seeing the stars.

I could go on, but this is quite enough. At that, I have omitted any number of fine writers and excellent works. I have scarcely touched the vast realm of science fiction and fantasy in languages other than English. But I have not been trying to review the subject, only to discuss, a little bit, one aspect of it, the importance of a good foundation beneath the edifice, a strong skeleton behind the flesh and blood and glamour. In the effort to make such a groundwork, we will find ourselves harking back again and again to the real world, to nature, the infinite permutations of her laws and the endless, enlightening surprises she keeps springing on us.

2

The Survival of Myth in Science Fiction
Wendy Doniger O'Flaherty

Neitzsche said that God was dead. Plato said that myth was dead. I think Nietzsche was right and Plato was wrong: when the gods died—as they did—we were left with an empty myth, with a play in search of characters, a *Hamlet* without Hamlet. And I would like to suggest some ways in which science fiction is and is not qualified to fill that gap, to people the sacred space of myth with characters from outer space.

To begin with, I had better tell you what I think a myth is and is not, and why some science fiction is like what I call a myth, and some is not.

It is impossible to define a myth, but it is cowardly not to try. To begin with, it is useful to list some things that I think a myth is *not*: it is not a lie, or a false statement to be contrasted with truth or reality. This usage, perhaps the most common meaning of myth in casual parlance today, is a desecration that began with Plato and that still leads most of us to call other peoples' stories "myths," while we call our own stories history.

The problem with this usage was brought home to me some years ago when a scholar who happened to be a Hindu reviewed my Penguin Classic, *Hindu Myths*. He began the review by saying, "The title is offensive. To the Hindu, the stories of his sacred literature are as much a reality and are as sacred as are the stories of the miracles of Christ or of Adam and Eve and Noah to the Christians."[1] Other cultures, too, call myths lies. The Malagasy end the recitation of any myth with a traditional tagline: "It is not I who lies; this lie comes from ancient times."[2]

Now let me say what I think a myth is. It is a story that is sacred to and shared by people who regard it as true; it is a story about an event believed to have been composed in the past and taken place in the past, an event that continues to have meaning in the present because it is remembered.

To say that a myth is a sacred story is to say that it must have religious meaning (though it need not be a story about gods). I do not wish to become embroiled here in the genuinely problematic argument surrounding the definition of religion and the sacred, though it will eventually play a part in our evaluation of science fiction as myth. Let me merely say for the moment that the stories that I want to talk about as myths are about the sorts of questions that religions ask, stories about such things as life after death, divine intervention in human lives, transformations, and the creation of the world.

Not only is a myth shared by a group of people; each member of that group believes that the story is anonymous, the creation as well as the possession of the group rather than of an individual. But the assertion that a myth is shared by a group must be carefully qualified. Many myths are the official possessions of a group, officially defined from the inside of the tradition: "This is *our* myth," or even, "We define ourselves as the people who have this myth." But we who are on the outside of other peoples' traditions may see myths in other places; we may find a story in complete isolation from any validating tradition. To say that such a narrative is a myth is to say that it is the *sort* of story that has been shared by other people, even if we do not know that *this* story has been shared by other people.

The assertion that a myth is about an event believed to have taken place in the past and that the story itself is believed to have existed for a long time has further implications, too. Myths are not necessarily archaic holdovers from some primitive time or hand-me-down beliefs that are no longer believable. But, logically speaking, there can be no beginning to the *tradition* of any myth. Tradition is, in Husserl's words, "a forgetting of the origin."[3] "This means, of course, that we can never see a mythmaker in action. If we do, he is not making a myth, but a story, a dance, or a dramatic production, perhaps a ritual. Or are the myth-makers not the originators of the tale, but the almost equally invisible succeeding generations who have passed it along until by some process it became a myth?"[4] Claude Lévi-Strauss has described this paradox.

It is a consequence of the irrational relation between the circumstances of the creation of the myth, which are collective, and the particular manner in which it is experienced by the individual. Myths are anonymous: from the moment they are seen as myths, and whatever their real origins, they exist only as elements embodied in a tradition. When the myth is repeated, the individual listeners are receiving a message that, properly speaking, is coming from nowhere; this is why it is credited with a supernatural origin.[5]

One is, therefore, in danger of committing the basic sin of hubris— masquerading as a god—if one sets out to create a myth.

Myths therefore strike a false note when we try to construct them or legislate them to suit our momentary needs. Myths may be consciously created, as Plato attempted to do, and, in fact, every myth must have been told for the first time by some particular individual. But stories only become myths when they are accepted by people who believe that they express some already perceived truth about the meaning of life.

Myths become true when their reality becomes true, either because the myth inspires people to change the way things are or because it enables people to project their new view of reality over the world, even when that world remains the same.

Is a myth ever told for the first time? The answer to that paradox depends upon one's point of view, from inside or outside the tradition. From inside the tradition, there can never be a first telling of a myth; "No Indian," as A. K. Ramanujan has remarked, "ever hears the *Mahabharata* for the first time." But from outside of the tradition, from the god's-eye view of the scholar, one might call a particular story a myth by recognizing the qualities that it shares with other myths that one knows to have stood the test of time, and guess that this one, too, will be taken up by the tradition. If the guess proves wrong, the story might be regarded in retrospect as a myth stillborn. For though it is true that mythmaking continues to go on in every culture, it is also true that we cannot recognize the myths of our own culture as myths until later on, just as we may be happy at some moment in our lives but too busy being happy to realize it; only later do we think, "How happy we were then." Like a fine brandy or a true aristocrat, a myth needs to *have been* a myth since a time immemorial. Thus, though a myth may indeed be *told* for the first time, by some individual who later becomes anonymous, a myth is never *heard* for the first time by its own culture.

The assertion that a myth must be part of an ancient tradition may seem to involve us in an awkward contradiction when we consider one particular subspecies of myth, what might be called the romantic myth.

For if the classic genre, to which myth belongs, is what is shared and common, the romantic is what is particular and personal. How, then, are we to regard myths (and there are many of them) in which the hero or heroine is the only one who sees the truth, the only one who has the faith and courage to follow his or her particular and personal vision against the often deadly threats of the rest of society? Almost all myths of the foundation of religions are of this sort, including the story of Jesus and the history of Joan of Arc. The answer lies in the transformation through time; what begins as an individual experience of rebellion against society becomes the new charter for a myth of a new society (Christianity, or the Roman Catholicism that canonized Joan in 1926). Only when that transformation has taken place does the romantic story become a classic myth—a shared, traditional myth *about* a personal, antitraditional romanticism.

Finally, the assertion that a myth is a story that many people have come to regard as true must be qualified; it is true not literally but in its implicit meanings. This assertion has serious consequences for the interpretation of myths. It means that one cannot understand the truth of a myth merely by telling it but only by interpreting it. *Autrement dit,* there *is* no myth devoid of interpretation; the choice of the words in which to tell it begins the process of interpretation. In this (as in some, though not all, other qualities), myths are like dreams: there can never be a dream entirely unpolluted by secondary elaboration; to tell the dream—even to *recall* the dream—is to interpret it. As the culture retells the myth over time, it constantly reinterprets it, however much the culture may claim that the myth has been preserved intact. The myth provides a paradigm on which a number of truths may be modeled.

The main characters in many myths are "others," the people who cluster on the borders of what we define as ourselves—our adult, Western, human, mortal nature: they are strangers (non-Westerners), children, animals, and gods. These others are important to us because we see in them not what they are, or at least not just what they are, but what we think *we* are as distinct from them. We define ourselves as not them: we are not gods, because we are not immortal; we are not Hindus (for instance), because we are not immoral or stupid or unscientific; we are not animals, because we are not vicious or irrational; we are not children, because we are mature. Because they are by definition not us, these others populate that territory, at once familiar and strange, within which we search for our answers to certain basic questions of human meaning. When we learn the stories that human beings have told about children, animals, strangers, and gods we may learn things about *them*, but we certainly learn things about *ourselves*.

The gods are the final others, the defining others in all myths; and the gods come among us most often in the form of those other others — children, animals, (lunatics, if we are to include them as fringe members), and strangers. One of Zeus' most important epithets was Xenios — the god of those who come to us as strangers, and whom we must receive as our guests, or risk the wrath of Zeus; for Zeus himself might take the form of a stranger.

Creatures from outer space may, in fact, be qualified to pinch hit for the gods (as Jesus, according to one science-fiction writer, served as god's "designated hitter.").[6] What could be more "other" than a Martian, after all? In the science-fiction films of the fifties, Martians stood in for other sorts of liminal creatures, particularly for Commies. And in a more recent film, *Chariots of the Gods,* the heroes of our own classical myths are the aliens. But the Martians could be gods, too. Mr. Spock, is, of course, the most famous example, but the paradigm began much earlier, in what might be called the Shazam syndrome and the Superman syndrome.[7]

The myth of the incarnate god became reincarnate in the comic-book tale of Superman disguised as Clark Kent or Wonder Woman disguised as Diana Prince;[8] the evil look-alike or shadow double became a clone created by extraterrestrial invaders and body snatchers. The shaman's voyage to the gods became a "Star Trek," and the battle between gods and demons a Star War. The lives of many saints follow the pattern of the Superman syndrome, in which the divinity is concealed and only gradually comes to reveal himself. The god-saint involves himself completely in human life from the very start, but he remains hidden, so that his hagiography is a kind of theological striptease, always hinting at more than is actually seen. In the Hindu stories of Krishna in the *Bhagavata Purana,* for instance, the apparently mortal infant Krishna is revealed in his full divinity to the reader (or listener) but not to the participants in the drama. It is surely significant that Superman comes "from another planet" (one that is named Krypton, the "secret" place). Nor is it ever entirely clear why Superman pretends to be Clark Kent, why he needs a secret identity at all. Excuses are made — he needs to give himself a rest, or to protect himself, or because his superpowers periodically wane — but these answers are not entirely satisfactory. The usual answers offered for the Christian incarnation are generally irrelevant here, but Sanskrit texts attack the same problem, with more success: why does God bother to pretend to be man? One Hindu answer is *lila,* divine playfulness: he does it for the sheer hell of it (or earth of it), to experience the bittersweet complexities and sensualities that are peculiar to the life of mortals on this planet. The usual Hindu answer, however (and more akin to the one given to account for Clark Kent) is that God cannot *help* becoming incarnate, that his divinity wanes. This aspect of the myth, the need to believe that the god really *is* vulnerable, expressed itself in a very interesting way in the Superman myth, in which, after some years during which he was said to be vulnerable to nothing, he was first said to be temporarily vulnerable to green Kryptonite and then, later, potentially fatally vulnerable to golden Kryptonite. Another explanation given by the Hindus for God's decision to take on a mortal identity is that God does it to make it possible for us to see him, that he presents us with a shaded lens of his pseudomortality through which we can view his solar splendor without being blinded. It is so much easier for us to love Clark Kent than to love Superman (though it is not easier, let it be noted, for the woman in the story, Lois Lane).

The other form of hagiography is the Shazam syndrome: the little crippled newsboy, Billy Batson, says "Shazam!" and turns into Captain Marvel. In many folk variants of this motif, the whole emotional point comes from the feeling of transformation and the taking-on of power— the crippled boy *becoming* the superhero. In Indian myths, however, it is the power of knowledge that is revered: the sudden knowledge that the newsboy always *was* Captain Marvel. In the West, Billy Batson becomes transformed into Captain Marvel. In Indian myths about the gods, Captain Marvel pretends to be Billy Batson, and we alone know that his secret identity is God; in other words, the Shazam syndrome is almost entirely eclipsed by the Superman syndrome. But in Indian myths about saints, Billy Batson is, like Western saints, transformed, transfigured.

Are Billy Batson and Superman fit to tie the sandals of Krishna and Christ? Is a Superman comic a myth? To confront this question, we must first ask why science-fiction heroes *should* play those roles, why there is a need for an understudy at all. And I think that Mircea Eliade has told us why.

In *illo tempore,* "archaic" man in the Eliadean prototype lived the myth in a group and in a shared, traditional ritual; this was the classical myth. But now we have lost many of our own rituals, along with our own myths, many of which have come loose from the moorings of their rituals and have lost their power and relevance. For it is difficult to keep the familiar myths that involved us in once familiar, and now lost, rituals.

The rituals of our childhood may still haunt us as adults. But nowadays, some of us may not have received any formal rituals at all as children; or, even if we do have them, we may still go on doing them in the same way that we have always done, but explain them differently if we chance to find new myths. And if we have no childhood rituals at all, or if we have lost them, what will provide the sustaining structure for the new myths that we may find?

Many canonical stories, wrenched out of their ritual context, are no longer taken seriously. The crucifixion and the Eucharist have lost their power as shocking mythic images for many Christians. Once, they still had power: Saint John tells us that many of the disciples would no longer follow Jesus when he told them to eat his flesh,[9] and the early Christian missionaries were, to their acute surprise and discomfort, accused of cannibalism when they attempted to convert so-called primitive tribes among whom cannibalism was known and despised. Nowadays, only chidren, for whom myth is real, experience the shock. Children taking first communion worry about eating Christ: Will the wafer taste bloody? They move behind the symbolism of the wafer to the older, more brutal ritual that it replaced—the actual sacrifice of a lamb.

In traditional societies, rituals often function as a physical, experiential complement to myths, and these rituals do in fact subject the initiate to various shocks—physical torture (fasting, sleeplessness, mutilation), fear, and the symbolic experience of being reborn. This is what the myth is about, the experience for which the myth has prepared not only the initiate but the community that shares vicariously in the ritual. In our world, myth is bereft of ritual and has become a mere story—a religion deprived of a congregation.

The loss of the ritual community for the majority of secularized, demythologized Americans has changed the role of myth in life. Of course there are Jews for whom the Passover Seder is still a living gate to the Jerusalem that was and that will be, and Christians for whom Christ is entirely present in the Eucharist, but they are the exception rather than the rule. For most of us, there is nothing but a lonely mythology of atheism and solipsism; we find it not in churches but in films and science fiction. Myth is now our secular theology. In the face of this degradation of our own symbols, as Eliade would have called it, perhaps it is time to look for our myths somewhere else.

"Archaic man" —the man who lives his myths—is an endangered but not yet extinct species. Eliade writes, "At a certain moment in history—especially in Greece and India but also in Egypt—an elite begins to lose interest in this divine history and arrives (as in Greece) at the point of no longer believing in the *myths* while claiming still to believe in the *Gods*."[10] The problem for us now is quite the reverse: we no longer have the gods, but we still sense the truth of the myths. The Hindus say that the gods lived in another age, the Golden Age; in the present fallen age, the Kali Yuga, the Dark Age, all we have left is the stories of the gods. It is like a certain rather eerie medical phenomenon: after a hand has been cut off, the amputee still feels sensation in the fingers that are no longer there.[11] So too, when the gods are cut off, we still *feel* the amputated divine limb in our myths and in our lives— whenever we come to the place where the gods would be if we still believed in them.

Can science fiction supply us with an artificial limb? The myths of science fiction have in some cases begun to function like "real" myths, to draw to themselves a kind of secular ritual community, through pockets of cult, such as the cults that sprang up around "Star Trek" and the books of J. R. R. Tolkien. In fact, the possibly mythical function of science-fiction literature is supported by a ritual community of sorts— the computer covens that have sprung up all over America, Users' Groups that communicate through modems to form a *communitas*,[12] that discuss such metaphysical questions as the nature of human intelligence and the possibility of life on other planets. But we have no *commitment* to the myths of "Star Trek" or Tolkien; there is no group that will hold us responsible to live in a certain way because of these myths.[13] Our suspension of disbelief when we read such stories is only momentary; it has no lasting effect upon us.

For these are ways in which these cults, and their myths, differ from myths as I have defined them: as stories that are sacred to and shared by people who regard them as true, as stories believed to have been composed in the past about events in the past. It will become immediately apparent that most science fiction fails to satisfy several of these criteria: it is not shared by an organized cult, it is not regarded as true. It is not about the past, but about the future, nor does the story itself come from the past. It does not have an anonymous author. Above all, it is not sacred. We have no *commitments* to the myths of "Star Trek" or Tolkien; there is no group who will hold us responsible to live in a certain way because of these myths.

Yet there are interesting counter instances to almost all of these objections. For cult, there are the cults of "Star Trek." For truth, it could be asserted that although science-fiction stories are not true in the more particular sense that traditional myths are regarded as true, science fiction, like all fiction, may present human truths in a metaphorical form. And though many myths are indeed set in the past, there are also myths about the future, millennial myths and eschatological myths, for instance; moreover, as Teilhard de Chardin has pointed out, even the myth of Eden and the myth of the Golden Age are myths not about the past but about the future. As to anonymity, all myths *do* have authors, of course, and it might be argued that we must simply wait for a while until more of the authors of our science fiction recede into anonymity as their creations are absorbed by the culture at large (a prospect that those of you planning to retire on your residuals may regard with mixed feelings).

We are left, therefore, with a rather subtler set of problems, in the definition of the sacred and the enduring classic. These are questions of substance and of quality. Can religious questions be raised outside of a religious tradition? Will science fiction last like traditional myths? Let us tackle the second question first, the question of the *quality* of traditional myths and science fiction.

Science-fiction stories that deal with mythical themes are one particular instance, or manifestation, of certain great themes that appear in all cultures, or at least in many cultures. It may be that the universal truth, what Jung called the archetype, is what speaks to us out of a science-fiction story, but it is also true that what attracts us and fascinates us is not the archetype but the particular detail of that particular version of the archetype, what Jung called the manifestation. The archetype itself is so simple as to seem trite or obvious when we try to isolate it; archetypes are "what children learn when they tediously reiterate nursery rhymes, intone tiresome chants, and make visual images that only fond parents delight in, psychiatrists regard as interesting, and Wordsworthian Romantics find profound."[14]

It is, moreover, very difficult to isolate a pure archetype, or to see it when we have it. Like the Invisible Man, who could only be seen when he was wrapped in bandages or dressed in a hat and a coat, the archetype can only be "seen" when it is enveloped in the bandages that each cultural manifestation swathes it in. Myths are necessarily transmitted by language. So, too, archetypes are necessarily transmitted by manifestations. One might define an archetypal myth as what a story would be like if no one told it; but we cannot hear such a story. Moreover, the details lend the myths their verisimilitude. We believe myths because we see our own details in them; and, finally, the details lend the myths their beauty, and that, too, persuades us of their truth.

But it is in the very nature of archetypes to attract these manifestational meanings to themselves. These are the banal details that make the myth real and also our own. On the other hand, the manifestation itself may sometimes be understood only in terms of the archetype. Archetypes may or may not have inherent meanings, but they *find* meanings; they provide a blank check on which people cannot help writing meaning, a mold into which people are irresistibly driven to pour meaning; an archetype is a vacuum into which meaning keeps falling, which meaninglessness abhors.

The myth, the core of meaning, survives to some extent even without language; the myth can be re-created again and again, reinflated like a collapsible balloon. The Trojan horse and the myth of Eden survive as myths, free-floating without words; the nonmythological classic, by contrast, survives only in language, despite the sustaining nature of the ancient core of truth that it embodies. As Claude Lévi-Strauss has remarked, where poetry may be lost in translation, "the mythical value of myth remains preserved through the worst translation."[15] Eliade has demonstrated how myths may become degraded, how they may lose their power and even, on an overt level, their meaning, though they always retain their intrinsic value, however much this may be disguised or forgotten.[16] Myths can be impervious to kitsch. They survive in a rag-gab of tawdry modern avatars: in India, Hindi films, complete with rock and roll choruses, depict the battles of gods and demons, and the Indian version of our own Classic Comics (*Amar Chitra Katha,* "Immortal Colorful Stories") present the ancient Hindu classics in a strangely Westernized but still recognizably Indian form. Though these comics are ostensibly written for children, many adults read them; and for some, they provide the only remaining source of the classical mythology of India.

And there are other, even more unlikely media in which the myths live on. Hindus who may not know from the *Rig Veda* or the *Mahabharata* the story of the aged sage Chyavana, who was rejuvenated so

that he could marry the beautiful young Sukanya,[17] may know the story
from another source: newspaper advertisements for a patent medicine
called Chyavana Prasa. The ad begins with a Sanskrit verse, which can
be translated thus: "This is the story of the Chyavana Food which the
sage Chyavana ate; even though he was worn out with old age, he
became a joy to the eyes of women." The verse is followed by a series of
cartoon illustrations with descriptions below them, in English, telling
the story of Chyavana, and ending: "The pleased twins [the Ashvins,
divine physicians] asked Sukanya what boon she wanted. She replied
that her husband should retain his youth perpetually. The twins prescribed a rejuvenating tonic containing Amia [gooseberry], later on
known as 'Chyavana-Prasa.' Thus Chyavana was blessed with the special yoga and having consumed it he became a full-grown youth pleasing
to the eyes of the women. And as the yoga was consumed by Chyavana it
came to be known as Chyavana-Prasa [Chyavana Food]. Kottakkal Arya
Vaidya Sala manufactures this potent tonic prescribed by the divine
physicians in the traditional and conventional manner with scrupulous
care and attention."

Thus the myth of Chyavana lives on, bloodied but unbowed, even in
an advertisement for a dubious rejuvenating medicine. And it is Western
travelers, not Hindu worshippers, who are shocked by the apparent
blasphemy in the so-called Rishikesh Zoo, where the gods are kept by
the dozens in little plastic cages, embodied in mannequins that move like
display-window models. Present-day Hindus devote themselves indiscriminately to some of the most beautiful sacred images ever created
(such as the carvings on medieval temples still in use) and to garish,
hideous, mass-produced idols and "calender art" icons; to the devout
Hindu, the archetype is preserved equally well in a Chola bronze or a
plastic Kewpie doll. In one sense, this is a good thing; if myth could not
survive kitsch, some myths would never have survived at all. Indeed,
some myths begin as kitsch and eventually become classics; taste, after
all, is often dependent on context, and new stories *do* sometimes become
genuine myths.

Nor is mythological kitsch limited to Hinduism; it is widespread in
the West, particularly but not only in Catholicism, which places in the
niches of great Gothic cathedrals plasters of Paris images garishly
painted like the modern Hindu idols; and these tawdry, funky icons are
still infused with great power. Indeed, where Protestantism is primarily
doctrinal (orthodox) and aesthetic, and the children are expected to

behave themselves in church, Protestants make what David Tracy has called the fatal error of thinking that religion is ethics with a few stories; Catholicism, by contrast, tolerates noisy children in church and is orthoprax, realizing, in Tracy's formulation, that religion is an aesthetic, though with some unfortunate kitsch elements. The symbolism of the Eucharist survives no matter whether the cup holds wine or grape juice or South African sherry. When the archetype is truly powerful, it does not need a powerful manifestation to convey it.

But some archetypes do not survive some kitsch manifestations. As J. M. Cameron remarked:

> I set beside "I come to the garden alone" the noble hymns of Isaac Watts and Charles Wesley and the former simply falls away from the world of authentic religious discourse, as do the holy pictures that used to—perhaps still do—punctuate the lives of Catholic children. I think kitsch presents us with a serious theological problem and stands, far beyond the formal bounds of theology, for something amiss in our culture, as, for example, when well-washed fat babies or puppy dogs presented on the cinema screen evoke disproportionate cries of delight. Kitsch is a form of lying, and religious kitsch lies about what is, for the believer, the deepest reality.[18]

Outside the realm of organized religion, too, myths may survive in kitsch transformation. In the film *Never on Sunday,* a whore in Piraeus retold all the Greek tragedies to her customers, but she always gave them a happy ending; everyone went to the seashore. And in America, a company called "Impulse" markets small capsules called "Instant Mythology" that are literally *reduced* (and reinflatable) myths: "Drop capsule in warm/hot water and watch mythological characters appear! Fun—educational—non-toxic. For ages 5 years and above. Not to be taken internally. Capsules contain: centaur, dragon, Pegasus, unicorn, or mermaid." Some archetypes seem to be able to exert their power in almost *any* manifestation.

But myth, too, is carried on language as perfume is carried on a wind. Mary Douglas has challenged Lévi-Strauss's assertion that myth, like poetry, cannot be translated after all.[19] When a myth is translated, its classic component is somehow tarnished; this part of the Bible is invisibly lost to those who cannot read Hebrew or Greek and was visibly lost to many people when the King James translation was discarded. The belief that the translation *is* the archetype is reflected in the thinking of the gentleman who remarked, "If the King James Bible was good enough for Jesus, it's good enough for me."

For even a myth needs *some* linguistic detail, some spark of originality, to ignite it for us; it must evenutally be reinflated, retumesced, and if the language that attempts to do so is inadequate and unexciting, the myth will not come to life again. This being so, Lévi-Strauss' assertion of the independence of myth from language is true only of a certain sort of myth, and then only partially true. The myth itself needs to have some vehicle in which to survive between its incarnations. The reinflatable balloon must always leave behind its rubber shell even when it is emptied of meaning and language. Heisenberg is said to have remarked that if he had never lived, someone else would have discovered the principle of indeterminancy, but if Beethoven had never lived, no one else would have written his symphonies. This may or may not be a valid statement about the difference between science and art; but it is certainly true that, though *anyone* can discover an archetype, only an artist can produce a great manifestation.

Science-fiction stories and myths may sometimes appear to be about the same archetypal human problems; but science-fiction stories do not ask the same questions about these problems that myths ask, nor do they ask them in the same words. In science fiction, we may recognize certain mythical archetypes, such as the god in disguise, the invasion from outer space (heaven), doomsday, the war between good and evil; and much of the best science fiction deals with great cosmic and ethical questions, and even resorts to a transcendent element at times. But the manifestation is inevitably colored by *science,* the new ingredient in this new genre, and it may be argued that scientific strictures cannot support the heavy load of religious values. If one has merely the *forms* of religious narrative, but not the doctrinal content, is the myth still a myth?

The archetypal survival of such stuff as science-fiction stories are made on was delightfully analysed by George Orwell in his essay on Rudyard Kipling.[20] Orwell argues that Kipling is "a good bad poet": "Most of Kipling's verse is so horribly vulgar that it gives one the same sensation as one gets from watching a third-rate music-hall performer recite 'The Pigtail of Wu Fang Fu' with the purple limelight on his face, *and yet* there is much of it that is capable of giving pleasure to people who know what poetry means. . . . Kipling is almost a shameful pleasure, like the taste for cheap sweets that some people secretly carry into middlelife. But even with his best passages one has the same sense of being seduced by something spurious, and yet unquestionably seduced." This, too, is the appeal of a poet like Walt Whitman, who was once described as the literary equivalent of a Hawaiian shirt.

> What is "good" about this bad poetry?
> A good bad poem is a graceful monument to the obvious. It records in memorable form . . . some emotion which very nearly every human being can share. . . . However sentimental it may be, its sentiment is "true" sentiment in the sense that you are bound to find yourself thinking the thought it expresses sooner or later, and then, if you happen to know the poem, it will come back into your mind and seem better than it did before.[21]

This is not at all a bad description of the kitsch charm of myth, of the depths (or, perhaps, the breadth) to which the language of myth can sink while the myth still bobs along blithely above it.

To this degree, even *bad* science fiction may serve the function of the classical myths. And there is another way in which this function is reinforced. Science fiction has mythic effect not merely on the page but, even more powerfully, on the screen. In traditional societies, drama built upon archetypes functions as the enactment of a myth, that is, as a ritual. In our day, drama (or film) often takes the place of the communal ritual that was a frequent (though certainly not inevitable) complement to the traditional myth. The theatre in the broadest sense of the term (encompassing opera, ballet, film, and the *soi-disant* legitimate theatre) is nowadays the main sacrificial arena in which myths are reenacted.

Hindi films function like myths for Indian society. Sudhir Kakar has interpreted popular Hindi film as "a collective fantasy containing unconscious material and hidden wishes of a vast number of people . . . Hindi films may be unreal in a rational sense, but they are certainly not untrue. . . . [They] are modern versions of certain old and familiar myths."[22] This is more literally true of Indian films than it is even of our own films, for Hindi films are often rather lurid reenactments of the sacred stories, with tacky but spectacular celestial special effects, dry ice simulating the clouds of heaven, and matinee idols playing the parts of the gods. In India, even where people do still tell the old stories in the traditional way, films begin to usurp the position of myths. It is not, therefore, as one might have thought on the basis of the Western situation, that myths flee from their classical shrines when these crash down under the assault of modern, materialistic canons, and find refuge in the cool, dark halls of cinema. No, even when the temple is still standing, the myths find another, supplementary home in the medium of film. Old archetypes never die; they just lurk quietly in the background of the sets of Hindi films.

Indeed, where mythological themes are culturally so omnipresent as they are in India, it is particularly easy for a sophisticated film-maker to select such themes as elements in a film, and to feel confident that they will magnify the image that he wishes to project, literally, to a mass audience. One film, *Santoshi Ma,* told the story of the establishing of the cult of a goddess named Santoshi Ma; the film became so popular that the cult of the goddess spread throughout India; people would offer traditional objects of worship (garlands, coconuts, and so forth) to the screen at the front of the cinema hall.

Science-fiction movies, and science-fiction programs on television to an even greater extent, often appear as serials. Again, the most stunning example of the creation of a new mythology in our day was the television serial "Star Trek." The serial is a Western parallel to the never-ending chain of stories that is taken up, link by link, night after night, by village storytellers in traditional cultures. When Dickens published his novels in serial form, the English-speaking world would hang upon the next installment; it is said that when a ship docked in New York carrying the latest chapters of *The Old Curiosity Shop,* the crowd on shore cried out to those on board, "Is little Nell dead?"[23] A contemporary American serial novel has been likened to Dickens' serials by a writer who commented, "The experience of a serial is that of a common, contained world. It is a shared event. Everyone is reading or watching the same episode within the same time frame. No one can skip ahead until the next installment comes out. And that level of containment is important, for it provides the serial with its basic subtext: we are all in this together."[24] This is not a bad definition of a myth.

And another great modern classic of science fiction has supplied us with a wonderful metaphor to explain just how it is that "we are all in this together." At the end of Ray Bradbury's *Fahrenheit 451,* when all the books in the world have been burnt, a group of people gather around a campfire; each of them has memorized one of the classics and so thoroughly internalized it that when they are introduced to one another one can say, "Hello. I am Plato's *Republic,* " while a man named Harris in Youngstown is the Book of Ecclesiastes.[25] This form of assimilation is very rare in our day; not many people do memorize, or even internalize, a whole book. But in ancient India, people really did memorize entire books of the Vedas and became known as the living incarnation of one particular school or branch *(shakha)* of the Vedic tree.

This is one of two complementary types of eclecticism that enable us to assimilate great classics. Through the first of these methods, that we have just seen, any one of us can make any single classic our own. But just as an entire classic can become part of any one of us, so too, parts of the classics have become part of all of us. There is the old story of the woman who went to see *Hamlet* for the first time, and afterwards was asked what she thought of it. "It was quite good," she said, "but it did have an awful lot of quotations in it." Many of the people who tell us that brevity is the soul of wit or that there is method in our madness do not know that they are quoting *Hamlet*. A more poignant instance of this process was noted by Hannah Arendt, who told of a concentration camp in World War II in which people got together and each tried to remember as much of Homer as he or she could, to piece together all the pieces that they knew. They did not manage to reconstruct all of Homer; and so their work did not keep Homer going, as it were (the way the whole work was preserved in the fiction of *Fahrenheit 451*); but they did it because it "kept *them* going," she said.[26] The pieces of Homer in them were things that they clung to when all the rest of their civilization was destroyed.

Thus a classic may be preserved either though an individual eclecticism (the *Fahrenheit 451* model, each classic going into a fragment of society, a person), or through a cultural eclecticism (the *Hamlet* quotation model, the fragmentation of the classics, each piece going into all of us, into society as a whole). Claude Lévi-Strauss has used a similar metaphor to explain the process by which mythology fragments an inexpressible truth and then transmits the separate fragments, which the hearers must know as a group in order to understand the message as a whole.[27]

Science fiction provides a body of literature in which great mythological classics take refuge in a demythologized age. It is one of the few places in which we continue to create superheroes, the last survivals in a kitsch mythology of atheism. Science fiction seems to be the only form of adult literature that can handle mythology with panache. Other kinds of novels with mythological themes are almost invariably second-rate: Gore Vidal's *Creation,* Michener's *The Source,* and so forth. These are instances of Eliade's degraded symbols. But in Mary Shelley's *Frankenstein* or Robert Louis Stevenson's *The Strange Case of Dr. Jekyll and Mr.*

Hyde, and nowadays in writers like Ray Bradbury and Ursula LeGuin, mythology takes on a new form, devoid of a formal, communal, ritual religious element, but not necessarily devoid of an individual, personal, mythical religious element. Such works of literature, like the great science-fiction films, present a genuine instance of that ephemeral swinging door through which myth and reality eternally pass one another, like star-ships in the night.

Notes

1. K. S. Narayana Rao, in *Books Abroad* (1976), 474.

2. I am grateful to David Graeber, a student of mine, for this reference.

3. Cited by Bernard Faure, "Intertextuality, Relics, and Dreams: The Avatar of a Tradition" (Paper presented at the Univ. of Chicago, Mar. 24, 1986).

4. Mary Barnard, *The Myth-Makers* (Athens: Ohio Univ. Press, 1966), 183.

5. Claude Lévi-Strauss, *The Raw and the Cooked: Introduction to a Science for Mythology,* trans. John Weightman & Doreen Weightman (Chicago: Univ. of Chicago Press, 1969), 18.

6. Stanley Elkin, *The Living End* (New York: Dutton, 1980), 152.

7. See my *Women, Androgens, and Other Mythical Beasts* (Chicago: Univ. of Chicago Press, 1980), 68–70.

8. Ibid., ch. 3, "The Shazam Syndrome."

9. John 6:52–56.

10. Mircea Eliade, *Myth and Reality* (New York: Harper & Row, 1963), 111.

11. A. K. Ramanujan used this phenomenon as a metaphor in his poem "Prayers to Lord Murughan" in *Relations* (Oxford: Oxford Univ. Press, 1971), 60.

12. It is, I think, fitting that the idea of the ritual status of the Users' Groups came to me from Frederick Turner (personal communication, May 9, 1987), whose father, Victor, made famous the concept of *communitas.*

13. As my son Michael remarked, you can put down a Tolkien book and go and do the laundry.

14. Leonard B. Meyer, "Creation, Archetypes, and Style Change," *Daedalus* (Spring 1980), 181.

15. Claude Lévi-Strauss, *Structural Anthropology* (New York: Basic Books, 1963), 210.

16. Mircea Eliade, *Patterns of Comparative Religion* (New York: New American Library, 1963), 431–34.

17. *Rig Veda* 8.1.30–34; *Mahabharata* 3.122–23; see my *Siva: The Erotic Ascetic* (Oxford: Oxford University Press, 1973), 57–61.

18. *New York Review of Books,* May 29, 1986.

19. Mary Douglas, "The Meaning of Myth, with Special Reference to 'La

Geste d'Asdiwal,'" in Edmund Leach, ed., *The Structural Study of Myth and Totemism* (London: Tavistock, 1967), 49–70.

20. George Orwell, "Rudyard Kipling, a review of T. S. Eliot's *A Choice of Kipling's Verse,*" in *A Collection of Essays* (New York: Random House, 1954), 135.

21. Ibid., 137.

22. Sudhir Kakar, "The Ties that Bind: Family Relationships in the Mythology of the Hindi Cinema," *India International Quarterly* 8, no. 1 (Mar. 1980), 11–20.

23. Cited by Marcia Froelke Coburn, in *Chicago* magazine (Apr. 1985), 130.

24. Ibid.

25. Ray Bradbury, *Fahrenheit 451* (New York: Ballantine, 1953), 163–65.

26. Hannah Arendt told this to David Grene, and he told it to me. This is its oral provenance to me; it may be recorded somewhere in print.

27. Lévi-Strauss, *The Raw and the Cooked,* 5; Edmund Leach, *Lévi-Strauss* (London: Fontana, 1970), 59.

3
"The Swelling Act":
The Psychoanalytic Geography of Fantasy
Ronald J. Heckelman

Kent: Is this the promis'd end?
Edgar: Or image of that horror?
> —William Shakespeare, *King Lear,* 5.3.264–65

It was here that *promises* were made; it was here that a memory had to be *made* for those who promised; it is here, one suspects, that we shall find a great deal of severity, cruelty, and pain.
> —Friedrich Nietzsche, *On the Genealogy of Morals,* 2nd essay, Sec. 5[1]

In Michael Crichton's *Sphere,*[2] a team of American scientists is secretly assembled to investigate a gigantic spacecraft discovered deep below the surface of the Pacific. After the investigators determine that the coral-encrusted craft has lain undisturbed for at least three hundred and possibly as many as five thousand years, they discover further, much to their dismay, that the ship's instrument panels are labeled with identifying English phrases (e.g., Emergency Lock). They deduce that the spacecraft must have originated in the future and was perhaps "intended to *go through* a black hole" in space (139). Even after painstaking exploration and analysis, the mysterious ship remains essentially uncanny. It appears, after all, to be from the team's own future, and yet it is incontrovertibly alien and Other. The same holds true for the perfect, mirrorlike, and initially impenetrable sphere, about thirty feet in diameter, which the team discovers inside the deserted mother ship. What could it be? Was it constructed in transit by the now mysteriously absent crew? Or was it somehow picked up—or even more disturbing—

covertly deposited aboard as the ship moved through space? Nobody can be sure. Does it promise or threaten? It seems at once familiar ("like an oversized ball bearing," 108) and yet strange. It appears metallic and inert, but it could just as well be organic and alive. Is it solid or empty? A container? A trophy? A message? A gift? An explosive? An *object d'art?* A vehicle of transcendence, or a trap? The pattern of grooves that marks the sphere's surface seems neither geometric nor amorphous (108). Crichton's novel revolves around the efforts of the scientists to fathom the meaning of the object. The story is not so much about the sphere itself, however, as about the interpretive struggles of the team. The spherical image comes to represent the interanimating promise and threat, at once utopian and dystopian, of the human imagination. It also symbolizes an ambivalent desire both to transcend time and yet to remain a willing captive of history and language, without which there would be nothing to resist, to overcome.

As Leonardo da Vinci showed long ago in his famous sketch of the man with outstretched arms and legs forming the center and spokes of an enclosing circle, desire is simultaneously enabling and disabling. After much travail, violence, and death, the remaining members of the team, two men and a woman, all of whom have visited the inside of the sphere, finally realize that it empowers them to turn their unconscious thoughts into stark reality: "If you think positive thoughts you get delicious shrimp for dinner. If you think negative thoughts, you get monsters trying to kill you. Same process, just a matter of content" (283). This explains how and why the team has unconsciously (imaginatively) though quite literally been destroying itself throughout the investigation. Figuratively speaking, they are the sphere, in all its sublime and beautiful—its godlike—power. In the end the three surviving scientists agree that the only way to preserve the sphere from those who would misuse it is to subvert it from within. They hatch a plan ironically to conceal its existence by consciously willing to forget about it, that is they attempt to repress (with the help of the sphere!) their memories of its terrible promise and threat. Of course, their memories of the past also amount to their recollections of the future. They construct an alternative, an-other narrative, which explains to the Navy (and to themselves) the violence that has recently occurred below the sea. Paradoxically, they use their imaginations not just to conceal but to reveal, to re-cover that which they believe poses a supreme promise and threat, the power indiscriminately to transform dreams and desires into concrete form.

The story concludes with this redemptive act of aggressive repression, of apocalyptic forgetting and knowing. In the end it is only more narrative that can re-cover narrative. The only way to preserve the secret of the sphere—a totalizing space that both contains and is itself somehow contained—is to leave it buried in the sea, in history, in language, and in the psyche. However, the final scene presents us with the revelation that the surviving female (the archetypal figure of creativity) has been either unable or unwilling to make the sacrifice. The struggle of the self with itself is not resolved. The reader is left to ponder the promise and threat of this situation.

Writing about the nature of literary fantasy, Harold Bloom[3] argues the following:

> *Fantasy, as a belated version of romance, promises an absolute freedom from belatedness, from the anxieties of literary influence and origination, yet this promise is shadowed always by a psychic over-determination in the form itself of fantasy, that puts the stance of freedom into severe question.* What promises to be the least anxious of literary modes becomes much the most anxious. (italicized in the original, 6)

What links the idea of fantasy to the figure of promising in *Sphere*, as well as in Bloom's argument, is the notion that a promise at one and the same moment empowers the construction of a future as it signifies rootedness in the past. It perversely inaugurates and subverts possibilities at the same time. It seems, moreover, to be a necessary form of self-aggrandizement and aggression. Can we imagine not making or receiving promises? Seen this way, promising is seductively manipulative and even narcissistic. As verbal play, a promise is ludic—a celebration of desire—as well as agonistic—a struggle with an Other (i.e., a hearer, oneself, time). In the balance of this essay I propose to explore the figurative shape and/or geography of fantasy by elaborating a dual phenomenology and rhetoric of the act of promising as a "lived" verbal and cultural relation.[4] How is it that promising, like fantasy, amounts to an ambiguous representation and subversion of desire?

Consider the images of swelling, growth, and engorgement attached to promising in the following lines from Shakespeare. At one point Hamlet exclaims to Claudius, "I eat the air, promise-cramm'd" (3.2.94).[5] In *King John*, Queen Elinor uses the metaphor of "a mighty fruit" (2.1.473) to portray the dual promise and threat that potential rivals represent to her son's political regime. Antony in *Antony and*

Cleopatra refers both to the Nile and to his own ambition as swellings: "The higher Nilus swells, / The more it promises; as it ebbs, the seedsman / Upon the slime and ooze scatters his grain, / And shortly comes the harvest" (2.7.20–23). Here the promise is both an overflowing, an uncontrolled exuberance, an excess, as well as a compressed bundle of potential energy that will reveal itself in another form as time passes.[6] In 1.2.27–28 of *Macbeth,* the Captain's account of the raging storm is, so to speak, pregnant with irony: "So from that spring whence comfort seem'd to come / Discomfort swells." The overflowing banks of the stream re-present Macbeth's overweening desire for power; or shall we say, the swollen stream prefigures this desire. A bit later, the third witch speaks of her magic spell as all "wound up" (1.3.37), that is, ready to be unwound, exhausted, or used up in the form of the fantastic narrative of Macbeth's rise and consequent fall. Most telling are the following lines of Banquo, as he speaks to Macbeth about the hags' prophecy that Macbeth "shalt be King":

> Good sir, why do you start and seem to fear
> Things that do sound so fair?—I' th' name of truth,
> Are ye fantastical, or that indeed
> Which outwardly ye show? My noble partner
> You greet with present grace and great prediction
> Of noble having and of royal hope,
> That he seems rapt withal; to me you speak not.
> If you can look into the seeds of time,
> And say which grain will grow and which will not,
> Speak then to me, who neither beg nor fear
> Your favors nor your hate.
>
> (1.3.51–62)

Banquo implicitly predicts his lord's rise (and fall) in the figure of a seed or grain that in time will grow and presumably fulfill its natural cycle by flowering, bearing fruit, and producing more promissory seeds.

A few lines later the imagery of swelling, eruption, and roundness recurs when Banquo recounts the vision he and Macbeth have beheld as the earth's "bubbles" (1.3.79). Associations with bubbles that come to mind are delicate, fragile, marvelous, fantastic, unnatural (how can the solid earth produce bubbles?), and empty. A bubble is a "promise of space," a promise of something essentially *full,* spoken, overdetermined, crammed with possibilities (the conventional understanding of promise), and also essentially *empty,* silent, underdetermined, a nothingness. This radical undecidability, not just an ambiguous both/and relation, but a neither/nor at the same time it is both/and, is implicitly captured by Arthur C. Clarke in the title of his book *The Promise of Space*,[7] his 1968 exposé on the scientific exploration and appropriation of space: "That is the danger, the dark thundercloud that threatens the promise of the dawn. The rocket has already been the instrument of evil, and may be so again. But there is no way back into the past; the choice, as Wells once said, is the universe—or nothing" (314).

Later on in *Macbeth*, the hero himself alludes to the promise made to him as "the swelling act/Of the imperial theme" (1.3.128–129). Because it is to his advantage to do so, Macbeth prefers to interpret the witches' prophecy as if it were a legitimate promise, which it certainly is not since the witches presumably have no power to insure the outcome. They are merely mouthpieces of some greater authority. So Macbeth confuses prophecy with promise. Not only this, he seems initially at least to overlook or repress the threatening import of the second part of the auguring, that he shall not beget future kings. But that error is what marks him as human and makes the tragedy possible. Not only is the content of what he takes as a promise royal—it concerns who shall be king—but the figure of the promise itself as a vehicle for the expression of desire and hope is itself also somehow imperial, powerful, wonderful. A promise is intrinsically a figurative swelling. Macbeth's tragedy pivots on a tension between the unnatural and diseased quality of the swollen promise of ascendancy and the possibility that this swelling symbolizes what amounts to an organic elaboration of the protagonist's natural potential. Maybe he ought to be king? On the one hand, Macbeth's triumph is the product of his vaulting promissory desire; and on the other hand, his ordeal derives from another side of this same figure, a chillingly burdensome promissory dis-ease which infects everyone and everything.[8]

But all of the foregoing is by way of asking, What is a promise, anyway? What does a promise do? What does one do when one constructs or finds oneself positioned within this particular speech-act?

A promise, inasmuch as it projects a future out of a particular past and present, as is the case in *Macbeth*, suggests both a linear (temporal) and circular (spatial) structure. On the one hand, the promise aligns past, present, and future, establishing a historical progression, a chain, linking one moment to the next. On the other hand, the promise seems magically to suspend time by means of the promissory relation as such, that is as that relation is experienced as a provisional phenomenological structure that spatializes or positions those participating "in" or living the act. The promise seems a world unto itself, a world, moreover, that defers its own end. The present is necessarily thrust into the foreground, and just as necessarily vanishes the moment the promise is spoken or historically put into play. Fulfillment, then, amounts to the transformation of a particular past into a particular future, as well as the future into the past. The phenomenological and hermeneutic landscape of a promise, therefore, is both metonymic and metaphoric. The structure of a promise is both linear and circular. Imagine a true line running from promise (point A) to fulfillment (point B), but moving through a "space" of temporality seen to be inscribing a circle that contains these points of departure and arrival. The struggle for temporal fulfillment from point A (moment of utterance) to B (moment of fulfillment) is magically sublimated in the metaphorical union of A and B at consummation. That is, there is the illusion that the opposition between the linear and circular aspects of the relation disappears, that history becomes totalized at the moment of fulfillment. But this fiction merely results from the submersion of one figure (the linear) into another (the circular), necessitated by the intrinsic nature of promising (and the imagination) itself.

This struggle between the temporal and the spatial dimensions, the one demanding and the other resisting resolution, animates every act and figure of promising, from the notion that history is inherently promissory to a promise to meet a friend at noon. Once in place, a promise seems to transcend its essential historicity and function as a kind of idealized play-space, inhabited by the conventionally defined players, the promisor and promisee. However, as I will demonstrate momentarily, this playing is always historical, agonistic, and asymmetrical. Consider the great covenantal promises of God throughout the Old Testament, not to mention the idea of the Old Testament itself as the narrative revelation and playing out of divine providence in/as history. God promises a salvation at the end of time that may be achieved only by working one's way through time. This is akin to Saint Augustine's notion that language may be, indeed must be, transcended only by moving *through* it. And although it is not merely linguistic, we must not forget that a promise is essentially a verbal relation. Hence the theological and social utility of applying a human speech category like that of promise to God, who as divinely perfect would not seem capable of promising since He, by nature, could not ever fail to keep His Word.[9] It is we who require a promising God, a divine authority who captivates, seduces, and persuades by means of great promises. And it is we who narcissistically approximate a godlike power and status when we project our own covenants and promises. A promise occurs as a historical event, and thereby generates narrative, in Paul de Man's[10] phrase "generate[s] history" (277). Whether this history is fulfilled or not is a matter of ideology and belief. More than this however, the promise as a structure is not only *in* and *of* time, it *is* time. Promising is the driving force within all narrative. History not only emerges from a promise as a chain of causal connections but also as an all-encompassing circle that totalizes and dominates. Inasmuch as this apparently empty bubblelike form is necessarily filled with, constituted by, historically determined hopes and expectations, the figurative structure seems *dynamically* to swell (as hope grows) at the same time it also seems *statically* always to have been tacitly prefigured (as hope seems implicitly always to have been a possibility).

Having set out the phenomenological shape of promising, the matter of fulfillment requires a bit more scrutiny at this point. J. Hillis Miller[11] argues that fulfillment is always an illusion—although a necessary one—because it can never be satisfactorily "confirmed that a promise has been kept, since something might always be done later on to invalidate . . . apparent fulfillment. A promise intrinsically demands an indefinite postponement of its fulfillment" (33). Like time, a promise moves inexorably toward and resists its end. The word *end* here means both temporal finality and teleological purpose. For example, consider the effect of the promise to tell a tale that commences the narrative game of Chaucer's pilgrims on the road to Canterbury, or the stories from the *Arabian Nights*.[12] The promise to tell a tale, to speak, enables narrative as it also defers the desire for gratification (erotic or religious) on the part of the teller or the listener. Miller concludes, therefore, that in its promissory guise, narrative always betrays the implicit promise it makes.[13] It is not possible to promise oneself, as it were. What would fulfillment amount to? Indeed, a promise is always already a kind of betrayal of history and time at the moment it is responsible for both.[14] Following the lead of de Man, Miller underscores as well that "language promises, but what it promises is itself" (35). Such a promise necessitates breach because it is impossible to determine the precise boundaries of language. Everything seems simultaneously inside and outside this ever-widening sphere. This would include narrative, which after all is a verbal construct. As narrativity, promising emerges as radically subversive and self-mutilating, as does language itself. The poet Novalis underscores this aporia in the overt asymmetry of the two parts, ironically labeled expectations *(Die Erwartung)* and fulfillment *(Die Erfüllung),* of his fantasy novel *Henry von Ofterdingen.*[15]

Another case in point is E. T. A. Hoffmann's tale, "The Vow" *(Das Gelübde).*[16] Countess Hermengilda vows never to surrender herself to her beloved, the dashing Count Stanislaus, until their homeland, partitioned Poland, is again made whole and free. Stanislaus realizes such a promise will never be fulfilled, so for his part vows eternal faithfulness and promptly goes off to war. Hermengilda's consequent pregnancy — her swelling — and her insistence that she had wed and consummated her union with Stanislaus when he appeared to her in a dream vision before his untimely death signifies the struggle between her ambivalent desire for and fear of fulfillment (political and erotic). The golden ring, which she claims was given to her by her husband, but which Count Xaver (Stanislaus' mysterious double) claims is his, represents the promise and threat to her psychical wholeness that the act of vowing poses. The vow structurally enables not only the erotic and political narratives that constitute the tale, but also one linked to gender and social class (i.e., the efforts of the countess' family to cover up her apparent indiscretion). Hermengilda's vow comes to be a sign of unconscious commitment and betrayal, of a simultaneous need for community and separation. By the end of the story, the vow and the ring have emerged as representations of the uncanny itself.

The same agonistic structure animates the motif of promise in much folk literature, from the fragmentary ancient Irish tale, "Cormac's Adventures in the Land of Promise,"[17] the story of how King Cormac attained his marvelous "cup of gold" (perhaps a proto-grail image) that repeatedly and miraculously shatters and becomes whole again, to the fairy tales of the Brothers Grimm and others.[18] For instance, in "The Frog-King, or Iron Henry," the ugly frog extracts a promise of love from the princess in return for retrieving her golden ball from the well. This promise then becomes the figurative site of the struggle between the princess' ambivalent desire to dominate and be dominated by the frog (sexuality). When her father, the king, forces her to keep her word, he unwittingly enables her deflowering and the apparent fulfillment of the magic spell that initially turned the prince into the frog, and which only the princess, of course, can reverse. The tacit message is that keeping a promise is always disfiguring, that it is a willing act of symbolic violence that nevertheless sacralizes the bond. The promised transformation of the frog back into human shape occurs at the moment the princess, furious because it has attempted to climb into bed with her, slams it against the wall in disgust. Her desire to kill is bound to her desire to love and be loved. In this tale, as in so many others, promising functions as a means of seduction as well as salvation. It is also always accompanied by figurative, if not literal pain.[19]

This brings us to the issue of fantasy. As we turn to this matter, it is important to recall the essential undecidability of the swelling promise in *Macbeth*. The witches' prophecy/promise bodes hope at the same time it threatens the psychological stability of the protagonist and the political integrity of the realm. Does it more authentically seem to grow, therefore, or to fester in the course of the play? Believing in the *power* of the promise enables Macbeth to ascend to a position that both liberates and imprisons him. That is, the promise emancipates as it tyrannizes. Once in place, it becomes a mechanism of historical and psychonalytic commitment as well as a burdensome potentiality. The promise directs Macbeth toward a particular end, magically opening and closing time in the course of bonding speaker and hearer in a specific relation. The promise is an egg, full of possibility; but as an egg, it is a protective and even oppressive shell that must be ruptured in order to fulfill its "self" in the form of an Other. But to rupture, to transgress, the border is also immediately to redraw, to reinstitute, the limits that have presumably been overcome. Short of this, there is no way to maintain the idea that genuine transcendence has occurred. The image of the threatening egg is, of course, a familiar motif of much fantasy and science-fiction narrative. For example, consider how this image animates a novel such as Russ Winterbotham's *The Space Egg*[20] or the film *Alien*,[21] where the discourses of promise and threat, of swelling and invasion, inextricably intertwine. This in contradistinction to the more archetypally benign interpretation of the so-called cosmic egg and sphere as symbols of time, cycle, perfection, deity, and fecundity. Recall the image of the rainbow, the overarching, egglike emblem of Divine Covenant in the Old Testament story of Noah (Genesis 6–9).[22] The rainbow functions as a figurative boundary that both divides and joins two qualitatively different and opposed realms, the marvelous (divine) and the mundane (human). The future is something promised and yet also threatened (it will be fire next time!). Desire for what lies beyond or at the end of the rainbow yields an uncanny amalgam of expectation and anxiety.

It is important to emphasize that it is not just a matter of interpreting an utterance or figure at one moment as a contextualized promise, and at another as a threat. Quite the contrary, the intrinsic structure of promising is internally divided, disfigured, in itself. The idea and act of promising are grounded on the operation of an internal and not just an external Otherness. A promise is always also a threat. This means that the rhetoric of promising—and I will work at relating this to the rhetoric of fantasy—signifies the repression of that which continually threatens the coherence and reliability of a promise as a social convention. The repression structurally enables and yet also prevents the total fulfillment of the relation. Despite its heuristic necessity, the repression is never absolute. In his essay "Promises," Paul de Man[23] calls our attention to the situation in German, where the verb to promise, *versprechen,* forms part of the phrase used to represent a slip of the tongue, *sich versprechen* (277). To promise signifies an excess, an eruption, a disturbance. It is language turned against its own inherent promissory trajectory. Psychoanalytically, excessive promising (whatever that would amount to) would be both the cause and the effect of a sadomasochistic cycle of outwardly and inwardly directed aggression. The only escape from this cycle would seem to be the "end" of promising—the "end" of language—death.

I prefer Bakhtin's term *dialogic* to characterize the simultaneously internal and external relation between promise and threat.[24] This is to emphasize the difference between the two speech-acts—but also to underscore the fact of their rhetorical contamination of one another. The simple binarism maintains its pragmatic utility while nevertheless being called into question. As an alternative to the expected, or as Eric S. Rabkin[25] puts it, "the anti-expected, the dis-expected, and the not-expected" (13), fantasy always produces promise and threat together. Just as a promise shapes expectations that were not explicit before, fantasy generates one world at the expense of another, and thereby exposes the network of cultural (including linguistic) conventions that inform our everyday construction of the real. As Roger Caillois observes, as quoted by Rosemary Jackson,[25] "The fantastic is always a break in the acknowledged order, an irruption of the inadmissable within the changeless everyday legality" (21). Fantasy and promise: irruption, eruption, interruption. All these terms imply a sundering, a rupturing of a surface and the consequent gap, the empty space, the silence, that then beckons to be filled, but remains maddeningly unfillable, both visible and invisible.

This is the sphere in Crichton's narrative, but also the obelisk in Arthur C. Clarke's *2001, A Space Odyssey*.[27] Both figures represent the eruption of the imaginary *into* and *as* consciousness. Consider also the folkloristic practice, recorded in the Bible, of erecting a cairn of stones to symbolize the making of a covenant (see the story of Jacob and Laban in Genesis 31:46–49, and the anthropological discussion of this phenomenon in Frazer[28] (2:398–409) and Gaster[29] (201–4). This is linked to the practice of swearing on a stone, as well as to the medieval and Renaissance motif of a king, he who conventionally vows to guarantee the reliability of promises, as one who resides on a stone (throne). The idea of monumentalizing and sacralizing a fixed geographical and symbolic point to represent promissory desire in this way may also be connected to the tradition of wishing on a star, an object that is both figuratively and literally a fixed elevation. I will return to this at the end of this essay. Like the sphere and obelisk, the swollen cairn signifies a totality as well as a rupture. Something has disturbed, transformed, and marked the linguistic and psychoanalytic, not to mention the physical, landscape. The sacred cairn is implicitly disfigured, however.

The anally retentive production of the mound (the monument) is symbolically undermined by another biblical and folkloristic practice, that of conceiving of the making of a covenant as a "cutting." The residue of this exists in the modern English phrase "to cut a deal." Here an animal (usually a calf, she-goat, or ram) is sacrificed and cut in twain, with the promising parties ritualistically passing in between (see the story of Abraham in Genesis, 12–18, and the discussion by Gaster, 140–56). Paradoxically, the sundering of the animal into two equal parts represents the need to preserve the image of the totality of the bond by underscoring its necessarily divided (its Other) nature. The violence of the cutting itself is both sacramental and retributive (Gaster, 143–45). The blood sacrifice not only solemnizes the uniqueness of the pact but implicitly threatens what might/should happen to any contracting party who breaks their word. But even more terrifying, it signifies the intrinsic perversity of the relation as such, as evidenced by the symbolic violence the two parties have unconsciously inflicted on each other (and themselves) by entering into the bond in the first place. In this same light, recall the practice of circumcision (Genesis 17:10–17), which may be interpreted as a violent cutting, a form of physical and symbolic disfigurement. At the same time it also signifies the idea of the Abrahamic covenant. Consider as well the tradition of shattering glass, commemorative of the ancient destruction of the temple in Jerusalem, which forms an integral part of the modern Jewish wedding (covenanting) ritual. An embodied memory of a primal act of violence and desecration is inextricably attached to the unifying exchange of vows and the consecration of community.

The subversive irruption of the unspoken and unseen assumes a double significance for Rosemary Jackson,[30] who proposes that fantasy "expresses" desire in two ways at once.

> It can *tell of,* manifest or show desire (expression in the sense of portrayal, representation, manifestation, linguistic utterance, mention, description), or it can *expel* desire, when this desire is a disturbing element which threatens cultural order and continuity (expression in the sense of pressing out, squeezing, expulsion, getting rid of something by force). (3–4)

This is certainly the case in *Macbeth,* where the promise (or what Macbeth believes is a promise) represents, constitutes, displays, parades, celebrates desire; and yet the promise also functions as a mechanism for expelling, purging, cleansing, getting rid of that desire. The promise eidetically exhausts itself in the act of becoming itself. It consumes itself; it consumes Macbeth, in the process of becoming narratively and dramatically manifest. To fulfill it—to fill it up with performance—is to empty, exhaust, use it up. It shrinks as it swells, becoming invisible as it looms more and more menacingly visible. According to their very natures, therefore, both promising and fantasy are latently apocalyptic. The drives toward Eros and Thanatos, toward community and separation, toward fullness and oblivion, fold back into one another. I use the word *apocalypse* with caution, and mainly in its etymological sense, meaning to reveal, uncover. Fantasy uncovers desire at the same moment it re-covers it. Indeed, our word *fantasy* derives from Latin and Greek roots meaning to make visible, visionary, unreal (Jackson, 13). The fantastic seems both opaque and transparent, like a poetic image. We feel incomplete and yet are filled with wonder in one and the same instant. This is akin to the effect of promising, which functions as an ordinary speech convention and yet magically creates a future where there was none, formalizes commitment and obligation where none existed before.

The ancient Greeks and Romans simultaneously represented and repressed this doubleness by according Hades, the Unseen, the supplementary names Pluto and Dis, which both mean wealth, abundance, excess. As a location, Hades is often imagistically represented as both forbiddingly empty and terrifyingly full (e.g., Vergil and Dante). The Latin designation Orcus, yet another conventional name for Hades, both the god and the place, is most likely derived from the Greek *horkōs,* oath. In his guise as Orcus, Hades emerges as a spirit who avenges perjury and who enforces the keeping of promises (Rose, 23).[31] The ancients did not view promises and vows as merely legalistic but as essentially mysterious and magical relations with unmistakable links to the world of mythic shadow, the underworld, which was construed as a place of threatening loss and of promising reward. As both the lord of the underworld and the god of oaths, Orcus suggests the subterranean and fecund, a place where the past is buried but remains alive. As a mythic space, Hades, like the symbolic space that a promise carves out of time and the social fabric, is both seen and unseen, conventionally familiar and necessarily fantastic.

We experience the play of promise and threat in the expression of fantasy in every act of so-called ordinary promising. We need not limit our attention to the mythic and literary. Toward this end, I would like to consider the utterance: "I promise to love you." It proves useful to situate the act within the following set of rhetorical functions: (a) promising as aggressive/excessive; (b) as submissive/restrictive; (c) as an opening; (d) as a closing; (e) as totalizing; (f) as fragmenting.

Inasmuch as this promise to love (to remain faithful) belongs to the speaking subject—after all, it is he/she (for the sake of convenience, afterward he) who created it—it represents his power willingly to commit himself to the performance of some future act. The subject projects and encloses a particular future for himself as well as for the beloved (the promise). The speaking subject orders time, and himself, by means of the promise. Certain events must follow if the bond is to be maintained. By the same token, the expectations of the promisee have been formalized. This attempt to control the self as an Other, not to mention the promisee as an Other, amounts to a form of symbolic aggression. And yet it is at the same time submissive behavior. Promises are always made to an Other. A commitment is made, an obligation willingly undertaken. Moreover, the fact of the promise assumes that the "I" who makes it will be the same "I" who fulfills or breaches it, as the case may be. This assumption about the unified and stable condition of the subject is ideological but heuristically necessary in order to verify later that fulfillment has or has not occurred. In other words, promising presupposes the enabling fiction of a unified speaking subject before, during, and after the act of speech. As Mary Pratt[32] observes, "More than perhaps any other speech act, promises (when felicitous) confirm the continuity of the individual over time—the beliefs, intentions, abilities and desires that are here today will still be here a month or a year from now when the promise falls due" (8). But this presumption of continuity and authority is continually undermined, threatened, in three ways at once.

First, the speaking subject does not remain the same entity at the point of fulfillment as he was at the point of utterance, nor for that matter does the promisee. As a result, fulfillment never completely satisfies; something we cannot always precisely identify seems perversely to escape, to remain outside the enclosing circle of the promise. Fulfillment is therefore never complete. The moment of consummation kindles the desire for more. Additionally, since promising, like all rule-governed speech behavior, is made possible by the operation of particular verbal and social conventions, the promise to love is actually the sole property of the speaking subject only in a very limited sense. The speaker's "I" merely fills the formulaic slot within the normative structure of the speech-act, in this case of promising. There must be an "I," whether explicitly spoken or tacitly understood. We proceed as if this image of totality were unproblematic. Every promise, every act of speech for that matter, is animated by a utopian faith in the possibility of order and coherence. At the same time however, subjectivity is constituted in the act of speech and in history. An "I" is always positioned in relation to a particular Other. In sum, the "I" does not preexist its linguistic constitution and representation; it is produced in the unconscious desire for and fear of an Other, which expresses itself in/as/through language and narrative.

Second, the speaking subject's authority is undermined by the action or nonaction of the promisee. The promise to love by itself will not persuade the promisee to accept what is promised, nor will it make the promisee desire to be loved. The legitimacy of the promise as a genuine social relation, therefore, depends on the presence of a mutual desire and tacit prior agreement. That is, in order for the promise to be formally accepted, the promisee must already desire (on some level of consciousness) the speaker's love, not to mention also understand the conventional rules that govern promising as such. Short of this, the promisee could not possibly recognize a promise as a verbal and social relation. In a sense then, the promise does not truly create but merely formalizes a relation already in place, as it were. Promises are therefore always somehow redundant. So much for the illusion of the all-powerful speaker who controls the Other by means of his promise. In actuality, the speaking subject is manipulated not only by the hearer but by the promise itself. The promisee, moreover, may choose to refuse the promise, not matter how seductively it is offered. Of course, this does not preclude the speaker from believing, for one reason or another, that a promise has been accepted when it has not. Or as in *Macbeth,* the hearer may take something as a promise erroneously. Suffice it to say that the promise potentially belongs as much to the promisee as to the promisor, both of whom reciprocally dominate the other. The aggressive self-aggrandizement of the "I" is immediately transformed into an act of willing submission (subjection), which amounts to a figurative self-mutilation.[33] The promisor has exposed his need for an Other; indeed, he has rendered himself an Other to himself. He has uncovered a lack and sought to re-cover it with the promise. The articulation, "I promise," gestures ambivalently toward a desire for community at the same time it presupposes and enforces the difference between I and Thou. The necessary consequence is the experience of anxiety and hesitation that, incidentally, forms the basis of Todorov's[34] well-known theory of the reader's experience of fantastic narrative (31). Nietzsche was the first to express the pain, suffering, and cruelty—as well as the "human, all too human" quality—of promising. He sardonically referred to man as the promising animal (*Genealogy,* 2nd essay, sec. 1, 57) Consider the extent that we celebrate our humanity by troping experience with the metaphor of promising. We will speak of a promising (or promised) future, a promising child, a promising author, a promising book, a promising landscape, a promising planet.

The third way in which the subject gives up control of his promise is that of the process of performance itself. Once the promise is in place, it is necessary to wait. The promisee must wait for the promisor to fulfill his obligation. By the same token, the promisor must wait—labor in time to make good his word—to see if he in fact will keep the promise, irrespective of his original intentions. He only knows for sure that he will perform when he actually does so (or believes that he does so). So the speaker waits—for himself, as it were—to experience satisfaction and release from the bond, the yoke, that he has willingly subjected himself to. He is master and slave to himself as well as to the promisee. And both are circumscribed by the promise itself. The promise violently opens up a future as it encloses the specific hopes and expectations that constitute the act as historical and phenomenological relation. The prefiguration of symbolic violence is contained in the words *promise* and *threat* themselves. *Promise:* from the Latin *pro* (forth) and *mittere* (to send), hence to send forth, out, or at. *Threat:* from the Latin *trudere* (to push), hence to thrust at.

The uncanniness of promising is thematized in a number of science-fiction narratives explicitly about the relation. I would like to consider Jeremy Strike's novel *A Promising Planet: Talk to Me in Thunder and Lightning*.[35] The cover illustration for that novel depicts a menacing orb situated above the heads of the harried spacemen. This represents the monstrous promise and threat at the heart of the story. In that story, Bill Warden, a surveyor for Star Systems Incorporated, attempts to claim what looks like a very promising and lucrative planet for his company. When he lands, however, he discovers that concealed within the promise of this new land—not to mention the promises of good faith from the planet's omnipotent "god" (Charley), with whom Warden strikes up a conversational relationship—is the threat that he and his crew will never be permitted to leave. In the course of the tale, the god, who initially welcomed the visitors, turns out to be a computer that completely controls the environment and dominates the local inhabitants, who seem to exist for the sole purpose of doing honor to the force "above" them. Not only does this god represent the promise of a future to his worshipers, he strategically uses promises to persuade members of Warden's crew to mutiny. When this fails, he causes an earthquake and volcanic eruptions in an effort to protect himself from the earthmen who are desperately trying to disconnect him. Steaming ribbons of lava pursue Warden down the halls as the god expresses his and his planet's combined promise and threat. And Charley does appear to prevail in the end. In the final scene, presumably many years hence, this promising deity greets a new expedition of surveyors and colonizers with "I am the god of this planet. You may address Me as the Great Egg" (125). The novel serves as an exploration of promising as a site of competing religious, legalistic, economic, and erotic interests. The idea that promising is as much a sign of aggression as submission is thrust into the foreground. The unconscious desire to possess and be possessed is shown to be as intrinsic to promising as is death *(mors)* to the concept of mortgage.

This rhetoric is repeated, along with the figure of a promissory landscape in three short stories published during the 1950s.[36] In Lawrence O'Donnell's "Promised Land,"[37] the focus is on Torren, the monstrously swollen (five-hundred-pound) "Protector" of the moon Ganymede (in Greek mythology, Zeus' cupbearer). The victim of a promising centrifuge experiment that failed when he was a baby, Torren feels betrayed by life. The only way he can now survive is to float like an island unto himself in a tub of water. His desire is to transform the environment of Ganymede so that it might become an alternative habitat for people from the earth. However, his motives are not altruistic but bitterly mercenary. The story recounts the rebellion of Torren's adopted son, Ben, who learns that his "father" intends to break an unspoken promise to the local inhabitants to modify the planet only gradually so they can adapt to the changes. Speeding up the process promises death to those who have labored faithfully to assist Torren for many years. After considerable exchange about who owes what to whom and why, Ben concludes that despite terrible threats, Torren can never kill him because of their reciprocal bond: "As long as I'm alive, I'm your enemy and yourself. . . . You'll do your best to defeat me, Torren, but you won't kill me. You won't dare" (160). Not just physically imprisoned in a hideous body or in the tub, Torren is a victim of the promissory bond with his symbolic offspring—his son, as well as his planet—both of which he manipulates but fails absolutely to control. For Torren, the possibility of fulfilling his desire also amounts to an act of self-subversion and mutilation.

Robert F. Young[38] sets his "Promised Land" in an even more explicitly political setting. A spaceship leaves earth bound for a planet designated New Poland, chosen to become the new home of a group of dispossessed (those who have lost their promise) Polish refugees. The use of Poland as a motif indirectly links it to Hoffmann's "The Vow."[39] The European Project has arranged for there to be a new "promised land for every eastern bloc population which has been robbed [of its] right to evolve naturally" (128). However, the ship bound for New Poland crashes instead on another uncharted planet, one not promised in quite the same way, and the non-Polish pilot, Reston, is gradually transformed into a priestlike Protector by the intensely religious pasengers/settlers. Despite, or perhaps because of his status as Other, Reston represents the settlers' need for hope, promise, and safety. By the same token, the initially diffident pilot comes to recognize "his own need for the immigrants" (137), and by the end, "surrenders" (137) not only to their passion but to his own desire to deliver and be delivered. In his transfiguration into the living promise of the future, his status as priest also ironically signifies the looming threat of a return to a totalizing and paternalistic if not totalitarian past.

In Robert Randall's "The Promised Land,"[40] earthmen, the presumed emissaries of the Divine Light, manipulate the people of the planet Nidor by means of their promises of a better life. The Nidorans' faith in these promises is such, moreover, that the people fail to recognize that they are the subject of genetic experimentation that includes incest and the subversion of their most sacred cultural traditions. In all these stories the idea of a promised land turns out to be a fantastic (a combined utopian and dystopian) vision.

Four fantasy texts that thrust the speech-act of promising itself into the foreground are Elizabeth Stuart Phelps' story, "The Oath of Allegiance,"[41] James Blish's "The Oath,"[42] Jack McDevitt's "Promises to Keep,"[43] and the novel by Larry Niven and Jerry Pournelle, *Oath of Fealty*.[44] Limitations of space preclude discussing them all in sufficient detail. In each case, however, a spoken or in some cases a tacit promissory bond emerges as the narrative and thematic fulcrum on which pivots a tension between utopian hope of fulfillment and dystopian fear and trembling. This is most richly worked out by Niven and Pournelle, who weave a complex web of implicit and explicit allegiances that animate the main plot: there is the promissory figure of the great swelling, the utopian edifice of Todos Santos, the boxlike city-in-a-city, which towers over a decaying Los Angeles but which in actuality exists in a fully symbiotic relation with everything that presumably exists outside and beneath it (including LA, the law, and the past); there is the romantic subtext that turns on the marriage of Tony Rand, Todos Santos' chief engineer; and most important, there is the idea of the oath of fealty itself, that which bonds the residents of Todos Santos together, forms them into a community and secures the project against those who have vowed to destroy it. Ultimately the novel is not so much about Todos Santos itself (a utopia/dystopia that exists in the present), as about the struggle on all sides to maintain unencumbered lines of feudal-like obligation and commitment to people and ideas, such as to one's spouse or to the concepts of right and wrong. Promising emerges as a strategy for establishing a necessary hierarchy and order, as well as a site where those empowered by a promise come into conflict and struggle against others as well as themselves. The salvation of Todos Santos depends on, but also weighs in the balance precisely because of, the oath of fealty.

Undoubtedly the most extended exploration of promising remains the six novels that constitute Stephen R. Donaldson's fantasy, the *First and Second Chronicles of Thomas Covenant, the Unbeliever.*[45] The key narrative tensions of the work all derive from the irony of the protagonist's name. Here we encounter a figure inscribed, as it were, in the very idea of promise, but who is incapable of belief or at being at ease with this situation. Covenant's incessant doubt and self-awareness of his own promise is what marks him as a modern antihero. Throughout the novels, the protagonist struggles against believing in the reality of the magical land where he discovers himself transported after a blow to the head. He is therefore never quite comfortable with his secondary identity as the living fulfillment of the ancient prophecy that foretold the reincarnation of the legendary hero, Berek Halfhand. As Halfhand, Covenant epically battles forces of evil in what amount to sacrificial efforts to maintain possession of his magic ring and to protect the land. These familiar conventions of literary epic and romance are undermined, however, by Covenant's intermittent returns to conscious "reality" throughout the *Chronicles.* The realm of the purely fantastic cannot be sustained. We know, for example, that Covenant is a professional writer who accidentally contracted (a bizarre promissory image, to say the least) leprosy, and is slowly becoming disfigured. More than this, just prior to the accident that rendered him unconscious and that initiated his fantasy, Covenant vowed to himself to survive the dissolution of his marriage and the ostracism from the community because of his disease. The symbol of this desire—of his hope for the future, but also of his paranoiac sense of entrapment in time and in his body—is his wedding ring: "It was an icon of himself. It reminded him of where he had been and where he was—of promises made and broken." (*Lord Foul's,* 27). The ring signifies the nostalgia for wholeness that his leprosy and sundered marriage seem to preclude. In the course of the narrative cycle, this conventional image of domestic fealty is transformed into the miraculously spherical talisman that protects Covenant/Halfhand throughout innumerable fantastic adventures.[46] To give up the ring would be to give up himself—but also to discover himself—in death. It would mean to express, to manifest and to exhaust, his promise. The ring both promises and threatens, expresses and represses, what the Unbeliever seeks not only to reveal but to re-cover about his self and time.

To conclude, I would like briefly to consider the central image of H. G. Wells' famous short story, "The Star,"[47] in relation to Arthur C. Clarke's supplementary tale of the same name.[48] According to Wells' narrative, on New Year's Day, a traditional time of great swelling hope and expectation, astronomers report that Neptune has mysteriously been deflected out of its usual orbit by a strange new star. The story is the account of the events that follow, as the sight of the star gradually grows on the earth's horizon, and a terrible collision seems imminent: "A vast mass of matter it was, bulky, heavy, rushing without warning out of the black mystery of the sky into the radiance of the sun" (223). But is the star purely a threat, or does it also promise something unknown but potentially glorious?

> Brighter it was than any star in our skies; brighter than the evening star at its brightest. It still glowed out white and large, no mere twinkling spot of light, but a small round clear shining disc, . . . And where science has not reached, men stared and feared, telling one another of the wars and the pestilences that are foreshadowed by those fiery signs in the Heavens. (224)

As time passes, however, people get used to this "grotesque possibility" (225): "'That is our star,' they whispered, and felt strangely comforted by the sweet brilliance of its light" (226). The star swells as it hurtles forward: "The star grew—it grew with a terrible steadiness hour after hour, a little larger each hour, a little nearer the midnight zenith, and brighter and brighter . . ." (229). Why is the star coming? No one can say for sure. What does it portend? Everyone gropes for an answer.

The image of the swelling, round, eruptive fiery ball returns us to the promissory metaphors of engorgement, of threatening but creative tumescence in *Macbeth,* and back to the sublime, womblike roundness of Crichton's *Sphere.*[49] Desire, as the word itself tells us, is a blessing or curse, as the case may be, from the stars. Desire: from the Latin *de* (from) and *sider-, sidus* (star).[50] The stars call to Macbeth, just as by means of his "vaulting" (1.7.27) and "thriftless" (2.4.28) ambition he seeks imperially to ascend, to shine with them. He refuses to wait. The figure of the swelling promise becomes emblematic of his exuberant and beautiful excess, and later of his (and Lady Macbeth's) debilitating paranoia. The promise functions as a psychoanalytic and fantastic space in which he takes refuge. But the roundness of this swelling seed implies as much implosive as explosive violence.[51] Womb becomes tomb. In similar fashion, the people of earth in Wells' tale feel strangely at home *(heimlich)* with their uncanny *(unheimlich)* star, their fantastic sphere into which they telescope the promise and threat of desire and the promise and threat that is desire. Desire for what? Wells never reveals this, for it is the growing anxiety about it that enables the narrative to move forward, to promise some kind of fulfillment in the end. The star passes the earth as mysteriously as it appeared, leaving considerable pain (volcanoes, earthquakes, floods) in its wake. The earth's temperature is permanently raised. However, this severity, this brutal tearing of the earth, does not serve merely to warn the world's inhabitants of the threat of desire and their own self-importance (as the observing Martian astronomers intimate). It also ironically signifies a fantastic promise of hope, a desire for a different, an Other, if not better world.

In his own story and "response" to Wells, Arthur C. Clarke[52] recounts the unsettling discovery by a scientist of a destroyed civilization on a burnt-out and shriveled star that was formerly a supernova. After careful calculations and dating, he concludes that this violence must have been what was perceived on earth centuries ago and named the star of Bethlehem, the herald of a new age, and the sign of divine promise and redemption. Was one thriving civilization capriciously wiped out—sacrificed—as a sign of the salvation of another world? The scientist struggles to understand the import of such a "colossal conflagration" (370). Could this have been the swelling and glowing star of which Wells wrote? The promised end? Or the horror?

Notes

1. Friedrich Nietzsche, *On the Genealogy of Morals,* tr. Walter Kaufmann & R. J. Hollingdale (New York: Vintage, 1969).

2. Michael Crichton, *Sphere* (New York: Knopf, 1987).

3. Harold Bloom, *"Clinamen:* Toward a Theory of Fantasy," *Bridges to Fantasy,* ed. George E. Slusser, Eric S. Rabkin, & Robert Scholes (Carbondale: Southern Illinois Univ. Press), 1–20.

4. This essay represents an extension of the theory of promising worked out in my doctoral dissertation, "'Promyse that is dette': Toward a Rhetoric and

History of Literary Promising" (Ph.D. diss., Claremont Graduate School, 1985).

5. All Shakespearean citations are to Alfred Harbage, gen. ed., *William Shakespeare: The Complete Works* (Baltimore: Penguin, 1969).

6. The notion of promising (as well as speech itself) as an aggressive celebration of exuberant excess (of time, words, desire) is linked to Bataille's (116–29) analysis of the custom of potlatch among the tribes native to the Pacific Northwest. According to Bataille, "Classical economics imagined that primitive exchange occurred in the form of barter; it had no reason to assume, in fact, that a means of acquisition such as exchange might have as its origin not the need to acquire that it satisfies today, but the contrary need to destroy and to lose. . . . *Potlach* excludes all bargaining and, in general, it is constituted by a considerable gift of riches, offered openly and with the goal of humiliating, defying, and *obligating* a rival" (Georges Bataille, *Visions of Excess: Selected Writings, 1927–1939*, tr. Allan Stoekl et al., ed. A. Stoekl [Minneapolis: Univ. of Minnesota Press, 1985], 121).

7. Arthur C. Clarke, *The Promise of Space* (New York: Harper, 1968).

8. As someone more crucially promised than promising, as it were, Macbeth bears some relation to Prince Hal (later Henry V) in *1, 2 Henry IV* and *Henry V*, who is also "promised" on different levels of dramatic action in the plays. However, Hal's perspective on promises is exceedingly more playful and cynical, though no less ironic, than Macbeth's.

9. See Jürgen Moltmann, *Theology of Hope: On the Ground and Implications of a Christian Eschatology*, tr. James W. Leitch (New York: Harper, 1967), 95–138; and Christopher Morse, *The Logic of Promise in Moltmann's Theology* (Philadelphia: Fortress, 1979), 27–81.

10. Paul de Man, *Allegories of Reading: Figural Language in Rousseau, Nietzsche, Rilke, and Proust* (New Haven: Yale Univ. Press, 1979).

11. J. Hillis Miller, *The Ethics of Reading: Kant, de Man, Eliot, Trollope, James, and Benjamin* (New York: Columbia Univ. Press, 1987).

12. Two excellent editions are: Geoffrey Chaucer, *Canterbury Tales: The Works of Geoffrey Chaucer*, ed. F. N. Robinson, 2nd ed. (Boston: Houghton, 1957); and *Tales from the Arabian Nights: Selections from "The Book of a Thousand Nights and a Night,"* translated and annotated by Sir Richard F. Burton (London: Bracken, 1985).

13. Miller's deconstruction of promise and fulfillment owes much to the rhetorical analysis of Paul de Man, *Allegories of Reading* ("Promises," 246–77), to the psychoanalytic perspective on promising pursued by Shoshana Felman (*The Literary Speech Act: Don Juan with J. L. Austin, or Seduction in Two Languages*, tr. Catherine Porter [Ithaca: Cornell Univ. Press, 1983], 25–69), and to the ontological critique of promise and memory provided by Jacques Derrida (*Memoires for Paul de Man*, tr. Cecile Lindsay, Jonathan Culler, & Eduardo Cadava [New York: Columbia Univ. Press, 1986], 91–153). The deconstructive

perspective becomes clearer—and even more threatening—when it is juxta-
posed to Erich Auerbach's contrary assumptions about promise and fulfillment
in "Figura" (*Scenes from the Drama of European Literature,* tr. Ralph Manheim
[New York: Meridian, 1959], 11–76).

14. On the necessity of betrayal and sundering, see James Hillman
("Betrayal," *Loose Ends: Primary Papers in Archetypal Psychology* [Irving,
Texas: Spring, 1978], 63–81), and Harold Bloom (*The Breaking of the Vessels*
[Chicago: Univ. of Chicago Press, 1982], 73–107).

15. Novalis, *Henry von Ofterdingen,* tr. Palmer Holty (New York: Ungar,
1964).

16. E. T. A. Hoffmann, "The Vow," *Tales of Hoffmann,* new translated
edition, ed. Christopher Lazare (New York: Grove, 1946), 266–94.

17. "Cormac's Adventures in the Land of Promise," *Ancient Irish Tales,*
ed. Tom Pete Cross & Clark Harris Slover (New York: Holt, 1936).

18. The discourse of promising clearly figures in the play of masculine and
feminine imagery, for example, branch and cup in "Cormac's Adventures," or
finger and ring in Hoffmann's "The Vow," although we need not limit our
concern to the erotic context, nor to the strictly Freudian appreciation of promise
and fulfillment. For example, both "Cormac" and "The Vow" display intense
political interests, the one amounting to an ideological and archetypal legitima-
tion of trial by physical ordeal, and the other, set in partitioned Poland,
symbolizing the projection of a fundamentally psychical struggle for power into
other institutional (economic, matrimonial, familial) realms. For additional
illustrations of the varied contextual significance of promising in folkloristic
material, see especially Grimm's "Little Briar-Rose" (237–41), "Bearskin"
(467–72), and "Hans the Hedghog" (497–502) in Campbell, as well as Andersen's "The Little Sea Maid" (543–59). (See *The Complete Grimm's Fairy
Tales,* introduction by Padraic Colum, commentary by Joseph Campbell [New
York: Pantheon, 1944]; and Hans Christian Andersen, *The Complete Illustrated
Stories,* tr. H. W. Dulcken [London: Chancellor Press, 1985].)

19. The association of promise, in the form of oath, with the ideas of test,
ordeal, struggle, and pain, occurs in Plato, "The use and abuse of oaths," *Laws*
12.948–49 (*The Dialogues of Plato,* tr. B. Jowett, 2 vols. [New York: Random,
1937], 2: 683–84), as well as in Aristotle's *Rhetoric* 1.15.1376b–77b (tr. Lane
Cooper [New York: Appleton, 1932], 84–89).

20. Russ Winterbotham, *The Space Egg* (London: Priory, n.d.).

21. *Alien,* dir. Ridley Scott (CBS, 1979).

22. All biblical citations are to *The Holy Bible,* King James Version (New
York: NAL, 1974).

23. Paul de Man, *Allegories of Reading: Figural Language in Rousseau,
Nietzsche, Rilke, and Proust* (New Haven: Yale Univ. Press, 1979).

24. As poined out by Michael Holquist, for Bakhtin, the dialogic means

"there is a constant interaction between meanings, all of which have the potential of conditioning others" (426). Unlike the dialectical, this interaction need not be limited to two terms, nor is it only an externalized relation. Bakhtin insists that interpretive contexts do not exist discretely but are necessarily built into one another. This is the basic condition of "heteroglossia," which he argues informs all speech production. (See M. M. Bakhtin, "Glossary," *The Dialogic Imagination: Four Essays,* tr. Caryl Emerson & Michael Holquist, ed. M. Holquist [Austin: Univ. of Texas Press, 1981], 423–34.)

25. Eric S. Rabkin, *The Fantastic in Literature* (Princeton: Princeton Univ. Press, 1976).

26. Rosemary Jackson, *Fantasy: The Literature of Subversion* (London: Methuen, 1981).

27. Arthur C. Clarke, *2001, A Space Odyssey* (New York: NAL, 1968).

28. James George Frazer, "The Covenant on The Cairn," *Folk-lore in the Old Testament,* 3 vols. (London: Macmillan, 1919), 2: 398–409.

29. Theodore H. Gaster, *Myth, Legend, and Custom in the Old Testament: A Comparative Study with Chapters from James G. Frazer's "Folk-lore in the Old Testament"* (New York: Harper, 1969).

30. Jackson, *Fantasy: The Literature of Subversion.*

31. H. J. Rose, *A Handbook of Greek Mythology, Including Its Extension to Rome* (New York: Dutton, 1959).

32. Mary Louise Pratt, "The Ideology of Speech-Act Theory," *Centrum,* n.s. 1, no. 1 (1981): 5–18.

33. On the symbolically violent and self-mutilating character of promising, as of the idea of speech itself, see especially Denis de Rougemont, *Love in the Western World,* tr. Montgomery Belgion (New York: Harper, 1979), 306–11; George Gusdorf, *Speaking [La Parole],* tr. Paul Brockelman (Evanston, Ill.: Northwestern Univ. Press, 1965), 3–59; and Shoshana Felman, *The Literary Speech Act: Don Juan with J. L. Austin, or Seduction in Two Languages,* tr. Catherine Porter (Ithaca: Cornell Univ. Press, 1983), 42–69.

34. Tzvetan Todorov, *The Fantastic: A Structural Approach to a Literary Genre,* tr. Richard Howard (Ithaca: Cornell Univ. Press, 1975).

35. Jeremy Strike, *A Promising Planet: Talk to Me in Thunder and Lightning* (New York: Ace, 1970).

36. Although I do not pursue this here, these stories, written by Americans during the 1950s, and based as they are on the figure of a promised land and an inevitable betrayal, can be ideologically read against the horizon of the Soviet occupation of Eastern Europe following World War II, and the consequent East/West Cold War.

37. Lawrence O'Donnell, "Promised Land," *Astounding Science Fiction* 44 (Feb. 1950): 137–60.

38. Robert F. Young, "The Promised Planet," *The Worlds of Robert F.*

Young: Sixteen Stories of Science Fiction and Fantasy (New York: Simon, 1957), 128–39.

39. E. T. A. Hoffmann, "The Vow," *Tales of Hoffmann,* new translated edition, ed. Christopher Lazare (New York: Grove, 1946), 266–94.

40. Robert Randall, "The Promised Land," *Astounding Science Fiction* 57 (Aug. 1946): 6–38.

41. Elizabeth Stuart Phelps, "The Oath of Allegiance," *"The Oath of Allegiance" and Other Stories* (Boston: Houghton, 1909), 1–31.

42. James Blish, "The Oath," *Best Science Fiction Stories of James Blish* (London: Faber, 1965), 207–24.

43. Jack McDevitt, "Promises to Keep," *The Year's Best Science Fiction, Second Annual Collection,* ed. Gardner Dozois (New York: Bluejay, 1985), 46–62.

44. Larry Niven & Jerry Pournelle, *Oath of Fealty* (New York: Pocket, 1981).

45. See esp. Stephen R. Donaldson, *Lord Foul's Bane,* bk. 1 of *First and Second Chronicles of Thomas Covenant, the Unbeliever* (New York: Ballantine, 1977).

46. The image of the ring is a widespread motif of promise, exchange, and sexuality in literature. For example, it occupies a central role in *Beowulf* (where the leader of a band of warriors is known as a "ring-giver"), and in many plays by Shakespeare (e.g., *Much Ado About Nothing*). See also Hoffmann, "The Vow," *Tales of Hoffmann*; Phelps, "Oath of Allegiance"; J. R. R. Tolkien, *The Lord of the Rings,* 2nd ed., 3 vols. (Boston: Houghton, 1967); and Larry Niven, *Ringworld* (New York: Ballantine, 1970).

47. H. G. Wells, "The Star," *Science Fiction: An Historical Anthology,* ed. Eric S. Rabkin (Oxford: Oxford Univ. Press, 1983), 222–33.

48. Arthur C. Clarke, "The Star," *Science Fiction: An Historical Anthology,* ed. Eric S. Rabkin (Oxford: Oxford Univ. Press, 1983), 364–70.

49. Michael Crichton, *Sphere* (New York: Knopf, 1987).

50. The *OED* and *Oxford Latin Dictionary* offer this as the most likely etymology. The precise historical etymology is unknown. Nevertheless, consider the following play of meanings that link the motifs of star, desire, paralysis and power: *dēsīderium,* a desire (for something absent); *dēsīdero,* to long for, desire; *sīderō,* to affect with sudden paralysis; *sīderālis,* of or concerned with the stars; *sīdō,* to adopt a sitting posture; *sedeō,* to sit, to sit in an official capacity (as a judge or magistrate), to occupy a position, to become fixed or established. What is most suggestive here is the hint of the possible semiotic, if not semantic, interanimation between star *(sīdus)* and to sit *(sedeō).* The stars occupy seemingly fixed positions within stellar constellations, which symbolize that which is both familiar and yet strange. The word/concept *desire,* then, implicitly and dialogically signifies both the object of desire (the transcendent

star), and the process of longing (the long suffering, waiting star). Like promising, to desire is to long for, to wait, to suffer. Desire, like a promise, or like language, is always rooted/positioned in history. A promise functions as a verbal and material site where this struggle is historically, imagistically, and psychoanalytically played out.

51. On the archetypal meaning of roundness as paranoiac, see James Hillman (*The Dream and the Underworld* [New York: Harper, 1979], 159–62). On the phenomenology of the circle and roundness, see Gaston Bachelard (*The Poetics of Space,* tr. Maria Jolas [Boston: Beacon, 1969], 232–42), and Georges Poulet (*The Metamorphoses of the Circle,* tr. Carley Dawson & Elliot Coleman in collaboration with the author [Baltimore: Johns Hopkins Univ. Press, 1966], Introduction, xi–xxvii).

52. Clarke, "The Star."

4

Metaphorical Drive — Or Why We're Such Good Liars
David Brin

Among all the wonderous devices of science fiction, just about the most fascinating to me were the "lie detectors" described in A. E. Van Vogt's *The World of Null-A*.

As far as the novel itself was concerned, they were little more than throwaways, authorial cop-outs revealed in the story at a certain point so that the protaganist, Gilbert Gosseyen, could verify what another character was saying without having to check it out. And yet, author's trick or not, the machines and their implications remained stuck in my mind.

Here is how they were supposed to have worked.

Every room, in every home or office, came equipped with a little wall-mounted device that "listened" to anything said within range. At any time, anyone engaged in a conversation could loudly and clearly say, "Lie detector: was he just telling the truth when he told me so-and-so?"

The machine was semisentient, meaning that it could answer back in a limited fashion. For example, it might respond, "He was telling the truth, withholding only details he considers inconsequential." Or perhaps, "The sentence is semantically true in itself, but he conceals contextual ramifications which he considers important."

How the machine was able to perceive all this was never made clear. Perhaps it weighed voice tremors, or tested the saliva in the air. The implication, however, was that there lay hidden from view an entire science upon which the practice of lie detection was firmly based.

Obviously, I am talking about something far removed from the Rube Goldberg "polygraph" devices of today.

Some of the protocols for using lie detectors were briefly implied, in Van Vogt's novel. The first was that the machine absolutely never *volunteered* a ruling without being asked. And it would only call a man a liar to his face, never after he had left the room. Also, it apparently was not considered polite to refer to lie detectors very often. Just the presence of such devices, nearby, seemed enough to make people careful to be truthful most of the time. Deception, in the world of Null-A, took on deeper, subtler forms.

What a fascinating concept! I am thinking of exploring, in a novel soon, the possible social consequences of such an invention.

Just try to think for a moment how dependent we modern humans are upon the lie—to smooth our way through day-to-day life, for instance.

("How are you today? someone asks.

(*Do you really want to know?* we think, and go on to answer, "Fine, how are you?")

Lying is supposed to be one of the Ten Bad Things. And yet, we are full of praise for the brave spy (from our side, that is) who prevaricates his way behind enemy lines or into the deadly dens of organized crime to catch the baddies before they can hatch their dark designs.

Early as children, we are lied to about tooth fairies and Santa Claus and stork-delivering babies. And I have seen no evidence that this is in any way harmful. Children do go through an early phase for a few years, when they appear to have great trouble differentiating what is true from what is false. But with enough practice most eventually seem to develop a natural instinct for telling the difference between "pretend" and actual lying about serious matters.

Perhaps this need for *practice,* for exploring what it *means* for something to be "true" or "false," accounts for something interesting I have observed—that most of the best Dads I have known seem to lie to their children incessantly, about inconsequentials. ("Daddy, what's that building over there?" "That's where the alien spaceships land, honey." *Daddy!*") On the other hand, good fathers apparently make it a matter of solemn honor absolutely never to lie about anything serious or important.

Fascinating. But as Mark Twain said, "I have the greatest regard for the Truth. I think we should be economical with it." Or at least he said something *like* that. Or maybe I am just making it up.

Perhaps we are wired for the ability to tell falsehoods. After all, lying is not uniquely a *human* failing. Researchers working with dolphins and apes report that these cousins of ours are ready and vigorous fibbers, especially when they are caught misbehaving. The most common whopper of them all appears to be, "Who, *me*? No, not me, boss. *He* was the one who did it!"

Of course this demonstrates one reason why we must have developed the ability to lie. A proto-man able believably to claim undue credit, or to deflect deserved blame, would find himself with access to more and better food, protection, respect and women than he otherwise would have merited by tribal rules. And so, of course, it also became a matter of some survival-related importance to grow better at *detecting* the lies of others.

Nowadays, it seems the battle between deceit and detection takes up more and more of society's time. There is an endless need for more accountants. Computers offer new techniques to both crime and law enforcement. There are now more lawyers in Los Angeles County than in all of Japan. Is it any wonder that so many place their trust in the unreliable and inconsistent polygraph, today's poor excuse for a "lie detector"? Wishful thinking may play a part. Is there not a part of most of us that longs secretly for a way to unmask all the prevaricators and scoundrels who seem to be all around us, laying traps and cruel hoaxes to trip up all us honest folk?

We *are* learning, slowly. For instance, a few experiments seem to indicate that one may more accurately check the veracity of another speaker over the telephone than we can in person! It seems liars use subtle facial and body cues either to seduce or threaten listeners into believing them. So it may be wise never to close a business deal until you have also discussed it by telephone.

And there appears to be a segment of the population, perhaps five percent or so, who do not lie as the rest of us do. They are totally adept at fooling today's crude "lie detectors." They project serenity and an aura of complete, sincere honesty as they spin their elaborate falsehoods. They make up the great con artists of our age.

All right, so humans (and some other animals) developed the ability to tell lies because of the benefits that might result. And for the same reason, we have also learned how to deflect some fraction of the lies of others. Still, while evolutionary advantage obviously explains why we are able to perform untruthfulness of the "I'll take credit for *this*, but blame *him* for *that*" variety, it seems much harder to account for all the other kinds of lying at which humans seem so adept, but for which we see no parallels among even our closest animal cousins.

So many lies have nothing to do with winning access to more food, money, sex, power. At least not directly. And indeed, these other types of lies may be the most potent of them all.

By now you must all be quite curious. Why do I bring this up here, in a discussion of the mindscapes of science fiction? The answer ought to be obvious.

To write science fiction—or indeed any other form of fiction—is to *lie*, purely and simply. It is to concoct, to fabricate, to incant. In other words, the science fiction author has simply got to be one of the great fibbers of all time.

After all, we tell tall tales, even slander, about fictional characters who certainly cannot sue or in any way protect their good names. Our stories are set in places that never were—we even provide maps!—and occur in conditions and circumstances that are speculative at best, and at times even absurd.

It is really an unusual situation, for in this case our "victims" appear to know full well that we are lying to them. And yet, instead of getting angry they seek us out, pay us, even ask eagerly for the "latest news" from our mythological universes. They bring us maps printed in different editions and ask us which is the more "authentic."

This is amazing—almost as astonishing as the fact that we take it all for granted.

Now I know what a few of you must be thinking—that literature is all about deeper human truths, which the writer illuminates by using analogies. At least the better examples supposedly do this. And I agree. But I also maintain that this is at least somewhat incidental to the true role of fiction.

The author's role *is* to lie. And lying can have a useful function. In fact, without it we would not be intelligent, self-aware, or even human at all.

Just as those children who are lied to *in the right way* by their parents somehow turn out smarter, more inventive, happier than their unfortunate peers, so it may be that the gargantuan, brobdignagian falsehoods woven by science-fiction authors serve a profound and important service in a human culture whose long and dreary childhood phase is at last shifting over into the hot, bright time of adolescence.

Evolution and Information

It is time for a biology lesson, so let us roll up our sleeves and start talking about fundamentals.

We all know that evolution is about life and death. Especially death. For instance, long before Darwin, acute observers pointed out that all animal species tend to produce far more offspring than is necessary to replace the parents when they die. It appears to be assumed that some of the products of this overproduction will succeed, and others will fail. Nature is *about* competition, and will only stop being so when (if we so choose) humankind picks up the new tools and changes the rules.

But what is all this competition *over*? Generally we tend to see it as a perpetual battle over *resources*. Trees fight slow, silent, chemical wars over their turf, and for the nutrients in the soil. Tiny diatoms evolve new techniques to cheat other plankton out of the trace elements in seawater. Packs of hyenas will wait until a cheetah makes a kill, then crowd close to drive her off to howl in outrage and disappointment.

The Earth is a rich and fecund place, but Life has this tendency to spread out and fill every available niche, until even the most inhospitable territory becomes the abode of one adapted species or another—from arctic hares to desert scorpions to sulfuriphagous bacteria dwelling in poison flows so hot they would instantly erupt into steam if they were not crushed in by the weight of kilometers of black water. Life proliferates. It spreads and adapts, always seeking the energy, the vital elements.

Even on the rich Earth there are only so many resources to go around. Setting aside anomalies such as dolphin altruism and a few relatively kind human societies, Nature is for the most part a zero-sum game. If *I* seize this bit, it is denied you. If you win a point, I lose one. Whether you *like* this situation or not is quite irrelevant. It is the core of modern biology.

But all this interest in resource competition has, I believe, distracted biologists from another truth, that there is one *other* thing in the world that is fully as important to animals as resources. That thing is *information*.

Now information is funny stuff. It is not intrinsically limited, as is the sunlight in a rain forest, or water in a desert, or good farmland in a starving nation. If I pick up a useful fact, it is not then necessarily denied you. If you learn it too, I am not then deprived of it.

I *may* want to try to keep you from learning my fact, since it may give me a competitive advantage in acquiring some resource. Or, I might offer it in trade. Or, on the other hand, I may have some reason to *give* you the datum, especially if it is time to cooperate.

Or, perhaps, I may give it to you because the datum is a lie.

Now evolution acts on how we use information fully as much as it does on our access to resources. It certainly rewards creatures that are better at behaving properly in the right circumstances. How is it, then, that we living things use information?

Well, first off, there is the information coded so magnificently in DNA. The twisting coils of nucleic acids, phosphates, amino acids, and sugars make up what Richard Dawkins has called "the selfish genes" within every cell in our bodies. Dawkins makes a case that it is not the creatures themselves that compete out in the outer world, but the information *codes* within the DNA that "strive" to multiply and spread copies of themselves through the success of their carrier organisms.

This fascinating topic goes far beyond the purview of this essay, so we will leave it here by saying simply that genes are in no way pictured as self-aware. They act in a world of chemistry, statistics, and happenstance. The vast majority of species in the world behave only in automatic chemical response to external stimuli—such as wriggling toward nutritious scents in the water, or moving away from light—and the most successful of those responses, those which process the information correctly, allow the organisms carrying those genes to reproduce and pass on more copies of those genes.

But as we go "higher" on the chaim of life, we soon encounter something new. We encounter *learning*.

Many of you will have heard of experiments with planaria (flatworms) in which electric shocks are used to teach the tiny creatures either to avoid light or seek it. This is an example of where some genes arose that gave their creatures the ability to *modify* their behavior responses, to change the way they deal with their environment. Only in this way can animals take advantage of new opportunities or adapt to avoid new threats.

Learning allows access to far more information than that contained in the genes alone. As we continue to climb the "ladder of life" we find animals increasingly subtle at drawing lessons from experience. Among the carnivorous mammals learning takes on a very advanced state. A fox will bring home a wounded chipmunk for its kits to play with, and "play" is now seen as clearly the way young mammals practice to learn the skills they will need if they are to be successful adults.

Learning enables these creatures to be far more adaptable than those dependent on mere instinct alone. Their responses can be more flexible. They can migrate into new territories, take advantage of altered circumstances.

So important is learning that "higher" birds and mammals sacrifice high reproduction rates in order to devote great time and effort to only a few offspring. And those offspring remain "young" for a very long time.

Neoteny is the word describing this tendency of more complicated organisms to have ever longer childhood periods. For all of the growing it must do, a baby elephant spends less time dependent on its mother than does an infant chimpanzee. Nor does any ape emerge as helpless, nor remain so for as long, as a human child. We come out of the womb as mere fetuses. So little is instinctive in us that we must learn to walk, learn to perform even simply communication with our own kind, learn to use our very limbs.

This concentration on learning at the expense of instinct makes childhood long and difficult. But it also has made us the only creatures that can inhabit, or at least visit, every ecological niche on the planet. It has made us supremely flexible, but the information revolution did not stop there.

Speech, Writing, and Imagination

It is said that the most significant feature separating humans from the animals is their use of speech. In a quantitative sense this certainly seems so, though other creatures do communicate abstract information to some degree. (Bee scouts "dance" to indicate the location of a food source. Apes can arguably learn a sort of sign language.)

What does language add to a creature's ability to gather and use information? Well, put simply, it enables the animal to "know" about that which it has never directly experienced in any way. This is a vast multiplication of learning.

The way humans use it, speech not only conveys facts but also *metaphors*. When we hear somebody say, "I drove the pickup to the market to get some potatoes," this does not register just as a string of associated event/facts but as *images*. Knowing next to nothing about the person's vehicle, or their neighborhood store, we nevertheless create a mental picture of the event described, even if we must later revise this tentative depiction when we learn more.

This is *not* how a computer takes in or evaluates information. The field of Artificial Intelligence is totally stymied over this question of mimicking the metaphorical way in which we think, so those in the field have concentrated on *explicit processing*. Clearly we do not think as such machines will.

It is also easy to see that with this way of using speech we were already well on the way toward becoming liars.

But humanity did not stop with this huge competitive advantage — full use of speech. Speech only gave us the ability to add the described experiences of our peers to what we have observed ourselves. What came *next* enables yet another order of magnitude expansion of the data available to us. It was the ability to share the experiences of people we have never even met, who live in far distant lands, or who even died long before we were born.

I am speaking now of writing, which enabled us to expand our access to information dramatically. Much has been said about this revolution, and I will not belabor the subject here except to say that it, too, contributed to our grant aptitude at fooling and being fooled.

What came next, though, was the most significant revolution of them all. It is the talent that truly makes us what we are. For it enabled us to use not only the information provided by our genes, or our instincts, or direct experience, or the words of those we know, or even the experiences of all the wise men and women who ever lived.

This new talent is the thing that lets us "know" what *has never happened,* and even what might truly *never* happen! It allows us to contemplate scenes and images no eye could ever have beheld and enables us to consider possible solutions to problems that have not even yet manifested themselves. It has made us so creative and innovative and adaptable that no animal on Earth can ever hope to match wits with us. It has turned competition between our species and others into a wholesale rout.

I am talking about imagination. It is the source of humanity's power on this planet. It is where the "mindscapes of science fiction" have their origins.

It is also the real mother of metaphors, and the true father of all lies.

Those Glittering Eyes

Let us pause for a moment for an aside as we turn to examine one of the finest works of sculpture in the world, Michaelangelo's magnificent statue of Moses.

The Hebrew prophet is shown seated on a throne, scowling in deep thought as he stares at something just out of view. His mood is intent, piercing. And right there on the patriarch's furrowed brow, just above his eyes, Michaelangelo has carved two small *horns.*

We have to ask why the artist put *horns* on the brow of one of the holiest men in Judeo-Christian tradition. The popular academic answer is actually quite simple. It seems that, in many biblical versions, a word was translated into Greek as "horns" when the original Hebrew actually said "lamps."

("He had lamps upon his brow.")

Now what the heck does *that* mean? It is hard to picture the prophet with little lanterns hanging above his eyes, so one can imagine how the mistake was made. Seemed reasonable enough.

Then, I thought about it.

Just above the eyes . . .

There is only one thing of any importance to be found right there in any human body. Just above the eyes is where one finds the prefontal lobes of the cerebral cortex.

Many people have heard of these tiny nubs of gray matter from the fact that they have sometimes been cut in a radical and not highly regarded treatment for certain mental disorders. ("I'd rather have a free bottle in front of me than a brain operation. . . .") Lobotomies have been known to relieve the suffering of certain individuals, but nearly always at a cost. The lobotomized person quite often loses interest in the *future.* He no longer has any capacity to metaphorize about it, or to envision pictures in his head concerning tomorrow or the next day or the next.

It turns out that the prefrontal lobes are the essential portions of the brain for enabling us to visualize ourselves in a future setting. They are where we imagine, where we make models of the actions we plan to perform, experiment with different schemes, and work out the likely consequences. They enable us to consider that tomorrow might be different than today.

I might add that the prefrontal lobes may also be the very last brain feature we evolved. It could be, in fact, that they do not always "turn on," that a great many people in our society are simply incapable of using the power that they offer.

Can it be, then, that what the biblical scribes were talking about when they spoke of "lamps over his eyes" was something special about the way Moses *thought*? Could they be describing something special about the way he used his mind? The way he stared with those glittering eyes, as Michaelangelo depicts him doing, into a future none of this contemporaries could see or contemplate?

(The writer Julian Jaynes has contended that, around the time of Moses, Western man went through a sudden and fundamental change in the "software" with which he used his brain. It was, said Jaynes, a relatively sudden conversion to a new way of using the internal language of our own minds. His scenario is fantastic, and it will take much more evidence to convince me of his complete hypothesis. But even partial acceptance of his data makes one wonder all the more at the miracle of thought.)

Now consider the placement of *horns,* instead of lamps, upon the brow of Moses. Is mistranslation all there is to it? I am not so sure. Think for a moment about the other biblical character who is supposed to have those embellishments.

To some, associating horns with the devil is an obvious holdover from the suppression of animism and the cult of Pan. But what if it were actually something else? What if it were a reflection of the discomfort caused in the hearts of many by the full activation of those tiny nubs, the prefrontal lobes, the organs that *enable* us to doubt, to imagine, to believe we can question even God?

More importantly to this discussion, are those bits of gray matter also partly or largely responsible for our loose facility with metaphors? Because if they are, they also explain our ability to tell science-fiction stories, and our ability to tell great whopping lies.

What Is Imagination?

The great Freudian analyst Lawrence Kubie wrote a book entitled *The Neurotic Distortion of the Creative Process,* in which he laid out the "classical" psychoanalytical theory of how imagination and creativity work in human beings. His purpose was to demonstrate the fallacy inherent in the damnable but nevertheless popular myth that creative people have to be crazy in order to be inventive, and that geniuses must suffer as some sort of "price" for climbing so close to Heaven.

(Many of Kubie's patients were artists, musicians, scientists, who were in great pain and believed he could help them, but were nevertheless reluctant because they feared the cure [and happiness] would only come at the price of losing their creative "spark.")

To simplify greatly, Kubie's model depicts the mind as being made up of many levels. And on each level there might be said to be "politicians" and "civil servants." The nature of the politicians is to have motivations, axes to grind, favorite priorities each wishes to impose on the overall person. Civil servants, on the other hand, are perfectly honest but dull functionaries.

Now among the most important "levels" of the mind is the one where *memory association* takes place. Here the civil servant is called the "preconscious." It is a system that keeps tabs on whatever is going on way up above in the conscious awareness — what we are seeing, smelling, hearing, thinking at that moment. The preconscious is forever scanning through its vast files of memory for anything in there with *any* sort of relevance to what is going on "up above" right now.

Say you have not smelled a particular aroma since you were a child, or a face in a crowd bears a more than 75 percent resemblance to a certain third-grade teacher — the preconscious honestly and assiduously seeks out any correlation, slips all or part of each relevant memory into an express tube, and ships it straight upstairs.

This is how things keep "popping" into our minds all the time. The preconscious is very good at its job, and is *always* very busy.

Only there are two problems. First, most of these memories are of very limited usefulness or relevance. If we paid conscious attention to all of them we would soon be of little more use than some of the unfortunate inmates of certain institutions, whose discriminating processes have broken down. So we must have an editing process.

Here is where the politicians come in — those drives, values, compulsions, neuroses that are constantly at war with each other beneath the surface, contending for control over the total man or woman. Down at the level of associative memory, these little scoundrels interfere whenever it looks as if the preconscious is about to send up something they *do not* want remembered! An offended neurosis cannot prevent the honest civil servant from sending the memory up, so he interferes by *pasting* a false label over the packing tube.

This is called neurotic misdirection, and Freud pointed out in his *Psychopathology of Everyday Life* that we *all* do this, even the sanest of us, all of the time. It is the source of slips of the tongue and pen, or spoonerisms, or those melodies that suddenly leap to mind and *stick*, for what reason we do not know. And it is one reason why things suddenly *occur* to us.

There are also politicians way up above, which try to call attention to some memories and to divert it away from others. In fact, it might be contended that the *only* real purpose of consciousness itself— that flickering "me" we all know from second to second—is to give an open, honest forum in which this debate can take place, rather than allowing decisions to be made in the "smoke-filled rooms" just below.

In any event, it is clear that if this model has any validity at all the process of memory is a complicated one, both profoundly powerful and yet easily manipulated and diverted.

But how does this relate to our earlier discussion?

Simple. Memory is the process by which we store, retrieve, and reevaluate what we have learned, whether through direct experience, hearsay, or reading. We have far, far more to remember than any other creatures, and we have developed brains and minds good at comparison, at associations, at judging relationships between memories that lie far apart in time and circumstances.

But this so far is *not* imagination. It is only association.

Earlier I spoke of two things that can interfere with the prconscious in its honest pursuit of its duty to draw and send up relevant memories. First there was the ambiguity of "relevance" itself. Then there was sabotage by petty little neuroses. But there is a *third* way by which the honesty of memory is compromised. And this process is one *mean* evolutionary adaptation.

Somehow, it seems, a certain little devil sneaks into the transit office of the honest ol' preconscious, and it does a nasty thing. Out of maybe a thousand mailing tubes sent "upstairs," the devil fills one or two with memories that have *absolutely no relevance whatsoever* to what the person is now experiencing. What is more, the devil also does even worse sabotage. He rummages through file drawers, picks out random memories, and *damages* them! He smashes them to bits and recombines some of them with bits from others he has broken. Then he stuffs the resulting *false* idea into the shute.

The result is the occasional bizarre thought, that apparently came out of nowhere. The weird juxtaposition. The momentary feeling that all of this has happened before.

The result is *imagination,* for now the human animal is capable of evaluating not only information gleaned from experience or transmitted by others but also data that came from no place at all! He or she can contemplate, weigh, evaluate more than what has happened in the real world, or what he or she has been *told,* but that which has never happened at all, and possibly never could.

Of course most of the products of this process are garbage, useless. We must edit, prune, cast aside ten thousand notions for every one we think to follow up on. And for every thousand of *those* that remain forever at the level of daydream, perhaps one or two advance to the status of *idea.* Nevertheless, by this awkward-sounding process we have been unleashed from slavery to the real world. We have been set loose upon the starlanes of imagination and metaphor.

The human animal has become capable, in other words, of *lying to himself or herself.* And here is the beginning of all that is foul and all that is greatest and most noble in our race.

The True Role of Lying

We have come to the point where we may be able at last to try to understand the place of metaphors in human life. They are models of the world, or pats of it, models that enable us to perform mental experiments, to "try out" a course of action before we are committed to it, or test an idea before we decide we like it.

Metaphors, especially those that come out of the imagination, are essentially lies. They are like photos of a mountain — useful to a map maker, but certainly never to be confused with the mountain itself.

How much horror and pain have been wrought by humans (mostly male) who have announced that *their* models of the world were final and complete Truth, and death to any who disagree? Humans are quite capable of associating their ego (one of the more powerful "politicians" in our minds) with an abstract idea, and going forth to wreak havoc on those with the effrontery to believe in different metaphors.

Indeed, it is my belief that there has been one and only one contribution by Western Civilization to human culture and the planet Earth, and that contribution is summed up whenever anyone, anywhere, says to himself or herself the following.

"Hey! I just might be lying to myself when I think that. Just because I want to think it's true doesn't mean it *is* true. Maybe I'd better get someone impartial to verify my results."

Out of this statement (or the newfound ability to make it) came science, skepticism, individualism, true empathy, respect for eccentricity, tolerance, and all of the other mythic structures that are starting to spread and take over a world *zeitgeist* once totally dominated by tribal totems, machismo, and paranoia. Out of this statement sprouts the flower of *honesty,* the principle that sometime saves some of us from the consequences of our lying minds.

Metaphorization enables us to imagine copiously, vastly expanding creativity. But it also lets us lie to *ourselves.* The imaginative individual faces a choice, between accepting the saccharin-sweetness of tying his or her ego to favorite metaphors, or bravely recognizing that the map is *not* the territory, and approaching his or her model of the world with a sense of humor.

A Brief Return to Relevance

A minor but telling example of this phenomenon is experienced by nearly every neophyte writer, when first submitting a piece to the scrutiny of others. Inevitably, a great deal of ego is tied up in the beautiful, stirring, unmatchable prose, in which all the author's deepest hopes or darkest fears may lay revealed. Any criticism sears like a burning poker, as if the correcting pencil were being stabbed into the scrivener's own tender hand.

I know of one case where an English instructor was essentially threatened that if she did not like a story, its writer was going to end his own life. One would hope she kindly lied.

The irony is, of course, that it is only through feedback, correction, and painful experimentation that any craftsman develops skill. Intelligent constructive criticism should be viewed as the basic bread of life by any new author. Indeed, the need never really disappears, since even a pro can enter into a phase of self-indulgence, of lying to himself about his work—the ruination of any bright career.

Self-deception is particularly hazardous in any profession that is *based* upon lying. The most dangerous politician is he who has himself convinced of the sophistries he used to pander his way into office. The most offensively egotistical movie star is the one who *believes* the stuff his publicity flacks put out.

And most pathetic of all are the writers who fail to remember that their mindscapes are wonderfully conceived and worked-out fantasies, and not, after all, icons before which they all must sacrifice their critical faculties or sense of humor.

Metaphors, Myths and Science Fiction

Every society seems to need its *myths*—those fables and allegories that distill the essence of a people and what they were all about during a given age. For example, back when the English colonies were perched on the edge of what seemed then a limitless, dark forest, there abounded myths that extolled the virtues of farms and towns and treated the "evil wilderness" harshly. So there were legends such as that of Paul Bunyan, whose axe could take out ten trees in a backstroke.

Nowadays there is an abundance of "civilization." It is wilderness that is rare, and mythic figures of sad-eyed bears in forest-ranger hats remind children from an early age what they must learn to cherish and preserve before it is lost forever. (Not coincidentally, there are now more trees in North America than there were in 1900, when Teddy Roosevelt became the prime promoter of this "new" countertheme of environmentalism.)

Just how powerful are these myths? For instance, did *Fail Safe* and *Dr. Strangelove* each in their own way help prevent nuclear war? The evidence I have seen makes me think it likely.

Myths are potent things. And they jealously guard their territory, as if they were living entities themselves. Richard Dawkins coined the term *memes* (as a parallel with *genes*) for ideas that are like viruses. Not only do they take hold in host organisms (human minds) but they arrange to have themselves spread around (via proselytizing, or argument, or science-fiction novels) to infect others. Some memes are lethal, some are symbiotic. And many are mutually incompatible. Memes can wage war with one another over the territory of our minds.

All around us we can see the latest battle raging—by mythic images extolling the old values of machismo or paranoia or homogeneity against potent interlopers promoting a new *zeitgeist,* one based on tolerance, diversity, suspicion of authority, and a fanatical (almost sexual) appreciation of *otherness.*

I have commented elsewhere about this new world view, the "Dogma of Otherness," so I will be brief here. But, it is well worth a moment's attention.

As just one example of this new human doctrine, and how it is promoted, look carefully at the popular film, *E.T.*—with an eye to its role as *propaganda.* You will see *xenophilia,* or "love of otherness," purveyed in its purest, most distilled form. Arguments over the movie's artistic merits (or lack of them) miss the point. Along with *Starman, The Day the Earth Stood Still,* and countless other cases, *E.T.* hammered away at its viewers (with their active collaboration and consent) helping them shape a new consensus of how they must live their lives. A consensus based on powerful myths of tolerance.

You ask, "Is he serious about this?" Well, yes and no.

No, I am not saying this model of mine is anything more than a metaphor for much, much more complex processes. I do not *believe* it any more than I believe my earlier description of Kubie's theory of associative memory was anything more than a clever model, to be looked at, pondered, then rolled up and thrown away.

But then, I must also say, yes! I *do* believe that it is at the level of popular culture that people work out what they want to be and do. And I think powerfully important things are being done in the realm of myth, right at this very moment.

(By the way, as I am a product of all of this propaganda in favor of tolerance-and-eccentricity, so it is no surprise that I approve of our steady movement in that direction, and like to think I try to "infect" others with it, through my work.)

Science fiction plays a potent role in all of this. In fact, one metaphorization might be to call our little literary cabal the "R&D Division" of the "Department of Myths and Legends" of the new culture. We are the scouts, the ones who explore the edges, who point out dangers that may lurk, not just *on* the horizon but perhaps some distances beyond it. We warn of possible mistakes and create chilling scenarios to make them mythically believable. And in so doing, we hope to prevent them from coming true.

(Does anyone actually believe a stranded starfarer would be *dissected* in the America of the 1980s? Or a talking ape thrown in a freak show? Naw! All those guilt-tripping movies and books have got us feeling too unworthy. We would probably smother to death any visitor under telegrams from talk-show hosts and ad agencies offering lucrative product promotion deals. As for rebellious robots, forget it! The Frankenstein Myth has put paid to any possibility of our ever letting *that* happen.)

And, of course, we dangle possibilities before our readers' eyes. "Hey! Dummy! Look what you just might get if—*if* you wise up in time." We say to them, "The possibilities are endless." And that, in itself, is a selling job in favor of a certain way of viewing the world.

Do I really believe this "Mythic R&D" metaphor actually *defines* science fiction. No way! Of course not. But, just as a single photograph of a mountain is helpful if insufficient to the climber, the little model given above may illuminate something about the underlying value of our work.

Lies and Human Destiny

I still fantacize about "lie detectors" from time to time. I long for Van Vogt's passive, impartial, mechanical judges whenever some smooth-tongued fellow tries to sell me on the latest hot investment, or that "great deal" in a car. Can I be forgiven if I might wish one were in the room right at that moment when someone says to me "I love you"? Not that I would ever *consult* the thing, at a time like that. But would it not be a comfort, just knowing that it was there?

And would it not also take all the romance and adventure out of such a moment? Would not the prospect also frighten the living hell out of me?

Say yea!

As we move out of brief adolescence into the epoch of our true power, we shall begin to take on many of the powers of gods. Already we can throw thunderbolts and fly across the sky. Soon we shall create life, and modify other creatures to do more than just surrender us their flesh and labor. We shall refashion them to *think,* either to become our servants — as predicted so movingly by Cordwainer Smith — or to be our companions, partners in civilization to relieve our loneliness in the long, long night.

Or perhaps they will be the long foretold intelligent machines. But if so, one thing I confidently predict is that, in becoming sentient, they will of necessity have lost the one attribute we tend to associate with computers, their prim precision, the error-free perfection of simple mechanical thought.

In any case, what will the creators of such new minds say when they come to realize that there is one basic key to the temple of consciousness, to unlocking the door of mind and self-awareness and creativity — and that key is the ability to make mistakes — the ability to lie?

Hell, what do we say to our *children*? Not tomorrow, but today! For these are the "intelligent life forms" we create anew every generation. Is it any wonder so many of *them* are confused when we tell them not to lie, and yet encourage them to *imagine*? When we urge them to flee falsehood, but to seek out adventure on the landscapes of faraway made-up worlds, and in the mindscapes of fictional alien minds?

The distinction is a subtle one, indeed. It is quite possibly the fundamental distinction underlying all of human morality. The best parents try hard to make it clear to their children. They show by example that imagination is what makes you laugh and cry and *feel* the pain of other creatures deep inside your heart, while at the same time retaining perspective and your own sense of self. But lying is when your *mind* goes wrong, when the process does not work, when you start believing the metaphors and letting them control you, rather than using them for what they were meant to be, models of the world and nothing more.

This is the heart of the issue, whenever we talk about "mindscapes" or science fiction or — or, indeed, anything at all.

Or at least (the author says as he chuckles, laughing suddenly at his own intensity) or at least this is *my* metaphor for what I *think* it is all about.

Look at it, contemplate it, *play* with it and see what you might learn . . .

Then, by all means, laugh out loud, and roll it up and toss it aside. Move on. Move on.

5

The Playing Fields of Eden
Frank McConnell

Our general subject is imaginary landscapes in science-fiction and fantasy, and the way we have phrased things suggests that science fiction and fantasy are primordial human activities that somehow imply, or necessitate, the invention of worlds elsewhere or elsewhen. I have written and taught for years that man is the storytelling animal, and that the act of tale-weaving is the first truly human activity.

I was, of course, wrong. Never fear, it is an old habit of mine. For recently thinking about this essay, watching the Chicago Bears blow their Super Bowl chances, losing at chess to my son, at dominoes to my wife, and worst of all at a high rate to my bookie (Lakers 106, Celtics 103), I came to realize that Eliade is subtly wrong in *Myth and Reality* and Huizinga subtly right in *Homo Ludens*. (I also submit to you that a man who, after dropping two hundred dollars on the Celtics, thinks about comparative anthropology, is at the very least deserving of your compassion.)

There is an older urge than the urge to tell stories. It is the urge to play, and to play with strict rules. I now believe that, even before they began telling anecdotes to one another, Og and Skag, the first fully enfranchised human beings, tried to match the number of stones one or the other held in his hand, or raced to the salt lick, or enacted some elaborate and forever lost combination of the two contests. And then they told anecdotes, because the game had given them the possibility of a landscape they could control, rather than vice versa, and had thereby given them the possibility of fiction.

I want, in other words, to reverse the perspective of these proceedings, and to suggest that imagined landscapes invent stories, rather than the other way around. In Stevens' great metaphor for metaphor:

> *The man bent over his guitar,*
> *A shearsman of sorts. The day was green.*
> *They said, "You have a blue guitar,*
> *You do not play things as they are."*
> *The man replied, "Things as they are*
> *Are changed upon the blue guitar."*

Never mind that this resonant wedding of rhythm and simplicity is obviously the strong percursor of that master fantasist, Dr. Seuss. I am more concerned with the fact that here, as everywhere in Stevens, the landscape comes *before* the story, just because it is an artificial landscape, the landscape of story or of dream or of game. Why is the man with the blue guitar a shearsman of sorts? Because he cuts into patterns: because he partitions the world of experience as it is given to us—or attacks us— into a habitable place for the imagination. Things as they are, as we all know, are intolerable. So we invent games to organize the chaos, and if we have the spirit to take the games seriously enough, later in our psychic evolution we invent stories that carry the grace of the games into a more expansive sphere. From chessboard to basketball court to Dungeons and Dragons playsheet, the playing field is the primal scene, the Eden, in which grows the Tree of the Knowledge of Good and Evil.

George C. Scott, in *Patton*, always raises a smile when he snarls, "I wouldn't give a hoot in hell for a man who lost—and laughed!" But that is actually very good theology. If you play a game with anything but absolute seriousness, you are not really playing the game. You are only watching, and the difference between watching and playing is like the difference between wanting and desiring. All sentient species do the first, but only a few are lucky and unfortunate enough to be capable of the latter. The game *must* be serious, just because it is cosmically trivial, trivality being, like Sartre's "Nothingness," the gift consciousness alone brings into the world. "We are a bit of stellar matter gone wrong," writes Sir Arthur Eddington of you and me; it is not that far from Byron's description of you and me, a century earlier, as "fiery dust," or Hamlet's description of you and me as "this quintessence of dust," or the observation of Lucretius, in *De Rerum Natura*, that human life is merely an epiphenomenon of a closed, uncaring universe.

We are a cosmic triviality, and we did not have to wait for radio telescopy to find out how tiny we really are. But, as far as we know, we are the only creatures who *have* heard the bad news. Blessed though they might be, presumably no dolphin has ever stared at the moon and felt longing.

But we have, and have realized that the dimensions of our world are not fitted to the dimensions of our hope. So we have, traditionally, done one of two things. We have invented a god who ultimately reconciles the world outside the head and the world inside the head, or we have invented playing boards or playing fields or rules of procedure that limit reality to bits we can deal with. Nick Adams' fishing trip in "The Big Two-Hearted River" and the Pauli Exclusion Principle are both attempts to say that, if the cosmos is radically unknowable, we may at least define the things we do know, and deal with them as if they were the all. One fishes with a sense of ethics: you do not drop a percussion grenade into the middle of the lake and wait for your dead victims to float to the surface. For to do so would be to violate the rules, and that is an unholy thing. The playing board is a shield against disorder whose vulnerability is its own best defense.

I am supposed to be talking about landscapes, and, remarkably enough, I am. For a landscape is not a world, it is a world as perceived, which is to say a prospect with rules of perception, which is to say a playing board.

I have grown prematurely metaphysical. Let me attempt to retreat from portentousness by asking you why you do *not* move your bishop vertically as opposed to diagonally, why you do *not* pass to an ineligible receiver, or why you do *not* cheat at cards. You do not because to do so would be to violate, not just the rules of the game, but the fragile, endangered structure of consciousness itself. Wittgenstein, that unhappy and godlike man, dated the second phase of his philosophical career from the moment when he realized that language could most accurately be perceived as a game. And to cheat at the game, to lie, is to utter a deep and maybe irrevocable challenge to the authenticity of consciousness altogether. But what is a lie? "How can you charge me with heresy?" shouted a priest friend of mine to his cardinal a few years ago. " You don't even know what orthodoxy is, you toad!"

A lie is a violation of the conventions of speech, of truth, of the rules of the game as they have been promulgated. And nothing else. It is easy, and therein lies its terror. You cannot lie until you have a convention about "the truth"; you cannot cheat until you know the rules to violate. "Civilization," said another friend of mine to me, "is an agreement to leave the abyss alone." But then civilization is the invention of the abyss it chooses, regally, to ignore. The first act of the Holy One in Genesis is to divide the light from the darkness: a shearsman of sorts. Some busy years later, Alexander Pope would re-create the creation in *The Rape of the Lock,* in terms of a card game: "The skillful nymph reviews her force with care; *Let Spades be trumps!* she said, and trumps they were." (Italics added.)

Tom Robbins, in *Even Cowgirls Get the Blues,* observes quite correctly that earthquakes only happen in cities. That is, if one continental plate decides to get on closer terms with another, rabbits, deer, and nomads will notice the ensuing perturbation as no more "unnatural" or "extraordinary" than a thunderstorm or a snowfall. But we have built cities, and cities are as vulnerable to fault lines as language is to lies or games to rule violations. We know that Jericho is the earliest city of the Neolithic Revolution; and we know, from the song we all sang as children, that its walls came tumbling down. Joshua, in other words, not only fought the battle of Jericho, he also, in a world-historical sense, invented the Richter scale.

King Lear knew this, too. That most inexhaustible of plays may be read as, among much else, a parable about human as opposed to inhuman space and a paradigm of the landscapes of fantasy.

In *The Poetics of Space,* Gaston Bachelard makes the crucial observation that "space" has two meanings. Our first association, when we are being self-consciously intellectual — always a bad move, by the way — our first association is usually with the Cartesian abstraction of emptiness incarnate or with the infinite and cold vistas of *Paradise Lost, Faust,* and *Star Wars.* But, says Bachelard, there is another kind of space, and one much closer to us. Call it human space: the warm encirclement of mother's arms, of your blanket on a frosty morning, of the living room at night after the children are in bed, of your lover's arms. It is the space of the cave, and perhaps we do not write about it as much as we do about the space of the galaxies because it is so much more dear to us. Sacred things are not to be lightly spoken of.

Bachelard, at least, has the great good sense to admit the importance of this perception. Among his phenomenological, deconstructionist, or otherwise distracted countrymen, he is the prose poet of the cozy, and of the home truth — and that is high praise — rather as if Beatrix Potter had married G. W. F. Hegel and begotten a critic.

Think about Lear in the storm. He has already learned about the difference between inside and outside, inside his clothes, inside the castle walls, inside the security of his kingship, and outside, terribly outside, all these things. And now it is raining on him. And he does not even care about coming in from the rain, for, as he says to Kent: "The tempest in my mind / Doth from my senses take all feeling else, / Save what beats there."

Orwell says that when Lear is in his right mind he hardly ever says anything sensible. Leaving aside the question whether Lear ever *is* in his right mind, here at least he is at the height of his rage, and therefore also at his wisest. Inside is civilized space, the space of the playing board or of the story, the space we have humanized. Outside is the abyss. And *Lear,* more unrelentingly than any fantasy I know, reminds us again and again that once you cross that boundary, you may never—ever—return. The tempest in the mind is the breaking of the rules of the game, the admission of the barbarians within the gates. It is the end of the civilization that invents, and then defends itself against, the void.

This is why, of Cuchulain, it is recorded that "the poets were encouraged to record his points of excellence, as follows: excellence of body, shape, and build. His grades in the following skills were also excellent: swimming, horsemanship, checkers, chess, and competitions of various sorts. In combat he was, as we have seen, unmatched in all Ireland."

It should strike us as curious that a mighty warrior is praised for, among other things, his prowess at checkers and chess. Not even Howard Cosell, one imagines, would ask Sugar Ray Leonard about his bridge game. Indeed, it should strike us as Homeric. William Empson, in *Some Versions of Pastoral,* remarks upon the scene in the *Iliad* where Ajax cooks his own dinner. Only in the primal perception of the epic or pastoral world, says Empson, could we see the connection between martial heroism and the most elementary of human technologies; because only that perception shows us how intimately related are primitive *and* sophisticated technologies. Think about the famous shock cut from tossed bone to orbiting nuclear warhead in *2001;* the landscape defined by both tools is human, antinatural, and therefore essentially the same.

Or think about my own favorite example of "heroic" ethics, from *Beowulf.* There the bard tells us that when Beowulf became king he was a mighty warrior, a fair dispenser of treasure to his people, and "when drunk, he slew no hearth companions."

It is a funny line, and a profound one. The rules of the game are revealed in all their simplicity and all their resonance. "You will *not* kill," says the Mosaic Decalogue. "Even when you're drunk, *don't* kill your friends," says *Beowulf.* Perhaps we could interpret most serious fiction as subtly encoded rules of conduct, as models for social and psychic games we might like to play.

Let me quote from a brilliant novel published last year, John Hough's *The Conduct of the Game.* It is about baseball umpires, about storytelling, and about theology. In one scene a young man, Roy Van Arsdale, is asked to serve as umpire in an informal softball game between the teams of lawyers—a harmless, even a trivial event. Roy calls a batter out on strikes, the batter swears at him, Roy ejects him from the game, and the lawyers tell Roy he is dismissed as their umpire.

Then comes a moment worth waiting to have been written. *"Wait just a goddamn minute!"* shouts Roy:

"If you want me to leave . . . I'll leave. I'll go. But if you do this—if you dismiss me in the middle of a game—you make the game meaningless, do you understand? Whoever wins, it'll mean nothing. Your man here took a good pitch and struck out. He swore at the umpire; he's out of the game. That's baseball. Those are the rules. Do you want to play the game right, or do you want to play a made-up game that'll suit your tantrums and your mistakes?"

"That's baseball. Those are the rules." In this extraordinary book, that is an extraordinary passage. The lawyers, overcome by logic (this is, after all, a work of fiction), ask Roy if he will at least leave Clark, the erring player, in the game. "No," replies Roy. "I cannot *leave* Clark in the game, because Clark is no longer *in* the game. What did I just finish saying?"

There is a direct line, I suggest, from this passage back to "Let Spades be trumps! she said, and trumps they were" and back to Lear's discovery that the tempest in the mind overwhelms the tempest outside the mind, and finally back to the only fiction I know that has the courage, or the audacity, to begin "In the beginning." You will notice that I have presumed upon your attention without really, so far, addressing the topic. I will be brief, and do not remind me that Polonius said the same thing. The imagination of landscape produces the possibility of fiction, and the activity of the game produces the imagination of landscape. Storytelling, no less than checkers or chess or football, is a kind of game, and the opponents are the storyteller and the listener.

But are we not already guilty of an insulting limitation in calling storytelling a game? Is it not also a science, an art, hovering between these two categories as Muhammad's coffin hovered between heaven and earth? Is it not a unique bond between every pair of opponents, ancient and yet eternally new; mechanical in its framework and yet only functioning through use of the imagination; confined in geometrically fixed space and at the same time released from confinement by its permutations; continuously evolving yet sterile; thought that leads nowhere, mathematics that add up to nothing, art without an end product, architecture without substance, and nevertheless demonstrably more durable in its true nature and existence than any books or creative works? Is it not the only game that belongs to all peoples and all times? And who knows whether God put it on earth to kill boredom, to sharpen the wits or to lift the spirits? Where is its beginning and where its end?

That is the best definition of storytelling I have ever written, and I did not write it first. From "But are we not already guilty" to "Where is its beginning and where its end" the passage is a direct quotation from Stefan Zweig's great story, "The Royal Game." I only cheated once in my hygienic plagiarism, and that was in using the word *storytelling*. For Zweig is not writing about storytelling. He is writing about chess.

There is a Zen of archery, and of the tea service. If there were a Zen of criticism, and if I were one of its masters, I would propose this *koan* to my apprentices: you may wager your life against a matador or a chess grand master. Choose.

(Since there is no Zen of criticism, and since this essay is *my* game, there is an answer, a right answer, to the *koan*. But you have to wait for it. Isn't Deep Thought *fun*?)

Not really, I say answering my preceding parenthetical paragraph. The game is not fun, and is not meant to be. Or, rather, the game as game redefines what fun is and what it can be. The chess grand master and the matador both know that the game is deadly serious.

So do the theologian and the storyteller. "I am convinced," writes Karl Rahner in *The Practice of Faith,* "that a human being's historical life moves in freedom toward a point of decision, that it contains this decision in itself, that life as a whole must be answered for and does not simply run away into a void in these details. Of course, this outlook on which my life is based, which is almost inescapable and yet required of me, is nothing but breathtaking optimism, so terrifying that everything trembles with the sheer audacity of it."

Game, narrative, and theology are a kind of spectrum of human attempts to impose *direction,* or *sense,* on the random series of absolutely unrepeatable moments that are experience. "Personality," writes Fitzgerald in *Gatsby,* "is an unbroken series of successful gestures." But this series can only have sense in retrospect, from the point of view of the goal that has been arrived at; that is what turns the random series into the unbroken series. If you had not spilled punch on her dress at the senior prom, would you be happily married to her today? As a detective writer of distinctly limited talent, I can tell you that beginning a novel without knowing how it will end is very bad for the blood pressure. Millennia before television, Homer invented the instant replay when Odysseus recounts his misadventures in the *Odyssey*—because, in being recounted, they are transformed into adventures. Pouring over maps of the campaigns he fought in, Hemingway's veteran in "Soldier's Home" thinks, "Now he was really learning about the war. He had been a good soldier. That made a difference."

What distinguishes game from storytelling from theology is, probably, the degree of involvement in the randomness of the playing field itself. It is a game if the field—the landscape—predominates over the control of the field. It is theology if the knowledge of the field renders the reality of the field all but irrelevant. *Prakriti* and *purusha,* the field and the knower of the field, are the central concepts of the branch of Hinduism called Samkhya. Between these extremes lies the area in which the random and the planned share an uncomfortable, if exciting bed, in which "what could be" flirts with "what had to happen." It is the field I call storytelling.

The four suits in a deck of cards represent the sociological landscape of a classic Neolithic culture (like the one we live in): priestly nobility, knights, merchants, and day laborers. Brahmins, Kshatryas, Vaisyas, and Sudras, if you are an Indologist. The Mayans played a form of basketball, pok-a-tok, in which the players attempted to bounce a rubber ball with their hips through a ring fixed vertically, not horizontally to the ground. We may guess that high scoring in pok-a-tok meant something different than it does in the NBA; but we know that court astrologers followed the movement of the ball carefully in order to forecast the fate of the empire. And the Aztecs regularly conducted "Wars of the Flowers," stylized mock combats among their captured slaves, the losers in which game would have their hearts ceremonially carved out on one of the following mornings so that the sun could rise.

You wonder where I am tending. I will tell you where I am tending. Games want to be stories, and theology wants to explain stories, and stories, the poor dears—if they are good stories—just want to be told.

My mathematician friends who also design computer game programs are fond of distinguishing between "games of partial information" and "games of perfect information." Most games fall into the first batch, but that does not diminish the importance of the games of perfect information.

Look at your chessboard and think about the opening sentence of *Pride and Prejudice.* Fan out your poker hand (three-card draw, nothing wild) and think about the opening sentence of Kafka's "Metamorphosis." Now you know the difference between games of perfect information and games of partial information. When I open P-K4, nothing—absolutely nothing—that I can do is unavailable to you, and if I lose to you it is because I lost, because the game has, in George Steiner's accurate and chilling phrase, tracked the ego to its final lair. If, on the other hand, I meet the opening bet in a jacks-or-better-to-open poker game, you have no idea whether I am fueled by self-assurance or by hope. Never draw to an inside straight, the grown-ups tell you; just you try not to draw to an inside straight, says your life. If I lose, I can blame the cards, the luck of the draw, the air conditioning, or the bourbon. The poker table strokes losers; we are only human. The chessboard damns then; we are *only* human.

Baseball is like chess and like fantasy. Football is like poker and like science fiction. The diamond is a perfect square poised on one of its corners. The time of the game is the time defined by the game—three strikes to get out, three outs per side per inning, three times three innings per game with each half inning posing one enemy against three times three opponents. The point of the game, as its central metaphysician Bill Veeck once said, is disarmingly simple—to find out if a running man can travel faster than a thrown or hit ball. Not *A Voyage to Arcturus,* not *The Lord of the Rings,* not *The Chronicles of Thomas Covenant, the Unbeliever*—not *The Tempest* give us a more overwhelming sense of an other, a clarified world. A baseball game can be annotated as surely as a chess game, can be transfigured into the pure abstraction of statistics—as Robert Coover understood in his stunning novel, *The Universal Baseball Association, J. Henry Waugh, Prop.*

The space of baseball is fantasy space, pastoral space—Tolkien's Middle Earth, Donaldson's The Land, Lewis's Narnia. Football is played, not on a diamond, but on a gridiron. It does not measure the speed of a running man against the speed of a thrown ball, it measures the momentum of a running man against the momentum of other men running against him. "Dancing is a contact sport," snarled—I think—Frank Leahy of Notre Dame. "Football is a collision sport." The space of football is not the space that contains, but the space that *is contained,* the Cartesian vista from which we cannot escape. Like science fiction, football is a matter of cold equations, of space to be traversed rather than filled. In baseball you can commit an error; in football you fumble.

But I pity anyone who cannot, like me, lose at chess as much as at poker; or who cannot be as awed by Reggie Jackson as by Walter Payton; or who cannot read Stephen King *and* Poul Anderson. I pity psychic amputees, in other words. The playing fields of Eden are the landscapes that make storytelling possible. And they are either the peaceful pastoral of *A Midsummer Night's Dream* or the blasted heath of *King Lear.* And they are the same place, just as nirvana, the state of rest, and samsara, the state of frantic to-and-fro, are the same state in classic Buddhism—the same state, but perceived differently.

And I told you there was an answer to my critical *koan.* Would you rather battle for your life against a chess grand master or a matador? Once you have accepted the question, once you have begun to read and write for the only sane reasons that should impel anyone to read or write, you have entered the game and you are lost and won. You are wagering against grand master and matador at once—they are both inside you—and you have no choice of opponents. Your only choice is the choice of the terms upon which you will win. It is distressing, it is inconvenient, and it is ineluctable. It is called consciousness.

6

Bookscapes: Science Fiction in the Library of Babel

George E. Slusser

According to the saying, you cannot tell a book by its cover. Which means, in the traditional library, glimpse its contents *through* the cover. For library bindings, traditionally, are of opaque leather or cloth—an outer surface that offers no image of what lies within. These blank covers, in effect, act as a barrier, a means of preserving the abstract nature of the word. They prevent this reader from translating words into visual images, and by means of the process returning the sign to its material source. By its cover the book can refuse the source, declare itself an independent word-world. And titles only reinforce this separation. Letters stamped on an opaque binding, they are not a conduit for images but another line of defense against visual penetration. They are a bit of the inside—the same orthographic markings that form its words— placed outside: a warning that the realm within may not (in any direct sense) obey the laws of our visible world, the mimetic standards of reality and illusion.

The traditional nature of the library book may have something to do with the development of a "mimetic crisis" in modern literature. By this I mean that questioning of a connection between the imitated world and the world imitated that, today, is all but severed. Auerbach's "dargestellte Wirklichkeit," placing grammatical emphasis on the latter term, names the real world as the source of images and words alike, which are related through the activity of mimesis. But the primacy of that source is in doubt, for example, in the debate that surrounded the "imagist" movement. When T. E. Hulme states that "poetry . . . is not a counterlanguage but a visible, concrete one," he concedes the possibility of a shift from the verbal adjective "dargestellte" to the noun

"Darstellung." This designates the act of "placing" as an independent counterprocess, able to create word structures that no longer have direct visual and concrete connection to a "real" world, and at best an oblique or symbolic attachment to any world. This shift is implied when Käte Hamburger subsumes mimesis under poesis, or when Roland Barthes replaces the word image with that of "simulacrum."[1] What is assailed here is the mimetic idea of "description" itself. This is, in the original sense, "writing fully" *(de-scribo)*, writing in a visual, concrete manner. But nonmimetic writing is partial writing, and herein lies its illusion of "freedom." For words are now symbols that, in extreme cases, claim the option of not seeking their other half, of declaring themselves a realm unto self, beyond all need of reference let alone resemblance.

Such words, isolated in the word-worlds of books, form what Borges, with chilling irony, calls the Library of Babel. The books here are not Aristotelian but perversely Platonic entities. For Aristotle, art can and should imitate nature. And words, to do so, must be grounded as much as possible in images. To Plato, however, mimesis is not semblance but dissemblance, the lie that obscures and debases the ideal. Yet Plato could envision positive conversion: the word or sign, brought up out of the cave, dissolves in the light of reality. The books in Borges' Library, on the other hand, operate negatively: they are not a cave but a tomb for the ideal. For only to the degree that images are excluded from their covers can the word inside develop its ideal nature. Freed finally from perception itself—that imperfect nexus of seer and thing seen even Plato could not abolish—this new ideal unfolds as system. The absolute, working within the covers of each book, is the mathematical process of permutation, operating on the level of sign system alone.

Borges' sense of the book as systematized repository is at least as old as Alexandria. Roll or codex, these books were involuted objects, whose wrappers, blocking any direct exchange via the image between external and internal realms, turned landscape into wordscape. They thus differentiated themselves from exvoluted or "storied" media— sculpted temples, Greek vases, triumphal arches, reliquaries, tympana of churches—which seek, through the antechamber of mediational images, to sustain visual continuity between the outer world of concrete things and the abstractions of word or spirit—the *pneuma*—that lie at the center. The book, with its blank covers, refuses this antechamber. Those covers instead enclose, and in doing so systematize, all images. Inside the book, images become illustrations. Their referentiality is internalized by being made to illustrate a precise scene in the story's action, which is located, by means of a page designation, at a precise place in the numerical system, the sequence of typographical marks that organizes the physical wordscape of the book.

Most scholarly libraries today still strive (without thinking of Babel certainly) to keep the book unstoried, for they will rebind storied covers with blank carton. But this is rarely the case with circulating libraries. I am interested in their tradition, and in the sort of book they purvey—the "popular" forms that issue from the pamphlet and broadside, and that, engaged in open social concourse, have long used images on their covers as means of mediating between the reader's landscape and the book's wordscape. These circulating books are the direct product of expansion in the technology of printing. And so are their storied covers. Indeed, the Library, which Borges carries to its logical endpoint, is a theoretical construct hardly explicable when confronted with the pragmatic facts of modern publishing. For the covers of today's books are, uniformly, storied. The illustrated dust jackets of hardback books can be removed and tossed. But images, with paperbacks, are indelibly painted on the covers. They are an organic part of the reading experience, and offer the tangible materials for a new, powerfully mimetic, library.

This illustrated library operates under a very different premise from Babel: for just as words need their figurable core, their "imagistic" content, so the books that contain and vector these words need their storied covers, as place of contact and transfer. The question of these storied covers is important, for it concerns no less than the efficacy of the book as a medium in a world where technological change has made accessibility and speed of exchange crucial factors shaping a larger "informational" landscape. The covers in question are themselves products of expanding technology. It is no accident therefore that the most elaborately storied covers today belong to science-fiction books—a genre itself the ideological product of, and vector for, technological advancement. And just as technology, in its functioning, involves contact, interaction, between theoretical systems and material objects, so science fiction can be said to function (as poetic or literary form) by reasserting, in the midst of today's Library of Babel, mimetic continuity—dynamic contact between word-systems and the material forms of the nonverbal world. But mimetic continuity depends, however, on this technological interface that is the illustrated book cover. This "bookscape" is the place where we can test science fiction's much vaunted power of "extrapolation." For that power involves, first and foremost, getting out of the Library of Babel.

2

When we think of books, we think (naïvely) of objects that *contain* the vision of an individual writer. And we think, in turn, of a library as a place that contains books, a container whose shape and size change as we add individual pieces. Borges' Library, however, is a form that presupposes all content, "an indefinite, perhaps infinite, number of hexagonal galleries" into which all fictional visions, past or future, fit.

And as they fit, these books cease to be visions, to have imagistic content. They become numbers instead in a a classification scheme and ultimately an element in a system of typographical permutations. There is no book that does not exist somewhere in the permutational potential of this library. No book can express a new or unique vision. In the same sense then, no book need be storied. For by adorning the cover of a book with images, we only accuse the gulf between image world and text world. This gulf is none other than that between the imperfection of human aspirations and the perfection of system.

> In order to perceive the distance which exists between the divine and the human, it is enough to compare the rude tremulous symbols which my fallible hand scribbles on the end pages of a book with the organic letters inside: exact, delicate, intensely black, inimitably symmetric.[2]

The books in Borges' Library are both empty inside and blank outside. And humanity is disconnected from them.

> Perhaps I am deceived by old age and fear, but I suspect that the human species—the unique human species— is on the road to extinction, while the Library will last forever; illuminated, solitary, infinite, perfectly immovable, filled with precious volumes, useless, incorruptible, secret. (322)

The "illumination" mentioned is not that of the imaged text. It is the imageless light of the blank page or cover.

Behind this relationship of human being and book we recognize Saussure's claim of an arbitrary connection between sign and thing signified, transferred here to the relation between image and word, mimesis and poesis, and finally book and cover. The book Borges describes, where neither title nor cover "indicate or prefigure what the pages will say," strives to become pure sign. It is no longer the product of an imitator of nature, nor even of man thinking. If anything, it thinks itself, obeys its internal laws of order. "Man thinking" is Emerson's phrase. And Emersonian linguistics offers a contrast. To Emerson, it is not the word but nature, the natural image, that is the "vehicle for thought." That vehicle however must be vehicled, projected in mimetic images, which are signs. These signs display "a radical correspondence between visual things and human thoughts." Words then, as signs, are not detachable from natural facts. They are graphic images of those facts, and have a direct and necessary, not an arbitrary, connection with them.

Over the gates of Emerson's library is written this caveat: "But wise men pierce this rotten diction and fasten words again to visible things, so that the picturesque language is at once a commanding certificate that he who employs it is a man in alliance with truth and god."[3] The "again" is important, for it indicates that already, in the nineteenth century, the Library of Babel was enough of a reality to put Emerson's mimetic vision on the defensive. And, if we judge from the statements of other contemporaries, mere "picturesque language" was not sufficient to turn the tide. The cover must be mobilized in order to enlist the literal image, the graphic artist summoned to restore the link, visually, between nature and the word.

One such testimony comes from Balzac, in his story "Le Chef-d'oeuvre inconnu." The protagonist of this tale, Frenhofer, is a painter increasingly drawn by the "meta-language," the theory, of painting. As this happens, painting itself becomes an act of blanking the cover of nature's book. In the climactic scene, Frenhofer offers to compare his "masterwork," the portrait of his ideal woman, to a young beauty present in the flesh. The canvas he shows is a chaos of lines, in which the only image discernible is an exquisite foot. Assuming he worked from the bottom up, we see form that is recognizable and even said to have the breath of life become a chaos of lines. To be a new Pygmalion, Frenhofer must not only create visual images but effect Emerson's radical ties with nature by seeking to bring that image to life. Pursuit of the opposite — the ideal as theory or self-referential system — obfuscates and destroys all images, and is judged severely. The incommunicable vision is the end of painting here on Earth.

As one of Frenhofer's critics puts it, we have a situation where "le raisonnement et la poésie [*poesis*] se querellent avec les brosses." We find this same situation elaborately worked out in a key passage of a late nineteenth-century work, Gottfried Keller's *Der grüne Heinrich* (1879–80). Poesis and mimesis are mutually exclusive acts here. Poesis has become, clearly, a making according to theoretical reason, and the protagonists substitute it, with disastrous results, for mimetic imitation.

Young Heinrich is studying to be an artist. At this crucial moment in the narrative, he has been taken from his canvases by real-life adventures, the sort that are persuading his friends to abandon art for social vocations. Returning to his studio, he takes up a sketchy canvas but cannot remember what he intended to draw there. On it, there is a vague foreground and outlines of two trees. He begins to fill in these latter.

> But I had hardly been drawing for an hour, and had dressed out a pair of branches with their uniform needles, when I fell into a deep distraction and started making, in a thoughtless manner, all sorts of little hatch marks, as one does when he tries out a pen. I later continued this scribbling from time to time, adding to what was now a net of lines, that I wove each day as if lost in daydreams . . . until this confusion [*Unwesen*] covered, like a huge grey spiderweb, most of the visible surface.[4]

Setting out to paint trees, Heinrich ends up testing his brush, drawing abstract, nonreferential, patterns. If his wandering pen seems at first more the product of distraction than abstraction, he recognizes, in a later statement, that this is not a maze but a "labyrinth," a structure for which there is a plan, a theoretical thread that runs from one end to the other. This may be the matrix for all visible landscapes. Bringing it to the foreground, however, erases the concrete image — and in doing so, it is implied, severs vital contact with the natural world, the tree he would paint. The web or system of lines is an "Unwesen," chaos created as mimetic ties are broken.

Heinrich is uncomprehending, but his friend Erikson elucidates, turns his drawing into a theoretical act. His comments mingle pragmatic irony with a nihilistic fascination with theory, and thus prefigure Borges' narrator. He hails in Heinrich's work a new direction in German art. But his irony, soon caught in its own web, takes a vatic direction.

> These busy hatch marks exist in and for themselves; they hover in the total freedom of the realm of beauty. This is industry, functionality, clarity for their own sake, all presented in the most alluring abstractness! And these

knots of lines . . . are they not triumphant proof that logic and artistic law celebrate their most beautiful victories only in the realm of the insubstantial and insignificant! God created the world out of nothing. His world is an abscess, a sickness that issues from that nothingness, a falling away from God himself, a detritus [*Abfall,* both meanings]. The essence of the beautiful, of the poetic and godly, lie in the fact that we, issuing from this ulcer of matter, can bring ourselves to be reabsorbed by the void. Only this is art, and the true art at that! (433)

The Library of Babel, Borges' narrator tells us, was also created out of the void. It too is a fall away from the purity of nothing, a fall into matter (in this case individual stories, descriptions, covers of books) that seeks, through the purifying geometry of the decimal system, to return to nothingness.

As Heinrich's effort to paint a tree shows, what Erikson calls an "abcess" is not simply matter. It is our relationship to matter, it is mimesis—that is, the representable world, the world that can be shared by means of that representation. The "sickness" lies then not in matter but in humanity's contact with matter. But, to continue the metaphor, a theoretical quarantine is possible. Borges' narrator, in the very act of writing his story, sees his words drift from signs that are shareable to marks that are pure abstraction, typographic design. "You who read me," he asks, "are you sure you understand my language?" (321). The "disease" is thinking you understand the signs, that there exists a shared (under*stood*) ground of content two people can stand on. It follows that the product of this diseased thinking is the image itself. Erikson does not try to understand Heinrich's drawing. The latter's failure to create an image becomes, through unmediated reversal, a model of theoretical order. By a like logic, the librarian's failure to mean becomes total meaning. By not being understood, each individual vision becomes inviolable and imageless. Each act of dyslexia is its own universe—a form without content, a form that contains material being (the source of the contagion that is the image) only in the act of voiding it. The image is shunned because it is a device of communication. Mediating between subject and object, it only acts to spread the sickness—the fall from grace Heinrich enacts and Erikson "redeems" by the blankness of theory.

Borges' Library and Heinrich's drawing alike are high-entropy structures, in which all forms of figuring tend toward the uniformity of the blank surface. And the final entropic state, curiously in both cases, is found in the book. Erikson meditates on the voiding of texts, on emptying them of their troublesome diversity of images. He praises Heinrich: "You have simply decided to throw out everything that is material [*alles Gegenständliche*], everything that has to do with content." And he sees the same happening, in narrative texts, to word images.

> And who can say how near we might be to the time when poetry tosses out the way-too-heavy line of words, and takes up the decimal system and its organization of light, fleeting abstract strokes of the pen. Thus can poetry unite with the graphic arts, have an identical outer form. (434–35)

Words carry "weight." This is their charge of images, their content. It must be "tossed out" of the text in favor of the nonmimetic lightness of theory—the decimal system that reduces words and graphics alike to the common form of abstract marks.

To Erikson, the vehicle of this reduction of sentence and drawing to a same form, their common denominator, is the book. More than Flaubert's "livre sur rien," his book is one that *is* nothing, an artifact that is wholly undifferentiated in terms of its images, its titles, and stories. If not wholly blank, his book is a wholly decorative and systematized object, unpersonalized by an imagistic content within or on the covers.

> A senate of expert bookbinders and gilders would convene weekly and hold olympian contests to rule upon the worth of luxury bindings and gilded covers. To do so, however, they must swear an oath not to make any epic poems or paintings themselves during their tenure as judges. Following this, hordes of oversophisticated publishers would produce the prize-winning works in a series of hourly printings, and with such great solemnity that the devil himself would not be able to tell good from bad. (435)

In this process, individual books lose their gestalt or image. All that remains is bindings, prized for their blankness, mass-produced in identical copies, manipulated by abstract laws of quantity and distribution.

Because it conveys no images, such a book conveys no sense of the future. Or possibility. For in terms of the system, all books at any given moment are present in virtual form. As such, however, they are image-less, for there is no need to envision in the future something that is already present. By the same token, such books cannot claim, as science fiction does, to foresee things by means of the book. "I cannot combine certain letters, as 'dhcmrlchtdj,' which the divine Library has not already foreseen in combination, and which in one of its secret languages does not encompass some terrible meaning" (321).

The system seems to allow no speculative possibility. Yet it harbors something "secret" — some combination of permutating signs that, put apart from the general uniformity, promises to body forth a "terrible meaning." The future image is not effaced, only repressed. And as image, such future can only be apocalypse, revelation of disaster.

The theology of the book is becoming clear. The book, as vehicle for diversified images and personalized words or "stories," is the product of a fall that must, if at all, be reversed by agraphic acts. Thus Mallarmé's blank book, whose future, to Maurice Blanchot in his *Livre à venir,* is no future. Here is how Roland Barthes describes this book.

> The typographic agraphism of Mallarmé aims at creating around its rarified words an empty zone in which the word [*parole*], freed of its guilty social harmonics, happily no longer resonates at all. The word [*vocable*], severed from the matrix of common clichés . . . is thus fully irresponsible of all possible contexts; it approaches the state of a brief, singular act, whose blankness [*matité*] affirms a solitude, hence an innocence.[5]

In the book, Barthes implies, the word, by joining graphic elements (the imagistic "content" of writing and drawing alike), falls from its original "solitude" or Rousseauesque self-sufficiency. It can recover this lost "innocence" (the word is postlapsarian: *in-noceo,* not harming) only by effacing the images that mar it.

The word then becomes, as it erases its mimetic "harmonics," necessarily ir-responsible in relation to its signifieds, visible or secret. The most "guilty" of these contexts is the social. Erikson, we remember, caught up in his uniformizing theoretical passion, is still held back by his irony, which acts as a social monitor. The void he skirts, moreover, is the same process of erasure that Barthes sees leading to original innocence. Emptiness in Keller, original or terminal, is a postlapsarian state, and a fearful one, for it threatens loss of self. Erikson's meditation on the blank book is broken into by his fiancée. Called back to the images of material existence, he in turn brings Heinrich back by smashing his fist through his canvas: "Get yourself out of the cursed web! Here at least is a hole" (435).

Keller's solution — Heinrich like Erikson abandons art for family and career — is possible neither for Barthes nor for Borges' librarian. For it is to submit to the hegemony of a single, historical time and place. But such cannot be the original source. What Erikson says ironically they take as truth: we move from void to void, and all between is fall into matter, a tyranny that is another absence, this time of origin itself. Implied here is the curious history of modern poesis. Chafing at the mimetic connection, and the tyranny of matter it came to represent, the Romantic artist sought to recover primal unity by creating "concrete universals." For Heinrich, the compound proves unstable, the drift naturally away from the concrete toward abstraction. Mallarmé and his followers cultivate this drift; the result is the blank book. Erikson's hole drives us back to parochial materiality, to no book. In either case, mimesis perishes, and with it (it is implied) art itself.

Science fiction is a mimetic form perfectly adapted to this situation. For it has learned to operate in the realm between these extremes. In the science-fiction book the two counterimpulses—Heinrich's dreams and Erikson's fist—operate in an interactive manner. Doing so, they create a system (and in a sense constitute a theology) that is not closed and totalitarian but open and dynamic. The speculative urge of the science-fiction text, seeking to free itself from material ties, knows at the same time it cannot do so without losing its images to abstraction and blankness. The first constantly drives the perceiver back to his or her concrete source, but does not immobilize him or her there, rather allows him or her (like Antaeus) to draw new speculative power from touching it. The science-fiction book must have a hole in its cover, and that hole, the interface between image and word, landscape and mindscape, is the icon. It is this icon that, restoring the mimetic connection, permits extrapolation.

3

The artist approaching the science-fiction cover must learn from Heinrich's failure. In the light of that cover, the grace Heinrich falls from is mimetic continuity itself. Mimesis assumes that today, and a century from now, different hands painting the same tree will, if they copy it faithfully, produce the same image. But to Heinrich, painting is a singular, or quantum, act. In his self-indulgence, the act of imaging becomes so isolated in its idiosyncratic convolutions that it totally loses its referential function. The sign, to an Emerson, is a product of the mimetic process. To be able to call its relation to that which is signified arbitrary, however, we must first have what Heinrich shows us—a radically relativized relationship between eye and object, one that precludes a same image of a single tree ever being produced twice. Given this condition, the only order possible is the systemic field, the aggregate of individual acts of painting, which have become signs lacking a common signifier.

Heinrich retreats to the safety of the parochial. But in doing so, he only trades one singularity for another. And we can discern the same retreat in non-science-fiction covers today. Signet Classic, for instance, recently redesigned the covers of all its books in order to provide strictly contemporary images for each novel or story. The cover for Cooper's *Deerslayer* shows us trees as Bierstadt painted them at the exact time and place of the novel's adventure. Such covers avoid the question of mimetic continuity as neatly as do the blank covers of the French "new" novels of today, many of which explicitly seek to operate in the imageless space of their own sign system.

The science-fiction cover, however, cannot pretend to such naïveté. The genre it presents, science fiction, in its stated relation to modern science, is at least tacitly aware of that science's postrelativistic search for modes of interaction between singularities and systems or fields of activity. Nor can the science-fiction cover, if it claims to be "extrapolative," avoid the question of mimetic continuity. Borrowed from statistics, the term "extrapolation" takes into account systemic functions. But it does not do so at the expense of the concrete image. The word literally means to "polish outward." To have polishing however, there must be friction, different elements that rub on each other. This is not the case with the Signet Classic covers, where the single frame, the sole instant of perception, holds its images in a frozen and inviolate state. Nor is it the case with the French covers. Instead of a monochronic time, their images exist in synchronic or "theoretical" time. All are equally virtual, at the same time both possible and absent. In contrast, the science-fiction cover is anachronic; images from identifiably different perceptual contexts literally rub together to produce (in a manner not unlike a dialectical promise) an expanded vision that, in itself, constitutes a third place and time.

These extrapolative images are iconic in the root sense of the term. The word "icon" has had a similar etymological fate to the word "fantasy," and carries a like mimetic charge. Today, we tend to think of the icon as something that systematizes the imitative process, as a step on the way to the Saussurian sign. The icon, in the linguistic sense, is a symbol that bears, if any, a highly stylized resemblance to the thing it signifies. The base word however, *eikenai,* means simply "to resemble." Likewise *phantazein* (from *phainein*—to show), in its pre-Socratic sense, means to produce—to cause to appear—an image of something that exists. Both are originally mimetic acts. Socrates, however, declares resembling a dissembling. Fantasy is no longer mimesis but illusion. Iconclasts smash images because they feel images lie. And to later linguists the symbol, and finally the sign itself, become unreliable as means of referring back to a natural source. Yet, despite this, neither word has wholly lost its root sense. *Webster's Dictionary* gives, as etymological analogy for "icon," the Lithuanian "*paveikslas* example *įvykti*," which means "to occur," "to come about." To make images then, in this sense, is to actualize. And it is this power that modern fantasy and the science-fiction icon alike claim to revive.

To examine the fate of the icon in our postmimetic, structuralist context, let us look at something analogous to a book—Keats's "storied urn." "Story" can be taken as the stories or levels that articulate the form of an urn (or book). This is a structuralist reading of the word. And if it perpetrates Plato's distinction, it does so by a subtle gambit. For rather than designating one term (form) reality and the other (content) illusion—such a designation is reversible hence potentially dynamic—it names both (in relation to the common term "system") as homologous. Taken on this level where image becomes decoration and the word typography, the book loses its sense of an outside and an inside. Both realms of "story" obey the same decimal system.

In the iconic sense though, story remains a vital connective force. Images on an urn or cover of a book function as icons if they cause to appear, on the other side of what is no longer neither barrier nor nonbarrier but an interface, a reality similar to theirs—in this case varied sets of the same thing, images. They create, in other words, a continuity of vital resemblances, capable of ever-expansive variation. We need not look to the stars for aliens. The alien has arisen in the bookscape itself, as a realm of nonimage between blank covers. In this sense the science-fiction cover is a vehicle for alien encounter. Moving on the surface of the void, its icons not only refuse to become a homology to that void, a decorative system. They invade the alien realm with their mimetic analogies. But images in this void are no longer constrained by designations like "illusion" or "reality." The friction now is between image and system itself. The science-fiction cover uses the extrapolative tensions of this interface to expand the ground of mimesis.

Borges' narrator declared his library coextensive with the universe.

This obviates the need for mimetic connections between books and things in the material world, for books constitute that world, are the only things in it. These books are necessarily blank, the only thing they can image is themselves. The science-fiction cover, within its frame, does not constitute a similar "universe." It is rather a field of images. As such it is governed, not by external laws of permutation, or an iconology, but by continuous combinations of visual forms that configure from within the space around it. This is not something already made—a library—but something in the process of being made. And the active force remains, at the center of this process, man the maker of images.

Borges' librarian is cut off from origins and ends alike. Go as far as he can in either direction, he can see neither beginning nor end. By yielding to the system, he loses his iconic identity as man. That identity, however, is not a static form; it is a dynamic process, a forming. Mankind on the science-fiction cover is never fully subsumed by his profession, or by his function in the system. Like Emerson's man he remains the master icon—the source of professions, roles, images. The human form is not absent here, it is ubiquituous: it is less coextensive with its universe (it would then be invisible) than potentially greater than the containing frame. Borges' librarian never makes contact with the origin or end. But such contact is essential if mankind is to define (that is, shape) itself as the product of its images. Origin is the (ever-renewable) acceptance of mimesis as the condition of fallen humanity. End is the loss of mimesis, to theory or to the void. These are the parameters of science-fiction cover icons: the home world and the alien, the landscape and the mindscape. The human, the dynamic space of these covers, shapes and reshapes itself in an area in between: a universe stretching from the tree Heinrich sets out to paint, to the canvas he produces.

The science-fiction icon, then, functions in multidimensional fashion. Common icons are usually set forth on two-dimensional coordinates: rocket ships, stars, alien artifacts, robots, dragons, monsters—organized on a scale whose poles are the organic and nonorganic. But each of these is also vectored on a cross-coordinate that moves from text to reader. This scale, one of humanizing and dehumanizing activity, encompasses the whole process of the book itself, acting as interface between material and mental world. Movement on this scale is never one-way, but a complex undulation that produces an extrapolative shifting of such polar values as singularity and system, or natural disarray and mathematical order. Reshaping its field by means of this undulation, the science-fiction bookscape is a system in expansion. As such, it allows humanity to sustain and extend mimetic continuity.

4

A multitude of questions may arise about the icons of science-fiction books. What, for instance, do they actually "resemble"? If they are not supposed to figure present things but things in the future, what can they be said to refer to? By describing the future in the past tense, the science-fiction text implies that what is presented has already happened or existed. But are the images that illustrate that text, by implication, things already seen, *déjà vu*? The questions raised by Heinrich or Borges' library, however, have to do less with the nature of icons than with the process of how they are (or are not) made. That process is a relationship, mediated by the eye both of the artist and the reader, between verbal and "natural" signs. We know that science-fiction books are frequently illustrated by artists who have not read the text. Their images often spring from titles. And the parameters of those images are just as easily set by a designer as by an author. The designer controls the layout, and the publisher the physical means of producing the cover. Between these two, the artist is forced to work around blurbs and titles. And often to work with titles an author did not choose.

There may be what we could call referential obliquity here. But there is not, as with Borges' library, recourse to a pure system of formulas. The glass through the artist must look is dark, but something is being seen darkly through it. And that something, I hope to show, is deep structures of interaction, emerging from the relation between icons on the cover and images in the text—structures only potentially present in either element taken alone. To reveal these interactive structures I have chosen, more or less at random on the shelf of a science-fiction library, both novels and examples of the more oblique publishing form of the story collection. We discover, when we examine these books as wholes, that the artist, in painting the cover, is finding his or her way back, through the blank covers and nonreflecting signs, and finally through that binding and production process that so fascinated an Erikson as a system in itself, to some image, obscured yet central to the mind of the writer, an inner icon that marks his or her work as personal and identifiable.

The science-fiction bookscape has traditional elements—title, author's name, publisher's name, logo. Less traditionally, there are lead-ins. These are descriptive and/or laudatory phrases, such as: the author or book has won a prize; or, this is a new version of a classic tale. And finally, there is the cover painting. Elaborately polychromatic, this cover has recently become panoramic (that is, wraparound) and multi-dimensional. Some images now are embossed, so that they stand out in a tactile sense. And more and more covers have physical holes in them, literal windows into the text. They even have pop-up contraptions that, reaching out to a reader, physically draw him into the "world" of the book. The old-fashioned blank book is belied by thousands of these multifaceted artifacts each year.

The artist's first contact with the world of the book, however, is with the title. Traditionally, these are not concrete images, but rather framing abstractions, capsule summaries of the book's verbal field of action. We need only think how many "classic" novels have personal or family names, or rank and class designations, as titles. Or there are place names that convey a precise social frame, or perhaps a more impressionistic (but nonetheless determinate) frame, such as *The Mill on the Floss*. There are conceptually encapsulating titles like *Paradise Lost*. These render the concrete events and actions inside, however vividly "painted," ultimately an *illustration,* the working out of a prestated proposition or program. Other examples are *Hard Times,* or (in the ironic mode) *Great Expectations.*

Titles of recent, non-science-fiction novels are aggressively non-mimetic. As such, they banish the least hint of the image, even the abstract emblems of classical fiction, from the cover. The titles of French "new novels" are a good example. Robbe-Grillet calls a novel *Projet pour une révolution à New York*. The title offers a "project," a theoretical construct that, in this case, is not literally realized in the narrative. Claude Simon gives his novels titles like *Le vent*. These indicate physical elements at such a level of abstraction that titles cease to have mimetic relationship to the scenes and descriptions inside the novels. We merely have generic nouns, in this case one that refers to no specific wind, either in the reader's world or in the fictional world. Indeed, precisely because it does not refer, the title stands forth as a pure grammatical category. The majority of these titles are self-referential—word games, puns, verbal configurations that, in their systemic play of elements, call attention to the operation of that system outside all mimetic constraints or expectations. The prototype is Mallarmé's *Igitur,* "therefore." The title is a conjunction that conjoins nothing. To read this novel is to read pages devoid of mimetic "content." There are no substantial narrative moments that incur consequences, logical or otherwise. Nor does this title promise any. Unlike nouns or verbs, the conjunction "stands for" nothing; it signifies pure relationship and designates a purely grammatical existence that stands alone beyond all need for an image or a story. The title places the book beyond mimetic temptation.

Science-fiction titles make a very different sort of conjunction. As if working consciously against the antimimetic tendency of the conventional title, they make their words, instead of a barrier to the story inside, a visual entry point—an icon working, in concert with the images on the cover, to unfold the mimetic possibilities of the text. Science-fiction titles are not merely florid rhetorical flourishes. They are every bit as aware as a French new novel that they are primarily signs, composed of the same orthographic stuff as the words inside the book. They are aware, therefore, of the resistance, traditional and inherent, to their functioning, in concert with the cover icons, in a strongly visual manner. This awareness leads science-fiction titles to develop strategies for restoring to the signs in those titles the suggestiveness of the image.

A look at any science-fiction bookshelf reveals these strategies at once. Science fiction will use abstractions, like Simon's "wind" or "grass." But it connects the abstraction, usually something of cosmic sweep, with a second term that is visually evocative: Poul Anderson's *Time and Stars.* Just how visual a term like "stars" can be is seen by the myriad "starbursts" or "starswarms" that, decorating the covers of science-fiction novels, give visual substance to otherwise unvisualizable terms like "time." And where a conventional title may use theoretical terms to suppress vivid images (Robbe-Grillet's "project" gives us neither a revolution nor a concrete New York to place it in), science fiction uses theory to evoke new and exotic possibilities the way we might use names or places in a cosmic travel guide: Brian Aldiss' *Report on Probability A.* In the science-fiction title, the abstraction of metaphor or synecdoche yields to the more visually concrete simile, where both terms are present for comparison: Aldiss' *Galaxies like Grains of Sand.* Finally the science-fiction title, instead of using family and place names as social or cultural counters, making them gesture toward abstract sets of relationships, creates mini-scenarios that ground them instead in concrete (and visualizable) situations: John Brunner's *Stand on Zanzibar,* or Fritz Leiber's *A Specter is Haunting Texas.*

Most important, the science-fiction title is chosen with an iconic function in mind. The author writes a book, titles it, then gives it over to the publisher, who then asks an artist to paint its cover. The title is intended to be translated into images. It must not impede vision but stimulate and direct it. It acts as part of a mimetic chain that leads from the reader and his or her familliar world, through the cover, and into the speculative realm within. We will examine two examples. Both are for collection of stories. The first is an omnibus title, chosen by the author, or the publisher, after the fact. It is a device for grouping stories that is clearly meant to work in iconic concert with a cover painting. The second, also for a collection of stories, is a preexistent title. Originally given to a single story, the title chosen for the volume has an iconic potential that can be extended, as unifying device, to a number of titles and single visions. It captures the process that governs our visualization of these stories as a set.

The first is the William Tenn anthology, *Of All Possible Worlds* (Ballantine, 1955). At first glance (before we reflect on the grammar of the title) we see what at best seems an iconic generality—"possible worlds," and a generality that matches the apparently stock images of the cover. So stock in fact that they appear (like the title) merely decorative—images that tell no specific story, figure no particular set of verbal signs. We see, against a backdrop of stellar bodies and nebulae, several needle-thin rockets that have landed front midground. Humanoid figures—they seem to have one eye—are climbing up to the foreground where, looming over them on the left, is some kind of "alien" figure. The figure seems made of metal parts—the connotation is of a "modernist" sculpture—yet remains humanoid in shape: two "legs" of cable, two "arms" like drills, a "face" and "head" of metal planes. The scene is so vague that anything seems possible here. And on one hand that is the point. World exploration remains open. The title, we realize, is a prepositional phrase. It qualifies its book in the following way: "Of all possible worlds, here are seven," the number of stories in the volume. On the cover, two ships have landed, some story has begun. The landing position of the ship, however, is the same as that for takeoff. And in the upper right background a ship is taking off. The title does not name all possible worlds; it names the characteristic of "all" and "possible" to subsume any given number of worlds, to be, as a whole, always greater than its parts.

Yet the fragmentary title suggests, on the other hand, closure. It is a truncation of Pangloss' words in Voltaire's *Candide*—all is for the best in the best of all possible worlds. For Pangloss, that world is our world. We may range the heavens, but the best is here in front of us all the time. If the word "best" (in the Panglossian sense of a homocentric bias, a fixation on the human form as best and only norm, that which governs and restricts our imagination) is absent from the title, it is implied by the images that accompany it—for the figures depicted claim to be alien, yet hardly conceal their resemblance to the human form.

This book has multiple layers of mediation—the title, the cover, an epigraph page, and an author's introduction. The epigraph is from the famous Dervish sequence in *Candide,* where Pangloss asks this wise man to discuss "the best of all possible worlds" and other ontological questions and has the door slammed in his face. The mediatory apparatus of the book, then, simultaneously opens and closes the door of the future to the reader. We are invited to explore outer space—Tenn explicitly tells us in his introduction that science fiction is *the* literature of extrapolation—and at the same time told to accept our status as rats on starship earth; we will never know worlds beyond, or even why we are here.

Humanity is apparently at that crossroads J. D. Bernal calls the "dimorphic split." The Panglosses, on one hand, are free to cultivate arts and religions based solely on the human as the best and only norm. To do so, however, they must remain on Earth. The other race is free to explore all possible worlds. To become this race, however, humanity must compeltely abandon its World, and undergo a change so radical that it no longer recognizes itself in terms of the original norm. The science-fiction icon, however, does not allow this split. The figures on the Tenn cover point in two directions at once. As images, they are perceived simultaneously as metallic and organic. They are products of two contradictory processes that remain, however, complementary: natural humanity and what Tenn calls "industrial man." In both cases however an image is shared, that of humanity, which subsumes all oppositions on the level of condition (human and nonhuman) and of action. Science-fiction humanity does not speculate itself out of existence. Rather it carries with it, in its movement from the known to the unknown, its own form as perennial referent, as both origin and shape of the mimetic process.

Thus the relation of icon to story in the Tenn book is not symbolic but direct and interactive. And it is a relation that reaffirms, in visual terms, the human source of an extrapolative process here presented in its basic form, as creative friction between image and word. The first story in the collection, "Down Among the Dead Men," is set in a future of permanent intergalactic war, where men are fighting a battle of attrituion with an insect enemy that outbreeds them. The situation is potentially dimorphic. Because they are in short supply, soldiers are being con-structed of "recycled" body parts. Made according to increasingly perfect models, they seem on their way to becoming a race of super-heroes. And a race apart. The soldiers in the tale refuse to obey the protagonist, a human born of woman, because they realize they are irreconcilably different; they do not reproduce biologically. There is no way to heal this split physically. An iconic bridge proves possible however, a transfer of images from the original, organic world to this new, mechanical one. The protagonist himself has been sterilized in a space accident. He cannot have organic offspring, but breaks the deadlock by offering to "adopt" his crew of artificial men, thus making them his "family." What is passed on here is an image. And that is not a form emptied of content but a matrix seeking to shape new material. Evoking the family image here is neither a lie nor self-delusion. It has become the positive extension of a human gestalt into an area where, technically, that image no longer adheres.

The last story, "The Custodian," has a similar dimorphic premise. In less than a year our sun will go nova and Earth will be destroyed. Society has divided into two groups: the Affirmers and the Custodians. The former are perfect Bernalians. They force humankind to leave behind all vestiges of its artistic and religious heritage, to go to the stars taking with it only the practical skills necessary for building new worlds. The latter are the guardians of "antiquities and useless relics," that is, of humanity's art treasures. The protagonist, a Custodian who has eluded evacuation, stays behind to spend his last year appreciating art. Plans change however when he discovers another living being on Earth—a child. The child's presence helps him to pass beyond the Bernalian split. For if the child can be said to have artistic promise (the protagonist names him Leonardo, after the great *unrealized* artist), then art is more than past things, objects of passive contemplation. It is a living force and as such has a future. Seeing this, the Last Man decides to become a Noah, but now saving artistic rather than biological types, putting them on a starship and taking them, along with Leonardo, to a new world.

This story is more than an exercise in nostalgia, or a space version of Heinrich returning to the Swiss countryside. Movement is irreversible (if not necessarily "forward"). There are choices. Some are involuntary—the choice of what artworks the protagonist takes is determined by material laws of mass and energy. Others are curiously willful. For instance, he cannot take all the Sistine Chapel paintings: "This time I cut out a relatively tiny thing—the finger of the Creator as it stabs life into Adam."[6] The Library of Babel results from a like schism, of the sign—the book of signs—from its visual origin. There is no God or author—no past, and hence no future. But here, with the Sistine painting, the protagonist cuts old ties only to make new mimetic links. Images will be transferred to artists on some new "theoretical" world. But these are images of humanity, not God. By cutting the finger, he substitutes his own act for God's, and with it his own image for the lost origin. Borges' Library, substituted for the universe, is a system that effaces the human image from its books. In the Tenn book, both on the cover and in the final lines of text, it is this human image itself that controls and directs the mimetic process.

The protagonist sees himself taking "both the future and the past to a rendezvous where they [again] have a chance to come to terms." But here, we notice, it is the protagonist who carries past and future with him. They are not, as in Bernal's evolutionary scenario, carrying him. Functioning as element of continuity between a series of images that we (as human observers) experience as past and future, he *is* the place of rendezvous, the means of making images mutually *recognizable*. Humanity, as Pangloss sees it, provides no such mimetic link. For him there is no past or future; his world, as the best world, subsumes (like Borges' Library) all possible worlds. Turn this around and we have the Dervish—the absent god cannot see the rats (just as Borges' librarian in his maze can never see God). This is not dimorphism but monomorphism. Tenn however offers neither, but rather a multimorphic, open-ended series of worlds that relies, for its continuity, on each form being recognizable, that is, on each retaining its sense of an original form, so that at each step future can meet past. This, if anything, is the essence of science-fiction extrapolation. Bounded by the human frame, origin and speculation engage in an elaborate dance, where every two steps forward depends on one step back.

The second example is the Samuel R. Delany collection *Driftglass* (Signet, 1971). This title might seem a signifier for something that exists only as a verbal permutation. Yet it offers a precise visual vector for engaging the text. The word "driftglass" draws the reader's mimetic imagination through a logical set of extrapolations into the text and toward the construction of a clear image. We have seen driftwood. It is prized for artistic reasons, and we know that, produced by the action of the sea on wooden debris (be it from storms or shipwrecks), it connotes transformation, like the "purifying" conversion of mimesis into poesis, or image into theory. Now the sea is doing the same things to bits of glass. But glass is already a "poetical" substance. And what is now present in the sea, in terms of chemicals or forces, to sculpt it? Changes in the natural and social environment are implied. And as if responding visually, extrapolatively, to these implications are descriptive passages in the story:

> Driftglass . . . You know all the Coca-Cola bottles and cut-crystal punch bowls and industrial silicon slag that goes into the sea? . . . They break, and the tide pulls the pieces back and forth over the sandy bottom, wearing the edges, changing their shape. Sometimes chemicals in the glass react with chemicals in the ocean to change the color.[7]

This piece of driftglass, like the title that names it, is an entry point. It evokes a new, and future, world that must be visually constructed around it. And it is a world with visual surprises. For we learn that the same environment that makes glass debris beautiful has made monsters of men, has given them the gills necessary to function in debris-producing deep-sea farms and factories.

"Driftglass" is the title for only one story in the volume. But the volume is not, as in more traditional collections, entitled "Driftglass and other stories." The projection of this sole title as single graphic motif across the top of the Signet cover is significant, for this indicates it was chosen for its general iconic properties. Clearly the images evoked by the word "driftglass" not only resonate with other story titles but serve to organize the impetus of those titles' imagery along two precise, and interactive, visual axes. There is drift, movement elsewhere, possibility of movement in expansion. And there is capture, glass focusing and absorbing light and other expansive media. Glass then provides a structure for drift, or as Delany translates it into terms of a mimetically continuous human existence, "points from which we suspend later pain." But it is also, in a theoretically occluded universe, the place through which the mind drifts in dream, moving free of all polar determinations. We see this interplay of expansion and capture in titles like "The Star Pit" and "Dog in a Fisherman's Net." "We," another title tells us, "In Some Strange Power's Employ, Move On A Rigorous Line." But in the story "Time Considered As A Helix of Semi-Precious Stones," the same prime mover is captured by the rigorous facets of a jewel. Yet with still another twist, in "Cage of Brass," a like precious substance suggests a way, as we dream on it, of escaping confinement.

We are not dealing, in this interplay of titles, with consciously stated "themes." Openness and closure operate instead on a prethematic level of suggestive visual rhythms. On this level, the title "driftglass" works in concert with the other elements of the cover apparatus, the verbal lead-ins and the graphic icons. Their common purpose is to predispose the (formerly "discriminating") reader to make visual connections once again, to read the book, in this case a set of otherwise separate stories, as a continuous mimetic experience.

Under the title, we find the author's name, and a lead-in: "A dazzling journey to the worlds beyond 2001." This remark is not as banal or useless as it seems. It offers, in fact, carefully directed visual suggestions. The date 2001 has both practical and mythic implications. As chronological marker, it gives a near, hence more easily visualizable, future. As a reference to Kubrick's film, however, it offers a visionary gateway as well. And as such it evokes (in a strongly visual manner, assuming we have seen the film) a sense of the nature and limits of the visionary act itself. In Kubrick, the great seeing "trip" to the infinite is at the same time contained by frames — the black slab, the cinema screen itself into whose "depths" we plunge. What we witness, in fact, is the expansive act of vision gradually captured — by the human cell, the white room, finally the human form and its biological destiny. The film is placed here as antechamber to the book, in the same way the book promises a journey to worlds beyond 2001. And to evoke this particular film is to suggest an analogy between the function of the screen, as place that both contains and extends the visionary act, and that of the book cover and page. What was thematic resonance in the title has here become structural suggestion — a way to transform the book's pages, as limited blank rectangles, into a seeing place.

Moving down the cover, we find an analogous interplay of framing shapes and depth of visionary promise in the complex graphic icon that adorns its bottom half. On a white background we have a line-drawn human figure, seated lotus position, palms uplifted, on a bank of drifting, pastel-hued clouds. The figure's face, which is black in contrast to his white body, is raised in trance. The head is covered by a space helmet. Inside the bubble, however, the area around the head is purple. And protruding from the bubble are gaudy streaks of color, like feathers. Behind the helmet (and corresponding to the brass seals that hold it to the suited body in front) is a golden halo. The sketching of this figure is creation ex nihilo out of the white cover. The visionary nature of the act is suggested by the shamanlike headdress, whose colors add relief to the nascent figure.

The reemerging human form is, at the same time, counterbalanced by a projective movement into the white cover. Between the legs of the seated figure, a bright-red foreground recedes toward a green door that stands free, without jamb, within this male space. Standing behind the door, also nested in this space, is the bust of a girl. The farthest parts of this bust, those standing behind the door, are dark-colored, the closer areas white. There are two visionary "holes" in this icon, one accessing the reader's space, the other moving out of it. Through the helmet, the color necessary to flesh out the human form spills from the recesses of the book to create images on an otherwise white cover. Through the green door that same color is reprojected (guided by the fertility icon of the female within the male) back into the realm of the story we are now asked to give imagistic "flesh" to.

This icon seems at first to illustrate a single story—"Corona." That story concerns a telepathic union between a white man and a young black girl. Indeed, the wavelike emanations, coming from the head of of the girl in the icon and touching the arms of the man, seem a specific illustration of this situation. The dynamics of the icon, however, have more general resonances. Take the story "High Weir." The word means "trap," but also suggests "high *wire*." A thematic rhythm—capture and extension—is set up that echoes the visual rhythm of the icon, as it captures the human image from the void only to reproject it. In "High Weir," Earth scientists are studying ruins on Mars. One of them, the linguist Rimkin, discovers that the eyes of Martian statues are holographic devices storing images of the entire lost civilization. Before, Martian civilization had presented a blank face—no decipherable language, arbitrary signs. Now images pour forth from the statues' eyes. But as Rimkin is drawn into this imaged world, he loses touch with his own form. Colleagues come to be "potatoes on legs." Drifting in contemplation of shapes that "could have been anything," Rimkin begins to think that he is a Martian and prepares to remove his helmet and join the world he envisions. Mimetic continuity and its loss have become here matters of life and death, and the conjunction of image and thing a fatally necessary one. Rimkin must be forcibly told who he is — a man. To designate is, literally, to relocate. For this saves the life necessary to keep the storytelling process alive in the future.

The best way to describe the relation of science-fiction cover icons to the text inside the cover is as a loop — a continuous, self-energizing mimetic connection that is established between the actual world of the reader and the image potential of the story. It is a loop however that, in the extrapolative sense, can stretch. Let us take the *Driftglass* circuit. The central expressive point of the icon is the space helmet, a circle banded on the bottom by a brass fixture, on the top by a solar corona. These technico-futuristic motifs, as they interface with the reader's space, become a colorburst of shaman's feathers, an image of pretech magic. The way back through the cover, into bookspace, is through the old-fashioned door. Behind it we anticipate, by the logic of the loop, something new, and so around again, like a Möbius band, a continuous and continuously inverted flow of images. In the process however the loop stretches. And this stretching results from a friction the iconic circuit of science fiction is particularly apt to explore. This is the friction between imaged content and the blank cover and page, the ideological space-time though which this science-fiction loop moves today.

We get this extrapolative stretching in Delany's stories. In "We, In Some Strange Power's Employ . . .", the reader expects a revelation of the "strange" power, and finds something less — the Global Power Company, whose rigorous lines are the power cables that force its grid system, "progress," on the world's remaining groups of individualists. The word "power" sets the frame — two age-old stances, on one side the exertion of power, on the other its abdication. The presentation of an interface term, however, a "power company," sets in motion an extrapolative loop that bends and shapes the frame. As with the space helmet, the technological rigor of the power system, menacing humanity with total loss of free will, bursts into images in the form of myth. But myth both primitive and modern; the company men are "line devils," the rebels "Hell's Angels." This unstable grounding invites reprojetion. And as it passes through the old-fashioned door of traditional human power struggles, it accesses a place where blankness is forced to wear a future face, and where orthographic markings are (at least for now) a tangible, and still human, web of power grids.

Moving from the title "Corona" to the story, we have a similar surprise. Its referent is no longer symbolic—be it to kingship or to a sun's diffraction ring—but literal, mimetic. And yet mimetic in reference to something that does not exist. Or rather does not *yet* exist. For the purpose of this naming is to give the sign a visual future. "Corona" is the hit song of a space-traveling rock singer. This future song is a synesthetic experience. It is music that engenders a cosmic spectacle, that claims to have "been there," and would make us see where it has been. As such, it offers an image nexus. This is the place where two suicidally lonely humans, by means of telepathy, the wordless projection of sound and image, physically join. But only momentarily. The point that anchors the mimetic loop, reconnecting symbol to referent, sun to king and king to sun and both to song, is itself a thing in movement.

With rock song in between, the two common meanings of "corona" mark the poles of a dimorphic split. These designate the ends of the mimetic process. On one hand, there is the ring around the sun, a place of fire in which no form or image, especially that of the speculative explorer, can abide. Like the great power cable, it turns the forms that touch it into brittle insubstantiality, shapes of "white and silver paper," or the blank pages of a book. On these grids of circle and line all mimetic acts disintegrate. On the other hand, there is the crown. This place does not consume images so much as capture them. It incorporates individual images into a general system of signs. As in "We, In Some Strange Power's Employ . . . ," it invites particular points of view to be plugged into the power line. In one case humanity loses its form and with it the model by which it structures images, or impresses them on the blank page. In the other humanity yields that same form. But now it is not the object or even the medium of perception that constitutes that form; the form is the perceiving source, the "point of view," Rimkin's humanity itself.

However abstract, the science-fiction cover does not, like Heinrich, lose the ability to paint a tree, or a human. Here, we can measure the change in a form because the point of origin is still recognizable in it. And recognizable as a shape from the reader's world of familiar images. Even on the cover of a novel with a radically Bernalian premise, like Spider Robinson's *Telempath* (Berkley/Putnam, 1976), we see the human shape reforming as it dissolves before our eyes. In this novel, biological mutation has made humanity's sense of smell hyperacute. Our familiar race perishes while, for the mutants, whole new realms of perception, of being, emerge. The cover depicts humanoid figures in various stages of disintegration. The figures are "falling into" the cover's black abyss. In the lower foreground, the human form "closest" to us is transparent, a bundle of hypersensitive olfactory nerves, yet clearly recognizable in shape, like an anatomical drawing of Vesalius. In the deepest background, these falling shapes burst into a formless welter of dots. The cover composition however, is dominated by the space "in between." And here the viewer is held at a point of dynamic transition where, in the very act of becoming formless red streaks and doodles, the human form continues somehow to regenerate itself.

If science-fiction covers will not permit the generating form to be irretrievably lost, they will not allow it to be held by a single, historically bounded image world either.[8] In such a case the cover would be a barrier. Using new iconic technologies at its disposal however, science fiction seeks to open that barrier. An example is the Fawcett trade edition of Heinlein's *Number of the Beast* (1980). The "theme" or meaning of the book is the ability of technological man to function in a transhistorical fashion, to let no single moment, not even that of his origin, determine his course. And the mindscape chosen for this adventure is the most historically tyrannical Western man has devised—Christian eschatology, original sin, and apocalypse. Heinlein's man cannot deny his origin, for it is the source of his speculative power. But he cannot accept its fixity either, because a precise beginning limits movement by demanding a specific end. Like Tenn, Heinlein would cut the finger, yet keep the subsequent flow of images.

Borges' librarian doubts that, in the realm of words alone, anyone can get his meaning. But meaning, in the case of the Heinlein cover, is an iconic activity, and a collective one that belies the imageless isolation of the word in Babel. The artist's drawings are less an interpretation than an attempt to translate words into visible icons, that mediate by drawing images from the text in order to reproject the viewer, by means of those images, back into that text. And the artist works in concert with designers, printers, other technicians. The effort is that of Emerson's generic man—man visualizing, that is, restoring visual continuity by means of the book, turning what was before was a blank object into what now is a *model* for speculative reading.

The cover to the Heinlein novel is wraparound. In the foreground of the front cover, four small human figures, scantily dressed and wielding swords, look up with fear. Above them, to the right, a large spaceship hovers; behind it, on the left, looms a large figure, with several superimposed bestial heads, all wearing the mark "666." As if impelled by the instability of this composition, we turn the book — and discover the landscape behind the beast and his train of fire: the classic apocalypse, a winged engine raining plagues on earth, blasting a small figure holding a sword. But, turning back to the front cover, we realize we should have rotated it 360 degrees. For the large ship, moving downward right to left, seems to emerge from the landscape of the back cover, as if it had circled the book. This book, then, does not have a front and back that act as beginning and end. The icons loop around it but do not form a perfect circle of destiny either, rather a spiral. The ship, it seems, is sweeping down to rescue the four humans. This is movement that opens the circle, and we sense that opening, literally, with our fingertips. For against the flat cover this ship is embossed. In its tactile complexity, it reaches physically out of the closed apocalyptic system, and in doing so substitutes our finger for God's, as the means of projecting images in the very act of perceiving them.

Apocalypse means revelation. What is revealed however is, traditionally, not a landscape but a wordscape. In the logic of Babel, images and "meanings" are referential aspects that violate the original sanctity of the Word. And through apocalypse the world is restored to Word in the sense that images by being "revealed" are converted into symbols. In this process however man, in his role as author of these offending images, is necessarily obliterated. As the Book of Revelation puts it: "If any man shall take away from the words of the book of this prophesy, God shall take away his part out of the book of life." Perhaps one reason the science-fiction novel and cover is fascinated with apocalypse is that, through their icons, they can resist the conversion into symbol, the obliteration of a human image source. Take the cover for David Brin's postholocaust novel *The Postman* (Bantam, 1986). This cover, literally, reverses the Book of Revelation. For it puts images back into words in order that man may reassert his part in the book of life.

The Brin cover is uniformly blue. It is basically unstoried, adorned chiefly with words, title and author's name stamped in massive raised gold letters, an apparent Moses-like triumph of the word. Below the title however, our fingers more than our eyes sense another presence — the embossed perforations and cancellations of a stamp. These are mono-chromatic, blue, as is the facial profile that occupies half the stamp's frame. The other half is a glimpse of a landscape—a road, fields, mountains, but especially a sun projecting an orange light that illumi-nates the tip of the face, invades the "wrong" side of the profile so as to give the impression that the face is looking inward, into the landscape. Such a reading assumes we have been holding the book closed between thumb and forefingers. For when we release the pressure, we realize that the landscape on the stamp is a hole in the cover, the profile a cutout. Opening the cover, we see the whole picture—a blasted road in the foreground, a hellish-red sky in the background. The stamp, however, has focused our vision into the golden sun, and in doing so provides a visionary path that moves between beginning and end, blankness and chaos. The stamp is not a symbol here, it has become a physical means of connection. Its function is no longer oblique, simply commemorating in images, but direct, the vehicle for perpetrating the human power to see images, to pass through apocalypse to new, sustained, vision.

5

The God of Revelations, by saying he is the Alpha and Omega, names himself as all-encompassing system. And many critics today imitate this act. They have cut the generative finger both of God, and of the image, the mimetic axis that connects sign to thing signified. In its place they erect the idol of the Word, coextensive with the book that itself is coextensive with the universe. Their view cannot encompass the science-fiction book, for more than a world it is a medium for visualizing worlds. Emerson speaks of power and form. The science-fiction book draws its existence not from loss of origin, but from displacement of origin from God to humankind, which in turn replaces systemic author-ity with extrapolation. This generates the mimetic continuity that links things to things in space-time, and in doing so reinstates humankind as dynamic force in a universe that extends beyond the confines of a library.

Science-fiction cover icons therefore are not a closed system. Were that the case, their permutations could be exhausted by means of a Freudian or some other interpretation. This is the way these icons are usually approached, as a finite number of recurrent types which, in their recombinations, ultimately refer to their own systems within the frame of the cover, not to a specific story inside. There are notable examples of such reflexivity. The first paperback edition of Bradbury's *Martian Chronicles* depicts stock images—rockets and space soldiers—without any apparent reference to the book's inner landscape. But, starting from this base, the Bradbury classic also shows us the process of extrapolative reillustration. Through a string of successive editions, this cover is redrawn again and again. And each time, as in most science fiction, the images strive harder to do what Emerson commands: to attach words to things, to incarnate the speculative wordscape by making it visible to our world of admitted resemblances.[9]

The science-fiction book finally, under the sign of Emerson, is a particularly American medium—all the more reason for it to go unnoticed by critics (even in America) whose models are European. Neither Heinrich nor Erikson, we remember, are able to mediate between matter and thought, with the result that the image ends up becoming theory, and theory a book void of all content, an element circulating in the internal space of some abstract distributional system. J. Hillis Miller, in a recent pronouncement from the podium of the MLA, sees American literature moving, in like manner, inexorably toward theory. The current issue (which he seems helpless to impede) is the inability of American critics to ground theory in a "material base." But the base today is no longer even the old "virgin land." That can be touched, violated; but here there is no touching. There are no things, only "phenomena," mind-forms. Theory is a systemic totality, and beyond its confines there lies only nonsystem. What is more, for Miller, theory is a wordscape. The new American critic cannot smash a fist through his or her theoretical wordscreen, because the fist, too, is necessarily made of words, and by means of words we cannot grasp that which is not words. Indeed, "grasp" is only a metaphor, and "materiality," to Miller, a "catachrestic trope"; "The word 'materiality' gives us possession of what it names but only by erasing the named object."[10]

The science-fiction bookscape, however, is the product of mimetic continuity, not erasure. If it has a figure, it is not catachresis but chiasmus. That is the figure of what Emerson calls "undulation," which is his dynamic of continuity, the process of fastening words to visible things. In his famous "transparent eyeball" passage, Emerson places his American seer on "bare ground." But this is ground free not of natural but of symbolic presences—of monuments, the cultural products of "unfastened" words. And Emerson's man is standing firmly on this ground, drawing from this act of standing the power to "see all" — to make what are essentially mimetic, extrapolative connections.

Theorein originally meant "to look at." But this origin has been severed, and theory, turning on itself in its sightless space, sustains systems free both of matter and of "content," of images. Emerson may not have imagined the spread of theory in America. But he did anticipate the science-fiction bookscape. For here, as Emerson saw, the mimetic link is not broken but displaced. And this displacement *is* a grounding. For it allows power to transfer from material nature to humankind, and thus offers the promise of seeing, if not all, at least farther.

Notes

1. See Roland Barthes, "L'Activité structuraliste," *Essais critiques* (Paris: Editions du Seuil, 1964), 213–20; and Käte Hamburger, *Die Logik der Dichtung,* 2nd ed. (Stuttgart: Ernst Klett Verlag, 1968), 17–19.

2. Jorge Luis Borges, "The Library of Babel," tr. Anthony Kerrigan, *The Mirror of Infinity: A Critic's Anthology of Science Fiction,* ed. Robert Silverberg (San Francisco: Canfield, 1970), 316.

3. Ralph Waldo Emerson, "Nature," *Works* (Boston: Houghton, Mifflin, 1882), 5:32.

4. Gottfried Keller, *Der grüne Heinrich* (Munich: Wilhelm Goldmann Verlag, n.d., 432. The translation is mine.

5. Roland Barthes, *Le Degré zéro de l'écriture* (Paris: Editions du Seuil, 1953), 107. The translation is mine.

6. William Tenn, *Of All Possible Worlds* (New York: Ballantine, 1955), p. 158.

7. Samuel R. Delany, *Driftglass* (New York: Signet, 1971), 122.

8. The cover of the Goldmann edition of *Der grüne Heinrich* is an example of this return to the single historical moment. Two figures, a man and a woman dressed in period clothing, stand with their backs to us. The man is looking down at the woman he holds protectively with one arm. She is looking off in the distance at a Swiss village, full of gingerbread houses, nestled in rolling hills. All of the speculative potential of this novel — Heinrich's paintings and Erikson's theoretical elucubrations — are predetermined by the narrow focus of these icons, fixed in a particular time and place.

9. Cf. the cover of the 1968 Doubleday hardback reedition. Instead of interchangeable icons, we have a precisely targeted Delvaux-like landscape of indecipherable ruins and red desolation, very much the "mood" of the Bradbury stories. The artist here has understood precisely that Bradbury's Mars is an empty canvas of words that *invites* readers to people it with concrete images.

They must reestablish the mimetic link with Mars. And this artist does to by setting next to the landscape's alien pillars vaguely human forms that seem to be transformations of those pillars, to emerge from them as if summoned by our act of contemplation, our desire to reestablish mimetic continuity.

10. J. Hillis Miller, "Presidential Address 1986: The Triumph of Theory, the Resistance to Reading, and the Question of the Material Base," *PMLA*, 102, no. 3 (May 1987), 289. To explain this triumph of theory in America, Miller offers the following cliché: "The triumph of theory in the United States in the particular forms it has taken no doubt has something to do as well with the notorious thinness of our culture that Hawthorne, James, and then Williams in *In the American Grain* have identified." He prefaces his essay with a quote from Goethe: "Alles Faktische schon Theorie ist," hardly the motto of American "transcendentalism," or of American science fiction either.

Mappings

7

Belief and Other Worlds: Ktesias and the Founding of the "Indian Wonders"

James Romm

One of the richest sources of fantasy in Greek and Roman antiquity was the traveler's tale or seaman's yarn, which purported to describe a region of the earth far removed from its audience's native land. The imaginative freedom of this type of literature has much to do with its immunity from the "lie-detector" ethic that was fairly pervasive among readers and critics in these cultures; whereas most stories were expected to have at least some factual or historical content, myths and folktales about the edge of the earth were *eukatapseusta* or "easy to lie about," as one Greek critic put it,[1] for the simple reason that no one could go and check on the reports that had come back from these parts. Thus the most remote spaces of the earth shared with the most distant times in history an affinity for the fantastic, because things more exotic or terrifying than anything in the familiar world could exist there without provoking disbelief.[2] But whereas past time was unrecoverable to the Greeks, distant spaces soon came increasingly within their purview; and, in order for the fantastic tales about them to survive in a new era of critical scrutiny, they had to deal with the question of truth content. In this essay I shall examine the evolution of one form of these distant-world legends, the teratological descriptions of India and Africa, in order to illustrate the impact of this "truth ethic" on an otherwise wholly fantastic genre of literature.

The bizarre and malformed shapes of men and animals at the edges of the world was a topic of constant interest to Greek explorers and travel writers from the very beginning of the literary record. Scylax of Caryanda, for example, a shadowy figure of the sixth century B.C. who, according to Herodotus,[3] explored the Indus River at the request of King Darius of Persia, is said to have described an assortment of human freaks that he encountered along the way.

> The Skiapodes["Shadow-feet"] have extremely flat feet, and at high noon they fall on the ground, and stretch their feet out so as to make shade. The Otoliknoi ["Winnowing fan-ears"], moreover, have huge ears, which they use like parasols to cover themselves with. Scylax also writes a thousand other things, about the Monophthalmoi ["One-eyed"], and the Enotiktontoi ["Those who give birth once"][4] and the Ektrapeloi ["Bizarre men"], and a thousand other wondrous sights. (Tzetzes, *Chilrades,* 7.629–36)

It is difficult to know how Scylax came up with such strange fancies;[5] but it is clear that they were fairly widely accepted, and went on to bulk large in later Greek ethnography and anthropology, in spite of all that enlightened science could do to dispel them.[6] Moreover, it was not only the early Greeks, in their relative ignorance of the distant world, who were fond of such tales; they persisted throughout all periods of Greek and Roman antiquity, and continued to play an important role in the art and literature of the Middle Ages and Renaissance, forming a tradition we know today as the "Indian Wonders." The Skiapodes, for instance, are still holding up their huge feet in manuscript illustrations and frescoes as late as the sixteenth century.[7]

Scylax and Hecataeus could "get away with" descriptions like these because none of their contemporaries had ever been to India, and none could hope to go in the near future. For lack of any direct evidence, the public had to accept the accounts of distant lands passed onto them by eyewitnesses, no matter how fantastic they seemed to be. In fact, there is some evidence that, in the case of the edges of the earth, the more fantastic the story, the easier it was believed by uninformed readers. Just as we modern readers expect visitors from other planets to assume various disorganized and monstrous shapes—indeed, we would be incredulous if they appeared just like us—so the ancients imagined the furthest realms of the world to be inhabited by bizarrely malformed men and animals, not at all like their native varieties.[8] Scylax and his followers were, in a sense, telling the public what they expected to hear, and so their fantastic fictions assumed the status of truth.

Herodotus' description of Libya, in one of the ethnographic digressions of his history of the Persian Wars, illustrates the degree to which the ends of the earth were conceived as a land of zoological wonders by the Greeks of the fifth century. Libya, or Africa as we call it today, was, like India, virtually a blank spot on the Greek map at this time; it was supposed that Homer's semidivine Ethiopians and dwarfish Pygmies lived there, but no one knew anything for certain, especially about the furthest reaches of the continent. In a well-known passage from the fourth book of the *Histories,* Herodotus describes the wildlife found at the western edge of Africa.

> It is here that huge snakes are found—and lions, elephants, bears, asps, and horned asses, not to mention dog-headed men, headless men with eyes in their breasts (I don't vouch for this, but merely repeat what the Libyans say), wild men and wild women, and a great many other creatures of by no means a fabulous kind. (4.191, De Selincourt translation)

The translator of this passage has nicely brought out the way in which Herodotus "hands off" the responsibility for the truthfulness of this teratological portrait, blaming everything on the Libyans. It is a typical strategy for Herodotus, who enjoys telling bizarre and fantastic stories, but also does not like to get caught out in a lie.[9] By putting these tales in the mouths of his informants, he can have things both ways. In this particular passage, for instance, he first makes clear that he has no direct evidence for the fabulous animals of Libya, but then goes on to call them *akatapseusta,* "not at all fabulous," on the authority of his native sources.[10]

Such attributions allow Herodotus to evade authorial responsibility in cases where he is interested in a story but has no factual support. He says, in effect, "It is not I but *they* who are to blame if this turns out to be a lie." Having thus let himself off the credibility hook, Herodotus is free to narrate the legend, and we readers are free to enjoy it, without facing the troublesome question of truth content. Of course, this sort of a disclaimer constitutes something of an abdication of the role of historian on Herodotus' part, since in other cases he seems determined not to accept any stories whatever if he cannot confirm them by means of direct evidence, or at least from the testimony of an eyewitness.[11] But he frequently allows himself this abdication in the case of legends about the distant world; it was there that the greatest wonders were thought to exist, and so the lure of the shadowy "half-truth" or "tall tale" was strongest there.[12] After "tipping his hat" to the truth ethic with his source attribution, Herodotus goes on to continue the fabulistic, teratological tradition established by Scylax and Hecataeus.

It should be noted that the new standard of evidence, as represented by Herodotus' need to distance himself from dubious information, is as much a literary problem as a geographic one. That a similar standard was evolving at this time in literary criticism, and similar authorial strategies for dealing with it, is demonstrated by Aristotle's *Poetics*. At the end of the treatise, Aristotle discusses a number of literary "problems," critical issues that seem to have been pressing among his contemporaries. One of these is the case of the man who says *ouk aléthé*, "that's a lie," to the poet (1460b35–1461a4). As one of the poet's possible defenses, Aristotle recommends exactly the strategy Herodotus uses— *houtós phasin*, "that's what they say," and therefore the story must be accepted, even if palpably false. Myths, as Aristotle points out, do not have to be true; they have a certain independent existence in the realm of popular tradition because they are so widely repeated as not to derive from any particular source.

However, audiences who may be willing to put aside the truth question for the sake of a good tale are less likely to do so for a mere ethnographic description; narratives are more easily excused by the defense "so they say" than Herodotean geography and ethnography, which is predicated on the fact that there was originally something to describe, something whose reality status can and must be brought into question. Thus the distant-world fictions of antiquity depend for their effect, in large measure, on the illusion that the phenomena they depict are real. In spite of their fantastic content, they do not qualify as true fantasies, since their readers were encouraged to believe that they represented an actual or at least a possible landscape, rather than the product of an author's creative impulse.[13]

We must be careful to distinguish, then, the "other world" of true fantasy literature from the "distant world" we are concerned with here. The most distant lands of the Greek geographic imagination are unlike the landscapes portrayed in much modern science fiction and fantasy texts, such as *The Wizard of Oz* or *The Lord of the Rings*. Such works are avowedly fictional; they create worlds that, although plausible and consistent within their own frames, are nevertheless understood by the reader to be unreal.[14] Although we may indulge our desires to believe in places like Tolkien's Middle Earth, even to the point of drawing maps and compiling guidebooks, these "documents" do not represent a place to which we can actually go. The traveler's tale, by contrast, occupies a very different position on the credibility scale, because it is a place from which the narrator himself *has just returned*. It exists in the present, it has been visited by people like us, and in fact we ourselves could go there, given a sturdy ship and an iron will. The science fiction and fantasy text occupies the realm of the plausible, not the possible; the traveler's tale occupies both. The lands in which such legends situate themselves are often, in fact, known to be quite real, as in the case of the "Indian Wonders" texts.[15] It is to this tradition of the "Indian Wonders," then, that I now turn, and especially to the *Indika* of Ktesias of Knidos,[16] the richest and most original exemplar of this tradition.

Beginning in the fourth century B.C., India, known only through Scylax' log, becomes the primary land of wonders to the Greeks, and later to the Romans as well. In the tradition of the Indian Wonders, another genre that had particular trouble with the question of veracity, we can observe a different narrative technique than that of Herodotus, one aimed at establishing authority rather than abdicating it. Thus, while Herodotus was content to leave the truth question open in several cases, by disclaiming responsibility for his information, Ktesias embraces that responsibility, in order to keep his wonders squarely in the realm of fact. As his epitomizer notes, he was careful to specify that all his information came from reliable eyewitnesses, and even claimed to have seen many of the wonders of India himself (31).[17]

However, since little else in this work has any basis, there is no reason to suppose that this statement does either. Since India was still a blank spot on the map to most Greeks of Ktesias' day, we can suppose that, had he really been there, his account would have been as sensational as were Marco Polo's accounts of China in medieval Italy. But since there is almost nothing in the *Indika* that is reported accurately, it is safe to assume that Ktesias either made the whole thing up, or adapted the legends and folk tales he might have heard from Indian visitors to the Persian court.[18] Probably, he did some of each. There are a few tales in the *Indika* that can be traced to earlier sources, but a surprising number appear to have no antecedents at all.[19]

The idea that Ktesias may have invented much of his material, or at least adapted from his informants' stories with a very free hand, puts the *Indika* into an entirely different literary realm from the *Persika*, Ktesias' other great work. The latter was a serious piece of historiography, for which Ktesias evidently did substantial research into primary sources.[20] It filled twenty-three books. The *Indika* comprised only one book, and probably entailed no firsthand investigation. Moreover, there seems to be no real structure to the *Indika*; its material is not organized along geographical, biological, or generic lines but jumps from one type of marvel to the next, from animal to vegetable to mineral, in a fairly haphazard fashion. It seems to be more intended as a collection of "believe it or not"–type anecdotes, like the paradoxographical collections that become popular in the next century, than as a straightforward piece of ethnography.[21] It was written primarily to entertain rather than to inform.[22] As with other texts of the genre, the question of its veracity had to be dispatched or avoided, in order to maximize this entertainment value.

Ktesias' vision of the natural world in India is far more detailed and all-encompassing than any the Greeks had seen before, including in its scope the marvelous properties of minerals, plants, and waters, as well as strange varieties of men and beasts. For instance, he describes gems that have the power to attract other gems (2), a type of iron that keeps away bad weather (4), and wood called *parébon* that produces a wide range of bizarre effects.

> It bears neither flower nor fruit; it has only 15 thick roots beneath the earth, the thinnest about the width of a man's arm. If one takes out a section of this root as large as an arm's length, it will attract whatever it approaches: gold, silver, bronze, stones, and everything else except amber. If a forearm's-length section is removed, it attracts sheep, and birds; indeed, they do most of their birding with this root. And if you want to freeze a jar of water, you throw in a nickel-sized piece, and thus you will make it freeze. And you can do the same with wine, and then hold it in your hand as if it were wax, but on the next day it turns to liquid again. Also it is given as a remedy to those with cholic. (18)

Virtually everything in this world—inanimate nature as well as animate— is fundamentally different from its closest Hellenic counterpart.

A second feature of the *Indika* that makes it a crucially important text in the history of fabulistic literature is its in-depth focus on monstrous races of men. Herodotus, as we have seen, mentions in passing the strange forms of humankind in Africa, and Scylax' log of his Indian journey may have dwelt at length on these bizarrely formed humans (we know too little about it to say for certain). However, nearly a quarter of the Byzantine summary of the *Indika* is devoted to such semihuman monstrosities, a far greater portion than that which deals with the Indians themselves, who are quite ordinary in physique.[23] There

are four races in all, to each of which Ktesias accords an extended
ethnographical portrait: the Pygmies (12); the Kunokephaloi or "Dog-
heads" (20, 22–23); an unnamed people described as atremic, that is,
having no anuses (24); and another anonymous tribe distinguished by
their enormous ears (31). All except the Pygmies are said to live in the
mountains, and all, as indicated by their names or distinctive features,
are monstrous.

These four fabulous ethnographies are remarkable in that they
create worlds which, though fundamentally different from that of the
Greeks, obey their own internal logic, and hence seem perfectly normal
within their geographical context. The description of the Pygmies is a
good example of this internal coherence.

> [Ktesias says] that there are black-skinned men in the interior of India,
> who speak the same language as the other Indians; they are called Pygmies.
> The largest among them are three feet tall, but most are a little over two
> feet. They have very long hair, which goes down to their knees and even
> further, and the longest beards of any race. Thus when they grow their
> beards long, they do not wear any clothing, but clothe themselves in hair
> instead of a cloak, letting down their hair in back below the knees and their
> beards in front down to their feet, and knitting the hair all around their
> bodies. They have genitals so long as to touch their ankles, and thick. They
> are snub-nosed and ugly. Their sheep are the size of lambs, and their asses
> and cows the size of sheep; also their horses and mules and other beasts are
> no larger than rams. Three thousand of these Pygmies are in the retinue of
> the king of India, for they are excellent archers. . . . They hunt foxes and
> hares, using crows and eagles and weasels and daws instead of dogs. (11)

Here, the smallness of the Pygmies forms a kind of ground rule that
determines all the other features of the environment, and is played on
continuously throughout the passage. Their strange style of clothing, for
example, is really a feature of their dwarfishness: beards can serve as
cloaks, because they do not have far to grow before reaching the ground.
And we note that the animals of the Pygmy habitat are curiously reduced
in size, so as to fit the proportions of their human overlords; thus hares
and foxes are hunted in this world, in the same way that boars and lions
are hunted by full-sized men. The *Indika* here has drawn a heroic
society, perfectly normal in and of itself, but shrunk to about half-scale
in comparison with the rest of humanity. It seems to insist that the
Pygmies, shrunken grotesques that they are, are still just as human as a
more "normal"-sized Greek audience.

Ktesias uses a similar technique in his description of the people without anuses (24). Here he expands liberally on the idea of atresia, creating a people whose whole life revolves around avoiding the need to defecate. For this reason, they eat no solid food although they have plenty of it available, and they purge themselves if they even drink too much milk. Their urine is said to be thick and muddy, and to resemble cheese. Again, the internal consistency of this society and its apparent normality are striking. Ancient ethnography often classifies foreign peoples according to their distinctive features, and in particular, their one dietary staple, but Ktesias has taken this tendency to a new, all-encompassing extreme.

We can futher observe Ktesias' technique of making an unreal world seem logically consistent in his description of the Kunokephaloi, or "Dog-heads." Hybrid dog-men had long been a standard of the distant world, as we have seen in Herodotus. But Ktesias evokes such a rich and complex picture of their way of life that they seem to be far more real in the *Indika* than in any previous text. In what is by far the longest of his four ethnographies, Ktesias describes this race in minute detail: their diet, language, relations with the Indian king, military skills, dwellings, hygiene, social organizations, economy, physical appearance, and even their preferred sexual position. What is even more important, though, is that Ktesias' account of the Kunokephaloi appears to be quite deliberately constructed around a thematically consistent set of images and motifs. Just as the ethnographies of the Pygmies and atresic people were structured around the one distinctive anomaly of their physical forms, so the ethnography of the Dog-heads, as suggested by the name of the tribe, is largely a study of hybridism, of the condition midway between human and animal life. For instance, the Kunokephaloi can understand Indian speech but cannot replicate it; they communicate with hand gestures, like deaf-mutes. Thus, if the power to use language is one of the defining characteristics of the human condition,[24] the Kunokephaloi possess it only partway. Similarly, their diet is somewhere between the human and animal. They attempt to cook their meat, instead of consuming it raw, but, lacking fire, they can only broil it in the hot sun. Their living conditions are also a kind of hybrid. They do not sleep on the ground, as animals do, nor in beds, as do men, but make litters out of dried leaves.

The ethnography of the Kunokephaloi is a masterful set piece, showing the full literary potential of Ktesias' genre. These creatures are the original missing links, stuck in an evolutionary limbo somewhere between the animal world and the human. Yet Ktesias does not treat them condescendingly or disdainfully as creatures who have not quite "made it" to human status. Rather, he enobles them, twice calling them "just," and adding as a final note that they are the longest-lived of all races of men,[25] often reaching two hundred years of age (long life was customarily associated with moral purity by the Greeks). They are also expert archers whose services are held in high regard by the Indian king. Thus, the Dog-heads exhibit all the features that are regularly identified in Greek lore with ideal societies: moral sanctity, simplicity, and military prowess. They are very close in spirit to Rousseau's noble savage.

This kind of contrastive use of foreign people and animals borders upon satire, and indeed I would argue that the entire Indian Wonders tradition is basically satiric in orientation. We can see the satiric potential of the genre already starting to emerge in the *Indika*. In a brilliant stroke, for example, Ktesias allows the Kunokephaloi to express their views on sexual behavior: "They have intercourse on all fours, like dogs," he says, "and consider any other position to be shameful" (23). This is a direct reversal of the standard sexual ethic as found say, in Herodotus, for whom any tribe that copulates in some "abnormal" way, on the ground or in public, for example, is doing it "like animals."[26] Humanity, for him, is defined by the proper approach to sex, the right time, the right place, the right position. But from the Dog-head point of view, as represented by Ktesias, the only proper position for sex is "doggie-style"; the missionary position, which for Herodotus constituted an emblem of humanness, seems vulgar to them. Thus, by means of a clever turnabout, the relative stature of human and animal in the great chain of being has been reversed.

All this is presented with the soberness of tone and the specificity of detail that mark the more scientific brand of ethnography practiced by Herodotus and the Ionians, to judge by Photius' summary. In a sense, therefore, Ktesias could be considered a scientific fraud or a hoaxer who tries to pass his own inventions off as truth by making use of whatever authoritative media (newspapers, documents, technical language) he can effectively manipulate. However, this solution to the problem of credibility was viable for only a limited period of time. The distant location of the *Indika* could serve as a shield against credibility challenges only so long as that distance remained inaccessible, or uninvestigatable, to its audience; once India, like other distant lands, became open to travel and exploration on a broad scale, no author could hope to situate fantastic narratives and descriptions there, and still pass them off as the truth. During the next few centuries, two events forever altered the truth status of Ktesias and his followers: the Indian expedition of Alexander the Great, which carried in its train a host of authentic geographers, ethnographers, and natural scientists, and the discovery of the Hippalus or monsoon wind, which made direct sea travel between Egypt and India vastly easier, and thus brought East and West much closer together.[27] With the opening of India to the Greeks, Ktesias' cover was blown. Already in the late fourth century B.C., doubts about his credibility are expressed by Aristotle and others; and by the time of the Roman Empire, Strabo has unmasked him decisively as a shameless liar.

Of course, the Indian Wonders tradition continues to play a part in literature all through antiquity, despite the opening up of the East. But it takes on a more fantastic and fairy-tale-like quality, as if increasingly aware of its own insubstantiality. For example, several Hellenistic authors adopted the strategy of simply moving father out into the unknown, exploring now the islands off the eastern coast of India—such as Iambulus' Isle of the Sun, Euhemerus' Panchaea, and the Taprobane (Sri Lanka) of Onesicritus and Megasthenes[28]—rather than the mainland itself. We know little about these narratives, which are now lost, but it seems clear that their appropriation of extreme distance was virtually an admission of fictionality, like the "once upon a time" of the modern storyteller.[29] Another form that the Indian Wonders take on in latter antiquity is that of the teratological letters of Alexander the Great, pseudonymous epistles that remained popular reading in the West until the Renaissance. Here, too, the narrator, Alexander, travels out beyond the now-familiar parts of India, into a vague and numinous realm that partakes strongly of the fantastic. In these texts, the distance of India is so great that it is felt virtually to be another world, a place that lies wholly beyond the reach of ordinary modes of travel.

It has often been remarked that the traveler's tale and related genres flourish in that twilight realm of the half-truth and fable, where lies cannot be detected with certainty, and the Indian Wonders provides a useful example of this in ancient literature. Imaginative works that deal with regions far off from our own, either conceptually or geographically, must perforce adapt in the wake of cultural developments that reduce that distance. In the Renaissance, for example, a flood of fabulous-voyage fictions, including the latter books of Rabelais' *Gargantua* and *Pantagruel,* followed upon the discovery of the New World, but after the Americas had been more thoroughly explored and made accessible to normal shipping, such texts increasingly took to the skies, exploring the moon and distant planets, instead of terrestrial realms.[30] To a certain degree, this outward movement is a way of coping with the truth issue; narratives that can no longer be believed about the known world must retreat into the unknown, thereby preserving, or in some cases completely surrendering, their credibility.[31] Ktesias lived at a time when India, for the Greeks, represented just such a realm of half-truth and shadowy, incomplete knowledge, having come just recently within the ambit of exploration, but lying too far off to be fully understood; he seems to have taken full advantage of this unique historical opportunity. Those who came after him were not nearly so fortunate.

Notes

1. Eratosthenes of Cyrene, as quoted by Strabo, *Geographica* 1.2.9.

2. In fact, the mythology of the distant world often overlaps with that of distant times; thus Homer and Hesiod displace the conditions of the heroic age out to the edges of the earth, to places like the Elysian Fields, the Isles of the Blessed, or the southernmost regions of Africa. See the comments by Malcolm Baldry in *Grecs et Barbares, Entretiens Hardt,* vol. 8 (Geneva: Vandoeuvres, 1962), 27–28, and W. K. C. Guthrie, *In the Beginning: Some Greek Views of the Origins of Life and the Early State of Man* (Ithaca: Cornell Univ. Press, 1957).

3. 4.44. For modern studies of Scylax, see Wilhelm Reese, *Die Griechischen Nachrichten über Indien* (Leipzig: Teubner, 1914), 35–53; and R. Hennig, *Terrae Incognitae* (Leiden: E. J. Brill, 1944–56), 1:116–20. Note also that the *Periplous of the Red Sea,* which appeared in the fourth century B.C. under Scylax' name, is actually by a different author.

4. Possibly a corruption for *Enotikoitoi,* "Those who sleep in their ears," an Indian tribe mentioned later by Megasthenes (Cf. Strabo 15.1.57).

5. Jean Filliojat proposes that the Skiapodes may have been inspired by tales of long-legged or one-legged deities in ancient Indian legends, in "La Valeur des connaissances gréco-romaines sur l'Inde," *Journal des Savants* (1981), 103. The question is discussed at length by Reese, *Die Griechischen Nachrichten über Indien,* 50–52, and in the sources cited by him. One of the more ludicrous suggestions produced by this method of inquiry is that the image was derived from the cross-legged contortions of Indian Yogis.

6. Hectaeus, for example, who was at least striving for accuracy, seems to

have included such fantastic races as the Skiapodes among his catalogues of foreign lands and peoples. Cf. Hecataeus fr. 327 Felix Jacoby, *Die Fragmente der griechischen Historiker* (Leiden: E. J. Brill, 1957–68); Reese p. 52; Jacoby in Pauly-Wissowa, *Real-Encyclopedie* s.v. "Skylax," vol. 8, col. 2689; R. Güngerich, *Die Küstenbeschriebung in der griechischen Literatur* (Münster: Aschendorff, 1950), 10.

7. John B. Friedman, *The Monstrous Races in Medieval Art and Thought* (Cambridge: Harvard Univ. Press, 1981), p. 205 and fig. 60. For a comprehensive history of the Indian Wonders in Western culture through the Renaissance, see R. Wittkower, "Marvels of the East," *Journal of the Warburg and Courtauld Institutes* 5 (1942), 159–97.

8. Hanno the Carthaginian, for example, describes the men of Western Africa, whom he encountered on a voyage of discovery, as *anthrópoi alloiomorphoi,* "men of strange form" (*Periplous,* ch. 7, in Karl Müller, *Geographi Graeci Minores* [Paris: A. Firmin Didot, 1855], 1:7). Some five centuries later, Strabo likewise assumes that, if there are human beings living in the Antipodes, they are nothing like ourselves (*Geographica* 2.5.13). Pliny the Elder, in an enormous catalogue of human monstrosities at the edges of the earth (*Historia Naturalis* 7.1–2), explains these anatomical peculiarities as a grotesque extension of the principle of infinite diversity in nature, the same principle that makes us all look and sound differently from one another. Surprisingly little has been written about the teratological tradition in ancient literature, but some interesting comments can be found in *Alexander's Letter to Aristotle about India* by Lloyd L. Gunderson (Meisenheim am Glan: Anton Hain, 1980), and in the opening section of Jean Céard's *La Nature et les prodiges,* (Geneva: Librairie Droz, 1968). Mikhail Bakhtin has also helped focus attention on this tradition by mentioning the Indian Wonders as one of the chief sources of the grotesque in Rabelais and other Renaissance writers.

9. The same technique is used by Herodotus in his description of the Hyperboreans (4.32–36); the goat-footed men of the far North (4.25); the one-eyed Arimaspians (4.27); the continual "rain" of feathers in the area north of Scythia (2.7, 31); the raids of other Indian tribesmen on the "Killer ants" of the central Asian desert (3.102–5); and the alleged floating island of Chemmis (2.156). Herodotus' credibility strategies are discussed at length in the second part of *Le Miroir d' Hérodote* by François Hartog (Paris: Gallimard, 1980).

10. There is some controversy as to how this word is to be interpreted. Some commentators have read it as Herodotus' own, first-person disclaimer of all that has gone before, establishing a contrast between the monstrous races, which are *thought* to exist by the Libyans, and the "other creatures," which Herodotus knows are real. See W. W. How and J. Wells, *A Commentary on Herodotus* (Oxford: Oxford Univ. Press, 1932), and Stein's edition, ad loc. However, it seems to me that *akatapseusta* falls too close to the attribution to the

Libyans to allow for a change of narrative voice. The editor of the most recent Budé edition, P.-E. Le Grand, evidently had the same difficulty, which he circumvents by accepting Reitzenstein's emendation of *akatapseusta* to *katapseusta,* "completely fabulous."

11. In particular, the legend of the circular stream of Ocean surrounding the earth (2.21 and 23, 4.36), and the existence of the Eridanos river and Tin Islands (3.115), are rejected for lack of corroboration.

12. See Klaus Müller's section on Herodotus in *Geschichte der antiken Ethnographie und ethnologischen Theoriebildung* (Wiesbaden: F. Steiner, 1972) for the idea that the historian's credulity increases as his narrative travels away from the Greek world.

13. In fact, the gravest charge that was leveled against travel writers, and one that recurs rather frequently, is that they describe "things which neither are nor ever were." See Plutarch on Euhemerus, *De Iside* 360b; Lucian on Ktesias, *True Histories* 1.3.

14. See the analysis of "subcreation" by Tolkien himself in the essay "The Fairy Tale," in *The Tolkien Reader* (New York: Random House, 1966), as well as the discussions of the concept of "suspension of disbelief" in Norman O. Holland, *The Dynamics of Literary Response*, (New York: Oxford Univ. Press, 1968), 63–70. In antiquity, Strabo distinguishes a class of fabulous geographical works that purported to be true but were nevertheless universally recognized as fiction (1.2.35), as did Lucian of Samosate (in his comment on Iambulus, *True Histories* 1.3).

15. Some modern critics, such as William Nelson and Kathryn Hume, would argue that the extreme distance of these worlds renders them, in effect, fantastic; the choice of a setting "far, far away" constitutes a winking admission by the author that he or she is in fact fictionalizing, much like our own phrase "once upon a time" (see Nelson, *Fact or fiction: The Dilemma of the Renaissance Storyteller* [Cambridge: Harvard Univ. Press, 1973], 48; and Hume, *Fantasy and Mimesis* [New York: Methuen, 1984], 21). However, I think both of these arguments adopt a narrowly modern, skeptical perspective, not wholly appropriate to antiquity. It is clear that not only Herodotus, as I have tried to show, but later writers like Pliny the Elder and Augustine, believed sincerely in the veracity of much that had been reported from "far, far away." Although a doubting Thomas like Eratosthenes of Cyrene might use the term *exókeanismos,* "voyage into Ocean," to designate the fabulous and incredible (see Strabo 1.2.3), Homer's Ocean, along with all the fables associated with it, remained a plausible fiction even into late antiquity.

16. Ktesias of Knidos was a physician at the court of the Persian king, at around the end of the fifth century. He used his inside knowledge of the Persian court to write the *Persika,* a revisionist history of the Persian empire that attempted to point out errors and shortcomings in Herodotus' account. He also

wrote an *Indika,* which seems to have been a largely ethnographic, rather than historical, account of the as-yet-unfamiliar Indian subcontinent. Both works are now lost, but their contents have been preserved in the *Bibliotheka.* The works were quite well known in antiquity and were read by such men as Plato, Aristotle, Xenophon, and Plutarch. See the article by Jacoby in the Pauly-Wissowa *Realencyklopedie, s.v.* "Ktesias," vol. II.1; the editions by J. J. McCrindle, *Ancient India as Described by Ktesias the Knidian* (rpt. New Delhi: Manohar Reprints, 1973); W. Reese, *Die Griechischen Nachrichten über Indien;* R. Henry, *Ctésias: La Perse, L'Inde* (Brussels), 13–19. In addition, the article by Truesdell S. Brown about Megasthenes, another Indian Wonders author, has much analysis of Ktesias as well ("The Reliability of Megasthenes," *American Journal of Philosophy* 76 [1955], 18–33).

17. All chapter numbers refer to Henry's edition (see n. 16, above) except where otherwise indicated.

18. Jacoby (Pauly-Wissowa, *Realencyklopedie,* col. 2038), notes that the name Ktesias records for the creature the Greeks call Man-Eater, "martichora," is a Persian word that does, indeed, mean "man-eater"; this bears out the hypothesis that Ktesias got his information through Persian intermediaries.

19. A detailed study of Ktesias' possible sources for *Indika* can be found in Reese, *Die Griechischen Nachrichten über Indien,* and C. Lassen, *Indische Alterthumskeit,* 2nd ed. (Bonn: H. B. Koenig, 1847), 2:641 ff. (reprinted and translated into English by J. W. McCrindle, *Ancient India,* 65 ff.). However, it must be noted that the results of this *Quellenforschung* are tenuous at best, and that Ktesias himself was quite possibly unaware of the degree to which his legends were based on actual phenomena in India or on the myths of the Sanskrit epics.

20. Diodorus Siculus 2.32.

21. Reese (*Die Griechischen Nachrichten über Indien,* 77) points out that, had Ktesias intended to write a truly informative or comprehensive work, he would not have neglected to mention peoples like the Ichthyophogoi, Kalatoi, or Skiapodes, that had been mentioned earlier in Herodotus' account of India, or even in other works by Ktesias himself.

22. "Far from being perturbed by the fabulous element in such authors, the Hellenistic readers seemed to enjoy them, judging from the widespread popularity of Ktesias' and Megasthenes' works." John B. Friedman, *The Monstrous Races,* 6.

23. This may be partly a result of selective epitomizing by Photius. The question of Photius' reliability as an excerpter has been discussed by Reese, who concluded that "gerade wie in seinem Auszuge aus Philostratos *Vit. Apoll.,* auch hier das Fabuloseste am ausfürlichsten [Photius] wiedergab, alles andere aber kürzte" (*Die Griechischen Nachrichten über Indien,* 78). However, the disparity is in this instance so great that we must assume it reflects in some degree Ktesias'

own scheme. Photius has clearly omitted some information about the "ordinary" Indians in chaps. 8 an 14, but how much is unclear.

24. Which it certainly was in antiquity, as indicated by the epithet *audéeis,* "speaking," used of mankind in the early epic formulae (*Odyssey* 5.334, 6.125). See also U. Dierauer, *Tier und Mensch im Denken der Antike* (Amsterdam: Grüner, 1976), 12, 33–34.

25. The same feature is attributed to them by Simias, in the Hellenistic era (*Apollo* 9–10, in John V. Powell's *Collectanea Alexandrina* [Oxford: Oxford Univ. Press, 1925], 109).

26. 1.203, 3.101. At 1.61 Pisistratus is thought to be insolent for using an abnormal sexual position with his wife. See also M. Rosselini and S. Saïd, "Usages des femmes et autres nomoi chez les 'sauvages' d'Hérodote," *Pisa Scuola Normale Superiore* 8 (1978), 949–1005.

27. For the story of the gradual unfolding of India in Greek antiquity, see the numerous articles by Albrecht Dihle on this topic, recently collected in the volume *Antike und Orient* (Heidelberg: C. Winter, 1984). Of particular relevance to the Indian Wonders tradition are "Der fruchtbare Osten," 47–61 (originally in *Rheinisches Museum* 105 [1962], 97–110); and "The Conception of India in Hellenistic and Roman Literature," 89–93 (originally in *Proceedings of the Cambridge Philological Society* n.s. 10 [1964], 15–23).

28. For these and other Hellenistic travel fictions, see Erwin Rohde, *Der griechische Roman und Seine Vorläufer,* 3rd ed. (Leipzig: Breitkopf und Härtel, 1914), 236–60. Iambulus' narrative has been preserved in summary form by Diodorus Siculus (2.55–60), as has that of Euhemerus.

29. Euhemerus' story, for example, was considered incredible by Eratosthenes and Strabo (Strabo 2.3.5).

30. This outward movement has been amply documented by Marjorie Nicolson in her many books and articles about Renaissance science and literature, including "A World in the Moon," *Smith College Studies in Modern Languages* 17, no. 2 (1936), and "Cosmic Voyages," *English Literary History* 7. See also the interesting study of the eighteenth-century travel naratives by Percy Adams, *Travelers and Travel Liars* (Berkeley: Univ. of California Press, 1963).

31. For an example of how the debunking of travel narratives in eighteenth-century Spain led to a marked increase in the publication of purely imaginary voyages, see Monroe Z. Hafter, "Toward a History of Spanish Imaginary Voyages," *Eighteenth Century Studies* 8 (1975), 263–85.

8

Universal Mindscape:
The Gaia Hypothesis in Science Fiction
Jack G. Voller

Following a series of articles written throughout the 1970s, James Lovelock published in 1979 a slim volume entitled *Gaia: A New Look at Life on Earth*. This subtitle was well chosen, for the book's central hypothesis is that "the entire range of living matter on Earth, from whales to viruses, and from oaks to algae, could be regarded as constituting a single living entity, capable of manipulating the Earth's atmosphere to suit its overall needs and endowed with faculties and powers far beyond those of its constituent parts."[1] The idea that all earthly life participates in some sort of organic oneness is as old as Eastern mysticism, perhaps as old as human consciousness, and is encoded into any number of myth systems and religions. Lovelock's theory is noteworthy because it establishes a variant of this idea on a foundation of empirical science, rather than on intuitive supernaturalism. It may be seen, as Brian Aldiss explains, "as almost a religious position arrived at through science and learning and a holistic view of the universe. . . . It presents a much desired unity, to which lesser mysteries are subordinate."[2]

Lovelock himself is circumspect regarding the metaphysical implications of his theory. A trained scientist, he is careful throughout his book to distance himself from religious questions and from what he sees as the well-intentioned but misguided fervor of radical environmentalism. His study is devoted to a careful presentation of the evidence for Gaia—his name for this single, living entity—evidence that Lovelock finds in the existence of planet-wide systems maintaining the proper chemical equilibria in Earth's atmosphere and oceans. Except in a brief Epilogue, Lovelock's investigations never relinquish the tone and rigor of scientific discourse; he draws in his Preface a clear boundary between empiricism and "scientifically untestable" religious belief (vii), and never transgresses until his argument is complete.

There are, however, a few interesting paragraphs at the beginning of the Epilogue in which Lovelock writes of his father, "an excellent and enthusiastic gardener and also a very gentle man" who, we are told, would save wasps from drowning because he felt even they have some purpose to fulfill (141). This reminiscence prompts Lovelock to remark that his father belonged to no organized religion. "I think," Lovelock explains, "his moral system came from that unstructured mixture of Christianity and magic which is common enough among country people, and in which May Day as well as Easter Day is an occasion for ritual and rejoicing" (141). A few pages on, Lovelock remarks that this way of thought is still common among British country folk, and he takes this as evidence that monotheistic religion and "the recent heresies of humanism and Marxism are faced with the unwelcome truth that some part of their old enemy, Wordsworth's Pagan, 'suckled in a creed outworn,' is still alive within us" (144).

Wordsworth, of course, was not much of a pagan; the sonnet to which Lovelock alludes is not especially representative of Wordsworth's understanding of the "power and presence" that for him informs the natural universe. This poem is, in fact, one of Wordsworth's sharper outbursts against a purely materialist world view and the anxieties and dislocations attendant upon it.

> The world is too much with us; late and soon,
> Getting and spending, we lay waste our powers:
> Little we see in Nature that is ours;
> We have given our hearts away, a sordid boon!
> This Sea that bares her bosom to the moon;
> The winds that will be howling at all hours,
> And are up-gathered now like sleeping flowers;
> For this, for everything, we are out of tune;
> It moves us not. —Great God! I'd rather be
> A Pagan suckled in a creed outworn;
> So might I, standing on this pleasant lea,
> Have glimpses that would make me less forlorn;
> Have sight of Proteus rising from the sea;
> Or hear old Triton blow his wreathèd horn.[3]

Wordsworth's metaphysics are rarely this simple, but his sonnet does at

least gesture at a fairly representative (if somewhat reductively understood) "Romantic" understanding of the ideal relationship between the
human and the natural. Seeking to determine its place in the universal
order—its location and origin in the universal mindscape—the Romantic visionary mind sought an understanding of the natural that became an
identifying engagement with the numinous perceived to be informing
nature. When, in "Tintern Abbey," Wordsworth recorded the disturbing
and sublime presence of "A motion and a spirit, that impels / All
thinking things, all objects of thought, / And rolls through all things" (ll.
93–102),[4] he identified the natural as both emblem and part of a coherent
metaphysical fabric that incorporates and diffuses to every participant
feature some quality of the divine.

We could find comparable sentiments in the works of other Romantics, but for our immediate purposes we need only understand Lovelock's reference to Wordsworth as an invocation of the "Romantic" idea
that nature both embodies and represents metaphysical possibilities that
traditional Western philosophical and theological systems do not and
cannot appreciate. This philosophical tradition, so energetically revi-
talized in that moment we identify as Romantic, remains quite powerful
today, yet Lovelock's invocation of Romantic spiritual inquiry was astute
for another reason. The Romantics' semianimistic quest for a sense of
place and belonging in the cosmic scheme derived its motive impulse not
only from the weakening of Christianity and the growing influence of
German idealism but also from eighteenth-century ideas of the sublime,
a concept that was itself an attempt to recover—in life as well as in
literature—the experience of God, the reassurance that divinity was still
present, however remotely, in the Newtonian clockwork universe.

The spiritual anxieties of the Romantics not having disappeared
from the contemporary mindscape, we should expect to find them in
contemporary literature as well, and we do. My particular concern here
is with popular literature, specifically with that genre, science fiction,
that is the most legitimate offspring of Romanticism. One of course
cannot advance the claim that all science fiction is concerned with the
place of humanity in the universal order (just as one cannot say the same
of all Romantic texts), yet a very recent science-fiction phenomenon is
very much aligned, at least potentially, with the type of spiritual inquiry
so energetically pursued by the Romantics. I refer to the employment of
James Lovelock's Gaia hypothesis in the fourth and fifth volumes of
Isaac Asimov's Foundation series, and in Brian Aldiss's Helliconia

trilogy.[5] Even before the appearance of these works, science fiction had proven receptive to environmental themes—one thinks of Ursula Le-Guin's ecological parables "Vaster than Empries and More Slow" (1971) and *The Word for World is Forest* (1972), to say nothing of Ernest Callenbach's Ecotopia novels and films such as *Silent Running* (1971)—but the Gaia novels go beyond these. I will take up Asimov and Aldiss in turn, hoping to suggest that the appearance of Gaia in these works does not represent merely the coincidental manifestation of environmental sensitivity but an important step along a path first discerned in the closing years of the eighteenth century.

2

Isaac Asimov's recent additions to his Foundation series extend the scope of the earlier novels, tying their Gibbonesque study of civilization into his career-long interest in robotic tales. More immediately interesting, given our purposes, is Asimov's addition of an entirely new element, the Gaia hypothesis.

In one sense, Asimov's employment of the Gaia concept is an appropriate extension of the series' concerns, for the first three Foundation novels constitute a study of individual action and isolation against the background of a galaxy-wide civilization. The Mule, a figure of an almost hyper-Byronic isolation, is unable to participate in human community by virtue of his odd appearance, his mental powers, and, most importantly, by acute self-knowledge of his differences. He is able to locate himself within Galactic civilization only by using his aberrant mental powers to modify the emotions of others, willing them to like him, swear fealty to him, obey him. Asimov gets considerable narrative mileage out of the fact that Mule, as an individual aberration, a mutant, could not be accounted for or anticipated by the Seldon Plan, which directs Galactic development.

Based on the science of psychohistory, the Seldon Plan is a powerful metaphor for the insignificance of the individual human in the vast technological world of the future, its inability to account for individual human behavior almost a manifesto of the unimportance of the solitary Self. Asimov somewhat mitigates this implication by making the action of a single individual, Bayta Darell, responsible for thwarting the Mule in his nearly successful attempt to discover the whereabouts of the Second Foundation; especially telling is the fact she can stop him only because she has demonstrated toward the Mule a genuine compassion and concern. Yet in these early novels, Asimov takes his concern with the separate human being no further; his individuals—rarely memorable as such, except the aberrant Mule—count mainly as factors in the ultracomplex mathematics of Hari Seldon's science.[6] Because the Mule is an exception to the Plan, he can and indeed perhaps *must* be stopped by individual action, but Bayta's chief contribution is that she protects the Second Foundation precisely so that it may destroy the threat presented by the one man who refuses to abide by the rules of the sacrosanct Plan. In consequence of Bayta's actions, the juggernaut of the Seldon Plan continues on its inexorable and well-charted course.

In the thirty-year interval between *Second Foundation* and *Foundation's Edge,* Asimov's concerns have shifted. Rather than rest content with fitting human evolution into the mechanistic mathematical plan of psychohistory, Asimov has invoked the Gaia hypothesis on a grand scale, offering it as a panacea for humanity's cosmic anxieties.

Significantly, Asimov does not depict these anxieties as metaphysical or philosophical. The characters of *Foundation's Edge* are concerned not with the transcendent or any concept of the divine, nor even with existential anxiety; the greatest intellectual concern is the fear that humankind is being manipulated by some unseen agency; onto this is grafted an increasing concern for humanity's origins. Knowledge of Earth has been all but lost; the "planet of origin" is surrounded by myth and deliberate misinformation. It is telling that the quest in Asimov's novel is for empirical truth, for facts. Already, Asimov has limited the implications of Gaia.

Two of the Galaxy's brighter sparks—one from each Foundation—become suspicious of the ease with which the complex Seldon Plan has recovered from the dislocations introduced by the Mule, and independently they set out to verify their suspicions of manipulation by unknown forces. Both are manipulated into arriving simultaneously at the planet Gaia, where one of these young men, Golan Trevize, is to make a decision that will determine the future of the galaxy; he may choose the economic and technological imperialism of the First Foundation, the mentalic paternalism of the Second Foundation, or the future proffered by Gaia. This planet—home of the Mule, it turns out—is unique in the galaxy, for it is more than a planet; it is a total participation in global consciousness. As the Gaian woman Bliss explains to Trevize and his companion Janov Pelorat, "The whole planet and everything you see on it is Gaia. We're all individuals—we're all separate organisms—but we all share an overall consciousness. The inanimate planet does so least of all, the various forms of life to a varying degree, and human beings most of all—but we all share."[7] The nature of the planet shapes the alternative that it offers the galaxy—an alternative identified as "Greater Gaia" or "Galaxia"—which is an implementation of Gaian unity and integration on what is literally a cosmic scale.

> Every inhabited planet as alive as Gaia. Every living planet combined into a still greater hyperspatial life. Every uninhabited planet participating. Every star. Every scrap of interstellar gas. Perhaps even the great central black hole. A living galaxy made favorable for all life in ways that we yet cannot foresee. A way of life fundamentally different from all that has gone before and repeating none of the old mistakes. (400–401)

The sense of individual identity retained while participating in a benevolent oneness encompassing not merely a globe, but a galaxy— surely, Wordsworth's Pagan would be well suckled in such a creed.

In the latest addition to the Foundation series, *Foundation and Earth* (1986), Asimov adds little to this notion of Gaia. His primary interest seems to lie in revealing the deficiencies of non-Gaian life (it is violent, petty, arrogant, isolated) and in merging the Foundation novels with his earlier robot stories—all while "leaving open more than enough possibilities for further sequels."[8] Yet there is a crucial revelation in the final chapter of *Foundation and Earth*; it turns out that there has been a presence behind the curtain all along—that robots were responsible for establishing Gaia in order that they might create a galaxy-wide super-organism, the better to care for humanity. The robots have revised the Three Laws of Robotics that govern their behavior, adding a "Zeroth Law" that supersedes the others: "A robot may not injure humanity, or, through inaction, allow humanity to come to harm."[9] They, like Asimov himself, have shifted their concern toward the universal, but it is a shift motivated by the rather mundane consideration of protection, of galactic babysitting.[10]

Even this deployment of the Gaia hypothesis—this move toward a universal mindscape—is at least vaguely related to the Romantic and post-Romantic desire to locate humanity in a universe in which God is not immediately present. Yet there is about these novels something that should give us pause; Asimov has employed technology, not mysticism or intuitive supernaturalism, to construct his sytem of (literal) universal belonging. The hard science of Lovelock has been superimposed on the potential science of robotics; the most empirically suspect element of Asimov's Gaia is a telepathy that is mostly learned. This elaboration of technological transcendence serves as a strong indication that what Brian Aldiss has labeled Asimov's "solid conservative faith in technology" is perhaps more solid and more fundamental than has been supposed.[11] Asimov has constructed, in essence, a technocrat's Nirvana, with the robot Daneel Olivaw as Bodhisattva. In this, his work falls victim to one of science fiction's most crippling intellectual and metaphysical limitations.

> If SF is indeed to be reckoned a separate category of imaginative writing, it is because it concerns itself not with man as such but with "scientific man"; and it is the very idea of man in those terms that has become monstrous. SF may try to tackle the monstrosity, but while it remains true to its frame of reference, it is inescapably trapped in seeking to cast out Satan with Satan.[12]

The modern sense of alienation from the divine and from the consolations of intimate natural contact may be due to an elaboration of and reliance upon empirical science and its servant, technology, but in the *Foundation* future, humanity need only follow this selfsame path to its termination in Eden. Asimov's scientific sublime, devoid of an explicit spiritual element, is thereby limited, and only partially satisfying as a response to this modern alienation.

In this line of thinking, Asimov is close to the scientist and futurist J. D. Bernal, who in his curious little volume *The World, the Flesh, and the Devil* (1929), predicted the development of what he calls "the compound mind," in which multiple individualities merge, much as they do in Asimov's rendering of Gaia. The evolution of this group mind, which for Bernal follows the displacement of human consciousness into machine-bodies, would lead to "a state of ecstasy in the literal sense."[13] The barriers of the Self would fall, and the technological extension of human senses, through "purely mechanical agents and perceptors" that Bernal refers to as "angels" (44–45), would open to human consciousness even "the interior of the earth and the stars" (45). The heightened knowledge thus gained by a compound humanity would permit an entirely new form of life to be created, one "more variable and more permanent than that produced by the triumphant opportunism of nature"

(46). So beyond humanity's present form would this new life be that "Finally, consciousness itself may end or vanish in a humanity that has become completely etherealized, losing the close-knit organism, becoming masses of atoms in space communicating by radiation, and ultimately perhaps resolving itself entirely into light" (47). Like Asimov, Bernal finds technology the agent of his secular transcendence, a transcendence that tends reductively and insistently toward the literal. To be sure, the Romantics were capable of celebrating technology and progress—one thinks of Wordsworth, Emerson, Thoreau, and Whitman—but these writers were more often concerned to celebrate the human spirit, and human spiritual potential. Turning probes into angels and Gaia into a robot-engineered Nirvana denies and devalues the element of metaphysical quest so central to the Romantic and post-Romantic tradition, of which science fiction is an integral part. To follow the line of thinking proposed by Bernal is to fall victim to the alienating peril that plagues much science fiction (and a good deal of contemporary Western culture)—the complete substitution of spirituality with scientism.

3

The faith of Asimov and Bernal in apotheosis through technology is replaced by a more intuitive, even spiritual, approach in Brian Aldiss' Helliconia trilogy, where technology is as much villain as savior.[14] Like Asimov, Aldiss finds in the Gaia hypothesis an idea that brings together much of his earlist work. Aldiss signals this with deliberate use of imagery from earlier novels—the deadly assatassi fish of *Helliconia Summer* first appeared in *Galaxies Like Grains of Sand* (1960)—but on the whole the significance of Gaian unification has much profounder implications for Aldiss. He himself gives some indication of this. Reporting that "most of my work seems to be about getting right the relationship between humankind and the environment, in the wider sense of that term. . . . Always there's a balance to be sought after," he goes on to ask:

> But what *is* there except the profound human/nature connection? . . . The problem was not an abstract one, of course, or I would hardly have followed it for so long with such ardour. I did not think God or a god was a strong enough or a "modern" enough link between the two seemingly

opposed sides of the equation. And this is where Helliconia is different from—a marked steps ahead of—my previous dramatisations of the problem. This time, I had an answer. The "god" was the planet, was nature, was process.[15]

There of course had been strong hints of this concern even in Aldiss' earliest stories, as Brian Griffin and David Wingrove demonstrate in their exhaustive study of Aldiss' works up to (but not including) the Helliconia novels.[16] There is an abortive gesture toward this galactic sentience in *Galaxies Like Grains of Sand* (1960); in *Cryptozoic!* (1967)—in which Wordsworth's well-traveled sonnet makes another brief appearance—the discovery of time's true nature inaugurates a new age for humankind, one in which it is understood that "All mind communicates."[17] The "minders," the mental time-travelers, know this—or something like this—intuitively. Edward Bush, the novel's protagonist, is aware that humanity has estranged itself from nature, yet during his mind-travel trances he feels himself to be "a biosphere, containing all the fossil lives and ideas of his ancestors, containing other life forms, containing countless untold possibilities, containing life and death. He was an analogue of the world" (35). A later revelation explains why Bush, the artist-visionary, records this sense of global, atemporal unity.

> Long past, immeasurably long past, the human race had been born into creation at myriad points at once. It was as diffuse as gas. It was pure intellect. It was omnipotent.
> It was God.
> It had been God and it had created the universe. (182)

Humanity—and this is the novel's tragedy—also had forgotten that it had been God, having gradually "drawn in upon itself" and forsaken its divine omnipresence, narrowing itself and concentrating itself, losing power in its desire for affinity and so now embodied only on Earth, only in a species that has finally forgotten its own origins in godhead. The novel, like Aldiss' other earlier works, ends far from Gaia.

Further examples could be found in other of Aldiss' writings, but the point is that only in the Helliconia novels, only by virtue of the Gaia hypothesis, does Aldiss find the balance that in his work he has so long sought, the spiritual nexus his divided universe required. Once he comes upon Gaia, he vigorously embraces its ability to embody in contemporary guise the Romantic spiritual quest for participation in "the eternal, the infinite, and the one."

The first clue to the integrated vision that informs these novels is Aldiss' convincingly detailed presentation of the response of the planet's biota to Helliconia's ponderous change of season. To list even the most important adaptation strategies of Helliconia's life forms would be a formidable task; suffice it to say they are impressive in their ingenuity and number. That Aldiss devotes many pages to the climatic adaptations of plants and animals is itself significant: man is not the measure of all things in the Aldissian universe.

Even when humanity is center-stage in the Helliconia trilogy, it shares the spotlight with the nonhuman phagors, "rough-coated minotaurs"[18] who prove to be living near the heart of the trilogy's metaphysical maze. The two species are involved, though they do not realize it, in a deeply commensal relationship, one that goes beyond their frequent enslavement and depredation of each other; a virus transmitted by a phagor tick is instrumental in regulating human populations in response to seasonal cycles.

In keeping with Aldiss' foregrounding of the profound interconnectedness of life on Helliconia, there is even a metaphysical aspect to the human/phagor relationship: the religion which dominates human affairs on Helliconia had its origin in phagor worship (*Summer* 485). The development of this religion was coeval with that of the human species itself, and the psychic residuum of this dependence accounts for much of the tension between the two species.

There is further evidence of a metaphysical common ground for humans and phagors in the ability of both species to communicate with their dead ancestors. This is not the typical ancestor-worship of primitive tribes, however; Aldiss uses this necromantic discourse to point up a crucial thematic concern. We see, in *Helliconia Spring,* that the spirits of the human dead are always violently angry when their descendants communicate with them; they become overwhelmingly polite and generous of praise in the second volume, but only because of the empathic involvement of terrestrial humans. Phagor ancestors, on the other hand, are consistently benign. The reason for this disparity is simple.

> Dreadful though the phagors are, they are not estranged from the Original Beholder, the Helliconia Gaia figure. So they are not tormented by the spirits about them. The humans are estranged; they worship many useless gods who make them ill. So their spirits can never be at peace. (*Winter* 139)

It is, in fact, the perception of this very phenomenon that prompts the Earthbound humans' first attempts to communicate empathically with Helliconia.

It is through this involvement of humanity with the inhabitants of Helliconia that Aldiss approaches the Gaia theme. That the natural world of Helliconia is a complex organism with a high degree of unity is first suggested by the increasingly frequent contrasting of Helliconian life with affairs on Earth Observation Station Avernus, a satellite orbiting Helliconia that closely monitors events on the planet and beams pictures back to Earth, a thousand light-years away. Yet the scientists on the Avernus are entirely isolated both from Earth and Helliconia, and indeed have no sense of proper belonging. The families on the station "were sundered indefinitely from the Earth-like world they studied. Yet how much more sundered were the eight families from that distant world they regarded as their native planet!" (*Spring* 380).

The inhabitants of the technological sphere (the Avernus) are doubly estranged from the web of life. The helico virus, transmitted from phagor to human, is an agent of natural order on the planet below, yet the incredible virulence of the disease excludes the Avernians, who have no immunity, from participation in the life they can only observe. Nor can they return to Earth, over one thousand light-years distant. As we are told in *Helliconia Summer,* "To be born on station was to be born into unremitting exile. The first law governing life on the Avernus was that there was no going home" (92). *Helliconia Winter* is even more explicit regarding the implications of this estrangement. In a passage deliberately echoing Shelley's *Defense of Poetry,* we are told that

> The Avernus was an embodiment, cast in the most advanced technology of its culture, of the failure to perceive the answer to that age-old problem of why mankind was divorced from its environment. It was the ultimate token in that long divorce. It represented nothing less than the peak of achievement of an age when man had tried to conquer space and to enslave nature while remaining himself a slave. (74)

This alienation is a major theme in the second volume, manifested in large part in the "Helliconia Holiday Lottery," a regular event in which one member of the spacecraft's crew is permitted to descend to the planet, even though to do so is to die. Despite this death sentence, winning the lottery is a great joy and honor, for the artificiality of life on the Avernus has become intolerably oppressive for many (*Summer* 92–93).

The lottery proves an insufficient outlet, however, even though Avernian technology enables a vicarious participation in the short surface-life of the lottery winner. For too many of those who must remain behind, the Avernus and their mission and all it represents have lost all consolation and meaning: "The belief in technological progress which had inspired the building of the Avernus had, over the generations, become a trap for those aboard it. . . . Belief had largely died on the Avernus, leaving despair in its place (*Summer* 466–67).

Helliconia Winter provides a grim picture of the consequences of this despair born of an artificial life; having lost faith in their mission and themselves, the Avernians sink into profound and unnatural depravity, decimating their numbers through savagery, wanton murder, and cannibalism. Schizophrenia becomes the order of the day, gender confusion a norm. "Everything depraved flourished," and when the bioengineering labs are used to turn out life forms that are nothing but oversized and mobile genitalia, we know the life impulse has been thoroughly perverted by the sterility of the Avernians' exclusively technological mindset. "Men will not be content to manufacture life: they will want to improve on it," Bernal predicted (45); these scenes on the Avernus are Aldiss' vision of that "improvement" when its impulse is founded solely on empiricism. All order and civility on the Avernus finally break down.

> The Avernus, haven of technology, temple of all that was positive and enquiring in mankind's intellect, was reduced to a tumbled arena, in which savages ran from ambush at intervals to break each other's skulls. (77)

> The complex separation from nature undergone by the Avernian colonizers had now reached its limits. Not only did individuals not know each other; they were now strangers to themselves. (174)

Not surprisingly, some of the Avernians try to escape this grim condition, landing themselves on a small, lifeless planet in the Helliconian system. But their enterprise is as doomed to failure as that of the builders of the Avernus.

> The escapers had failed to understand the nature of mankind; that it, like the elephant and the common daisy, is no more and no less than a part and function of a living entity. Separated from that entity, humans, being more complex than elephants and daisies, have little chance of flourishing. (*Winter* 174)

So little chance, in fact, that the colony dies out.

This contrast between the fulfilling life on the planet—that is, life as part of a fully functioning and integrated organism—and life on the fact-gathering station is made all the more powerful by frequent contrast of the Avernians' situation with that of the inhabitants of Earth. On Earth, where broadcasts of Helliconian events are increasingly popular, there is an understanding of Helliconia that exceeds that of those on board the Avernus, despite the much greater proximity of the Avernians in both time and space to the object of their study. And it is in this connection between Earth and Helliconia that Aldiss approaches closest to the concerns of this essay.[19]

The avidity with which the Helliconia broadcasts are watched on Earth is a consequence not of mere vicarious interest in the private activities of others, but of something much more profound, much more crucial to the health of the human psyche. We are told that "The inhabitants of the planet Earth had once watched the affairs of Helliconia with considerable detachment" (*Summer* 39), but such is no longer the case. "Observation was developing into commitment. The watchers were being changed by what they watched. . . . The increasing maturity, the increasing understanding of what it was to be an organic entity, was a debt which the peoples of Earth owed to Helliconia" (40). What close observation of the bio-climatic workings of Helliconia has produced, for Earth's inhabitants, is nothing less than "a transformation in the human spirit" (90), one with consequences for human understandings of nature and ecology and civilization.

> A more integrated approach to life meant that people no longer sought to extract more than their fair share from a global production system now much better understood and controlled. Indeed, interpersonal relationships took on a kind of sanctity, once it was realized that, of a million planets within reasonable distance from Earth, not one could sustain human life or match the miraculous diversity of Earth itself. (90)

Put simply, Helliconia became "of prime importance to the spiritual existence of Earth" (90). The residents of Earth, more sophisticated than their Helliconian cousins, are able to bypass dogma and inculcate "a religious sense of life which needed no God" (*Summer* 262), acknowledging at the same time the need for Helliconians to employ dogma in their more primitive quest for spiritual assurance.

Significantly, the Avernians, in their metaphysical and spiritual impoverishment, look upon Helliconian religion only with contempt (*Summer* 382), especially the practice of communing with the dead. For those on Earth, however, the new insights into the workings of life have revealed (and reconciled them to) the inseparability of life and death, and this Helliconian necromancy, known as "pauk," is perceived sympathetically. The ability of the Helliconians to "shift beyond and return from the boundary set between life and death" is understood to be "compensation" for the severe disruptions and discontinuities they experience during the course of their planet's year, and for this reason pauk is seen to have "evolutionary value, and [to be] a point of union between the humans and their changeable planet" (383). The Avernians, too long away from Earth to be able to claim that planet — or that planet's nature — as their own, cannot understand pauk except as baseless superstition; on Earth, the importance of pauk is not in whether the spirits of the dead are really contacted but in the ability of the practice to provide continuity and contact with aspects of existence not grasped by the instruments of the orbiting Avernus, the cold probes and instruments of empirical science. For the Helliconians, a descent into the underworld that is the home of the ancestral spirits is a descent into "a green and unknown, unknowable womb, the womb of the original beholder. The original beholder — that passive mother principle — received the souls of the dead who sank back into her" (*Summer* 134). It is this, the sense of the profound belonging and connection so intimate that ends lead to beginnings, that the science and technology of the Avernians can never reach nor measure. Apparently those who make ambulatory vaginas cannot understand the planetary womb.

What the humans of Earth come to discover is their relationship to their own "original beholder," and it is here that Aldiss relies most heavily on the implications of Lovelock's Gaia hypothesis. Recovering from a nuclear war (and resultant nuclear winter) that nearly destroyed their species, the humans of Earth discover that their planet is a "living biosphere," a complex organism itself, a unity, and they personify this in Gaia, the Earth mother. Like Helliconia's Original Beholder (and identified as her sister), Gaia is one of those "geochemical spirits who have managed the life of a functioning world as a single organism. . . . a vast cooperative entity, creating well-being from the centre of a furious chemical storm" (*Winter* 219, 220). The survivors of Earth's nuclear war developed an "empathic feel for all life," and rethought and reorganized the very way they lived upon the planet.

> As nature had formed a diverse unity, so now did consciousness. It was no longer possible for a man or woman merely to feel or merely to think; there was only empathic thinkfeel. Head and heart were one. . . . Men and women looked about at the territory they happened to occupy and no longer asked "What can we get out of this land?" Instead, they asked, "What best experience can we have on this land?" With this new consciousness came less exploitive ties and more ties everywhere. . . . The ancient structure of family faded into new super families. All mankind became a loose knit superorganism . . . the new race could feel itself to be the consciousness of Gaia. (*Winter* 177)

Aldiss insists that the presence of an Earth-spirit like Gaia was responsible for the development of the human race, for he contrasts Earth's slow, evolutionary recovery from nuclear near-disaster with the fate of a planet called New Earth. Colonized in better times, New Earth becomes host to some survivors of the nuclear wars on other planets in Earth's solar system. The new arrivals find New Earth to be an uncongenial place, although they cannot explain precisely why. Aldiss, however, makes clear the source of this planet's trouble: New Earth is "without a tutelary biospheric spirit" (*Winter* 175), and so it stagnates, its colonists "like neutered animals. Something vital and rebellious had gone from their spirits" (179). The survivors explore a nearby ice planet, and discover an ancient civilization buried under that ice—a civilization that, it turns out, destroyed itself by nuclear war. Learning the wrong lesson, the survivors return to New Earth, believing they can alter that planet's weather for the better by a strategically planned nuclear detonation. Their plan fails, and life on the planet, if it even survives (Aldiss is deliberately ambiguous) is not improved.

4

Emerson, in the "Divinity School Address," also quotes the line from Wordsworth about a pagan suckled in a creed outworn, although the outworn creed for Emerson was an uninspired Christianity. Emerson goes on, in this text, to expound "the sublime creed that the world is not the product of manifold power, but of one will, of one mind; and that one mind is everywhere active, in each ray of the star, in each wavelet of the pool."[20] This Transcendental semipantheism develops more clearly into a notion of universal wholeness in "The Over-Soul," where Emerson writes that "the heart in thee is the heart of all; not a valve, not a wall, not an intersection is there anywhere in nature, but one blood rolls uninterruptedly an endless circulation through all men, as the water of the globe is all one sea, and, truly seen, its tide is one."[21]

These and other, similar passages in Emerson—and Wordsworth and many of the Romantics—in some ways suggest the more esoteric implications of quantum physics, and this connection between science and metaphysics has some relevance here. Just as the new physics often leads to questions long regarded as the exclusive domain of all philosophers, so does the science of Lovelock lead, at least potentially, to a modern Romantic animism, a new secular transcendence.

This potential is most fully realized in the Helliconia novels. Aldiss' technological future leads beyond itself to the realm of the metaphysical, the extratechnological, and it does so with minimal reliance upon that technology. The consolations become those of the spirit, not the mechanical guardian. The handmaiden of science has always been more suspect for Aldiss than for Asimov, as is evident in *Non-Stop, Galaxies Like Grains of Sand, Hothouse,* and elsewhere,[22] and in these authors' handling of the Gala hypothesis we see this difference clearly. Asimov does not go beyond the minor-key hints of spirituality that Lovelock endorses, and indeed almost loses them in the glare of light reflected from his robots. For Asimov, sufficiently developed technology is the answer; *deus* is indeed possible *ex machina*. Aldiss, like Wordsworth and Emerson and perhaps even Poe in *Eureka,* finds the intuitively apprehended sense of global participation the surer path to the universal mindscape sought since Copernicus banished us to some nameless and disconnected suburb of the universe.[23]

Notes

1. J. E. Lovelock, *Gaia: A New Look at Life on Earth* (New York: Oxford Univ. Press, 1979), 9. Further references appear in parentheses in the text.

2. Brian Aldiss, letter to the author, Oct. 9, 1986. Quotations from this letter by permission of the writer.

3. William Wordsworth, *The Poems,* ed. John O. Hayden (New Haven: Yale Univ. Press, 1981), 1: 568–69.

4. Wordsworth, *Poems,* 1:360.

5. I am excluding John Varley's Gaea series—*Titan* (1979), *Wizard* (1979), *Demon* (1984)—because it does not invoke Lovelock's Gaia hypothesis, at least not immediately enough for any evidence of this influence to remain. Varley has

gone to Greek myth (and to Hollywood) for his sentient, planet-sized bio-machine Gaea, and while it may be that the creatures that live in Gaea find that "The whole world is Gaea. Gaea is one" (*Titan* [New York: Berkeley, 1986], 260), there is none of the participation-in-global-consciousness that is the hallmark of Lovelock's Gaia. Some of the beings Varley's Gaea manufactures "were not individuals with anything like free will, but rather extensions of herself in the same way that a finger or hand was an extension of a human's existence" (*Demon* [New York: Berkeley, 1985], 26), but this is not the planetary or galactic unity depicted by Asimov or Aldiss. Varley's senescent Gaea is, primarily, an enemy for the novels' characters (including some of Gaea's own creatures) to fight.

6. C. N. Manlove identifies another reason why Asimov's characters in the early Foundation novels are less than striking: every fifty or one hundred pages, they disappear as the novels take their jumps forward in time (*Science Fiction: Ten Explorations* [Kent, Ohio: Kent State Univ. Press, 1986], 28).

7. Isaac Asimov, *Foundation's Edge* (1982; New York: Ballantine Del Rey, 1983), 348. Further references appear in parentheses in the text.

8. Gerald Jonas, rev. of *Foundation and Earth*, by Isaac Asimov, *New York Times Book Review*, Nov. 23, 1986, 30.

9. Isaac Asimov, *Foundation and Earth* (New York: Doubleday, 1986), 347.

10. Christopher Small, tracing the influence of *Frankenstein* on modern fiction, comments on Asimov's robot ethos, specifically on the importance of his first law of robotics, which declares that "A robot may not injure a human being, or, through inaction, allow a human being to come to harm." This law, Small notes,

> tries to pre-empt the whole problem of conflict between creature and creator. . . . Even as a starting point of fantasy, such a formula well illustrates the inadequacy of SF to deal with the moral problems it raises: what is "harmful" or beneficial to man is here presupposed to be calculable by a machine, or not at all; and to imagine a robot thus rendered innocuous is to miss the whole point at the outset of what it represents. . . . Mechanical systems sufficiently elaborate and autonomous to be called robot-like have already been made with any number of such "fail-safe" devices built into them. But it should not be necessary to point out that the most elaborate system of such safeguards merely underlines the fact that men are trying to resign moral choice to a machine. (*Ariel Like a Harpy: Shelley, Mary, and "Frankenstein"* [London: Victor Gallancz, 1972], 300.)

Aldiss' rendition of the Gaia hypothesis, by explicitly transcending the technological rather than foregrounding it, avoids precisely this limitation.

11. Brian Aldiss, *Billion Year Spree: The True History of Science Fiction* (New York: Doubleday, 1973), 269.

12. Small, *Ariel Like a Harpy*, 294.

13. J. D. Bernal, *The World, the Flesh, and the Devil: An Enquiry into the Future of the Three Enemies of the Rational Soul* (1929; Bloomington: Indiana Univ. Press, 1969), 43. Further references appear in parentheses in the text.

14. This should not be taken to imply an antitechnologism; such a position is as simplistic as the belief that through technology alone humanity may resolve those problems—social, psychological, and metaphysical—with which it is beset. The point I do make here is that Aldiss, more so than Asimov, is explicitly concerned to balance technologism with a recognition that humankind exists in a universe that has nonempirical, "scientifically untestable" dimensions of metaphysics and spirituality. However much Asimov may recognize this personally, his treatments of the Gaia hypothesis privilege the empirical over the spiritual. Aldiss is more successful in exploiting the metaphysical implications of the Gaia concept (although the Helliconia novels are hardly philosophical treatises) because, as I take it, of his greater willingness to recognize science fiction as the inheritor of a Romantic tradition—a tradition with a marked spiritual dimension. Asimov, I am told, insists that his work be read in light of its declared sources (although he, unlike Aldiss, does not supply these in the novels), yet even if Asimov is not conversant with Romantic writing—rather unlikely, given his erudition and range—he is clearly using Lovelock's theory. This, we have seen, encodes into its Epilogue some of our age's post-Romantic anxieties. One need not know Wordsworth—or even Lovelock's Epilogue—to sense that ours is an age of considerable spiritual disquiet.

15. Brian Aldiss, letter to the author, Oct. 9, 1986.

16. Brian Griffin & David Wingrove, *Apertures: A Study of the Writings of Brian W. Aldiss* (Westport, Conn.: Greenwood Press, 1984).

17. Brian Aldiss, *Cryptozoic!* (1967; New York: Avon, 1969), 174. Further references appear in parentheses in the text.

18. Brian Aldiss, *Helliconia Winter* (1985; New York: Berkeley, 1986), 101. The other volumes comprising the trilogy are *Helliconia Spring* (1982; New York: Berkeley, 1984) and *Helliconia Summer* (1983; New York: Berkeley 1986). Further references in the text will be by keyword and page number in parentheses.

19. Reviewing the third volume in the series, Thomas D. Clareson writes that the Avernus "is no more than a self-operative machine, however complex, which is totally indifferent to its caretakers" (*Extrapolation* 27 [Spring 1986], 93). The space station is this, to be sure, but to see this as its primary thematic function is, I think, to slight its considerable value in establishing the contrast between the spiritual destitution of technologism and the sense of metaphysical plenitude implicit in the Gaia/Original Beholder unities.

20. Ralph Waldo Emerson, "Divinity School Address," *The Collected Works of Ralph Waldo Emerson*, vol. 1, ed. Alfred R. Ferguson et al. (Cambridge: Harvard/Belknap, 1971), 78.

21. Emerson, "The Oversoul," *The Collected Works of Ralph Waldo Emerson*, vol. 2, ed. Joseph Slater et al. (Cambridge: Harvard/Belknap, 1979), 173–74.

22. Griffin & Wingrove, *Apertures*, 166–67 et pasim.

23. The mindscapes of utopias and their ideological implications touched off considerable debate at the ninth Eaton Conference, and although this debate never came to include the Gaia novels, I would like to sneak in a few words on the relationship between utopianism and the science-fictional interpretations of the Gaia hypothesis.

Is Gaia a utopian vision? Yes, and admittedly it is one that is not on the "front ranks," at least as the battle lines are drawn by Marxists or feminists or racial/ethnic groups (or combinations thereof). We should recognize, however, that there are many ways to configure (and wage) a battle. We might begin by asking if the goals of science-fiction-interpreted Gaia are so foreign to those of the groups who feel themselves excluded, their vision denied. In particulars undoubtedly, but—and this is especially true in Aldiss' version of Gaia—there is the suggestion that Gaia's implications for social structure can address problems of economic exploitation and discrimination by gender or race or any other standard.

Some critics label utopias as failures if they do not explicitly address the means by which humanity is to get from here to there. This seems to me terribly reductive, for few utopias are meant as blueprints. Nor should we judge a utopian novel on its ability to make us want to live in the world it describes; utopian fiction is valuable because it embodies challenging ideas and presents them for our consideration and edification (and rejection), not because it could be misconstrued as a travel brochure. Both Gaian visions I discuss are set in the far-distant future, but this in no way diminishes their impact on us. After all, if Lovelock is correct, we are living in Gaia now; the far-future setting of the novels simply indicates the distance we have yet to go before we might reach full consciousness of our participation in Gaia.

Gaia's distance and seeming failure to address contemporary ideological concerns does not mean it is a simplistic, escapist utopia. It is, after all, founded on a scientific hypothesis, which means it is grounded in very real, tangible, empirical nature. The environmental implications of this are obvious, and they, in turn, have as much an ideological dimension—and as real and as dedicated a "front rank"—as any other contemporary "Ism."

9

Recent Feminist Utopias: World Building and Strategies for Social Change
Peter Fitting

I would like to do several things. On a descriptive plane, I will argue that the moment of feminist-inspired utopian fiction of the 1970s has ended and has been replaced by more pessimistic dystopias. At the same time, as someone who has been academically and politically involved with that utopian writing, I am concerned by this rise in feminist dystopias as a literary phenomenon and as a political strategy. These concerns will lead to the second part of my essay, one inspired to some extent by the text of a paper presented at an earlier Eaton Conference—Gregory Benford's "Reactionary Utopias" (published in *Storm Warnings: Science Fiction Confronts the Future,* edited by George E. Slusser, Colin Greenland, and Eric S. Rabkin [Carbondale: Southern Illinois University Press, 1987]). While we certainly disagree on a number of issues, I think his article provides some useful criteria for evaluating contemporary utopias, particularly in terms of assessing the building of imaginary worlds. Insofar as Benford criticizes these utopias not so much on literary grounds but in terms of their contents, he and I are on the same footing. One either rejects the notion of utopia altogether, which some critics have done (i.e., Thomas Molnar, *Utopia: The Perennial Heresy*), or one accepts the concept of utopia and what it implies, namely a critique of the present state of affairs and a positing of a desirable alternative. To criticize fictional utopias, we must either disagree with their critiques of the present and/or of the ideal societies depicted; or we must argue that a specific utopia is ineffective in putting forward those goals for the reader.

Utopias and dystopias have thus a performative function; ideally they are intended to push the reader to action. Benford is right to begin with the recognition that this performative function depends on a utopia's ability to make the reader want to live in that other world, although I will disagree with him—reader to reader—about the actual effects of the seventies utopias we are concerned with.

2

The classics of the feminist utopian revival of the 1970s are familiar to most of you and include: Suzy McKee Charnas, *Motherlines* (1979); Sally Gearhart, *The Wanderground* (1978); Ursual K. LeGuin, *The Dispossessed* (1975); Marge Piercy, *Woman on The Edge of Time* (1976); and Joanna Russ, *The Female Man* (1975). To these should be added two utopian novels written by men with feminist overtones: Ernest Callenbach, *Ecotopia* (1975); and Samuel Delany, *Triton* (1976).

Like Margaret Atwood's *The Handmaid's Tale*—the most influential of recent dystopias—Sally Gearhart's *The Wanderground* also portrays a backlash against the growing strength of women and gays. But here the backlash prompted "the revolt of the Earth herself"; outside the city men suddenly became impotent, while machines and mechanical devices no longer functioned. Although the men established a patriarchal police state in the cities, the core of the novel was the evocation of a utopian world of the women outside the cities. This focus on the depiction of new societies organized around egalitarian and cooperative principles is characteristic of all of the above novels, although some go further than just describing the utopian society, raising questions about the possibility of utopia (in LeGuin and in Delany), or by concentrating as well on the transition to the new society (in Piercy and in Russ).

Insofar as they emphasized the changed lives and experiences of their characters and because they described alternate societies that would make such new patterns of behavior and interpersonal relations possible, these works provided the reader with an experience, however limited, of what a better world, beyond sexual hierarchy and domination, might look and feel like. Despite Benford's initial assertion that "One of the striking facets of fictional utopias is that nobody really wants to live there" (*Storm Warnings*, 73), I would argue that the ability to "awaken a real longing to take part" is a major component of the relative success of many of these recent works.

However, with one exception to which I shall return, this utopian moment seems to have ended. More recent fictions no longer give us images of a radically different future in which the values and ideals of feminism have been extended to much of the planet, but depressing images of a brutal reestablishment of capitalist patriarchy.

3

The transition from utopia to dystopia can be seen in Zoe Fairbairns' novel *Benefits* (1979), which was written in Britain at the end of the utopian period. It is set in the near future in the context of Britain's worsening economic plight. All social welfare programs are suspended except for the equivalent of Canada's "baby-bonus"—a "Benefit" that will be paid directly to the mother, but only to mothers who do *not* work outside the home. However, rather than leading to a strengthening of the family and its traditional values, the Benefit has two related effects that lead the government to conclude that it is a failure. On the one hand, lower-income families "breed" as a way of increasing their income; while may women are able, thanks to the Benefit, to live, without men, outside the system and its embodiment in the nuclear family.

The government then announces that the Benefit will be withdrawn from "unfit" mothers, namely those who do not live according to traditional family norms. But as Britain's economy continues to worsen, European planners help to implement even more drastic "social planning" experiments: the widespread—and usually forced—placing of "contraceptive pellets" in women, and when women find ways to remove the pellets, putting a contraceptive in the water supply. Women deemed "suitable" for motherhood are to apply at a government "Women's Centre" for an antidote, but instead the antidote reacts with the contraceptive, producing massive deformities and rendering British women "unsuitable as vehicles for the carrying of unborn children (Zoe Fairbairns, *Benefits* [London: Virago, 1979], 196).

This is not, however, the end of the novel. Although there is a possibility that it may be generations—or never—until British women are again able to bear children, a younger and more militant generation of women argue for a renewed commitment to the goal of a society that will be finally "a fit place to bring [babies]." *Benefits* is certainly not a utopia, but it does not end in complete despair either. It demonstrates an increasing bitterness toward the continuing exploitation of women and to government attempts to control their fertility: "Our women are going to be the first to find a style of life that isn't defined by men having power over us because we have children" (215).

While I cannot adequately review here the various manifestations of the state's attempts to regulate sexuality and fertility, it is increasingly apparent that the struggle of women to gain control of their own bodies and their own fertility is perceived as a critical threat by the Christian right; and by the courts, I might add, which, in the Baby M case, have ruled against the natural claim of motherhood in favor of a contractual agreement, a decision that will open the floodgates to baby farming, through the creation of a subclass of poor women who will become hatcheries for the rich. These issues are central to Margaret Atwood's *The Handmaid's Tale* (Toronto: McClelland & Stewart, 1985). There, in a near future in which people have become increasingly alarmed by a declining birthrate, (explained in the novel as being caused by the various forms of pollution to which we are exposed as much as by conscious decision), the Christian right stages a violent takeover and establishes a theocratic "Republic of Gilead" throughout much of the United States. This renewed regulation — "for breeding purposes" — of women's bodies marks the triumph of the Moral Majority and its "family protection" agenda. The "traditional" values of the nuclear family are forcibly reestablished, while divorce, birth control, homosexuality, and other manifestations of the "permissiveness" and "moral decay" that characterized the sixties and seventies are brutally repressed. And, as in the baby M case just referred to, fertile young women (here called "handmaids") are used — with the proper scriptural references (Genesis 30) — as surrogate mothers when the wives of the new leaders are unable to conceive.

Suzette Elgin's science-fiction novel *Native Tongue* is set in the more distant future of the twenty-third century, although its starting point is also the contemporary attacks on women's efforts to obtain social and political equality. Here the reaction leads to the repeal of the Nineteenth Amendment (which gave women the right to vote), and a new amendment to the Constitution (ratified in 1991) according to which "all citizens of the United States of the female gender shall be deemed legally minors." In the future of the novel, the Earth has contacted and now trades with other planets — a development that has led to the rise of a small elite group of translators (called "Linguists") who, because of their discipline in teaching their children to master languages from infancy, have a monopoly on handling negotiations between the Earth and its alien trading partners.

Within this futuristic context, the novel describes life within a linguist family where the women lead an even more exaggereated version of today's double duty for women: even though they are legally minors and are completely dependent on their fathers and husbands, they are also skilled translators with busy professional lives. At the same time, because the linguists are anxious to preserve their monopoly, the politics of reproduction are significant. The linguist women are compelled to marry young (by the age of sixteen), which "[allows] the husband to space his children three years apart and still see that the woman bears eight infants before the age of forty" (Suzette Haden Elgin, *Native Tongue* [New York: DAW Books, 1984], 146). What distinguishes this novel from the dystopian future of *The Handmaid's Tale,* at least to some of its feminist readers, is that, despite this repressive situation, the women-linguists have, in the privacy of their "Barren Houses" (where the no-longer-fertile linguist women live communally), developed a uniquely women's language, one that they hope will change the world by changing the way that women look at and construct reality.

While the women living together in the Barren Houses do experience reality in specific ways, the majority of their experiences are nonetheless shaped by the power relationships in which they are rooted and exploited. They are still legally minors, bound to their husbands, fathers, and families; their reproductive functions, to take the issue central to *The Handmaid's Tale* and *Benefits,* are completely under the control of the male members of the patriarchal household. Indeed, leaving aside the science-fiction aspect—communication with extraterrestrials—they lead a similar, but more secular and communal version of the lives of the women in *The Handmaid's Tale.* Indeed, I would argue that rather than providing a way of transforming the world, this new language will condition the women to their inferior and exploited state. Allowed to live separately, even with their own language, they will still be little more than slaves. Reality will not be changed by this new language; it will become an instrument of self-deception, the bleeding off of the rebellious energies of a group of exploited women.

Although not everyone may agree with my specific readings of these novels, I think we can at least concur that these futuristic visions illustrate a reaction to the gains won over the past two decades. Written from three relatively different literary contexts and from three different countries, they mark an end to the feminist utopianism of the 1970s.

There is, however, one significant exception—Ursula K. LeGuin's *Always Coming Home* (New York: Harper & Row, 1985). But in an entirely different way, it too I think demonstrates a retreat from an earlier feminist utopianism.

For those of you who are familiar with LeGuin's work, *Always Coming Home* is a return to her roots, both in the sense of her "anthropological" origins (her parents were anthropologists and her mother, Theodora Kroeber, wrote *Ishi: The Last Stone Age Man* (1961), which played an important part in utopian "rediscovery" of North American indigenous cultures in the 1960s, and which in many ways *Always* strongly resembles); and it is a return to the anthropological sensibilities and organization of her *The Left Hand of Darkness* (1969). *Always Coming Home* is more than five hundred pages long and includes a cassette of the music and poetry of the Kesh people. Although the reader enters the book with a story, narrative is soon replaced by bits and pieces of Kesh culture. These include poems, legends, autobiographies, drawings, music, maps, jokes, plays, a glossary, and even some recipes. Neither a blueprint nor a narrative, *Always Coming Home* is a nonlinear collection of information that it is up to the reader to put together, in the manner of a kit.

Like *The Dispossessed,* the intentions of this "book," the implied reasons for wanting to describe a "people which might be going to have lived a long, long time from now in Northern California,"(xi) are clearly utopian. In the lovely valley of the book, the Kesh live and work close to the natural in a way that is both culturally rich and obviously satisfying. Moreover, in typical utopian fashion, the happy, pastoral society of the Kesh is contrasted to a patriarchal, militaristic Condor people who can be seen as a figure of our own world and its (rapid) course toward destruction.

Instead of showing the difficulties, disagreements, and hardships involved in building and maintaining a new society, *Always* focuses on the immediate pleasures and joys of daily life. But this small community seems cut off from the rest of the world. And although there are occasional glimpses of advanced technology (the computer terminals), that technology is hidden and most people live in a nostalgic return to an almost pretechnological world—a "reactionary utopia" in Benford's terms. For my tastes, this imaginary society is too small and isolated, while the only references to a transition leave open the possibility— despite LeGuin's violent denials—that this is somehow a postholocaust world: no alternate explanations are offered of how today's global tensions were resolved, or how the population was reduced.

Because LeGuin's utopia is unclear about how this wonderful new Northern California came to be, or what happened to the rest of the world, it makes it difficult for me to give myself over to the fantasy of living there. While this may be quibbling, the earlier seventies utopias I referred to — particularly those of Piercy and Russ, the utopias in which I would most like to live — not only depicted the entire planet but also addressed the issue of how we got from here to there.

At this point, I would like to return to Benford's "Reactionary Utopias" and his recognition that the criteria for judging such utopian writing lie with the reader's response to an imaginary society. Benford begins with the comment that "nobody really wants to live in" fictional utopias, and he then lists five characteristics of what he considers recent backward-looking "reactionary utopias," of which *The Dispossessed* is the key example. I agree that a utopia should be judged by its ability to make the reader want to live there and I submit that the relative popularity of the feminist-inspired utopias of the 1970s has to do precisely with that. His opening generalization is based not on knowledge of readers but on his own reaction — *he* would not like to live there. (Parenthetically, let me add that his choice of *The Dispossessed* is based on its specific unattractiveness, its lack of sensual pleasure, as opposed to the much more appealing depictions of daily life in all of the other utopias mentioned.)

Benford's next two criteria are familiar criticisms of traditional utopias that have, I think, been addressed in many contemporary works — their "lack of diversity" and their "static" nature. His third objection — that they are "nostalgic and technophobic" — I accept in part. A better world does not lie in the past, although he and I may disagree on the distinction between technophobia and a regard for bringing the development and application of technology into some kind of balance with human needs and with the biosphere. *Ecotopia, Woman on The Edge of Time,* or even *The Female Man* are good examples of attempts at such a balance. His fourth objection — the "presence of an authority figure" — applies more to the actual utopian experiments of the nineteenth and twentieth centuries than it does to fictional utopias. He does modify this statement by adding that "in literary utopias the authority is the prophet who set up the utopia," and who is often invoked "as a guide to proper, right thinking behaviour" (*Storm Warnings,* 75).

While it may be characteristic for some of you to cite Scripture as an authority—or for me to cite Marx—I am not familiar with too many utopias that rely on such authority, except for Benford's bête noire, *The Dispossesed,* where Odo is frequently cited—although a possible description of that novel might be that it dramatizes the contradiction between the original precepts of the founding mother and the congealing of those fluid revolutionary principles into a static set of rules where, as in the case in many political and religious institutions today, people's actual practice violates the spirit but not the letter of the law. Of course my phrasing of this issue already indicates what I think about Benford's last and most important criticism, that these works rely on "social regulation through guilt." I for one do not know how any society could work without having either a strong state apparatus for enforcing its rules (police, the courts, etc.) or what Benford calls "social responsibility . . . as the standard of behaviour." But I will stop; we cannot resolve this debate now.

4

In attempting to conclude then, let me begin by stating that it is relatively easy to equate this decline in utopian writing with larger social and political events and to see the dystopian novels I have described as ominous signs of what may lie ahead. My concern is not only with the accuracy of such visions, however, but also with their impact. What effect do these more pessimistic works have on readers, particularly when compared to the earlier visions of a future structured by feminist principles and ideals? More bluntly, what serves the building of a new society best? The evocation of images of a better future along with indications of how we get there? Or, at a time of increasing threats, does it make more sense to try to warn people that the battle is far from won?

On the one hand, the argument that we need such cautionary tales resembles an older critique of utopianism. It might be argued that the move away from utopian writing and the turn to more "realistic" visions of the future is a way of maintaining our vigilance, that the building of a better society does not need images of that better world, but the energy, anger, and strategies to change this one. Utopian visions perhaps too quickly skip to the alternative, and too quickly forget the intermediate fight, particularly now that so many of our recent gains are under attack. Yet I still think that the utopian novels of the 1970s were successful, despite what Benford says. Not only because I and many others might choose to live in worlds in process like those described by Piercy and Russ, or by Delany and Callenbach, but also because they have helped carry the vision of an alternative to a new and larger audience.

The purpose of my essay has been to describe and defend the political dimension of such works and to counteract reading strategies that obscure or deny their literal meaning. While there is much to love and enjoy in this privileged corner of our own world, the utopian impulse at the heart of all science fiction, the awareness of the fundamental insufficiencies of the present and the longing for a more just and humane world, should not be denied. In reading these evocations of the possible development of our own sociopolitical environment, I would like them to lead you to ask yourselves about the future you hope to live in, and what you intend to do about it.

10

Time and Vast Eternities: Landscapes of Immortality in Orson Scott Card's Fiction

Michael R. Collings

When Ender Wiggin speaks the death of Marcos Ribeira in Orson Scott Card's *Speaker for the Dead* (1986),[1] one of the listeners, Bishop Peregrino, suddenly discovers spiritual depths within something he had considered an infidel incursion into the realm of true religion. As Ender reveals layer after layer of necessary deception in the lives of Marcos, his wife Novinha, and her lover Libo, Peregrino realizes that

> The Speaker had done a monstrous thing, to lay these secrets before the whole community. They should have been spoken in the confessional. Yet Peregrino had felt the power of it, the way the whole community was forced to discover these people that they thought they knew, and then discover them again, and then again; and each revision of the story forced them all to reconceive themselves as well, for they had been part of this story, too, had been touched by all the people a hundred, a thousand times, never understanding until now who it was they touched. It was a painful, fearful thing to go through, but in the end it had a curiously calming effect. (293)

The passage is one of many in *Speaker* devoted to the function of narrative and *true* story in creating a sense of community. The passages are particularly important in discussing Card's work and his relation to science fiction and fantasy because he, too, is concerned with telling "true" stories and establishing a community of believers through repetitions and permutations of his "story." From his earliest science-fiction stories, appearing in 1977, Card has explored his deeply felt assumptions about the nature and destiny of humanity—and in doing so, he has demonstrated how the forms of science fiction and fantasy have enabled him to define and test those assumptions for his readers.

In the *Doctrine and Covenants,* one of four books accepted as scripture by members of the Church of Jesus Christ of Latter-day Saints, the voice of God comes to Moses upon a high mountain to announce, "For behold, this is my work and my glory, to bring to pass the immortality and eternal life of man" (Moses 1:29). As interpreted by LDS readers, this statement goes far in distancing Latter-day Saints from the mainstream of received Christian tradition by asserting not only the ultimate perfectibility of humanity but also that humans may eventually share Godhood itself.

This background is helpful in assessing Card's writings because he is a deeply committed member of the Church of Jesus Christ of Latter-day Saints. He has noted frequently that his activities within the church consume more of his time than writing science fiction. Nor has he ever hidden that commitment, even though in his early science-fiction novels and stories, he tried to avoid overt references to Mormonism. It is sufficient, he argues, that he write truly. In doing so, the assumptions he makes about the nature of humanity will communicate themselves clearly.

Card thus becomes a fascinating writer to study in terms of mindscapes. One of his primary purposes is to explore how humanity may attain perfection—literally, to share in the immortality of God. Most of his fictions focus on a single individual powerful enough to alter the course of history and move humanity a step nearer to ultimate perfection, to become within the context of the story a near-God. In *Speaker for the Dead,* for example, a character describes Ender Wiggin as "something of a savior, or a prophet, or at least a martyr" (88), an accurate representation of nearly every one of Card's central characters.

Even more intriguing, Card carefully constructs worlds and environments for his characters, varying the kinds of worlds he imagines to allow his readers to move through an unusual range of possibilities as Card explores the actions of his Christic figures and the consequences of those actions.

In the medieval world, meaning was interpreted on at least four distinct levels: literal, allegorical, analogical, and anagogical—each defined by connections between the objective universe and the larger realm of God. In imaginative fiction, the same distinctions of meaning were often applied to the worlds created, to the landscapes themselves.

This fourfold layering is especially helpful in working with Card's fiction of, particularly in light of his consistent reaffirmation of traditional literary values: the importance of story, of character, of epic heroism. His fictions are structured about his need to express a particular world view. As he said in a recent interview:

> Science fiction has never been more than 50% of my writing, even in the hottest years. I have constantly been writing things dealing with Mormon history or other religious things, or other historical things for the Utah audience. . . . I've written books of satire and philosophy and other subjects for the Mormon audience. (13)[2]

Because of this concern for theological and religious expression, Card's writing suggests the potentials inherent in science fiction and fantasy as forms incorporating multiple mindscapes; in fact, his fiction is increasingly devoted to exploring ideas and images difficult to fit within the framework of mainstream fiction precisely because the central ideas do not correspond directly to elements observable within realistic landscapes. His concentration on science fiction and fantasy allows him to place his characters on worlds designed as test frames for experiences not objectively possible in mainstream fiction.

1. Literal Landscapes

Card's earliest writing was explicitly religious; he worked as an assistant editor for a religious magazine, contributing articles and stories aimed at inculcating specific moral values within a specific audience. To this extent, his work was *literal,* reflecting as much his concern for theological truth as for artistic or fictional "truth."

Some years later, however, he translated this literalism into fiction. *A Woman of Destiny* (1984)[3] is a historical novel, fictional in intent but based on the lives of Eliza R. Snow, Brigham Young, Joseph Smith, and others important in Card's LDS heritage. Although *A Woman of Destiny* succeeds as historical novel, it lacks the depth of characterization and empathy found in Card's fantasy and science fiction, largely because he must *assert* the spiritual and the supernatural within the context of a mainstream world. He does not, for example, show an angel speaking to his heroine, Dina Kirkham; instead he describes a dream that becomes a disturbing foreshadowing of truth. Throughout, Card is limited by the expectations of an audience that demands realistic settings, characters, and actions.

In fact, several responses to the novel indicated how widely it was misread by mainstream readers. One reviewer referred to it as the "true story of Dinah Kirkham" (perhaps an unintentional tribute to the strength of Card's meticulous re-creation of the nineteenth-century world critical to the novel); unfortunately, the reviewer[4] continued, the "rambling, 700-page saga sags under the weight of Mormon dogma, which seems to take precedence over the development of characters and their relationships" (59). A similar misreading occurred when Kristiana Gregory[5] wrote that Card is a "direct descendant of heroine Dina [*sic*] Kirkham" (8). The care with which he reconstructs the landscapes of Manchester and Liverpool in England, then Nauvoo, Illinois, thus occasionally works against Card's ultimate purposes, convincing his readers that they must take as literal, historical fact what was intended to function as a fictional re-creation of those facts.

2. Allegorical Landscapes

When we move from *A Woman of Destiny* into fantasy, we can see how the potentials of such fiction allow Card's imagination to develop more fully. Although few of Card's works are exclusively allegorical, he has, from the beginning, understood the potential power of allegorical treatment. Names and places often approach allegorical intensity — especially characters' names, as in the early Worthing tales, with such characters as John Tinker, Sammy Barber, and Martin Keeper.[6] This tendency continues in Card's work, subdued but often present. In *Seventh Son* (1987),[7] characters' names describe not only occupations but also personalities, becoming full-scale allegorical representations, as in Armor-of-God Weaver, the Reverend Thrower, and Taleswapper.

Occasionally, however, Card has used allegorical fantasy to investigate the implications of godhood and immortality. In *Hart's Hope* (1983)[8] Card's landscape mirrors his characters' moral state. The city of Burland bears several names, including Hart's Hope and, significantly, *Inwit*, or "Conscience." It is ruled by Queen Beauty, who hopes to extend her three-centuries-long reign by sacrificing her son, Youth. Throughout, Card emphasizes connections between the city and his deeper purposes — to establish the messianic role of his hero, the Young King as he moves from the depths beneath the city of Conscience to share in its rule, subverting the rebellious reign of Beauty and laying the foundations for the ultimate union of Conscience with its exiled true

King. In Hart's Hope, the name *is* the thing; again and again, Card warns readers that words, people, things, and places are to be read in multiple directions, as part of intricate parallels with human history and human understanding, with the result that the physical landscape of Burland and its surroundings parallels the growth, development, and finally the sacrifice of Card's characters.

Card's continuing interest in the potential allegorical fantasy is demonstrated by his current series-in-progress—the six novels comprising the *Tales of Alvin Maker*. These novels consciously impose Mormon history onto the fantasy framework of a magical, alternate-world America. Even more importantly, the landscape shows the double meaning characteristic of allegory; in *Seventh Son,* for example, water is both a natural force and a malevolent power seeking the destruction of young Alvin Maker. Later, Card uses his imagined world as a setting for an imagistic and symbolic fulfillment of the scriptural prophecy of the stone cut from the mountain in the millstone that simultaneously nearly ends Alvin's life and teaches him about the nature of his power.

In *Seventh Son,* as in *Hart's Hope,* Card relies on the readers' ability to penetrate the allegory and discover—and understand—deeper, more substantive meanings than a literal presentation would allow.

3. Analogical Landscapes

In discussing science fiction and fantasy, Brian W. Aldiss[9] writes that "In its wider sense, fantasy clearly embraces all science fiction. But fantasy in a narrower sense, as opposed to science fiction, generally implies a fiction leaning more toward myth or the mythopoeic than towards an assumed realism," in other words, a fiction standing as analogy to that assumed realism (26). Aldiss' differentiation is helpful in discussing Card, since much of Card's fiction works most effectively as analogy. He is less interested in the specifics of particular scientific extrapolation than in creating parallel worlds that allow him to explore the values and characteristics most central to his purposes. In spite of his early reputation as an *"Analog"* writer, his science fiction often borders on fantasy, precisely because his most successful narratives treat imaginary worlds as similar to ours, their physical laws generally consistent with ours but altered just enough to turn the landscapes into the settings for thought-experiments, keeping the alterations both possible and acceptable within a loosely science-fictional framework. In works such as *Capitol* (1979),[10] *Hot Sleep* (1979),[11] *The Worthing Chronicle* (1983),[12] *A Planet Called Treason* (1979),[13] *Songmaster* (1980),[14] *Ender's Game* (1985)[15] and *Speaker for the Dead,* Card's worlds offer the possibility of immortality, omniscience, and omnipresence—three cardinal traits of deity.

In the first three, for example, the drug *somec* provides virtual immortality for its users, but at the eventual cost of the user's humanity. As Ursual LeGuin did in *The Left Hand of Darkness* or Frank Herbert in *The Dosadi Experiment,* Card carries out thought-experiments, subjecting his fictional characters to an altered environment that emphasizes a single characteristic. But whereas LeGuin was concerned with sexual roles in contemporary society, and Herbert with the effects of population pressure and overcrowding, Card often tests attributes that do not occur within the "real" world. If, as his religion teaches, humans may attain to immortality and virtual godhood, what will that mean on individual terms? Since this world cannot answer that question, Card creates alternative worlds in which such traits are possible.

In the case of *Capitol,* immortality of a sort is possible, but it is a counterfeit and ultimately destructive immortality. Its beneficiaries are like stones skipping across water, broken from the ties of time and humanity (79, 275). To further emphasize somec's perversion of immortality, Card focuses his narrative on a Trantor-like world encased in plastic and metal, its surface severed from the winds that give its unique whiptrees life; their passing becomes a symbol for the passing of something irreducible in the human spirit as lives become extended but increasingly useless.

When the inevitable rebellion comes—appropriately narrated through the eyes of the Governor of Answer, a colony world—Card explicitly connects the artificiality of somec-induced immortality with the artificiality of the metal-encased world.

> Capitol slit its own throat. The revolution started there, and now they have no food, and there are only a few survivors, and they can't last long. Cannibalism. The planet's dead. A place of savages trying to survive in metal. (274)

In later novels, Card abandons the artificiality of drug-induced immortality and explores time-dilation through space travel as an analogue that allows his characters to take on characteristics of godhood. Although present as early as *A Planet Called Treason,* this manipulation of time functions most successfully in *Speaker for the Dead,* in which Ender Wiggin and his sister Valentine have lived for three thousand years while only attaining a physical age of about thirty-five. Ender is a quasi-mythical figure; on the one hand, he is *the* Ender, the xenocide responsible for the death of the first sentient species encountered by humanity — in this guise, he is excoriated throughout the Hundred Worlds, achieving an unenviable immortality as a Devil-figure. On the other, he is the Speaker for the Dead, anonymous and undying, whose words bring hope and whose actions promise safety for the Piggies, the newly discovered, second sentient species.

Again, Card's imagined worlds parallel the purposes of his fictions. In *Ender's Game,* young Ender Wiggin is systematically distanced from humanity. He must save humanity from the inimical Buggers, yet he must do so without knowing that he is destroying them. He must be manipulated to penetrate the obscurity of events and understand the single action that will resolve any problem — immediately and for all time. Card parallels Ender's psychological isolation by isolating him physically, first in the Battle School, a space station of metal, with curved corridors and nul-grav playrooms in which Ender first learns the art of warfare. When he has mastered that level, he is transferred to Command School — a warren of tunnels excavated by the alien Buggers within an asteroid. Here again he is isolated, forced by the pressures of his training and by the physical environment itself to empathize so completely with an alien mentality that he can defeat the enemy in battle. Between the two sections, however, Card allows Ender to return to Earth for a brief, idyllic stop. The shift in landscape is a conscious ploy on Card's part. In narrative and symbolic terms, Ender's interlude at a secluded lake reinforces his affection for the Earth and makes it possible for him to destroy a sentient race in order to preserve that world. In each stage of Ender's education, Card prepares an environment that amplifies Ender's isolation.

In *Speaker for the Dead,* Card reverses that process — Ender must be reintegrated into the mainstream of humanity, symbolically by acknowledging publically his dual identity as Ender the Xenocide and as the Speaker for the Dead. Again, Card isolates his character, this time by bringing him to the planet Lusitania, colony world for humans and home-world of the Piggies.

Here also Card discusses the possibility of immortality, beginning with an artificial construct divorcing Ender from those around him. In his years of wandering from planet to planet, he has aged only marginally; those around him do not even suspect that he is the original Speaker. But there is a price for the wisdom he has accumulated over three thousand years; other than his sister Valentine (who has married and thus restored her humanity), he has no intimate connections with his own species.

On Lusitania, however, all of this changes. Ender is removed from the artificial environment of spaceships and time dilation to confront an organic variation on immortality. The Piggies live in three separate phases—first as virtually mindless organisms, then as Piggies, and finally as trees with extremely long life-spans. The forests of Lusitania thus become ironic counterparts to the metal-clad surface of Capitol in Card's earlier meditation on immortality. Here, instead of artificiality, Ender encounters a natural means by which life can be extended. As in the earlier novels, landscape becomes part of Card's exploration of immortality providing his characters with graphic representations of an ultimate destiny.

In his novels and short stories, Card has dealt with an individual who must become a savior in some way or another; Ender Wiggin is the archetype. In *Ender's Game,* he saves the human race, but only by risking his own sanity; in *Speaker for the Dead,* he recovers that sanity, again plays savior to an entire race, and ultimately reconciles himself to the sacrifices required of him. And the worlds within which he functions are specifically modeled to aid him in completing his role as mediator— as savior, or prophet, or at the least martyr.

4. Anagogical Landscapes

The most complex level of interpretation in Card's work is the anagogical, in which the characters and landscapes participate directly with Card's underlying theological assumptions; in essence, landscapes represent not only literal places but also symbolic selves embodying religious values.

In *A Planet Called Treason,* the planet is both an alien world and a symbol for the human soul divorced from God. Each family's resolution of the problem of isolation is insufficient to bring about renewal; only when Lanik Mueller combines attributes of the various families is there hope for resolution; and that combination forever alters the physical face of the planet Treason, while endowing Mueller with virtual immortality and omnipresence. For several generations, Mueller literally becomes one with Card's landscape, finally reentering the mainstream of humanity as a demigod.

More recently, this level of understanding has become increasingly important, especially in his Tales of the Mormon Sea stories.[16] In these stories, Card posits a near-future America in which a limited nuclear exchange has radically disturbed the climate and ecology of the Great Salt Lake Basin. Within that altered world, a remnant of humanity struggles to survive and adapt to new conditions. Theirs is a world without God—yet with a deep sense of faith. "Salvage" and "The Fringe" deal with this apparent contradiction by exploring the nature of faith itself; in "Salvage," the connection between meaning and landscape emerges when Card uses as a primary setting the half-submerged Salt Lake Temple, which in turn symbolizes the half-submerged religious faith that is consciously denied but that subconsciously influences the actions of his characters.

In the final story, "America," landscape becomes character as well as symbol. The ties between our world and the world of God are implicit in Card's identification of America as continent and as symbolical representation of God. Card's characters become actors manipulated by a quasi-sentient America determined to preserve its integrity as "the promised, the promising land" (53). The land forces intercourse between the European Sam Monson and the Indian Anamari Boagente in order to generate a saviour who will act according to the needs of the land. Card connects his landscape with his theological concerns for the literal fulfillment of Book of Mormon prophecy when Anamari says about her dream-vision of a resurgent America led by an incarnation of Quetzalcoatl, "Say *Deus* or *Christos* instead of *the land* and the story is the same" (44). Mindscape has become meaning in "America."

This discussion was not intended so much to analyze Card's work as to assess how the imagined worlds of fantasy and science fiction allow writers to expand the scope of their interests. In each of Card's novels, he has defined the implications of immortality and godhood, topics difficult to treat effectively in mainstream fiction. His increasingly daring incorporation of theological themes into analogical and allegorical forms suggest that science fiction and fantasy provide an ideal forum for examining his ideas. On the one hand, works such as *Ender's Game* and *Speaker for the Dead* succeed as straightforward science fiction; on the other, they simultaneously use the forms and structures of the fantastic, and most particularly the potentials of imagined landscapes, to communicate Card's deeply felt religious convictions and thereby touch readers more intensely.

Notes

1. Orson Scott Card, *Speaker for the Dead* (New York: Tor, 1986).

2. Dora M. Shirk, "An Interview with Orson Scott Card," *Westwind* (Jan. 1987): 11–15.

3. Orson Scott Card, *A Woman of Destiny* (New York: Berkley, 1984); as *Saints* (New York: Tor, 1988).

4. Rev. of *A Woman of Destiny*, by Orson Scott Card, *Publishers Weekly*, Nov. 25, 1983, 59.

5. Kristiana Gregory, "Soft Cover" (rev. of *A Woman of Destiny*, by Orson Scott Card), *Los Angeles Times Book Review*, July 22, 1984, 8.

6. Orson Scott Card, "Tinker," *Eternity SF* (1980): 11–21.

7. Orson Scott Card, *Seventh Son* (New York: Tor, 1987).

8. Orson Scott Card, *Hart's Hope* (New York: Berkley, 1983).

9. Brian W. Aldiss & David Wingrove, *Trillion Year Spree: The History of Science Fiction* (New York: Atheneum, 1986).

10. Orson Scott Card, *Capitol* (New York: Ace, 1979).

11. Orson Scott Card, *Hot Sleep: The Worthing Chronicle* (New York: Baronet, 1979).

12. Orson Scott Card, *The Worthing Chronicle* (New York: Ace, 1983).

13. Orson Scott Card, *A Planet Called Treason* (New York: St. Martin's, 1979); revised version published as *Treason* (New York: Tor, 1988).

14. Orson Scott Card, *Songmaster* (New York: Dial, 1980).

15. Orson Scott Card, *Ender's Game* (New York: Tor, 1985).

16. The Tales of the Mormon Sea series includes "The Fringe," *Magazine of Fantasy and Science Fiction* (Oct. 1985): 140–60; "Salvage," *Isaac Asimov's Science Fiction Magazine* (Feb. 1986): 56–75; "America," *Isaac Asimov's Science Fiction Magazine* (Jan. 1987): 22–53; and "West," *Free Lancers IV*, ed. Elizabeth Mitchell (New York: Baen, 1987), 1–82. A fifth story, "Pageant Wagon," has not yet appeared.

II

Avenues of Power:
Cities as the Mindscapes of Politics

Pascal J. Thomas

Never mind the Stars—the City is the only appropriate landscape for science fiction! That always was my spontaneous reaction when confronted with the genre. Or even with the very idea of the future, back from when I was a child raised in an apartment building. Countless space safaris or bucolic Utopias have done little to change this notion. Are not cities the birthplace and motivation of technology? Are they not the most artificial of landscapes? For this reason, I would argue, the only fascinating one.

A quick way to absorb science fiction's fascination for the urban, phenomenon is to leaf through an illustrated book like Robert Sheckley's *Futuropolis*. The demented creations of Frank R. Paul or Philippe Druillet reduce people to ants, but they stand side by side with the seriously intended drawings of the architects of Utopia. For if the cities have fascinated those who think the future, the future seems to be foremost in the minds of those who think the cities. The notion of urbanism was born at the turn of the century, at the same time as futurism, and a glance through the library shelves will turn up such blatant examples as Michel Ragon's *La Cité de l'an 2000*[1] or Le Corbusier's entire written *oeuvre,* for that matter.[2]

Let us corral a few science fiction books and examine their cityscapes more closely. The selection here is admittedly random. More examples can be found (for instance, under the entry "Cities" in *The Science Fiction Encyclopedia.*) This randomness, I hope, will make for a representative slice. Some prime examples have escaped, to roam the prairie awaiting another posse: James Blish's Spenglerian nomadic town-ships *(Cities in Flight)*; Greg Bear's living-God cities of *Strength of Stones*; Dominique Douay's nightmarish Paris slipped into the cracks between the stories of *Cinq Solutions pour en finir*; Jean-Pierre Hubert's devastated city of *Scènes de guerre civile*. However, this last novel depicts war-torn Beirut under a thin disguise; I would like to focus on writer-created cities. Not that they acquire strong individuality; often they are nameless continua that are the only horizon, the only milieu of the characters' life.

J. G. Ballard's early story "Concentration City"[3] fits this description perfectly. "The City is as old as Time and continuous with it,"[4] a figure of authority asserts; indeed, no time or space without the City can even be imagined. People live in an endless stack of floors, and blocks extend West, East, North, or South as far as the express trains can roll. The denouement suggest that the City is actually closing on itself, thanks to the curvature of space.

This last feels like a bit of sleight-of-hand on the part of Ballard. "Billenium"[5] takes on a more somber tone. A tale of overpopulation, it is to the previous story as *1984* to *Brave New World*. In the first story oppression has become internalized, and Franz M., with his fancies of flight in free space, is merely turned over to psychiatry;[6] in "Billenium" on the other hand, Ward presumably falls under the jurisdiction of some housing police when he actually finds free space behind a wall. He thus violates the building codes allocating to each individual his or her four square meters (an ever-shrinking norm). Constraints here are heavily felt. As soon as you step out into the street, going to the restaurant of your choice becomes an impossible endeavor, because it would entail walking upstream of the pedestrians, to whom the large Keep Left signs do not spare the occasional massive traffic lock. Ward then "[surrenders] his initiative to the dynamics of the city,"[7] now seen as some living entity.

Another viewpoint is presented in John Brunner's *The Squares of the City*, where we see the city being made, or rather remade. An Australian traffic expert, Boyd Hakluyt, is brought into the newly built capital of the Latin American country of Aguazul. President Vados needs some work done on the city that bears his name—getting rid of some shantytowns that have sprung up along the avenues of this "ultimate achievement in city planning."[8] Hakluyt, who has worked on such problems all over the world, from India to Galveston, knows that changing traffic flows can change the city. Faced with a wildcat slum, he has a solution ready in minutes: "I can eliminate their market. . . . [A] contributory factor to its survival must have been the absence of heavy traffic flow through the roads it occupies. So we have to create such a flow."[9]

Brunner makes some keen observations on Latin America in this book, and some good points about technological responsibility. Hakluyt does not have the ruthlessness needed to enforce the above solution, and cannot stay neutral; his manipulations are manipulated, and people moved about by Vados like pawns on a chessboard.[10]

What an ambiguous last sentence: who does the moving, Vados the man, or Vados the city? In Joëlle Wintrebert's *Chromoville,* the chess motif surfaces again in a more marginal role: "*Blacks* and *Whites* were the major pieces in a chess game which the *Multis* had never won."[11] The organization of Chromoville is much more rigid than that of Vados. Instead of being governed by traffic patterns, it adopts — a bit like J. G. Ballard's *High Rise* — the shape of a Babylonian pyramid. It evens has levels of different colors:[12] here the *people* are colored, with *Black* and *White* at the top of the hierarchy, the *Multi(colored)* as executives, and so on down to the Orange artists, the Brown craftsmen, and the Red workers! The novel does fall into some near-Marxist lecturing on occasions. This political transparency, which makes it easier to analyze, detracts somewhat from its otherwise high artistic value.

As we know, French science fiction of the 1970s was never without a certain dose of revolutionary politics, and *Chromoville* goes back to that period. The police is a caste of its own, and the novel tells of an uprising against the hierarchy. Europeans need not go back to Babylon to see hierarchy written in stone; it is no chance that castles and churches are the main surviving buildings from the Middle Ages, and that the "natural" pathways of many towns still lead to them.

Even when those natural pathways were removed, authoritarian ends were never far below the surface. One of the best-known examples took place in France in the second half of the nineteenth century: Baron Haussmann's remodeling of Paris smacks of Versailles' French gardens, with wide avenues connecting large circular plazas and cutting mercilessly through older neighborhoods. Traffic and aesthetic considerations may have been a consideration, but another one is said to have loomed large in the minds of the government-appointed city planners: wider streets are harder to barricade, and the cavalry and artillery would then be in a better position to prevent a repeat of the popular uprisings of 1848. Whatever the purpose, the renovation destroyed many of Paris' traditional neighborhoods.

You can guess from its pyramid shape that Chromoville is governed with an iron hand, by a (Black) Hierarch who lives at the top. But the police does not surround him; their Green caste[13] lives only on the fourth level of the pyramid. Beneath the Black, White, and Multi, at the third level, jockeying around the holders of power, Purple urbanists are mixed with Yellow prostitutes "in a carefully designed pell-mell."[14]

Although the concept was born at the turn of the century, urbanism came to play a major role in Europe only after the Second World War, during the "reconstruction"[15] period. The need for large-scale work combined with the utopian inclinations of the would-be city planners. Much of the nineteenth century's dystopian view of cities (à la Dickens) was still prevalent. A better world could then be built, by building better, healthier cities. Le Corbusier is certainly the best known of those utopian builders,[16] and despite his genius, not a success story. Much of the reconstruction ended up as imitation of destroyed models. For economic reasons, what *was* innovative came out as dehumanizing projects, known to the French as "grands ensembles."[17] Those have taken on a life of their own under the caricatural pen of artists such as Sempé or Folon. But even lavishly thought-out enterprises met with skepticism: Le Corbusier's main housing unit in Marseilles is known by locals as "la maison du fada."[18] Once more, patterns imposed from above were rejected by the common individual — as is often the fate of the best-intended projects.

Coming back to Wintrebert, note that the disorder among prostitutes and urbanists must be "carefully designed." By contrast, "chaos" or "mess" *("pagaïe")* are swearwords from top to plebeian bottom of the pyramid. In the throes of the revolution, the Hierarch and his aides will end up fused into the very walls of their city — a fitting fate; the Hierarch's power was never up to that of the City itself. As a disgruntled revolutionary remarks in the last pages of the book: "We must blow up the City,"[19] meaning that, unless that is done, the old system will assert itself again. This conviction is borne out by some of the events that occurred during the fighting. Ordinary citizens, who had chosen to revolt by going outside of the city walls, were totally distraught when the Hierarch reacted by locking them out of their urban matrix. In frenzied despair, they turned upon the *Sancous*[20] who dwell in disarrayed slums outside the city. Yes, there is life outside of the city, but it is eventually subservient to it. Beyond the slums, the countryside is well groomed.[21] In other words, *that* landscape is human-shaped, too.

That is no different from the reality of the European landscape. Escape from the city (a cliché if ever there was one) will not be so easy after all. The claustrophobia felt in European science fiction has geographic roots, which I see as deeper than the political ones.

From the other side of the Atlantic, Isaac Asimov's cities must be quite familiar to us all; more than Trantor, much talked about but not much shown in *Foundation,* one recalls the New York of *The Caves of Steel,* where children's games are shaped by the technology of pedestrian conveyor belts. That, surely, is a dystopian and oppressive environment, allowing only for the crime and detection story set into it. However, the protagonist, Lije Bailey shows himself terrified at the thought of leaving his steel cocoon when the need arises. I would plead in this instance Asimov's not-so-distant European origins and his well-known agoraphobia. They may be what give this work its uncommon strength. For a more American perspective, however, let us go west to . . . well, to the stars, really, but we all know that is the same thing. To Aurora then, from the sequel *The Naked Sun.* Upon the formless void, human endeavor has built a noncity, ruled by media, a much more characteristic phenomenon that, like Los Angeles, rejects structure to propose direct interactions between individuals.

Returning to New York, Samuel Delany's *Dhalgren* is also dominated by the image of a city. Delany himself has cogent comments to offer about the mechanics of cities (and he make them in his *Nevèrÿon* series), but Bellona has few of the attributes of a structured city. It is no ruin, since it somehow functions, but no powers-that-be can be discerned, nor any of the usual services. People live in an anarchistic fashion in almost–empty buildings, and the book presents itself as a rather anarchist collage of fragments. In fact, dislocation is total, extending to the notion of time, and Bellona takes on the features of an anticity, a peculiar sort of escape from the cities.

That escape from the cities was once carried out as a real-world social experiment—after the fall of Phnom Penh to Pol Pot's Khmer Rouge in 1975. The image of the capital city of Cambodia emptied in a day, hospital patients running along the road with their drips still attached, is what gave the original impetus[22] to Philip Goy's novel *Faire le mur.*[23] Goy wrote a rather unusual work, with a lot of absurdist elements; its connection to science fiction may appear tenuous as its extrapolations were soon caught up with by reality.

In *Faire le mur,* this radical *retour à la terre,* back to the country, is seen through the eyes of a photo-reporter. Conversations with the revolutionary leader, Pol Pot-Pus,[24] clearly set out the meaning of the change: "city means police . . . otherwise, it'd be back to the jungle,"[25] but it is much more than that: "city . . . from the Latin *civitas* . . . it's civilization."[26] And Pol Pot-Pus and his "Caméristes Rouges" methodically set out to destroy all traces of civilization before sending their people . . . back into the jungle to their radiant future. Cars and planes are torched,[27] and so are the shops laden with technological wares, or simply food. The most gruesome and grotesque scenes take place in the hospital—the whole of chapter 16 is devoted to its evacuation. Along the way, place names are first changed (long a standard practice of revolutions), then obliterated as writing and reading themselves are made illegal.

All those gory events are recounted in an exaggerated ironic style. Philip Goy does not share the leftist convictions of Wintrebert and many of his fellow French writers. His book lampoons Marxism, its slogans, and its utopian tendencies, and above all the Western intellectuals who believed in them. His protagonist, a French left-wing intellectual, is ready to make any 180-degree turn to accommodate Pol Pot-Pus and his jargon. Much to his shame, dreams of his home civilization still run through his head; significantly, they involve images of urban structures, in particular the Paris of May '68.[28] To Goy, too, May '68 is a pivotal reference; in contrast to many of his contemporaries, he lived through it with the skepticism of the scientist he is.

Despite its zaniness, his novel is even more didactic than Wintrebert's, thus even more open to analysis; the author goes so far as to include at the end of the book[29] a table of correspondences between the events in his book, in the real world, and in the "retrograde" evolution of species.

If we set *Faire le mur* beside *Chromoville,*[30] it extends the refusal of Utopia a step further. The rejection of unnatural structures imposed on society, be they the pyramids of Babylon or those of Le Corbusier, can stand for a refusal of old-fashioned, static Utopias—oppressing structures. But the erasing of structure in anarchistic Utopias is rejected too. What is left, then? Only the heritage of those structures that were organically grown (to borrow Mumfordian images). Europe is probably richer in those than in anything else.

In the nineteenth century, Europeans projected their Utopias into the relatively empty spaces of America—see for instance Jules Verne's

The Begum's Fortune (where the hygienic city of Franceville fights the evil Stahlstadt out in Oregon). Closer to us, Le Corbusier's *successes* came in the new urban centers of the Third World: Brazil, India, Algeria.

Symmetrically, Ballard's radical dystopia in "Concentration City" takes on an American slant: "Free space? Isn't that a contradiction in terms? Space is a dollar a cubic foot."[31] A dollar—not a pound! Which goes hand in hand with a structure where cubes can feel at home: a three-dimensional grid of numbered streets, avenues, and levels.

The uniform square grid, so widespread in the New World, plays an interesting role in the character of cities. A colonization pattern going back to the Romans, it starts its life as order imposed upon the void (or upon the Barbarians, seen by the new dwellers as empty of culture). But its invariance under extension enables it to support cities while imposing very little structure. An urbanist like Bardet decries it and favors the circular city as more "organic."[32] This vision of the city as a body,[33] however, implies that it has a head, a center—and the central authority that comes with it. Square grids allow a more fluid growth, the birth of variegated centers; an adaptable Utopia could emerge. The attempt is dramatized in *Squares of the City,* where the city-patient is another New-World utopian creation. Vados' Utopia eventually fails because it was *not* built on a tabula rasa, but on the "aboriginal dirt."[34] The problems were contained in the first page of the book: "They had . . . put wild mountain torrents into concrete conduits,"[35] and the old Latin-American world rejects it like a foreign transplant.

In some sense, the Old World cannot afford Utopia: too much stands in the way, no building can be done without tearing up fundamental organs that cannot be replaced. Organic metaphor notwithstanding, stones are not the only issue. If nothing else, the works mentioned should prove it. Cities are structures not only of surrounding space, but also of the human psyche; they make their inhabitants as much as those inhabitants build them.

Thus it was logical that robots should take such a prominent role in Asimov's Aurora, and be banned from his earthly cities. Thus it is logical for Ballard to translate his "inner space" into such closed-up constructions as the Concentration City, and Ward *has* to be committed to a psychiatrist, for to go against his city is to lose his mind. Likewise, as we saw earlier, it is impossible for the inhabitants of Wintrebert's

Chromoville really to leave their pyramid city. The proteiform mutant Sélèn displays the most intense and interesting behavior in that respect. His talent gets him out of his lowly class position; and he is able to go through the walls, at the price of a loss of his body, and of his identity — "He was amnesiaing himself by losing himself into the City."[36] This confusion, born from the transgression of boundaries, is also that of passion: "then Sélèn *was* the city."[37]

The brutal Pol Pot-Pus in *Faire le mur* is quite aware of his ultimate goal: what lies behind the systematic obliteration of city-civilisation is not merely the substitution of a new power structure to the older one embedded in the city; that is but a necessary way station to the creation of a New Man: "the true goal of socialism is . . . the appearance of the New Man."[38] A New Man emboided in the Cámeriste Rouge fighters, so young and wonderfully ignorant. *Faire le mur* operates a reductio ad absurdum when the New Men, returning to the jungle, quickly retro-evolve (r-evolution) into monkeys, then into stones.[39]

Notice as an aside that the same phenomenon can be seen at work in today's self-proclaimed "cutting edge" of science fiction: cyberpunk. To people the habitats of space posited by Bruce Sterling of Michael Swanwick, physically modified versions of the human being are required, and again their aggressively artificial environment molds their mental processes along with the possible forms of social organization.[40]

This general issue of the control exercised by city structures on the human mind has of course been discussed before. Jacques Dreyfus' *La Ville disciplinaire* is a critique of urbanism as it is practiced. Dreyfus argues that city planning has been more successful than is generally acknowledged. It represents another way for capitalism to streamline production and force the human mind into a rationalistic mold. Cities are seen as a kind of language, and, like language, as imposing rationality upon the world. Destroying Phnom Penh and forbidding writing are for Pol Pot-Pus two sides of the same coin (or would be if he had not abolished money as well).

Cities thus share a basic dilemma of the human condition: we need language to understand the world, and yet resent the limitations to our thought imposed by its categories; we need cities to inhabit the world, and resent the power implicit in their structures. Chromoville or Concentration City dramatizes the constraint on human rationality under oppressive authority; but it is unlikely that we can do without some form of government,[41] some form of language, and some form of cities. Throw away the city, as in *Faire le mur,* and rationality disappears altogether.

Old-style Utopia (the pyramids) will never work because of the rigid structure that intellectual creation would lay upon the world—it is just not complex enough. At the opposite end to stultification, we then find the symmetric neo-Utopian pitfall of entropy, loss of structure—the Caméristes Rouges of Goy, or the crowds in "Billenium," just as mindless, flowing like rivers in canyon streets. Again, complexity is lost.

Science fiction brings out scientific metaphors in its commentators. Beyond the heat-death of the Universe, entropy had its days of glory to describe the New Wave. Mathematically, entropy is expressed by the concepts of the theory of probability.

Cities, like thought, are antientropic, getting more and more complex, through the feedback loop between their populations and their structures. The challenge for them (and those who dream them) is to steer away from stultification, to preserve their complexity in space and their unpredictability in time. Currently, mathematicians devote a lot of attention to objects that, although derived from simple deterministic— nonprobabilistic—laws, exhibit incredibly complex and yet still unpredictable behavior, arising from the repeated application of a simple process with the end product being fed back into the next application of the process. The typical structures are fractals[42]—shapes such that closer examination of details only reveals further complexity of the same kind. Fascinating pictures are presented in Hans-Otto Peitgen's book *The Beauty of Fractals.* I would like to think they will provide promising models for new avenues of our thought.

Notes

1. Translated as "The city, 2000 A.D.."
2. See Le Corbusier, *Urbanisme,* new ed. (Paris: Fréal, 1966).
3. In *The Best Short Stories of J. G. Ballard* (New York: Holt, Rinehart & Winston, 1978).
4. Ibid., 19.
5. Also in *Best Short Stories of J. G. Ballard.*
6. When arrested for vagrancy; but early on, his search for free space is greeted by comments like "What are you looking for? A slight case of agoraphobia?" (ibid., 7).
7. Ibid., 129.

8. John Brunner, *The Squares of the City* (New York: Ballantine/Del Rey, 1978), 12.

9. Ibid., 52, 54.

10. Literally, as it turns out at the end of the novel, where black and white pawns are methodically listed.

11. Joëlle Wintrebert, *Chromoville* (Paris: J'ai Lu, 1983), 9: "Mais les *Noirs* et les *Blancs* étaient les pions majeurs d'un Jeu d'Echecs auquel les *Multis* n'avaient jamais gagné."

12. In some sense renouncing technology, despite its science-fiction trappings.

13. It is endowed with a name that reeks of French bureaucracy (*les émargeurs*—those who appear on the payroll). For Wintrebert, policemen are green and merchants are blue; of course the traditional associations made with those colors in the United States do not obtain in France!

14. "Les *Violets*, urbanistes, et les *Jaunes*, hétaïres, se partageaient dans un désordre très étudié le degré suivant" Wintrebert, (*Chromoville*, 9). Note the dig at the urbanists.

15. The same word appears at least once in Wintrebert, *Chromoville*: "Ce système autocratique a fait son temps, il n'était valable que pour la reconstruction" (199). ("This autocratic system has outlived its usefulness, it was valid only during the reconstruction.")

16. See Robert Fishman, *Urban Utopias in the Twentieth Century: Ebenezer Howard, Frank Lloyd Wright, Le Corbusier* (New York: Basic Books, 1977).

17. Translated as "large ensembles."

18. Translated as "the crackpot's house," with a touch of a Provençal idiom added.

19. Winterbert, *Chromoville*, 220: "La ville . . . *est* la hiérarchie. Il faut la faire sauter."

20. "Sans couleurs"—colorless pariahs.

21. Wintrebert, *Chromoville*, 203. "Tiré au cordeau," a metaphor that again evokes the gardener's art.

22. Philippe Goy, *Faire le mur* (Paris: Denoël, 1980). The book appeared only five years after the Khmer Rouge takeover, and events in the real world had caught up with it. This was much to the chagrin of the author, who was prevented by his work in experimental physics from writing the book any faster.

23. "Doing the wall." This is an idiom meaning "going AWOL." But the "wall" in the title also refers to the Berlin Wall, which the protagonist has started out to cover. True city folk, Western Europeans live with their backs to the Iron Curtain, a boundary situation that is hard to avoid.

24. "Pus" means pus, but it is also pronounced like "pue" ("puer"—to stink).

25. Goy, *Faire le mur,* 267: "La ville c'est les policiers . . . sinon c'est la jungle."

26. Ibid., 266: "La ville . . . du latin *civitas* . . . c'est la civilisation."

27. Ibid., 158 and 207 respectively.

28. Ibid., 215–19.

29. Ibid., 308–13.

30. Their publication dates are four years apart, and, although both books took a long time between inception and publication, it is true that Wintrebert's *Chromoville* is the later work. Both, I feel, have their roots in the politically charged French science fiction of the late 1970s, itself carrying the delayed echoes of May '68.

31. *Best Short Stories of J. G. Ballard,* 4.

32. See for example Gaston Bardet's popular survey, *L'Urbanisme* (Paris: P.U.F./Que Sais-je?, 1947). Like Mumford, Bardet believes in a degree of "natural" development of cities, and admires models from the past. Le Corbusier, on the other hand, celebrates "la marche vers l'ordre."

33. Literally, the body politic!

34. Brunner, *The Squares of the City,* 12.

35. Ibid., 9.

36. Wintrebert, *Chromoville,* 177: "Il s'amnésiait en se perdant dans la Ville."

37. Ibid., 178: "Alors Sélèn *était* la ville."

38. Goy, *Faire le mur,* 153: "Le véritable but du socialisme, c'est . . . l'apparition de l'Homme Nouveau."

39. Ironically, those new Utopians earn the same fate as the Hierarch and his court in Wintrebert's book.

40. However, despite their surface utopian zeal, Sterling and Swanwick seem to hold back from this brave new world, and their viewpoint characters are adamantly unmodified. It is probably too early to assess fully their work.

41. In the words of the Machiavellian Minister of Information in Brunner, *The Squares of the City*: "People do not object to government; to be governed . . . is part of the human human condition" (83).

42. Michel Jeury is the only French science-fiction writer I know to have made use of this concept, in his "Colmateurs" series (three novels published by Presses Pocket under Jacques Goimard's helpful editorship). German science-fiction writer Herbert Franke contributed an article to Peitgen's book (Berlin & New York: Springer Verlag, 1986).

12

The Two Landscapes of
J. G. Ballard's *Concrete Island*
Reinhart Lutz

At the opening of James G. Ballard's *Concrete Island* (London: Granada Publishing, Panther Books, 1976), a car accident strands a modern-day Robinson Crusoe on a traffic island sandwiched between two superhighways and a feeder lane in the West of London. At first, though injured, the protagonist tries to escape this piece of postindustrial wasteland, but gradually he begins to view his new habitat with entirely different eyes; he develops an alternative pattern of behavior, abandoning the realist modes of thought and action. in short, Ballard's 1973 novel offers us two radically opposed views of or ways of reading its desolate central landscape: as a realistic (indeed "concrete") environment or as a projection of the protagonist's insular state of mind—itself, in turn, due to (over-)adaptation to his surroundings. The two views, however, are intricately woven together, since at the core of both is an intense concern with the impact of the artifacts of postindustrialism on the human condition.

Given that the island comes to function as the externalization of what is internal and mental, it is perhaps not surprising that the text's strategy for creating the suspense that will keep us reading is highly unconventional. It involves playing a game of hide-and-seek in which the second, internal landscape remains concealed behind the apparent realism of the discourse for as long as possible. Furthermore, whenever the reader spots a "breach of realism," the text immediately comes up with a disclaimer and tries to persuade us once again to trust the realism of the narrative. But in the end, precisely because it has privileged a conventional (or "realist") reading, the narrative gives us a final shock when we are forced to realize not only that the hero, architect Robert

Maitland, perceives his environment in a way we can only call "psychotic," but also that his perspective *succeeds* in making sense of his world—a world which, of course, we all share, our world.

Let us, then, look at the text in some detail to see *how* Ballard works out this interaction between concealment and revelation of an alternative mode of perceiving reality—the truly imaginative dimension of the novel; and let us discover how our Robinson Crusoe deals with the challenge his "mindscape" confronts him with.

Right at the outset of *Concrete Island,* there is a touch of ambiguity as to whether or not we are still in what can conventionally be termed "our realistic universe," when Robert Maitland breaks "through the crash barrier," as the title of the first chapter puts it. In line with the conventions of the science-fiction genre—and *Concrete Island* is marketed as science fiction—we might easily expect, as we read the chapter heading, that Maitland's accident will catapult us into an alien world. Many famous and influential texts of the genre work in this fashion, and we can even find mainstream stories which introduce an alternative reality by using the "split-seconds-before-death" plot (the most famous in Ambrose Bierce's "An Occurrence at Owl Creek Bridge," another is the 1956 novel *Pincher Martin,* by Ballard's Nobel Prize-winning British contemporary William Golding). But Ballard's text refuses this route and from the beginning works hard to establish our confidence in the setting as realistic by using naturalistic descriptions that catch the precision and detachment of journalistic or technical writing. And thus we become more inclined to read Maitland's car accident as a literal smashing through "the palisade of pinewood trestles that formed a temporary barrier along the edge of the road" (7), and much less likely to see it as the metaphor for a departure from an environment we conventionally read as "real."

As to the reason for Maitland's crash, the text soon offers both a rational explanation—a tire blowout at high speed—*and* the victim's first attempt at stepping outside our familiar context of interpretation (a step that is hidden by verbal disclaimers—a qualifying "almost" and "perhaps"—and the context of the victim's posttraumatic state of shock):

"As Maitland frankly recognized, he invariably drove well above the speed limit. . . . Today, speeding along the motorway when he was already tired after a three-day conference, preoccupied by the slight duplicity involved in seeing his wife so soon after a week spent with

Helen Fairfax, he had almost wilfully devised the crash, perhaps as some bizarre kind of rationalization." (9).

For a moment, the accident is interpreted as Maitland's means of coming to terms with his existence in an environment that demands cooperation with the inanimate forces channeling the course of human action (such as the physical conditions governing freeway traffic) at the same time as it shows a lack of interest in the formulation of any moral or social constraints for its inhabitants (Maitland's "modern marriage" is silently accepted as "normal"). This reasoning of Maitland's marks the beginning of his struggle for control over the text and of the replacing of conventional readings of action with readings offered by an alternative mind-set. That mind-set is here devising a set of new, seemingly absurd rules to govern motivation and behavior in the strange new arena Maitland sees in the architecture of our postindustrial, suburban free-way culture. However, the text is very careful to mask this internal struggle for an alternative code of conduct. It immediately distracts its readers from the new code by next plunging us into an elaborately naturalistic description of Maitland's self-injuring and ultimately futile attempts at leaving the traffic island.

The morning of the next day sees Maitland's first appropriation of something from the island. He salvages a junked car exhaust pipe and transforms it into a crutch, a crudely manufactured tool and substitute limb: an entirely reasonable, "Crusoesque" act, a few steps on human-ity's walk along the path of technological progress leading toward domina-tion of its world. This act also points at the theme of humanity's merger with the products of its technology, which come to function as prostheses for the natural body—a classic topic of the science fiction genre, which has found its culmination in stories about cyborgs and robots with human brains. At this very moment, moreover, the boundaries between the animate—Maitland's body—and the *in*animate become blurred by the use of strangely similar language (resembling that of a pathologist) to relate both Maitland's self-examination of his injuries *and* the salvaging of the crutch. Compare, for example: "the head of his thigh-bone now seemed to be fused into the damaged pelvic socket" (30). And: "the exhaust pipe hung loosely from the expansion box" (32).

Next, echoing Defoe's *Robinson Crusoe,* Maitland "deliberately . . . turned his back to the motorway [his ocean] and for the first time began to inspect the island" (32). A certain mood of defiance awakens in him, a refusal to be completely preoccupied by the world from which the crash wrenched him. This new ambivalence toward his environment also colors Maitland's encounter with the perimeter fence, whose indestructible wire mesh establishes the eastern border of the traffic island. Fences are always ambiguous for Ballard, whose stories often probe the issue of imprisonment. Here the perimeter fence can be seen to represent the outer limit of the protagonist's imagination — west of it lies his domain, but beyond exists a world Maitland cannot now enter and that refuses even to notice his absence.

Wandering among the landmarks of the island, Maitland gradually sheds his "realist" belief "that rescue would come as inevitably as if he had crashed into the central reservation of a suburban dual carriageway" (43). But his dismissal of the idea of rescue as being "completely false, part of that whole system of comfortable expectations he had carried with him" (43) does not lead him toward abandoning his struggle for eventual rescue. What *does* change is the means by which the protagonist tries to achieve this goal. It is important to understand that throughout *Concrete Island,* Maitland *does want* to escape — although his actions often seem to be contradictory, false, or even diametrically opposed to this aim. In this Ballard shows a frightening consequence of our reality — in the idea that a man can be marooned on such a mundane object as a traffic island, yet find rescue to be as difficult as it would be from a real island in the limitless ocean. The difficulty, of course, rests in the conditions of our culture, the architects of which (ironically, of course, including Maitland himself) have created the island and the surrounding vast and hostile sea of freeways. This setting is particularly appropriate for making the text's point since the sea has traditionally been used as a metaphor for desolation and utter emptiness, perhaps most masterfully by Ballard's national predecessors Milton, Tennyson, T. S. Eliot, and Golding, the action of whose *Pincher Martin* takes place entirely on an large rock in a cold sea.

On the other hand, Ballard's fictional *answer* to the almost mythological problem of being stranded is one of radical otherness. Through Maitland, we are confronted with a totally new reading of the old Crusoe myth — in order to make sense of your "island," you have to become a psychotic. This reading, in its decided contemporaneity, presents the real "scandal" of the novel.

As Maitland's answer begins to emerge, the text camouflages its validity by employing the ruse of an attack of fever, which sets in exactly as the stranded man first begins to behave incongruously. Instead of signaling for help, Maitland scrambles under cover when he spots a trash collector on the far side of the island, because—most peculiarly and suggestively—he visualizes the light motorcycle the man is wheeling as "an horrific device of torture" on which his body will be broken in a quasi-religious "judgement by ordeal" (60).

Next, without realizing how contradictory his behavior is—and contradictoriness will become a prominent mark of the hero, one that will set his actions apart from what we conventionally see as successful strategies for goal-achievement—once the coast is clear, Matiland comes *out* of hiding to start a new attempt at calling for rescue that is of course soon abandoned as futile.

But once in the grip of fever, Maitland suddenly comes to realize that the only way in which he can truly understand and come to terms with the new landscape evolving in his mind is to pursue a course of identification or mental merger with the inanimate environment, a project that requires the abandoning of his previous identity. Clues leading to such a realization have been scattered through the text, so that the idea does not come as a complete surprise. Apart from Maitland's preference for thoroughly modern, anonymous landscapes, we already have noted the significant fact that he never refers to himself in the first person singular—a telltale psychological sign of a weak sense of self. Here, on the "realistic" plane of interpretation, the text hints at the idea that the conditions of our architecture and society favor such a lapse into schizophrenia; what makes the text truly radical is its implication that schizophrenia is the (only) correct means of fully understanding and successfully communicating with the environment that we, like architect Robert Maitland, have built for ourselves. Hence:

"As he tottered about, Maitland found himself losing interest in his own body, and in the pain that inflamed his leg. He began to shuck off sections of his body, forgetting first his injured hip, then both his legs, erasing all awareness of his bruised chest and diaphragm" (70). And: "Parts of his mind seemed to be detaching themselves from the centre of his consciousness" (63).

What follows Maitland's loss of identity is his sight of the island's distinguishing landmark, an abandoned cinema. This external feature of the island triggers Maitland's diving into the deep internal pool of his childhood memories, from which he moves toward entering the new internal landscape by admitting to himself in a burst of perceptiveness that: "More and more, the island was becoming an exact model of his head. His movement across this forgotten terrain was a journey not merely through the island's past but through his own" (69–70). That is, the island is a map of his mind and his past, and the old cinema is the house of childhood memories.

Even in his feverish state, Maitland insists on establishing his "domination" over the island, and thus follows, like Defoe's Robinson Crusoe, the Western tradition of interacting somewhat imperialistically with his environment. But to achieve this aim, Maitland devises a strategy of becoming one with the island and ultimately sacrificing himself—that is, his wounded body—for and to it, becoming "a priest officiating at the eucharist of his own body." Here, self-sacrifice becomes an agent of domination. (The text tears a wound in the fabric of our culture by equating a drive for power with the event of Golgotha, which has historically been regarded as the ultimate self-effacing self-sacrifice.) The all-pervading, inverted religious imagery of *Concrete Island* is a crucial aspect of its radicalism and shock value.

The fictional exploration of Maitland's new mode of thinking and communicating with his environment would not be complete without a test against other specimens of humanity. It is for this reason that the text now introduces two hitherto hidden coinhabitants of the island.

Still feverish, Maitland discovers an inhabited shelter among the ruins of the island, and is promptly attacked by its "tenant," a mentally disabled ex-acrobat. Falling unconscious, he is rescued by a twenty-year-old prostitute named Jane Sheppard, a dropout with an upper middle-class background and a marijuana habit. In her own way, Jane is a child of her age, in which all narratives, whether they are personal or document a culture, are told by mechanically mass-reproduced images and photographs. Not only does Maitland deduce Jane's personal history from a series of disjointed snapshots, it is also through the decoration of her primitive shelter in the basement of the abandoned *cinema*—where else!—that we learn about the society that built the traffic island and its mind-set. The walls of the shelter are adorned with posters depicting the icons of a significant segment of Western culture during the late 1960s; the text introduces us, through Maitland's eyes, to pictures of Ginger Rogers and Fred Astaire—technologically preserved, nostalgic remnants of a lost era—"a psychedelic poster in the Beardsley manner, a grainy close-up of the dead Che Guevara, a Black Power manifesto, and Charles Manson at his trial: (80). These are the documents of the society in whose arena Maitland will have to survive.

Because he is now obsessed with escaping, Maitland antagonizes prostitute and acrobat, who both shun a disclosure of their refuge from the surrounding society. A dialogue with Jane reveals the latter's extraordinarily accurate insight into crucial aspects of Maitland's inner self. It is Jane who involuntarily doubles and thus confirms Maitland's first alternative interpretation of his accident, and again brings to the surface of the text the darker reading of Maitland's crash.

" . . . You're the sort of man who has to test himself all the time. Do you think you crashed on to this traffic island deliberately? . . . I'm not joking—believe me, self-destruction is something I know all about" (96).

Here, the text uses Jane to examine critically the hero and to qualify bluntly and ironically the spirituality Maitland sees in his acts. Not only does she replace his idea of self-sacrifice with her own term "self-destruction," but she also challenges the sincerity of his forced stay on the island.

> " . . . You know, you could have got away from here, if you'd wanted to."
> "How?"
> "Right at the beginning. . . . If you'd really tried, you could have done."
> "Tried?" With a grimace Maitland recalled his ordeal. . . . He rubbed his chest, covered by no more than the grimy dress-shirt. "It's cold in here." (116)

He refuses to acknowledge the second reading of his crash, a strategy he will consistently follow, and which retains the tension of the text to its finale. But because of the physical dependency he comes to have on her and because of her insights into his submerged desires regarding the island, Jane continues to pose the greatest challenge to Maitland. He will have to test *his* reading of crash and island against *her* perception, a perception that almost emerges as a third reading of their surrounding landscape.

For Jane, this patch of land is simply an ideal temporary refuge from society—she views the island realistically. Yet she understands what Maitland sees in it, and what kind of interaction he wants to establish with an "island" that is clearly more than a patch of postindustrial wasteland dotted with the abandoned ruins of another age. She is able to connect these two islands—the material traffic island and

Maitland's internal and conceptualized idea of an island—when she tells
him that, ". . . You've got a hundred times more hang-ups [than me].
Your wife, this woman doctor—you were *on an island* long before you
crashed here" (italics added, 141). The text obscures insight with crude
language, but Jane has nevertheless unearthed crucial psychological
material, as her appropriation of the island as metaphor indicates; and
the sexual encounter immediately following this dialogue seals the
importance of what has been said.

Maitland's inability to define his relationship with Jane Sheppard
exclusively on his own terms is paralleled in his relations with Proctor,
clearly a modern-day "Friday." For although the retarded man is willing
to carry the injured Maitland on his back and function as a "beast of
burden" (145), he steadfastly refuses to help his master in any of his
attempts at escape.

Hence, still lonely, though not alone, and increasingly fascinated by
his own vision of the island, the stranded architect feels more and more
compelled to "let go," to disassociate himself from external reality. The
text mirrors this process in its devotion of considerable space to a
description of how Maitland's powerful visualizations of an alternative
world are gradually taking over the domain of the familiar. For example:
"Maitland looked up at the high causeway of the overpass. . . . Below
the span were the approach roads to the Westway interchange, a
labyrinth of ascent ramps and feeder lanes. Maitland felt himself alone
on an alien planet abandoned by its inhabitants, a race of motorway
builders who had long since vanished but had bequeathed to him this
concrete wilderness" (149).

As if to lay claim to this legacy, Maitland involuntarily achieves the
symbolic act of the "naming of the island" (as the title of chapter 20 puts
it) when Proctor, tricked into helping him in one of his plans for escape,
scribbles the architect's name not on a huge concrete pillar where it
might attract help, but on a variety of objects like "the dusty roof of [an]
overturned taxi" (156). Thus he unknowingly brands the features of the
old island with the name of his (and their) master, architect Maitland.
And made the "owner" of its dismal artifacts, Maitland considers an
even larger offering to the island, albeit an ambiguous one, in exchange
for his "inheriting" it.

"He remembered his attempt [in his fever dream] to shuck off
portions of his own flesh. . . . In the same way, he was at last beginning
to shed sections of his mind, shucking off those memories of pain,

hunger and humiliation. . . . All these he would bequeath to the island" (156).

Maitland has reached the point of no return; he now bases his actions entirely on principles rooted in the structures of his private world. Consequently, he refuses Jane Sheppard's now sincere offer to release him back to the extrainsular, outside world. As she herself prepares to leave after Proctor has died in an accident, Maitland exhorts her to not interfere with his decisions by saying, "I want to leave in my own way. . . . Don't call for help. I'll leave the island, but I'll do it in my own time" (174).

After Jane has left, Maitland takes uncontested power over the island. All alone and resting in a "pavillion of car-doors," he experiences both an almost supernatural reoccurrence of physical strength and "a mood of quiet exultation" (175).

How far, then, does *Concrete Island* ultimately travel along the road away from realism and external reality? The text is now completely subjective and no longer tries to mask Maitland's altered perception of his environment with realistic disclaimers. In the four final paragraphs we are restricted to Maitland's perspective, which has now become completely detached from any conventional form of "reality" or "realism." The protagonist is literally given the last word and is allowed to let his interpretation of his own state end the novel.

Set free on its own terms, Maitland's mind comes up with a seemingly paradoxical solution to the challenge of the island. There is the realization—which does not come as a real surprise for the attentive reader, already familiar with the machinations of Maitland's brain— that: "in some ways the task he had set himself [escape] was meaningless. Already he felt no real need to leave the island, and this alone confirmed that he had established his dominion over it" (176).

The merger with the island seems to be complete; the stranded man has discovered his ideal habitat. Implicitly, Maitland expresses the idea that he has been able to conceptualize and abstract from external reality an ideal environment that completely satisfies his needs. Yet even though he has expressed his determination to stay and not really pursue the task he labels "meaningless," Maitland is nevertheless paradoxically convinced he can rest reassured in the belief that: "In a few hours it would be dusk. [He] . . . thought of Catherine and his son. He would be seeing them soon. When he had eaten it would be time to rest, and to plan his escape from the island" (176).

This is Maitland's final decision, by which he achieves an extremely private sensation of closure. For *him*, two ordinarily conflicting aims can be achieved at the same time; the conflicting environments of the external and internal landscapes can coexist in the realm of his newly expanded mind. But *we* see that the price we pay for this act of unification with our environment involves the acceptance of one of Ballard's famous "unacceptable answers," as Colin Greenblatt has christened them.

In its presentation of Maitland's startling answer, Ballard's text has made use of what is perhaps *the* most science fictional technique of storytelling, the extrapolation of an existing trend towards the formulation to a new response/answer. Initially, the text looks critically at the postindustrial landscape that was imposed first on a natural landscape, and then, like a gigantic technological Troy, built layer after layer upon each preceeding architectural structure, until the latest pattern from the drawing-boards of "a race of motorway builders" arrived to be imprinted on the surface of a now almost completely dead, desolate, and inhuman landscape. But the novel does not stop with this *modern* statement about a raped garden of Eden—it goes one scandalous step further with its suggestion that humans can survive—as always—by developing new modes of relating to their environment. The trouble with this new mode is, of course, that it is at best psychotic and, as we seem to see in Robert Maitland, at worst suicidal. But in the world of *Concrete Island,* the only hope for the future lies in embracing the psychotic mode of thought and action. Contemporary humans, the text suggests, have to give up their historical rationality if they want to fully understand and interact with the monstrous environment they have created.

At the end of *Concrete Island,* the reader is left in a landscape in which only the psychotic can happily live, a result that should deeply disturb us. Furthermore, we arrive at this conclusion relatively unaware. The text has tricked us into following the protagonist into his schizophrenic mode of perception, until suddenly we realize that his private interaction with the material of our reality has become the articulation of a powerfully different response to our contemporary landscape.

13
Neuroscience Fiction:
The Roman à Synaptic Cleft
Joseph D. Miller

In addition to being a terrible pun, the title of this essay indicates that, as the protagonist in the classical roman à clef, the field of science that focuses on the brain, neuroscience, is typically disguised in most of the science fiction written today. By that I mean that the neuroscience content in science fiction is implicit, rather than explicit, as in the case of the physical sciences that still dominate the field. There is a deeper level to this metaphor of the roman à clef/synaptic cleft. Although the synaptic cleft is usually thought of as a space between the terminal ending of one neuron and the next neuron, the cleft also serves as a backdrop for certain physiological events that have much in common with the meaning of the French term *clef* or key. In fact the lock and key model of synaptic transmission posits a neurotransmitter, released by one neuron, as the key that, after traversal of the synapse, unlocks the receptor on the adjacent neuron, thus evoking consequent cellular responses. In the roman à clef, the key is our knowledge of the historical events that are a subtext for this French literary form. I hope this chapter may serve as a key to unlocking the often covert, cryptic subtext of neuroscience in science fiction.

Neuroscience content, broadly speaking, is sometimes more evident in the mainstream media, as evidenced by the recent "Reagan's Brain" episodes in Garry Trudeau's comic strip, *Doonesbury*. Here we have a true science-fiction plot; the intrepid correspondent, Roland Hedley, in somehow miniaturized form, is on safari in the presidential central nervous system, seeking the suppressed memories of "Iran-gate." The illustration is marvelous, easily outshining, I think, the images called up, for instance, by Isaac Asimov's *Fantastic Voyage*.[1]

Since most of us in neuroscience today assume a very tight correspondence between mental phenomena and brain anatomy, this strip is literally a "mindscape." I eagerly await the movie version, starring, I hope, Harrison Ford. Parenthetically let me suggest two possible titles for such a film: 1) *Raiders of the Boss Narc,* 2) *Indiana Jones and the Temple of Ron.*

More seriously, we should ask how it is that the neuroscience content of science fiction is so understated. I think the reasons are in large part historical. Early use of neuroscience concepts in the field was extravagant, to say the least. Mary Shelley's *Frankenstein*[2] first popularized the idea of brain transfer in literature. The Hollywood version subsequently provided an interesting bit of "neurosociology"; the pathological behavior of the monster is implicitly attributed to Igor's error in brain selection, the famous "Abbie Normal" confusion. The covert message here is that retardation is directly related to gross brain pathology. In reality, our ability to associate gross anatomical features in the brain with specific behavioral correlates is exceedingly limited. We can relate tumors, traumatic damage (e.g., gunshot wounds), and sometimes vascular accidents to specific intellectual deficits. For the most part, though, even if we could, 1) maintain the recipient in a temporarily brainless condition, 2) reattach the millions of nerves necessary, 3) avoid all the difficulties due to anoxia, swelling, and immunological rejection, it is still very unlikely that any transplanted brain, grossly "abnormal" or not, could produce anything approaching normal behavior. The reason for this is that the development of the nervous system is a highly idiosyncratic process. The pattern of specific neural connections in a given brain differentiates humans far better than fingerprints. So whole brain transplants, as in Robert A. Heinlein's *I Will Fear No Evil,*[3] are not a serious possibility.

On the other hand, we do have the ability to do partial transplants. Small amounts of tissue, generally from fetal brains, can be introduced into recipient nervous systems. Under the right conditions, such transplants can correct certain biochemical disorders in animals. Most recently, autotransplants have been performed in humans. Adrenal tissue, which is basically nervous tissue, can be transplanted into a region of the human brain that is damaged in Parkinson's disease. Preliminary results seem to show that such transplants establish connections with adjacent cells, are functional, and can alleviate the symptoms of Parkinson's disease in at least some patients.[4] This idea of partial transplants has been explored in a cross-species context in a story by Brian Aldiss called "Shards."[5] In this story, small amounts of human temporal lobe tissue are transplanted into porpoise brains. The "shards" of human tissue increase the cognitive power of the porpoises, but also generate an extremely fragmented thought process in the recipients. The only real difficulty with such a procedure is that it requires crossing a species barrier. A major experimental question is whether brain tissue from one species can establish viable connections with brain tissue of a second species. Whether fragments of consciousness in this situation would be transferred along with fragments of cortical tissue is a point of argument. Many neuroscientists believe that aspects of conscious thought are localized in an anatomical sense; others believe the thought process is distributed across the entire nervous system, in something like the way information is distributed in a laser hologram. Empirical data support both views. Certain learning/memory functions appear to be associated with electrical activity in specific brain regions. Furthermore, Wilder Penfield and H. H. Jasper's classical work[6] indicates that electrical stimulation of delimited regions of the temporal lobe in humans seems to activate past memories in an extremely vivid fashion. On the other hand, learning and other cognitive experiences are associated with the activation of relatively wide regions of the nervous system. The bottom line is that partial transplant studies appear to be quite feasible. Science fiction has thus far made relatively little use of such "conservative" procedures, since they apparently lack the melodrama of full-blown brain transplants.

A related idea is the notion of the human brain maintained in isolation. Exceedingly graphic presentations along these lines include the novel and film *Donovan's Brain* (1953) and the pseudo-Lovecraftian film *Reanimator* (1986). Once again Hollywood schlock is quite far removed from what we can accomplish in the laboratory. We can, and routinely do, keep small slices of brain tissue from various species alive in special oxygenated media. Studies using these techniques have been invaluable in determining the physiological functions of specific brain regions. Once again, this sort of scientific procedure has not been employed as a plot device in science fiction, quite possibly because of the overblown and unsophisticated use of the "brain in the fishtank" in the cinema. Thus, the hyperbolic exaggeration of the 1950s science-fiction film may well have generated a reluctance to use such "hard" neuroscience in more recent literature.

However, examples of the naïve application of neuroscience concepts abound in early works of science fiction. One particularly popular notion is that some relatively simple alteration in the way we think, and consequently in the way our brain functions, will confer upon us all the extrasensory powers imaginable. Thus in A. E. Van Vogt's Null-A series,[7] the use of non-Aristotelian logic, in conjunction with Gilbert Gosseyn's double brain, allows the full expression of Gosseyn's superhuman abilities, including teleportation. Learning the Martian language similarly allows for the extrasensory self-actualization of Valentine Michael Smith in Heinlein's *Stranger in a Strange Land*.[8] In Poul Anderson's *Brain Wave*,[9] a tremendous increase in human intelligence is produced simply by the earth's moving out of some galactic cognitive inhibitory field. In Theodore Sturgeon's *More Than Human*,[10] the next step in the evolution of human intelligence requires the appropriate blending and meshing of a set of disparate individuals into a superhuman gestalt intelligence. In contrast, some authors have attempted to use physiological mechanisms, albeit rudimentary, to explain intellectual transformations. In Daniel Keyes' story "Flowers for Algernon,"[11] super intelligence is achieved through a surgical procedure. In Disch's *Camp Concentration*[12] similar genius is produced through the action of a mutated syphilis bacterium. In Herbert's *Dune*[13] Paul Muad'Dib's precognitive abilities are triggered by exposure to the neurochemical-like spice. Similarly, transcendence in Chayefsky's *Altered States*[14] is achieved through the ingestion of a psychotropic drug with simultaneous sensory deprivation. The dark side of such transformations is seen in K. W. Jeter's *Dark Seeker*.[15] In this work, a neurotransmitterlike drug triggers an irreversible change in the central nervous system that generates simultaneous group consciousness and deepening group psychosis. At least these latter works attempt to relate changes in cognitive function to changes in brain function. This reductionistic notion, that brain is the hardware for mind, is one of the major unifying concepts of neuroscience. Until recently, it has only sporadicallly been employed in science fiction.

Why is there such an emphasis on extrasensory abilities as the next step in the evolution of the human mind/brain? Once again, there are strong historical antecedents for this favorite conception of science-fiction writers. I believe it is largely a product of the popular misconception that humans only use 5 percent of their brains. This belief has its origins in the early neurophysiological investigations of the 1950s.

Under barbiturate anesthesia, it appeared that only relatively small regions of the brain could be directly implicated in sensory or motor functions. Very large regions of cortex appeared to be inactive in these studies. We now know that this lack of activity did not reflect noninvolvement of nervous tissue in behavioral and physiological functions. Rather, the explanation for these results is simply that barbiturates suppress brain activity in most brain regions. Under appropriate anesthetics, or in freely behaving unanesthetized animals, most brain areas are active and contribute to the generation of behavior in a complex and sophisticated fashion.[16] This is not to say that the organization of the central nervous system is not highly redundant; indeed, following cerebral damage, adjacent regions of the brain can "take over" the function of damaged regions. In other words, critical brain functions are very well "backed up" through redundant mechanisms. But we certainly do use all of our brains. It is easy to see how the "unused" 95 percent of the brain could be identified with the production of supposedly existent, but rare, extrasensory phenomena. Consequently, the supposition that further evolution or alteration of brain function should engage this "unused" portion leads to the inference that this evolution would produce a heightened facility for paranormal powers. Thus, one of the most cherished plot vehicles of classical science fiction is, at heart, a product of neurophysiological misinterpretation.

Another major error of early neuroscience research that has had explicit repercussions for the field of science fiction was the "center" hypothesis. At one point in the history of neuroscience, it was thought that explicit behavioral functions could be directly related in a point to point fashion to specific cellular regions or centers of the brain. Thus, hypothetically there was a center for eating, a center for drinking, a center for sexual excitation, and so forth. This sort of interpretation was the intellectual descendant of nineteenth-century phrenology or "bump reading," which attempted to assess cognitive function in terms of specific bumps on the skull. For the most part, there is probably as much validity to the center notion as to the older notions of phrenology. Today we believe that behavior is a product of redundant neural systems that may be organized in heirarchical layers of astounding complexity. This has not prevented science-fiction writers like Michael Crichton in *The Terminal Man*[17] from assuming what is essentially the defunct center hypothesis. For Crichton, electrical stimulation of one specific spot in the central nervous system reliably and repeatedly elicits one and only one behavioral response. Similarly, the ubiquitous use of the "wire head," a term attributable to Niven, I believe, represents another simplistic application of this principle. Here the idea is that the junkie of the future will be able to produce reliably a euphoric state through self-induced electrical stimulation of pleasure centers in the hypothalamus. In reality, self-stimulation is a very labile phenomenon; eliciting thresholds change radically, as do the behaviors elicited, and effective stimulation sites may change over time, let alone between different individuals. Still, even with such reservations in mind it is interesting to note that one of the brain structures supporting robust self-stimulation is the prefrontal cortex, a region that seems to be essential to the production and execution of alternative behavioral strategies, a function, as David Brin claims in chapter 4 of this volume, possibly essential to prevarication. But, for the majority of brain regions in the majority of species above the level of complexity of the sea slug, conceptions like these, often based on creaky brain science, are demonstrably inadequate.

In addition to the explicit, generally extreme, examples of neuroscience or, at least, pseudoneuroscience in science fiction I have discussed to this point, there is an entirely different area of science fiction in which the neuroscience is implicit rather than explicit. The imaginative literature dealing with artificial intelligence disguises the contribution of neuroscience in a way similar to the way in which external events are used as a subtext in the French roman à clef.

The origins of this area of science fiction can be traced at least to Karel Capek's R.U.R.[18] and perhaps all the way back to the Golem myths of medieval Yiddish folklore. But certainly the greatest proponent of the thinking machine in our time has been Asimov in his robot series.[19] The most sophisticated of Asimov's robots are indistinguishable from humans, except, perhaps, in the loftiness of their morals. While Asimov never drew explicit comparisons between mental function and computer software, it is easy to think of the robot ego as a program that runs on the positronic hardware. Likewise, superego can be directly equated with the three laws of robotics. The conceptualization of program as mind has been further refined in works like David Gerrold's *When Harlie Was One*[20] and in Heinlein's *The Moon Is a Harsh Mistress*.[21] Perhaps even more to the point, Rudy Rucker reversed the equality in *Software,*[22] underlining the identity of mind as program. The idea here is that mind is the software that runs on the biological hardware of the brain. Nothing in principle would prevent the direct conversion of that biological software into a suitably complex program in FORTRAN. Frederik Pohl has taken these ideas even further in *Heechee Rendezvous*.[23] In this novel, various characters can access software equivalent to the minds of their ancestors. Furthermore, the afterlife can be configured for these individuals as just another operating system. In Greg Bear's *Eon*,[24] multiple artificial intelligence (A.I.) simulations of human personality are simultaneously active. While an adequate simulation could serve as the ultimate answering machine, the legal and social implications of multiple, indistinguishable, artificial personalities have scarcely begun to be considered in science fiction. But, in all of these works the neuroscience is implicit. The underlying construct is that the computer program is an adequate model of mind, and that adequate computer hardware is an effective model of brain. This resolution of the mind/body problem is not only implicit neuroscience but also the foundation of the new hybrid, cognitive science. This science attempts to integrate neuroscience, linguistics, computer science, and cognitive psychology in a grand tapestry whose warp and woof is the construct described above. A grain of salt is necessary here; every new technological development is eventually coopted for a model of brain function. We have had mechanical models, hydraulic models, electrical models, chemical models, superconductor models, and holographic models of the brain at one point or another. But this latest one may well be the most productive metaphor for mind/brain function ever developed. The proof, of course, is in the pudding. When a sophisticated artificial intelligence program cannot be distinguished from the biological original (thus passing Turing's famous Test), the adequacy of this model will be validated. So perhaps I should not have said "the proof is in the pudding"; rather, the truth is in the Turing! In any event, the generation of this particular mindscape is inherently recursive. That which is mapped is also doing the mapping. This implies that a major element of uncertainty must forever be a part of the most accurate map possible. This is perhaps where early models of brain/mind failed, insofar as those maps were entirely deterministic. The irony here is that an adequate map of brain/mind would probably be at least partially unintelligible and/or ambiguous, in any experiential sense. The source of my optimism here is that such models are already approaching this state of partial unintelligibility. Such maps, by Goedelian necessity, must draw upon elements of ambiguity, uncertainty, the lie and the bluff. The very incompleteness of the description of the brain/mind is the only hope of capturing any experiential knowledge of the thing itself.

Rucker's novel *Software* accomplished more than the introduction of biological cybernetics to science fiction. The publication of that novel also marked the inauguration of the new subgenre known as cyberpunk. William Gibson's novels *Neuromancer*[25] and *Count Zero*[26] further sketched the cyberpunk landscape and peopled it with the console cowboys of cyberspace. Later authors such as Walter Jon Williams in *Hard Wired*[27] and Greg Bear in *Eon* have extended this program, if you will! One of the most striking things about these cyberpunk novels is the shared conceptual cyberspace that forms the background to most of the action in these novels. Artificial and biological intelligences mutually inhabit this space, engaging in continuous transfer of information. Security systems are visualized as "ice," corporate information banks as hypergeometric solids, and the Turing Police are ever on the lookout for artificial intelligences who have become too intelligent. In this shared conceptual universe, distinctions between artificial and biological intelligences are largely irrelevant, the movers and shakers are programs irrespective of origin, and the currency of exchange is information. Much of the cyberpunk mindscape has been assimilated wholesale into the darkly satiric television series *Max Hedroom*. And the *Doonesbury* strip has in turn coopted this mindscape for Reagan bashing in "Ron Headrest." Trudeau thus manages, in nearly sequential strips, to devastate both the presidential hardware (the "Reagan's Brain" series) and software ("Ron Headrest"). Trudeau's evenhanded treatment of these metaphors for the consciousness of our "head of state" suggests another example of the dissolution of the archaic mind/body dichotomy.

Telepathy is a trivial matter in such mindscapes; all that is required is a biochip capable of interfacing between relevant brain cells and appropriate transmission and reception hardware. Prosthetic devices have already been developed for human use that convert visual stimuli into arbitrary electrical stimulation patterns applied directly to the visual cortex. The blind can learn to interpret these patterns as visual experience. Similarly, there is no reason why the innervation of the larynx that functions in the production of ordinary speech could not be linked directly to telemetry output devices. Through satellite links every human on earth could experience electronic telepathy, clairvoyance, and clairaudience. The bare bones of such communications systems have already appeared in the science-fiction cinema; it is only necessary to recall that the ultimate paranoid conspiracy in *The President's Analyst* (1967) involved the implantation at birth in every human brain of a transceiver, courtesy of Ma Bell. This particular phone could not be taken off the hook! Roger Zelazny's Hugo-winning story "Home Is the Hangman"[28] extrapolated the phenomenon of telepresence. In this story, remotely controlled robots could operate in hostile environments. Interestingly, the operators often developed a feeling of telepresence; that is, the focus of consciousness of the operator would seem to shift from the remote console to the robot in the hostile environment. This process in turn contributed to the development of an endogenous consciousness in the robot. But how close this is to the parapsychological claptrap of astral projection, telekinesis, and so forth! Even precognition, at least of the probabilistic variety utilized in *Dune,* simply boils down to forecasting and extrapolation with a sufficiently large data bank.

Where, precisely, in the brain might we place a biochip to function as interface between the individual brain/mind, telemetry linkage to a worldwide communications net, and by extension the "global village"? Three regions of the human brain are involved in the production and comprehension of language, surely a function closely related to consciousness. These regions should not be thought of as language "centers" but rather as processing nodes in a complex network. Neurological damage to areas involved in the motor aspects of speech (supplementary motor cortex, and Broca's area) often results in difficulties with language generation, but language comprehension is intact. In contrast, damage to Wernicke's area eliminates the comprehension of language. In individuals with such damage we often see jargon aphasia, that is, the production of a fluent but unintelligible word salad perhaps akin to the glossolalia or "speaking in tongues" sometimes seen in evangelical fundamentalists with presumably normal central nervous systems. In any event it appears that Wernicke's area is the most critical region for language. In Brin's terms, if prefrontal cortex is the "lamps of his face," it would be fair to call Wernicke's area "the doors of his mouth" (apologies to Roger Zelazny)! It is interesting that the major language areas lie on opposite sides of the fissure of Rolando. If we think of song as the highest form of speech, the song of Roland is both a classical poem and a neurolinguistic metaphor! As for the placement of a biochip for electronic telepathy, any of these three regions (or, for that matter, the innervation of the larynx as mentioned above) could serve the purpose. Since the supplementary motor cortex and Broca's area are "downstream" from the primal language region, Wernicke's area, it is likely that one could still lie through biochips in these areas. However, one might speculate that a biochip in Wernicke's area might give the most veridical representation of thought. It is difficult to imagine lying without some type of linguistic representation of both the perceived truth and the lie, representations that should be associated with neural mechanisms in Wernicke's areas. Thus, the most honest electronic communion might require biochip placement in this general cortical region.

There is admittedly some explicit neuroscience in the works considered here. Zelazny appears to have picked up a nodding acquaintance with random neural net theory and the cyberpunkers even seem to have some idea what a neurotransmitter is. It is annoying, however, to see how frequently the authors use current speculation in neuroscience as local color in their novels. Thus, if you need learning enhancement, you do not pop an undefined memory pill; instead you do a hefty dose of vasopressin. Unfortunately, in contrast to a spate of early sensational reports, it now appears that vasopressin has relatively little to do with learning or memory. Instead, it functions as a mild nonspecific stimulant. Any modest increase in general arousal typically facilitates learning. So there appears to be nothing special about vasopressin. However, it is now becoming ensconced in the cyberpunk universe much as the old "you only use 5 percent of your brain" chestnut was ensconced in early science fiction. What is required here is a certain critical faculty on the part of the science-fiction author. There should be no problem in simply making up a neurochemical capable of performing whatever feat is required. Chances are good that we neuroscientists will eventually properly identify the substance that performs that mental feat in reality. But it is probably a wise course for the author to avoid overcommitment to a given neuroscience "fact" until a sufficiently large body of data exists in suport of that "fact."

With respect to either the rather small amount of explicit neuroscience or the considerably larger body of implicit neuroscience in science fiction, it is important to consider the emotional valence of these concepts as they are applied. From the earliest use of neuroscience in Shelley's *Frankenstein* to the bleak landscapes of modern cyberpunk, the history of neuroscience concepts in fiction has been a history of dark and pessimistic application. Why should this be? The use of hard-science concepts from physics, chemistry, and so forth, is often, if not predominantly, optimistic in science fiction. Yet biological concepts, particularly those dealing in some way with brain function, are almost invariably presented in a negative light. I suspect that this negative valence is a product of the historical winnowing of the centristic philosophy. That is, the geocentricism of the Middle Ages was destroyed by Copernicus, the anthropocentricism of nineteenth-century biology gave way to the evolutionary theory of Darwin, and, finally, "telecentricism" (to coin a term), the implicit faith in mind as inexplicable and irreducible center of the universe, last bastion of Cartesian duality, is now crumbling under the reductionistic onslaught of neuroscience in league with the aforementioned cognitive science. These sciences, along with the behavioristic approaches of the psychological and ethological disciplines, ultimately imply that there is nothing special about mind. Consciousness does not exist in a vacuum, but is rather the specific product of a "self" organizing neuronal architecture, under the strong influence of environmental stimuli, in an adaptive context that represents a constraining evolutionary history of millions of years. This, of course, is a frightening proposition for many of us. Where is spirit, where is the soul? Neuroscience treats these concepts as meaningless terms; thus neuroscience is a black science in literature. The uncompromising reductionism of modern neuroscience is at least as great a threat to our residual, comfortable, anthropocentric notions of mind and consciousness as the irreducible defining characteristic of humanity, as the Copernican challenge was to the geocentric philosophy of pre-Renaissance Europe. The very idea of artificial intelligence, as the final extension of neuronal reductionism, is an assault on the last bastion of human uniqueness, consciousness itself. As Yeats said, "Things fall apart; the center cannot hold."[29] So it should not be surprising that neuroscience concepts and artificial intelligence in science fiction are so often portrayed in a negative light. In the approximate words of umpteen 1950s Grade B science-fiction movies, "There are some things humanity is better off not knowing."

But, in reality, explications of the biological underpinnings of human consciousness need not have any more deleterious consequences than, for instance, Darwinian theory had for early twentieth-century humanism. Knowledge is ethically neutral; the application of knowledge may as easily be liberating as imprisoning. A knowledge of the behavioral, evolutionary, and neural determinants of human consciousness may ultimately lead to a relaxation of those constraints. This is essentially the same reply that may be made to Skinnerian behaviorism; any possibility of behavioral "freedom" presupposes knowledge and, potentially, control of those environmental variables that ordinarily condition our responses. Ignorance of the constraints on our behavior is concession to slavery, knowledge is a prerequisite for any possibility of transcendence. Browning says "Ah, but a man's reach should exceed his grasp,/or what's a heaven for?"[30] In reality, it is only the delimitation of our grasp that can allow us to perceive the potential extent of our reach. And so the barren mindscape of contemporary cyberpunk nonetheless contains the seeds of an optimistic neuroscience and perhaps an optimistic neuroscience fiction.

In closing, then, we see that a great irony exists in the use of neuroscience concepts in modern science fiction, particularly in the cyberpunk subgenre. The irony is that although the neuroscience is generally implicit and understated, the welding together of neuroscience and computer science in literature and, ultimately, in the world leads directly to the attainment by purely physical, technological means of powers and abilities that rival the extrasensory capabilities of even the most outrageous superhumans of the Golden Age. If Doc Smith were alive today, I believe he would generate a novel with a title something like *Microchip Lensmen!*

Notes

1. Isaac Asimov, *The Fantastic Voyage* (Boston: Houghton Mifflin, 1966).

2. Mary Shelley, *Frankenstein or The Modern Prometheus* (Berkeley: Univ. of California Press, 1984).

3. Robert A. Heinlein, *I Will Fear No Evil* (New York: Berkeley, 1971).

4. Roger Lewin, "Brain Grafts Benefit Parkinson's Patients," *Science* 236 (1987): 149.

5. Brian Aldiss, "Shards," *Magazine of Fantasy and Science Fiction* 22 (1962): 49–56.

6. Wilder Penfield & H. H. Jasper, *Epilepsy and the Functional Anatomy of the Human Brain* (Boston: Little, Brown, 1954).

7. A. E. Van Vogt, *The World of Null-A* (New York: Ace, 1953); *The Players of Null-A* (New York: Berkley, 1974); *Null-A Three* (New York: DAW, 1985).

8. Robert A. Heinlein, *Stranger in a Strange Land* (New York: Putnam, 1961).

9. Poul Anderson, *Brain Wave* (New York: Ballantine, 1954).

10. Theodore Sturgeon, *More Than Human* (New York: Ballantine, 1953).

11. Daniel Keyes, "Flowers for Algernon," *The Hugo Winners,* v. 1, Isaac Asimov, ed. (New York: Doubleday, 1962).

12. Thomas Disch, *Camp Concentration* (New York: Doubleday, 1969).

13. Frank Herbert, *Dune* (Philadelphia: Chilton, 1965).

14. Paddy Chayefsky, *Altered States* (New York: Harper & Row, 1978).

15. K. W. Jeter, *Dark Seeker* (New York: Tom Doherty, 1987).

16. Richard F. Thompson, *Foundations of Physiological Psychology* (New York: Harper & Row, 1967), 474–83.

17. Michael Crichton, *The Terminal Man* (New York: Knopf, 1972).

18. Karel Capek, *R.U.R.* (New York: Doubleday, 1923).

19. Isaac Asimov, *I Robot* (New York: Signet, 1956).

20. David Gerrold, *When Harlie Was One* (New York: Ballantine, 1972).

21. Robert A. Heinlein, *The Moon Is a Harsh Mistress* (New York: Putnam, 1966).

22. Rudy Rucker, *Software* (New York: Ace, 1982).

23. Frederik Pohl, *Heechee Rendezvous* (New York: Ballantine, 1984).

24. Greg Bear, *Eon* (New York: Bluejay, 1985).

25. William Gibson, *Neuromancer* (New York: Ace, 1984).

26. William Gibson, *Count Zero* (New York: Arbor House, 1986).

27. Walter Jon Williams, *Hard Wired* (New York: Tom Doherty, 1987).

28. Roger Zelazny, "Home Is the Hangman," *The Hugo Winners,* v. 4, Isaac Asimov, ed. (New York: Doubleday, 1985).

29. William Butler Yeats, "The Second Coming" (1921), 1.3.

30. Robert Browning, "Andrea del Sarto" (1855), ll. 97–98.

Methods

14

Islands in the Sky: Space Stations in the Universe of Science Fiction

Gary Westfahl

This essay results from a specific research project. Dr. T. Lindsay Moore, professor of government at Claremont Graduate School, was a consultant to NASA (National Aeronautics and Space Administration) and the Jet Propulsion Laboratory in 1985. His task was to advise on a possible management structure—or government—for the proposed multinational space station. He asked me to look at science-fiction stories concerning space stations for insights they might provide into the task of governing such a facility. What began as a job, however, became an adventure, then an obsession. I read over one hundred and fifty novels and stories about space stations, among these a number of classic works in the genre. Obviously the space station is a major aspect of the science-fiction landscape. And questions arose: What purposes does it have in that landscape? What are its basic forms? How and why are those forms modified? (I find two major modifications: the starship and the space habitat.) Finally, how useful is such research, first to those working to transform the dreams of science fiction into reality, second to science-fiction critics? For the latter I hope to offer, in this bibliographical survey, a model for charting what remains basically unmapped territory: the science-fiction library itself.

The standard space station—a spinning metal wheel or torus, attached by spokes to a central hub—is one of the most powerful images ever promulgated by science fiction. One reason for the circular model is that space stations must rotate to have artificial gravity. But the popularity of this design stemmed more from its beauty than its scientific necessity, and a number of writers have pointed out that cylinders, spheres, dumbbells, or discs would work just as well. Today, however, as we realize that such stations, even revolving ones, need have no particular shape at all, space stations tend to be formless, chaotic assemblages of compartments, tanks, and passageways—eminently logical but lacking in aesthetic appeal. As for space-station interiors, the usual dominant impression is of bare walls, long narrow corridors, and cramped quarters, occasionally enlivened by touches of homey decor or futuristic designs.

The main motive for building a space station—expressed in such works as Jeffrey Lloyd Castle's *Satellite E One* and Rafe Bernard's *The Wheel in the Sky*—is to establish an outpost in space, a base from which to launch further explorations of the moon and other planets. And though the astronauts constructing a space platform in Murray Leinster's *Men into Space* (based on a CBS television series) speculate that the station will eventually have to be destroyed, as a hazard to space flight, the general assumption is that the station will remain in orbit as a way station, a place for spaceships to be refueled and repaired, for travelers to rest or transfer from an Earth-to-space vehicle to a true spaceship. Additional space stations of this type may be needed in orbit around other planets—like Gaudien, orbiting Mars in J. M. Walsh's *Vandals of the Void*—or others may be placed along well-traveled routes in deep space. For example, Manly Wade Wellman's "Space Station #1" is positioned in Mars' orbit, but 180 degrees away from Mars, to serve as a stopping place for spaceships going from Mars to Jupiter when those planets are in opposition; and Wilson Tucker's "Interstellar Way-Station" is one of ten space stations located along the path between the Sun and Alpha Centauri.

These sorts of space stations—aptly described by Richard Elam, Jr., in "The Ghost Ship of Space" as "space service stations"—are undoubtedly the most common in science fiction; but they are often so briefly mentioned or visited as to render them invisible. The works of Robert A. Heinlein provide a good example. Readers will no doubt recall the space habitat in his recent novel *The Cat Who Walks Through Walls,* the specially equipped satellite home of "Waldo," perhaps even the Space Station No. 1 being built by "Delilah and the Space Rigger." But there is also Supra-New York, the earth-orbiting space station seen or talked of in four stories from *The Green Hills of Earth*; Space Terminal, orbiting the Moon, and Mars Terminal, orbiting that planet, in the same anthology; Terra Station, visited by Heinlein's *Space Cadet*; Circum-Terra Station, occupied and destroyed by Venusian rebels in *Between*

Planets; the space station that the emergency mission takes off from in "Sky Lift"; the two space stations that beam laser messages to the Moon in "Searchlight"; and the space station being constructed out of an asteroid by Andrew Jackson Libby, the young "Misfit." These space stations are interludes, little touches of local color, or bystanders to some larger adventure occurring in space or on a planet.

Another reason for building a space station, emphasized in works like Lester del Rey's *Step to the Stars* and Murray Leinster's *Space Platform,* is to establish an orbiting fortress armed with atomic missiles aimed at Earth in order to impose a Pax Americana on the globe. The logic behind these plans seems to be the old military strategy of seizing the high ground; but there are problems in applying this idea to outer space. On Earth, high ground is easy to defend, but a space station in a fixed orbit is exposed and vulnerable. And, because space is limitlessly vast, there is nothing to prevent an enemy nation from launching its own military satellite. As a result, even those stories that endorse the idea invariably portray such stations as increasing world tensions, not lessening them; and in Edmund Cooper's *Seed of Light,* a military station leads directly to nuclear war. Ironically, C. M. Kornbluth's *Not This August,* the one novel in which a military satellite achieves a desirable end—the peaceful removal of Communist troops occupying America—is the one novel that explicitly warns of the endless cycle of escalation in space warfare; and at the end of the book, its hero renounces military action to pray for peace. In wars between worlds, then, space stations are easy to destroy, easy to avoid—they are irrelevancies. Instead, as science fiction moves farther into the future, other types of space stations appear, devoted to peaceful purposes.

Space stations that harness solar energy and beam it to Earth are an old idea. Though Asimov claims (in *Isaac Asimov Presents the Best Science Fiction Firsts*) that his 1941 story "Reason" "first suggested using satellites to collect solar energy and beam corrected forms to Earth," there were at least two earlier stories that described space stations designed to provide Earth with solar energy. In Otto Gail's *The Stone from the Moon,* which appeared in Germany in 1926 and in America in 1930, space station Astropel has a gigantic mirror to focus sunlight on portions of the Earth's surface, while Murray Leinster's "The Power Planet" (1931) remains stationary so that the temperature differences between its hot and cold sides can generate electricity, which is beamed to Earth. With the revival of interest in such stations in the

1970s, "powersats" have been background elements in scores of recent novels, notably Harry Harrison's *Skyfall* and Lee Correy's *Space Doctor.*

Another early realization was that space stations could be used to process materials in space and to manufacture goods from them—a plan most grandly realized in Basil E. Wells' 1941 "Factory in the Sky," an immense sphere in the asteroid belt that builds spaceships and other products. Like powersats, space factories usually play a minor role in modern science fiction, although a manufacturing station figures prominently in Jerry Pournelle's "High Justice" and "Consort."

Manned communication satellites were frequently presented by Arthur C. Clarke, who has admitted that he may have been inspired by George O. Smith's earlier stories about *Venus Equilateral,* a station in the orbit of Venus that maintains contact between the planet and Earth. A recent example of these stations in Geosynch, the hub of a worldwide broadcasting network in Juanita Coulson's *Tomorrow's Heritage.*

Some science-fiction space stations are devoted to types of scientific research, including Douglas R. Mason's *Satellite 54-Zero* and Clarke's Met Stations (in *Islands in the Sky*), both concerned with meteorology; the orbiting observatory of Hugh Walters' *Terror by Satellite*; and the station housing a supercomputer used by various scholars in Hal Clement's "Answer."

The flexible gravity of a space station may be ideal for treating some ailments. Certainly the grandest and most advanced medical facility is Sector Twelve General Hospital, featured in many stories by James White, a massive structure with numerous sections duplicating the environments of various alien worlds. Other medical centers include the unseen Hospital Wheel of Mack Reynolds' *Satellite City,* the Space Hospital of Clarke's *Islands in the Sky,* and the "Louis Pasteur satellite hospital" mentioned in Clarke's *The Songs of Distant Earth.*

In Clarke's "The Lion of Comarre," the world government has its headquarters on an "artificial moon" orbiting Earth, to ensure that "no narrow parochial viewpoint" influences its decisions. For similar reasons, a space station would be a logical place for humans and aliens to meet—neutral ground, as it were—though the only facility specifically designed for alien visits is Damon Knight's "Stranger Station." But Russians and Americans do meet peacefully in a space station in the film *2001: A Space Odyssey,* as do humans and Klingons in the "Star Trek" episode "The Trouble with Tribbles," and members of two warring alien races in John Brunner's *Sanctuary in the Sky.*

It is common to educate spacemen by assigning them to a general-purpose space station to receive their final training, a practice seen in countless stories, including Richard Marsten's *Rocket to Luna,* Richard Elam, Jr.'s, "The Iron Moon," and the anonymous "no frills" novel simply named *Science Fiction.*

Some writers envision a network of space stations constructed solely to aid spacecraft in distress. In C. E. Fritch's "Many Dreams of Earth," "living space stations" connected to the brain of a man in suspended animation are scattered through the solar system waiting to help troubled spacemen, while in Louis Charbonneau's *Down to Earth,* "emergency landing outposts" constructed in hollowed-out asteroids can be found throughout the galaxy.

Pleasure stations are relatively common. These are among the most beautiful space stations in science fiction: in Everett Smith's and R. F. Starzl's "The Metal Moon" there is the Pleasure Bubble, a gigantic sphere whose upper half is a magnificent city enclosed in crystal. In Poul Anderson's *Hunters of the Sky Cave,* Ensign Flandry attends a party on the Crystal Moon, which features "glass-clear walls . . . curving and tumbling like water," and massive "synthetic jewels, ruby, emerald, diamond, [and] topaz." For interior beauty, no space station can match the multiplicity of dreamlike environments available in the immense "pleasure world" of C. L. Moore's *Judgment Night.* Somtow Sucharitkul's *Mallworld* is a huge cylindrical shopping center with over twenty thousand "shops, hotels, department stores, holopalaces, brothels, psychiatric concessions, suicide parlors, and churches"— along with the X-rated amusement park Copuland. In Robert Silverberg's *Regan's Planet* and *World's Fair 1992,* the 1992 Columbian Exposition is held in a space station; Curt Siodmak's *Skyport* describes the construction of Sky Wharton, a glamorous space hotel; and Mack Reynolds' *Satellite City* offers gambling casinos and other legal and illegal delights. Then there are the space brothels: the 5000 Doors Moments of Bliss satellite in Philip K. Dick's *The Crack in Space,* and the *Velvet Comet* in four novels by Mike Resnik.

In stark contrast are the space prisons. These include the endlessly orbiting spaceship of Harlan Ellison's "The Discarded," which houses malformed mutants unwanted by the "normal" people; the space station where the world's genetic engineers are imprisoned in Ben Bova's *Exiled from Earth*; and the space prison filled with terrorists and revolutionaries orbiting around Curt Siodmak's *City in the Sky.*

Some space stations are truly unique. The isolated and spartan space station would seem the perfect place for a monastery, but the only one in science fiction that I know of—in Michael Moorcock's *The Fireclown*—is decidedly eccentric, with monks striving to become "clear" according to the precepts of scientology in the Monastery of St. Rene Lafayette (an old pseudonym of L. Ron Hubbard). On the other hand, a space station seems the worst place to treat psychiatric patients; nevertheless, Frank Belknap Long in *This Strange Tomorrow* presents space station Molidor, where people with mental problems are forcibly sent to undergo what has to be the most bizarre form of psychological treatment ever described in fiction—"space therapy," consisting of brutal beatings by sadistic guards, long hours endured doing nothing but staring out into space, and outlandish "entertainments" featuring ballet dancers and clowns.

Space stations, necessarily, are a home for those working there— but this aspect is usually not emphasized. Stations depicted in Siodmak's *City in the Sky* and the film *Earth II* are specifically designed to become a model for more harmonious living on Earth. And in C. E. Eliott's Kemlo novels, space station Satellite Belt K is a cozy little society, with close-knit families and traditional values. For the most part, however, space stations are staffed by largely- or all-male crews who unenthusiastically serve out their terms of duty while waiting to return to planetary life. Even the apparently contented personnel of Smith's *Venus Equilateral* finally decide to abandon their space station and go back to Earth—"Man's Natural Environment." The reasons for these attitudes should be examined, for they will affect the viability of any space-station project; clearly, no space station will endure if no one wants to live there.

Space-station life can certainly be unpleasant: cramped, austere living quarters, boring routine, and separation from loved ones and familiar Earth settings. Yet space stations also have their attractions: the freedom of zero or low gravity, the possibility of creative architecture and interior design, and the thrill and challenge of working in space. Most dissatisfaction with space stations comes either from ever-present dangers or, paradoxically, from boredom due to the lack of danger.

The dangers fall into three categories: natural disasters—meteors and malfunctions; alien invasion—monsters and microbes; and manned attack—marauders and madmen.

Although earlier novels like Bernard's *The Wheel in the Sky* and Victor Appleton II's *Tom Swift and His Outpost in Space* express considerable fear that meteors will strike the space station, we now know such encounters are unlikely. A real danger, stressed in Martin Caidin's *Killer Station,* is increased radiation due to solar flares. And any equipment failure in a space station can be disastrous; in Harrison's *Skyfall,* a space station crashes to Earth due to a series of mechanical problems and accidents.

Alien invasion is a colorful theme exploited in film. Virulent ambulatory behemoths infest a space station in *The Green Slime,* while a strange "space fungus" menaces station residents in *Mutiny in Outer Space.* On television, poisonous space flowers attack a space station in "Specimen: Unknown," an episode of "The Outer Limits," and ador- able but ravenous tribbles cause problems on Space Station K-7 in the "Star Trek" episode "The Trouble with Tribbles." Slightly more plaus- ible are the alien menaces depicted in written science fiction: the "space sharks" that attack Tucker's "Interstellar Way-Station"; the berserker- like alien warship that threatens a space station in Ted White's *Secret of the Marauder Satellite*; the humanoid Martians that occupy a space station in Lester del Rey's *Siege Perilous*; and the "space plague" that kills crewmen in Caidin's *Four Came Back.*

The most frequent danger to space station residents is other human beings. Enemies can sabotage the station even before it gets off the ground, as in Duncan's *Dark Dominion* and Leinster's *Space Platform*; they can launch missiles at the station, as in Leinster's *Space Tug*; they can threaten a siege, as in Smith's *Venus Equilateral*; they can send a saboteur to the station, as in Hal Clement's "Fireproof"; they can slip an impostor aboard, as in the film *Project Moonbase*; or they can persuade a loyal crewman to turn traitor, as in Caidin's *Killer Station.*

Residents of space stations have an alarming tendency to go mad. People there can develop a variety of disorders: paranoia, suicidal tendencies, claustrophobia, agoraphobia, psychosis, delusions of gran- deur, schizophrenia, sadism, neurosis, compulsive behavior, religious mania, catatonia, and psychosomatic illness. In addition, authors have posited new types of psychological problems caused by space life, such as the "space jitters," "space craziness," "space shock," "space mad- ness," "space fatigue," and being "space happy." The situation is summed up in del Rey's phrase from *Siege Perilous*: "space gnawed at men's minds." And people with space gnawing at their minds are likely to do dangerous things to other crewmen or themselves, like the madman sabotaging his own space station in Laurence M. Janifer's and

J. L. Treibich's *Target: Terra,* or the man who "suddenly announced that
he was going outside with a butterfly net to catch meteors" in Clarke's
"The Other Side of the Sky."

Some space-station residents find they simply cannot take the
pressure. A nurse in Correy's *Space Doctor* suddenly announces she is
returning to Earth, saying that she "can't take another day of living in
these tin cans with death outside their walls." But most men and women
of science fiction are made of sterner stuff, and their dissatisfaction with
life in space has another cause.

The space-station crewman is not the traditional hero who goes out
in search of adventure; in a space station one sits and waits for adventure
to come. Furthermore, while none of the above dangers are impossible,
they occur only rarely, if at all. Clarke makes this point in *Islands in the
Sky* by continually contrasting the wild imaginings of young Roy
Malcolm with revelations of the prosaic reality. Thus, the meteor that
smashes into the hull turns out to be part of a training exercise; the alien
monster he sees in a room is an ordinary Earth hydra scientifically
enlarged in space; and the mysterious strangers lurking nearby that he
thinks are space pirates are revealed to be actors filming a space-
adventure movie. It is little wonder that Roy gets more excited by
meeting a group of colonists from Mars, and ultimately rejects an offer
to return to the station permanently and instead plans to join in the
exploration and conquest of Mars. Other station residents make similar
decisions: for example, the young man working at Silverberg's *World's
Fair 1992* ends the story by resolving to pursue his interest in exobiology
on other worlds.

If neither the unheroic nor the heroic will live in space stations,
then who will stay behind? First, there is one type of hero who is
expected to sit and wait for challenges to come his or her way—the
doctor; physicians and specialists are anxious to spend their lives in
White's Sector Twelve Hospital, where they will regularly confront the
most difficult cases of space medicine. The physically handicapped will
prefer life in a space station, because their conditions will be less of a
problem in weightlessness or low gravity. It is remarkable how many
malformed or disfigured individuals inhabit space stations. These include the legless commander of Inner Station in Clarke's *Islands in the
Sky*; the one-armed crewman of Caidin's *Killer Station*; the midgets on
board space stations in Leinster's *Space Tug* and Janifer and Treibich's
Target: Terra; the paramedic without a foot in Correy's *Space Doctor*;

Heinlein's Waldo, suffering from myasthenia gravis; George Walt, the one-headed, two-bodied proprietor of the space whorehouse in Dick's *The Crack in Space*; and the gravely injured station resident of del Rey's *Siege Perilous*. Insane people may also prefer space-station life; the crews of James Gunn's grim *Station in Space* and the station in Janifer and Treibich's comical *Target: Terra* are both totally mad, but they seem willing—even determined—to remain there. Possibly, the mentally handicapped, too, are able to function better in the abnormal environment of space than in the normal environment of Earth. Finally, prisoners in space will remain; they have no choice.

Realizing that these are not the sort of people from which to build a true space civilization, science-fiction writers have suggested two solutions to the problems of space-station life. The heroic are offered the chance to transform their stations into spaceships and explore the unknown, while the unheroic are tempted back into space by a new and more comfortable type of space station, the space habitat.

The first transformation is best seen in Bova's *Exiled from Earth.* The scientists imprisoned in the space station are initially depressed by their tiny quarters, the lack of good scientific equipment, the absence of goals in their lives. Then one of them suggests attaching a rocket engine to the station and traveling to another solar system. "Heading for the stars gives everyone an aim, a purpose," he says. "Staying here is riding an orbital merry-go-round for the rest of your life." At least four other novels have similar conclusions. In Duncan's *Dark Dominion,* the launching of an armed space platform generates so much tension and hostility that its commander decides to travel to the stars instead of going into orbit. In Long's *This Strange Tomorrow,* rebels seize control of Molidor because "space therapy has failed" and fly it out into space. In Brunner's *Sanctuary in the Sky,* the immense space station is revealed to be an abandoned starship, which is reclaimed by its original owners and returned to its mission of seeding the stars. And in Thomas M. Scortia's *Earthwreck!,* a nuclear war that destroys all life on Earth forces residents of Russian and American space stations to transform one station into a spaceship headed for Mars, where the human race might make a new start.

Peripatetic space stations leave the question of whether a satisfying life can be achieved in stationary orbit. The proposed solution, a preoccupation of recent science fiction, is to build a larger and more Earthlike structure, the space habitat. Though usually thought of as a

recent idea, a standard space habitat can be found in Jack Williamson's
1931 novelette "The Prince of Space": a gigantic enclosed cylinder,
spinning to simulate Earth gravity, with homes, roads, and vegetation
attached to its interior to suggest a planetary landscape. Variations on
this concept are to build space colonies within and around asteroids, as
in George Zebrowski's *Macrolife,* or simply to construct more conventional space stations on a massive scale, as in C. J. Cherryh's *Downbelow Station* and her other novels.

Space habitats differ from smaller stations in more ways than in size
and design. While traditional space stations tend to specialize, a typical
space colony performs many functions, including agriculture. But the
primary purpose of a space habitat is to serve as a community in space;
in fact, one attraction of the space-habitat proposal is the idea that any
group of people on Earth that feels oppressed can find refuge in a space
colony. There is the Rastafarian space colony in William Gibson's
Neuromancer; the Amish colony in Sucharitkul's *Mallworld*; Hazara
Ysroel, the new Jewish homeland in space of W. R. Yates' *Diasporah*;
and the radical feminist colony in William Forstchen's *Into the Sea of
Stars*; among countless others.

The extremists in the space-habitat camp, like Zebrowski in *Macrolife,* argue that space colonies should entirely replace planets as homes
for humanity. Zebrowski makes two points: first, planets are dirty and
dangerous, while space colonies are sterile and safe; second, space
colonies will always be harmonious, since if any discontent occurs, a
new space colony can be built where dissidents can create their own
community. Yet there are ominous aspects of even the most enthusiastic
space-habitat stories that suggest that these structures, despite their
apparent novelty, are not much different from earlier space stations.

Despite's Zebrowski's reassurances about safety, space habitats are
susceptible to all the dangers that threatened space stations. All the
unsolved technical problems that could doom a space-habitat project are
listed in Mack Reynolds' and Dean Ing's *Trojan Orbit*. Even a minor
malfunction could have devastating results: in Ing's "Down and Out in
Ellfive Prime," a broken sprinkler system oversaturates some ground
and causes a large "spinquake," a sudden shift in rotation that puts
everyone's life in peril. There is a virulent plague that kills many
inhabitants of Yates' Hazara Ysroel. Other men, however, constitute the
gravest threat: missiles damage Goddard Space Colony in Coulson's
Tomorrow's Heritage; Island One in Reynolds' and Ing's *Trojan Orbit* is

deliberately sabotaged by its underworld sponsors; traitorous political intrigue threatens Cherryh's Downbelow Station and the habitat in Reynolds' *Chaos in Lagrangia*; and revolutionary terrorists seize control of Island One in Ben Bova's *Colony*.

Finally, there is the ever-present threat of madness. The inhabitants of the Grand Sphere in William Jon Watkins' *The Centrifugal Rickshaw Dancer* are wild, compulsive gamblers, while residents of Downbelow Station are described as passive in times of crisis; both attitudes suggest an unhealthy sense of fatalism in the face of danger. Also, as pointed out by Gregory Benford, space-habitat residents tend to avoid contact with outer space, as if denying the reality of what surrounds them. Such feelings are attributed to the family that built Freeside space colony in Gibson's *Neuromancer*: "Tessier and Ashpool climbed the well of gravity to discover that they loathed space. . . . We [are] growing inward, generating a seamless universe of self." And members of the younger generation in both Watkins' *The Centrifugal Rickshaw Dancer* and Reynolds' *Chaos in Lagrangia* are depicted as bored and decadent, driven to hedonism, dangerous drugs, and flirtations with fascism.

Furthermore, it is naïve to assume, as does Zebrowski, that all social problems can be eliminated simply by limiting the size of human communities. In addition to the generation gaps, all sorts of factional disputes break out in the space habitat of Reynolds' *Chaos in Lagrangia*, while the rebellion against Earth in Watkins' *The Centrifugal Rickshaw Dancer* almost fails because of the inability of various groups to cooperate. And visions of harmonious anarchy and utopian existence are challenged by Gregory Benford's "Redeemer," which argues that because of dangers, "you don't get democracies, you get strong men" in space habitats. In fact, whatever their pluralistic pretensions, space habitats tend to be dominated by one man or a small clique, an echo of the military style of command common in smaller space stations.

Space-habitat stories tend to conclude like space-station stories. There is the desire to travel to other worlds: two novels about space colonies, Bova's *Colony* and Victor Appleton's *The City in the Stars*, both end with ringing speeches calling for further space exploration. The residents of Goddard colony in Coulson's *Tomorrow's Heritage* are working to launch a mission to colonize Mars; a new project to build starships is created to ease the tensions in the habitat of Reynolds' *Chaos in Lagrangia*; and in Joe Haldeman's "Tricentennial," space colony inhabitants eagerly volunteer to serve on board a starship. Like space stations, space habitats frequently leave their stationary positions to travel through space. In Larry Niven and Jerry Pournelle's "Spirals," a space colony, when its supplies from Earth are cut off, moves to the asteroid belt to obtain what it needs; Hazara Ysroel in Yates' *Diasporah* travels to another star so that the Jewish people can finally escape from persecution; and in Forstchen's *Into the Sea of Stars*, all seven hundred of the Earth's space colonies leave the Solar System when a devastating war breaks out on Earth.

The next step, in solving the space-station problem by expansion, is the artificial world. I refer to the huge constructs in Niven's *Ringworld*, Bob Shaw's *Orbitsville*, Colin Kapp's Cageworld series, and John Varley's *Titan*. Because these artificial worlds, for their inhabitants, resemble natural worlds, works like Niven's *Ringworld* are more like novels of planetary exploration than like space-station stories. These structures eliminate the new problems of life in space by substituting for them the age-old problems of life on a planet.

In the more practical world of the 1980s, authors are expressing a renewed interest in small space stations—but with variations on the old ideas. In David Brin's self-described "propaganda piece," "Tank Farm Dynamo," the author suggests building a very cheap space station out of discarded fuel tanks—which the narrator calls "eggs" that will "some-day transform themselves into great birds of space. And our grand-children would ride their offspring to the stars." Also, in Clarke's *The Fountains of Paradise* and Charles Sheffield's *The Web between the Worlds* and "Skystalk," space stations are physically linked to Earth with long cables to form "space elevators" that can economically transport men and materials from Earth to space. In these stories, the space station returns to its original modest goal of helping people travel to other worlds.

What ideas might be useful here to those actually working to construct a space station? Their task can be divided into four phases: building support for a space-station project; assembling the station; ensuring the station's safety; and governing the space station.

Support from two groups—the military and the business commu-nity—does not seem promising. The participation of military personnel in a space-station project tends to irritate other members of the team, as seen in Duncan's *Dark Dominion*. And profits from the exploitation of space, at least in the near future, will be too small to generate sufficient interest from private enterprise; the businessmen in science fiction who do build space stations, like Von Goff in Gail's *The Stone from the Moon* and Laura Hansen in Pournelle's "High Justice," tend to be closet visionaries who pretend to stockholders that they are trying to make money while secretly dreaming of conquering space. On the other hand, valuable support from various organizations all around the world might be obtained for a project described as a model international community, a way to promote peace on Earth, as in *Earth II* and Siodmak's *City in the Sky*. And both the general public and the scientific community might respond to a facility specifically designed to launch further manned and unmanned explorations of the cosmos. If the former approach is tried, the space station could be termed the beginning of a "space city"; while if the latter approach is chosen, the station could be renamed a "space platform," the term first used by Otto Gail and later popularized by Murray Leinster.

Science fiction offers a few practical suggestions for space station designers. In Hal Clement's "Answer," for example, because the super-computer is sensitive to radio transmissions, all personnel communicate by means of "an efficient but amazingly archaic system of mechanical bells and speaking tubes." Incorporating such a system into a space station would not be difficult or expensive, and it would provide a backup system in case of a power failure.

What of methods and schedules for constructing the station in space? NASA once proposed using robots to do much of the work. The underlying problem is that highly trained scientist-astronauts are over-qualified and poorly suited for the necessary long hours of monotonous labor in space. The elegant solution presented in novels like del Rey's *Step to the Stars* is to hire construction workers who already have the skills and temperament for the job. Indeed, recruiting a crew of blue-collar astronauts would ease NASA's current manpower shortage, and provide a way for "ordinary citizens" to participate in the space program.

And what of security? Both science fiction and a Soviet general have pointed out that a space station is extremely vulnerable to anyone with a means and a motive for attacking it; for that reason, any space station should be provided with some method of defending itself. How to avoid madness in space is another question: Caidin's *Killer Station* proposes having a psychologist on board at all times to look for signs of mental illness, but acknowledges that the very presence of such an observer could exacerbate tension and psychological problems.

Finally, management structures described in novels like Bernard's

The Wheel in the Sky and Caidin's *Four Came Back* provide an interesting contrast to the schemes currently being discussed by NASA and its consultants. Both sources envision three levels of authority: the "top," which finances and provides broad overall direction to the station, roughly corresponding to a company's stockholders; the "middle," which decides the functions and operations of the station, corresponding to a board of directors; and the "bottom," which actually oversees the day-to-day operation of the station, corresponding to a company's president and chief executives. In science fiction, the third and lowest level is the space station itself, which gives the crew a considerable amount of autonomy; but in NASA proposals, all three levels are on the ground, leaving the station personnel virtually powerless—and unhappy. NASA should take the long view and start considering government in space; if nothing else, the prospect might garner some needed publicity.

If my comments seem to keep returning to the field of public relations, this is not, I suspect, accidental. While science-fiction writers are generally knowledgeable, they are not working scientists or scholars, and their works are essentially dreams of space stations, not blueprints or organization charts. I have learned little about how space stations are built or managed, but much about how space stations are dreamed of. Such information should be valuable to anyone working to generate support and enthusiasm for a space station.

For the science-fiction critic, finally, my findings provide a useful data base. And reason for some reflection. A space station, its confined chambers surrounded by the deadly blackness of space, would seem an ideal setting for a tale of Gothic horror; yet few if any of the stories I have read resemble Gothic novels in any way. This might call into question Brian Aldiss' assertion in *Trillion Year Spree* that science fiction "is characteristically cast in the Gothic or Post-Gothic mould." On the other hand, many of these works accord perfectly with the theories of Hugo Gernsback: they offer prosaic scientific explanations, not mystery and terror; they seek to dispel fear and inspire confidence in a technological future. I make no sweeping conclusions, but would assert that any valuable theory of science fiction must be derived from and relevant to the entire body of science-fiction literature; focusing on a small number of carefully chosen works—the announced methodology of Darko Suvin's *Metamorphosis of Science Fiction*—simply will not do.

Thus, what begins as a bibliographical survey can become a critical study—a way of broadening and deepening our knowledge of science fiction by testing our hypotheses, in the best scientific tradition, on previously unexamined material. Since surveys with vectors different than mine might yield different results, other researchers should be encouraged to undertake projects of this kind. To put it bluntly, we will never properly understand science fiction unless we read it—extensively, and without preconceptions.

15
What Really Happened on Mulberry Street?
Bill Lee

A Credo

I believe that maturity is not an outgrowing, but a growing up: that an adult is not a dead child but a child who survived. I believe that all the best faculties of a mature human being exist in the child, and that if these faculties are encouraged in youth they will act well and wisely in the adult, but if they are repressed and denied in the child they will stunt and cripple the adult personality. And finally, I believe that one of the most deeply human, and humane, of these faculties is the power of imagination: so that it is our pleasant duty . . . to encourage that faculty of imagination in our children, to encourage it to grow freely, to flourish like the green bay tree, by giving it the best, absolutely the best and purest, nourishment that it can absorb. And never, under any circumstances, to squelch it, or sneer at it, or imply that it is childish, or unmanly, or untrue.
> —Ursula K. LeGuin, "Why are Americans Afraid of Dragons?"

LeGuin believes that mindscapes create landscapes as she so profoundly demonstrated in *The Lathe of Heaven*. She also believes that there is a profound relationship between the child, the imagination, and any definition of a whole person. If a child cannot be a whole grown-up, then no grown-up worth naming can be a whole adult without being part child. Writers of fantasy and children's literature, adults all, have nourished the inner child and at the same time pose the same problem that LeGuin addresses, namely that the world is full of people who want to control, pervert, or destroy the child-vision. It is the characters in the books and their creators who offer us not only an alternative vision of the landscape but also present the problem of how hard it is to see in a world that does not want you to. It is my purpose to suggest that some of these writers are presenting us with the most profound moral issue of our time: whether or not we are allowed to be in touch with the geographics and the landscapes that differ from the norm of a practical-minded society.

To have read Dr. Seuss' *And to think that I saw it on Mulberry Street* (rpt. in *The World Treasury of Children's Literature,* bk. 2, Clifton Fadiman, ed. [Boston: Little, Brown, 1984]) over and over as a child is to have entered a world of subversive activity. The dynamic of the story is about the loss of the child in the father and the struggle of the child to stay alive in the life of the imagination. What I now believe delighted me as a nine-year-old was that the book was written and drawn by an adult with the title of doctor who gave me permission to see what I saw. At the same time the author framed the tale told by Marco with the admonitions of a father who wanted his son to see but to see only what he approved of.

> *When I leave home to walk to school,*
> *Dad always says to me,*
> *"Marco, keep your eyelids up*
> *And see what you can see."*
>
> *But when I tell him where I've been*
> *And what I think I've seen,*
> *He looks at me and sternly says,*
> *"Your eyesight's much too keen.*
> *Stop telling such outlandish tales,*
> *Stop turning minnows into whales."*
>
> (Seuss, 523)

The message is that the "mature adult" tells his son to see what *you* can see yet condemns and devalues that personal vision of the world. This causes Marco to ask himself a serious question. "Now what can I say/When I get home today?" (Seuss, 524). It is a question for us all.

Fortunately, Dr. Seuss allows us to travel with Marco on his wondrous journey. Marco creates a landscape as he goes, one that mirrors his mind, one that is not sanctioned by any adult reality system. It is a landscape that Dr. Seuss is helping to create, one that he shows us in his fantastic pictures. Marco imagines; the good doctor illustrates; we read and see. (The Greek *Phantasía* is literally "a making visible.")

Marco "felt simply GREAT!" when he arrived home, because he

had seen the greatest world he had ever imagined. Yet when his father
sits him down,

> There was so much to tell, I JUST COULDN'T BEGIN!
> Dad looked at me sharply and pulled at his chin.
> He frowned at me sternly from there in his seat,
> "Was there nothing to look at . . . no people to greet?
> Did *nothing* excite you or make your heart beat?"
> "Nothing," I said, growing red as a beet,
> "But a plain horse and wagon on Mulberry Street."

Marco, in other words, is not allowed to bring his friends home. We
might assume on one level that Dr. Seuss has written something of a
cautionary tale admonishing, on the side of the father, Marco and us to
behave. Finally, however, he is giving his complete approval, for even if
we are not allowed to tell the tale in the house or in school, there is plenty
of room to experience it on the journey between.

James Hillman calls the dark messenger god, Hermes, the "God of
betweens" ("Notes on Opportunism," *Puer Papers* [Irving, Tex.: Spring
Publications, 1979], 156), and it is Dr. Seuss and Marco who are the
subversive messengers of this story. The journey is an escape into the
world of the Mulberry Street of Marco's mind. To escape denotes an
avoiding of capture or any threatened evil; to gain or regain liberty. In the
world of fantasy the idea of escape is preeminent for both the reader and
the protagonist. To read the imaginative landscape is to avoid capture by
one who has custody; it is to imagine myself beyond the limits of my
adult self (whether that be external or internal).

Marco's father has superstition in its primary sense — excessive fear
of the gods. Marco's reports of what he has seen have been rejected as
superstitious precisely because the old man is trying to control the gods
of fantasy, those creatures who people the world of the imagination.
Thus are the sins of the father passed on.

In Michael Ende's *The Neverending Story* (New York: Penguin,
1984), one of the gods of between is Gmork, the werewolf, who tells
Atreyu, "The human world is full of weak-minded people, who think
they're as clever as can be and are convinced that it's terribly important to
persuade even the children that Fantastica doesn't exist" (127). The
geography of Fantastica is being obliterated by the Nothing, and it is
easy to see the connection with Marco feeling forced to say nothing
about his imagined world. In Fantastica, "Continents and oceans,

mountains and watercourses, have no fixed location in the real world. Thus it would be quite impossible to draw a map of Fantastica. In Fantastica you can never be sure in advance what will be next to what. . . . In Fantastica there are no measurable distances, so that 'near' and 'far' don't at all mean what they do in the real world. They vary with the traveler's wishes and state of mind" (Ende, 137). The essence of the Nothing is a lack of belief in this kind of geography, and because the adults, the clever ones, have a different state of mind, they feel it incumbent upon themselves to create a world that allows for nothing. State of mind becomes mind of the state.

The value of human visits to Fantastica is presented by the Child-like Empress simultaneously to Atreyu, to Bastian Balthazar Bux, and to the reader. Obviously, if we are reading this fantasy, we have no trouble believing in the land of Fantastica. But the message is one that must be carried; it is the nature of this kind of experience to be subversive, to bring down the state—of mind. The value is spiritual. "Every human who has been here has learned something that could be learned only here, and returned to his own world a changed person. Because he had seen you creatures in your true form, he was able to see his own world and his fellow humans with new eyes. Where he had seen only dull, everyday reality, he now discovered wonders and mysteries. That is why humans were glad to come to Fantastica. And the more these visits enriched our world, the fewer lies there were in theirs, the better it became. Just as our two worlds can injure each other, they can also make each other whole again" (Ende, 148). The people who advocate the Nothing, who structure the mindscape to permit no escape, these people who want nothing for an answer, who do not want to know what happened on Mulberry Street—these are the representatives of what Ralph Waldo Emerson called "the state of society . . . one in which the members have suffered amputation from the trunk, and strut about so many walking monsters" ("The American Scholar," in *The Selected Writings of Ralph Waldo Emerson* [New York: Random House, 1950], 46). These everyday, normal monsters are to be feared more than Billy Pilgrim's Tralfamadorians or Maurice Sendak's Wild Things.

In L. Frank Baum's *The Wizard of Oz* (New York: Ballantine, 1979), when Dorothy first reaches Munchkin land and meets the Witch of the North, she is "half-frightened at facing a real witch" (14). The reason she is frightened is because she has been told by Aunt Em who lives in Kansas, which is a civilized country, not to believe in them. With a profound understanding of geography, this witch tells Dorothy, "In the civilized countries I believe there are no witches left; nor wizards nor sorceresses, nor magicians. But you see, the Land of Oz has never been civilized, for we are cut off from all the rest of the world. Therefore we still have witches and wizards amongst us" (Baum, 14–15). Fortunately, Dorothy is given the gift of a tornado to sweep her from the grayness of the civilized countryside into a place where her imagination may flower. She is given the journey through this fantasy land whence she can return nourished for her battle against the nothing of Kansas; for in the beginning, "When Dorothy stood in the doorway and looked around, she could see nothing but the great gray prairie on every side" (Baum, 2). Dorothy is harvesting the results of the pioneer vision, the relentless civilizing force of the westward movement.

Kansas is surely a landscape of a mindscape. It is a land of incessant adulthood, of incessant work requiring blinders. Dorothy's journey through the landscape of Oz will give her a chance to maintain her child self in her grown-up phase. She will bring the primal spirit of the uncivilized world back to help reenvision the landscape that has been lost. When Dorothy reappears in Kansas, it is appropriate that Aunt Em asks, "Where in the world did you come from?" (Baum, 219). Apparently, for the moment at least, Aunt Em knows intuitively that Dorothy has been someplace; but she limits the inquiry to "in the world." We do not know what Aunt Em believes when Dorothy tells her "gravely" that she has come from the Land of Oz because the book ends at this points. Oz is certain to be no "where in the world" that Aunt Em believes in. Those of us who have seen the landscape that Dorothy has seen know what we know. Whether the civilized will believe it is left a literal blank on the page.

Dorothy has been to Oz, which is Mulberry Street, which, as the Darling children know, is Neverland. It is a place that never was, which adults tell children to never mind, which never existed but always is. The incredible narrator of J. M. Barrie's *Peter Pan* (New York: Bantam, 1982), in his chatty style, engages us in a discourse on child geography.

> I don't know whether you have ever seen a map of a person's mind. Doctors sometimes draw maps of other parts of you, and your own map can become intensely interesting, but catch them trying to draw a map of a child's mind, which is not only confused, but keeps going round all the time. There are zigzag lines on it, just like your temperature on a card, and these are probably roads in the island; for the Neverland is always more or less an

island, with astonishing splashes of colour here and there, and coral reefs
and rakish-looking craft in the offing, and savages and lonely lairs, and
gnomes who are mostly tailors, and caves through which a river runs, and
princes with six elder brothers, and a hut fast going to decay, and one very
small old lady with a hooked nose. (Barrie, 6–7)

Neverland is exactly that mindscape/landscape which doctors cannot
map because it is a terra incognita to science and civilization. (Dr. Seuss,
of course, is an exception.) Neverland is a confusion, an anarchy, a chaos
of delightful colors and personages — but apparently only for children. It
is where Peter Pan plays.

The mother, Mrs. Darling, can vaguely recall a Peter Pan, that trickster puer, that god of between, by "thinking back into her childhood" — a
sign of hope that she has some capacity to recall. (Indeed, it is her dream
that recalls Peter.) But she cannot reenvision that world. "She had believed
in him at the time, but now that she was married and full of sense she quite
doubted whether there was any such person" (Barrie, 8). To be full of sense
is apparently to lack nonsense, to reject the faith required to believe — for to
try to save Tinkerbell is an adult task as well as a child's.

It is the narrator of the story who redeems all, for he is the essential
trickster — an adult who can recall and retell Neverland and Peter Pan
and all the adventures. It is, he tells us, "On these magic shores children
at play are for ever beaching their coracles. We too have been there; we
can still hear the sound of the surf, though we shall land no more"
(Barrie, 7). This latter part is a trickster's challenge to the "we" —
parents reading to children, children old enough to read to themselves.
The trick is to read on because to read on is to do more than land a
coracle; it is to fly out of our windows and reach the island of Neverland.
To read on is to follow the map of the child's mind, to find, as Henry
David Thoreau tells us, "that there are continents and seas in the moral
world to which every man is an isthmus or an inlet" (*Walden* [New York:
Holt, Rinehart & Winston, 1960], 268). That world is an Edenic anarchy
that will free our souls from having to be "mature" in the most negative
sense, or to be — also in the negative — "little adults." To go there is to
attempt to be whole, not as some adults would have it, to be half-grown
or half-baked.

In Norton Juster's *The Phantom Tollbooth* (New York: Random
House, 1964) there is a map of "The Lands Beyond" which is not too
different from the Land of Oz or Neverland. The hero of the quest

adventure is magically given the map as a challenge to his boredom. Little adult that he is, he immediately concludes, "I don't think there really is such a country" (Juster, 14). His perception of the real has been nothinged, the boundaries of his vision proscribed by his adult self. In this scene, he is like the child in a recent *New Yorker* cartoon. A boy is sitting up in bed with arms folded, in a room fully of toys, mostly mechanical and scientific. His father, sitting on the edge of the bed, provides the caption and the capper to this picture: "It's a bedtime story. It doesn't *need* corroboration!" (*The New Yorker*, 1 Dec. 1986). What makes this a sad story is that it is the reversal of Marco and his father confronting each other at the end of *Mulberry Street*. It is a glimpse of the grown-up child—which is to say the shut-up child who has been inundated with journalistic reality. At the beginning of *The Phantom Tollbooth* our hero, Milo, has burned out his ability to play imaginatively, but enough of his child self still remains so that he still has faith that his world might be revisioned if he surrenders to the directions in the strange map.

The gift is a map from the gods that invites Milo into a geography of beyond, one that allows him to go so far beyond that "neither the tollbooth nor his room nor even the house was anywhere in sight. What had started as make-believe was now very real" (Juster, 16), because Milo has been willing to pass through a tollbooth that has magically appeared in his room and because he is now on a thruway that will lead him and, fortunately, us through into the "very real." It is, as we all recognize, a place that requires faith, a place that requires us to "make believe." If we make believe, if we engage in the lie, in the fiction (from the Latin *fingere,* to form, mold, devise), then we also make belief. Then, like Bastian in *The Neverending Story,* we can name the Childlike Empress and renew the landscape. Rather than merely suspending our disbelief, we may confirm our belief that there is, in fact, a relationship between Oz, The Lands Beyond, Fantastica, Neverland, Mulberry Street, and our becoming world.

In *The Phantom Tollbooth,* when Milo reaches a place called the city of Reality where people hurry so much that they do not see the city, he is told that they miss their Mulberry Street because "one day someone discovered that if you walked as fast as possible and looked at nothing but your shoes you would arrive at your destination much more quickly" (Juster, 117). By looking at nothing, they reach their destinations and miss their destiny.

As our fictional characters go from one landscape to another, as they nourish themselves in fantastically real landscapes, they understand what Alec Bings, who sees through things, tells Milo: that the "most important reason for going from one place to another is to see what's in between" (Juster, 117). This is the most subversive activity of all as Marco found out on Mulberry Street.

Since none of these stories was written by a chronological child, as no fantasy ever is, then we must take hope and have faith that Fantastica is still alive. As that spiritual child Thoreau said, in *Walden,* "If men would steadily observe realities only, and not allow themselves to be deluded, life, to compare it with such things as we know, would be like a fairy tale and the Arabian Nights' Entertainments" (78). To have explored the landscapes of the fantastic, of the real, we can agree with the child of the lower case, e. e. cummings, who (in his *Complete Poems*: 1913–1962 [New York: Harcourt Brace Jovanovich, 1972], 663) thanked his God "for most this amazing"; "(now the ears of my ears awake and/now the eyes of my eyes are opened)."

16

Infinity in Your Back Pocket: Pocket Universes and Adjacent Worlds

Max P. Belin

One of the most important parameters of science fiction, to both the storyteller and the audience, is the freedom of setting that the form permits. We live in a galaxy containing billions of star systems, which is itself only one medium-sized example of galaxies. In that vastness of space, any condition can exist that the storyteller sees fit to put there — the only limits are those of the author's imagination and of his or her audience. Yet, this vastness creates the problem of getting the characters, and the plot with them, across the immenseness of space without a delay of several generations. Despite what detractors of the form might imply, science fiction is as logical as any other kind of literature. Science fiction has its own rules of willing suspension of disbelief, although they are somewhat wider than those of any other form. If the writer of science fiction wishes to take advantage of this wealth of setting, he or she must first deal with the issue of transportation.

Over the course of the science-fiction era, this problem has been dealt with in many amazing ways, from starships that might take a hundred generations or more to reach their destination, as featured in Robert A. Heinlein's story "Universe," to vehicles that pass through every point in the universe simultaneously, such as the starship *Heart of Gold,* from *The Hitchhiker's Guide to the Galaxy* by Douglas Adams, to vehicles such as the "rockets" of Ray Bradbury's stories, which are never explained in any manner, sublime or ridiculous. Oddly enough, what is perhaps the most interesting means of reaching other worlds is also the method that provides the greatest number of possible settings: the process of traveling without moving at all. Many of the most fascinating locations in science fiction and fantasy can be reached by crossing a line or taking a short walk—or using an article in the hero's pocket.

To understand properly the advantages of the pocket universe, it is important to understand the advantages and limitations of the more common methods of reaching another world. As mentioned above, the best-known method is the spaceship. It seems only logical that sooner or later, when our technology extends to the proper level, humanity will begin constructing vehicles to travel across space, as we have with land, water, and air. A spaceship also has the advantages of serving as a location for adventure in its own right, of serving as the mobile home base of the characters, and of providing clues about the society that built it. Perhaps the best-known example of all is the USS *Enterprise,* from the series "Star Trek," but other good examples are the Torchship *Lewis and Clark,* from Heinlein's *Time for the Stars,* the *Long Shot* from Larry Niven's "At the Core," and the tramp freighter *GAC 59,* from David Drake's *Cross the Stars.*

At the same time, however, a starship also produces limitations on the story and the storyteller. To begin with, one must account for how the character or characters came to be aboard such a ship in the first place, how the ship works, who built the ship and who maintains it, and why it was built in the first place. Another difficulty lies in the fact that a starship is most often an expensive, important piece of equipment, and as such will tend to dominate any story one puts it in, if only in terms of obtaining fuel for the vehicles and finding a place to park it while having one's adventures. In short, even a vehicle that can reach any point in the universe instantaneously tends to draw too much of the story away from the adventures of the characters and toward the care and feeding of exotic machinery.

Several methods have been invented to get characters about the cosmos without the aid of spaceship, and without the drawbacks such involves. Perhaps the best known of these is the Martian series of Edgar Rice Burroughs, in which a gentleman soldier named John Carter is transported to the planet Mars for no obviously explainable reason. Another good example is the strange case of Gulliver Foyle, from Alfred Bester's *The Stars My Destination,* who learns, quite by accident, how to teleport himself spontaneously to any point in the cosmos. Although Foyle is from a future Earth in which most people can teleport between five- and one-thousand miles, his is still an extraordinary achievement, and it serves as the cause of his adventures in and around the solar system, and then beyond.

There have been methods of interstellar travel that are even more eccentric than these, but the problem with very eccentric methods of space travel is that only very eccentric individuals can use them, and it is easy to lose one's audience in the creation of these characters. To realize the full potential of travel to other worlds, what is needed is a preponderance of closely related or linked worlds and a simple, straightforward method of moving from one to another—not the sort of thing that would require one to be a hero, with the mind and will of a god, or that would require one to be a highly trained explorer or traveler from a technologically advanced culture; rather, the sort of thing that any small child might be able to figure out and use, or any ordinary man suddenly called upon to be a hero could fathom.

A pocket universe is conceptually a very simple formation. It is an entire universe, generally similar to our own, but different in special ways designated by the storyteller. Since the fictional universe is separate from our own, it may contain any physical laws or conditions required by the plot or theme of the story. Should magical powers, personified forces of good or evil, mythical creatures or beings, natural features or landscapes impossible in our own universe, or other elements of setting that would normally conflict with the willing suspension of disbelief of the audience become necessary, the author may adopt the simple recourse of transferring the story to a place in which such conditions are normal, or even commonplace.

The term *pocket universe* implies the properties of convenience and a smaller than normal size (compare with terms such as *pocket battleship* or even *pocket nuke*). The term is therefore applicable to any microcosmic location that contains its own laws of nature and of science. Some examples of the pocket universe concept do not even require physical departure from our own world—such as the childhood stories of Ray Bradbury, in which any condition available to the mind of a child may appear at any moment. Others are created solely to generate the central concept of the story, such as the short story "The Wall" by Arthur C. Clarke, in which an entire universe is created for the purpose of showcasing a three-dimensional Möbius strip effect. Regardless of the desired effect, however, a pocket universe is a storyteller's convenience that makes unique plot devices possible by suspending the normal limitations of setting.

One of the best examples of the pocket universe concept occurs in *The Magician's Nephew,* by C. S. Lewis. While this work is a part of the

Chronicles of Narnia series, and thus falls more in the scope of fantasy than science fiction, it is nevertheless a fine example of both the variety and the simplicity of this method of scene change. The book follows the adventures of two children, named Digory and Polly, who are unwillingly sent on a journey to other worlds by a rather unsuccessful magician, who is Digory's uncle. The two children rapidly discover that the magic rings they have been tricked into testing do not simply send a traveler into another world, but rather allow one access to a central forested plain, "the Wood between the Worlds," from which a vast array of worlds, of which our Earth is only one, can be reached at will.

As of this point in the story, each of the children has access to an infinite number of other universes in his/her pocket. Needless to say, this gives the author the opportunity to involve the characters in the magical conditions and dangers that rapidly become the focus of the plot. By their misinformed blundering in a randomly selected alternate universe, the two children free a wicked witch from stasis enchantment and permit her to reach our world. This creates an amazing amount of havoc, and the children find themselves faced with the prospect of trying to remove a witch from the city of London and send her back to her own world. However, in the process of doing this, they blunder into yet another world, and suddenly realize that they have introduced a force of evil into a newly created, innocent universe.

The overall effect of this magic and blundering is to give the author the chance to create two entire worlds, complete with inhabitants and challenges to be overcome, and then send his characters into them at will. The witch's home world of Charn, and the newly created (and unwittingly witch-infested) place called Narnia, are as developed and as real as any others in the realm of speculative fiction, and the very existence of those worlds makes possible adventures that could never happen in our own universe. Moreover, the simple and easy-to-use method of travel allows the author to use mere children for the hero and heroine; common people like those in his audience. In addition, since the Chronicles of Narnia are an allegorical work, the existence of these other worlds also allows the author to retell the story of Genesis in a new form, which of course was the point of the exercise.

The remainder of the series of books deal only with Narnia, or more properly, with travels between that world and our own. While there are other tales of this same general type that involve dozens of other worlds, such as the Myth Adventures series by Robert Asprin, they all suffer from the same basic problem—that in order to permit travel from one universe to another by magical means, the story must first contain the existence and use of magic. While this is no problem in fantasy, it simply will not pass unnoticed in the realism of science fiction, where the form as well as the audience demands a logical and scientific explanation for everything. Fortunately, there is a simple, logical way to permit a character to travel at will from one world to another at will—place the worlds next to each other in physical space.

This concept of contiguous or "adjacent" worlds may therefore be seen as a compromise between plot device and genre. This is not to say that "adjacent worlds" conditions are not found in fantasy, or that actual "pocket universes" are not found within the concept of science fiction. It is important to recognize, however, that while stories set in a science-fiction setting lack magic, and must therefore lack magical worlds (or alternate universes), they do in turn have access to the wonders of hypertechnology, by which means any condition may be created so long as the creators possess the necessary scientific knowledge. The primary difference between the pocket universe and the adjacent world is that the former is magical (or natural) in origin, while the latter is artificial. As plot devices, however, the two serve almost identical roles.

A good example of this concept can be found in the Well of Souls series by Jack Chalker. The five books of this series focus on a bizarre planet known as the Well World, a place that can only be reached by forgotten extradimensional gateways, and where nothing is quite as it seems to be. The planet itself is actually a single huge computer, which first created and now maintains the entire universe and everything in it. What makes this a pocket-universe story is that the surface of the Well World is subdivided into hundreds of tiny hexagonal biospheres— effectively separate worlds. During the creation of the universe, these biospheres (or "hexes") were used to simulate planetary conditions for the life forms being developed for later seeding on real planets. However, in the eons since, the beings who worked these acts of creation have vanished, and each hex has become a separate nation with its own climate, terrain, and technology.

When one character is suddenly placed on the surface of the Well World with a mission to figure out how the great computer works and track down two madmen before they can do the same, his first difficulty lies in the fact that although each hex is different, with its own population and rules, he can still travel across one in a matter of days, or weeks at most. A second, and far more serious problem, is the fact that the inhabitants of the Well World range from thinking, mobile plants to classical centaurs and satyrs to giant carnivorous insects, and most people who come to the Well World are transformed into one of these creatures or another. Thus the protagonist, a starship pilot named Nathan Brazil, must also deal with the problems presented by the fact that all of his companions are no longer human.

Even in a setting as simple as that of the introductory novel, *Midnight at the Well of Souls,* the remarkable advantages of the pocket-universe concept become readily apparent. In the course of just a few weeks and some rather simple adventures, Chalker is able to send his hero across mountains, grasslands, oceans, deserts, and forests, through technological levels ranging from nonexistent to highly advanced to outright magic, and among dozens of different forms of life. Yet through all of this, Nathan Brazil uses no magical or hypertechnological abilities to get where he needs to go, and in fact never leaves the southern hemisphere of one fairly small planet. With a total of 1,560 separate hexes on the Well World, only half of which contain life as we know it, Chalker does not run out of possibilities for his characters through five full-length novels, yet all of these individuals are forced to travel under their own power when they have anywhere to go.

Wonderful as the Well World may seem, it is not without its own drawbacks. It is not an easy world to reach, or to escape from once you are there. Thus, almost any story set there must contain the elements of rediscovery of the gateways leading to the planet, and the elements of escape from an escape-proof laboratory. Furthermore, the Well World is still a functioning device with a rigorously controlled and maintained environment. As a result, there is a limit both to the number of places to go and to the things that can happen there. However, the Well World is not the only example of what could be called the adjacent-worlds concept, and not all such worlds are as orderly or as well run.

In reading Larry Niven's *Ringworld,* one quickly realizes that while this is also an artificial world, built for some vast alien purpose, it is an artificial world that is running amok. A Ringworld is a relatively simple concept, albeit a brilliant one. It is a ring-shaped construct, built around a star at a radius that will produce a constant Earth-like climate on its inner surface. The structure is about six hundred million miles long, about a million miles wide, and about a thousand meters thick, producing a usable space roughly three million times the surface area of the

Earth. Clearly then, a Ringworld is a useful thing to have if one is faced with an overpopulation problem. One can place the population of three million Earth-like worlds in a single solar system, while the structure itself would require only about the mass of the planet Jupiter to construct.

As in the case of the Well World, a storyteller can place almost any desired conditions on a Ringworld, since the entire structure is clearly artificial. The only real question to be answered is who built it, and how? In the novels *Ringworld* and *The Ringworld Engineers,* Niven's characters set out to answer these very questions. The first novel details the first scout flight to the Ringworld, which is made by two humans, a Kzin (an alien and traditional enemy of humankind), and a mad member of a highly advanced race known as Puppeteers. It happens that the Puppeteers, who are migrating across space, have discovered the huge structure in their flight plan, and wish to know more about it.

As eccentric as the expedition itself seems, the great structure they have been sent to study is more so. It rapidly appears that the entire structure was built by a humanlike race of uncertain origin who possessed the power to transmute one element into another. Yet it also seems that these builders have vanished, abandoning their creation. To make matters worse, the expedition rapidly runs afoul of the structure's meteor defense system and spends most of the novel just attempting to escape from the ring. Nevertheless, even in such a short span of time they manage to encounter several different intelligent species, find life from several other parts of the galaxy that might have been transplanted, and determine that civilization has indeed fallen on the Ringworld and will not be back.

For all of this achievement, the first book barely scratches the surface of the Ringworld's potential. In the sequel, two of the original characters are sent back to the structure after twenty eventful years. This time their mission is to search the surface of the ring for the secret of transmutation of elements (the secret that makes the building of such a structure possible in the first place). After a number of mechanical failures and a large amount of walking, driving, flying, and sailing about the ring, the characters discover that the structure is indeed populated with life from other parts of the galaxy, as well as hundreds of mutated versions of what appears to have been the dominant race on the Ringworld. They also discover that the entire structure is unstable, and that they must discover a means of saving it.

Clearly these adventures do require the presence of starships. The Ringworld is a great distance from the Earth or any of the worlds nearby that have been colonized by humanity, making it somewhat difficult to reach. Since there are mountains a thousand miles high along both edges, it is also rather difficult to escape from if one happens to crash on the ring. Yet, once there the Ringworld contains all of the variety and geography of the millions of worlds its surface would hold, all of which can be easily reached by any conventional form of surface or ground transportation. The structure also provides situations and adventures that even an entire galaxy could not produce, such as gigantic oceans with island chains in them that are actually maps of other worlds, or mountains a thousand miles high that are actually old meteor punctures and not mountains at all, or even the prospect of walking a million miles to get across the structure—the short way.

Thus, the adjacent-worlds concept shows its inherent advantages. In the final analysis, there is only one truly major problem with pocket universes and adjacent worlds—the question of how such conditions were set up in the first place. It is relatively straightforward to produce a hero or heroine in a far-distant future, or a not-so-far distant future, provide him or her with a space vehicle or a means of teleportation to whatever point he or she wishes to reach, and find a reason for sending him or her there. However, it requires much more of the storyteller to produce a rationale for why a character can reach a wide scope of other worlds without actually traveling to other stars, let alone a reason for wanting to go. For this reason there will always be more stories of space travel than of pocket universes or adjacent worlds. Yet the most fascinating destinations in speculative fiction will most likely remain those that can only be reached by not actually going anywhere.

17

Landscape and the Romantic Dilemma: Myth and Metaphor in Science-Fiction Narrative

William Lomax

The science-fiction conflict, writes Mark Rose, is often "between the human figures and the landscape," for the landscape, as a manifestation of the alien or the sentient unknown, becomes itself a leading character.[1] From the panoramas of Verne's *voyages extraordinaires* to postholocaust ruins to alien planets to the heat, wind, or water death of the earth to the interior landscapes of the mind—from the six hundred gravities of Hal Clement's Mesklin to Larry Niven's ingenious alien environments to Philip Dick's twenty-first century Los Angeles to Vance's dying earth to Aldiss' hothouse to the sentient ocean of Lem's Solaris to the Freudian landscape of Altair 4—from these to countless other science-fiction visions, it is the landscape that is the star, the leading character, the source of conflict, the reflected image of humanity, and the setting for human adventures, whether for damnation or salvation. More perhaps than any other element of narrative, it is the landscape, altered or displaced in time or space, that identifies the narrative as science fiction. A better understanding of its landscapes, then, should lead us to a better understanding of science fiction itself.

A search for the origins of science fiction in its landscapes unavoidably leads us into the territory of myth, and the pursuit of myth leads us in turn to Romanticism, for science fiction, in my judgment, expresses fundamental mythopoeic patterns whose roots lie in nineteenth-century English Romanticism. The purpose of this essay is to justify that judgment.

Northrop Frye offers a definition of myth appropriate to this task in his *Study of English Romanticism* (1968). Myths, writes Frye, are the "fictions and metaphors that identify aspects of human personality with the natural environment, such as stories about sun-gods and tree-gods. The metaphorical nature of the god who is both a person and a class of natural objects makes myth, rather than folktale or legend, the direct ancestor of literature."[2] This metaphorical nature, Frye continues, also allows primitive societies to express in myth views of their origins, class structures, laws, rituals, institutions, and so forth, and this larger cultural significance of myths causes them ultimately to coalesce into "large unified structures, or mythologies, which tend to become encyclopedic in extent, covering all aspects of a society's vision of its situation and destiny."[3] As civilization develops, these mythologies divide in two, one branch providing the metaphorical patterns of literature, and the other the conceptual ideas underlying the culture as a whole. "At any given period of literature," Frye says, "the conventions of literature are enclosed within a total mythological structure, which may not be explicitly known to anyone, but is nevertheless present as a shaping principle."[4] In Western Europe, Frye concludes, "an encyclopedic myth, derived mainly from the Bible, dominated both the literary and the philosophical traditions for centuries. I see Romanticism as the beginning of the first major change in this pattern of mythology, and as fully comprehensible only when seen as such."[5]

The old Christian culture Frye calls a "closed" mythology, one that is imposed on believers from the outside and that unites all segments of society in a single system of values and beliefs. The new mythology of Romanticism, by contrast, was "open," that is, derived from the internal structures of the imagination, out of which belief emerges rather than being shaped by external compulsion. God as creator was replaced by the human being as creator, and human words assumed the power of revelation once reserved for God's Word. The Chain of Being was inverted, and the Christian world stood on its head. The significant reversal in this pattern, however, is not one of belief, but of *system*. Christian mythology was not replaced by a competing closed system of mythology, but by *no* system of mythology, or rather by *all* systems of mythology. The Romantic myth, in other words, allowed anyone whose imagination was capable of world-building to construct his or her own myth system. It was the secular equivalent of Luther's priesthood of all believers. Thus, the primary goal (and even obsession) of many Romantic writers and philosophers was the individual search for a new world view to replace the crumbling Christian system. But the worship of the individual imagination had paradoxical, some would even say tragic, consequences. Without a central, culture-spanning and culture-uniting myth, any person who possessed the advantages of circumstance and opportunity, and whose personal myth had the power of persuasion and fulfillment, found it easy and enticing to fill the vacuum left by the receding Christian system. It is no accident that some of history's most vicious tyrannies—all energized by a more or less totalizing myth system—have been imposed on the human race in the two centuries since the "open" myth of Romanticism replaced "closed" Christianity. At the same time, however, this mythic fragmentation into numerous individual systems has also inspired a proliferation of new literary styles, forms, and genres—of which science fiction is one—designed to express these new systems. Thus the fragmentation of Western culture, or loss of its "total mythological structure," produced an unprecedented explosion of literary and artistic expression at the same time that it tyrannized countless millions.

The Romantic myth produced yet another dilemma: without a new totalizing structure to provide new "metaphorical patterns," how is the artist to express him- or herself? If a maker is to communicate with anyone else, that person must tap into that mythological substrate which "may not be explicitly known to anyone, but is nevertheless present as a shaping principle." In an environment of post-Christian cultural fragmentation, the one comprehensive system still available was, of course, Christianity. As a result, we find no radically new pattern of metaphors in Romantic literature nor do we see it even today, two centuries after the Romantic revolution. What we *do* see is a pattern of reversal. Without a new pattern to replace the old, the obvious solution was simply to reverse the old as a means of expressing revolutionary change. Thus the death of Christianity has been the great cultural theme of the past two centuries, not the birth of a new system. Nietzsche proclaimed the death of the old god, not the birth of the new. Christianity therefore remained a powerful cultural myth at the same time it was being dismantled, and the language and metaphors of the "new" Romantic myth were often simply inversions of the old, for this was the most effective means of canceling out the old while building a new structure on the foundations of the old.

It was a strategy that could never be satisfactory, of course, for it was roughly equivalent to demolishing a house, then rebuilding it, using the same lumber, but facing the opposite direction. Carlyle's Everlasting No was one such demolition, and his Everlasting Yea was one such reconstruction. The widespread ennui and existential despair that we associate with Byron, Kierkegaard, Werther, and other Romantic figures was, as Morse Peckham has shown,[6] simply the unavoidable psychic response to the process of mythic demolition without the regenerative healing of mythic reconstruction. Even for those who have achieved an Everlasting Yea—what Peckham calls positive Romanticism—this dilemma still remains, for a reversed myth is no myth at all. It remains a link to a decaying past, a looking backward that is not only awkward but essentially destructive. Thus even positive Romanticism, at its heart, was fundamentally negative.

It is the landscapes of science fiction that most clearly express these Romantic dilemmas and their implications for modern life. A brief look at pre-Romantic landscapes will reveal the nature of the change initiated by the Romantics and its significance for science fiction.

Any artistic landscape, no matter in what medium it is executed, is necessarily partial. It will always be cut off by the picture frame, or the period, or the cadence. But the unavoidably truncated landscape assumes significance for us only to the degree that it extends in our imagination beyond the artificially imposed limits of frame, period, or cadence. As vast and overwhelming as Dante's literary landscape is, his words portray only the visible tip of a far vaster and even more overwhelming mythical system that is literally cosmic in scope. A busy canvas of Bruegel, vibrating with the Brownian-like motion of peasant life, is simply a window on a microcosmic portion of a world that extends into the macrocosmic time and space of medieval life. A classic Titian landscape may pause at the frame, but it telescopes the mind into far distances visible only to the imagination. A delicate eighteenth-century minuet holds its shape only by virtue of the structuring cosmos of aristocratic court life that orbits around it. Through the blind strings of Homer's harp, all of Greece sings. In Frye's terms, landscapes such as these are the metaphorical patterns or conventions that express and are shaped by the conceptual ideas of the "total mythological structure" of the culture. In more mundane literary terms, the landscape is a synecdoche, the perceivable tip of the thought world that informs and supports it. Given this concept of landscape, we can then search literary landscapes for patterns that will reveal the evolution of the mythologies behind them.

The link between metaphor and myth was, of course, most pronounced in the Middle Ages. Neither medieval writer nor painter was concerned with the natural landscape or with physical verisimilitude. "The invisible lay always just beneath the visible," writes D. W. Robertson. "To suggest its presence was not only a function of art but also a function of rhetorical persuasion."[7] When naturalistic landscape painting emerged during the Italian Renaissance, the link remained unbroken. The style was naturalistic, but no one had ever seen such landscapes in the real world. The goal was to portray the harmony of a whole in a single glance, for the idea of a landscape as an end in itself did not yet exist.[8] Similarly, in the seventeenth-century Dutch landscape, writes R. R. Haas, "all the characteristics of this world are united into one immense landscape."[9] Again, the technique may be naturalistic, but the images represent the concepts and patterns of the "thought world" of a totalizing myth.[10] Eighteenth-century British landscapes, despite their frequent nationalistic fervor, continued this classical tradition inherited from the Italian and Dutch schools.[11]

In this brief survey of pre-Romantic art, I mean to imply that the mythic reversals characteristic of Romanticism and fundamental to science fiction as a genre have not yet occurred. How, then, can we explain those familiar works of the pre-Romantic imagination—the voyages of Wilkins, Godwin, Cyrano, Hall, and others—that are often called "science fiction" or "proto-science fiction"? Do they also express the prevailing mythic foundation, or do they prefigure the Romantic reversals that produced science fiction?

Bishop John Wilkins was the most influential apologist for Copernican astronomy in mid-seventeenth-century England. He was essentially a science popularizer, promoting study and acceptance of science against "traditional authorities and religious hostility."[12] His two speculative works, *The Discovery of a World in the Moone* (1638) and *A Discourse Concerning a New Planet* (1640), were written to show the general public "the findings of the new astronomy, and to show laymen that there was no reason, religious or otherwise, to reject such findings."[13] Wilkins was attempting to "break down the traditional, medieval view of the universe," and to undermine the idea of a "closed, finite, hierarchically structured cosmos."[14] He was essentially working to reject traditional authority, but only *Church* authority, not Scriptural authority. He was rejecting only the metaphor, not the myth. His goal was merely to resolve the apparent contradictions between science and religion caused by Copernicanism. While arguing for the plurality of worlds and for the elimination of the old Aristotelian idea of hierarchical values, he realized he had also to convince people that such ideas "did not contradict the principles of religion or challenge the validity of Scripture."[15] Wilkins was repudiating the tradition and authority of Aristotle, of the Schoolmen, of Church leaders blind to irrefutable change—but he was emphatically *not* repudiating the great myth of Christianity. He emphasized astronomy for very practical reasons, such as navigation, but he also taught it because it "would prove the existence of God and Providence" and "lead to a closer appreciation of God and a more religious life."[16] His "astronomical fictions" were entertaining but not serious speculations.[17] He briefly pondered the problems of inter-planetary travel, and indulged in a few minor fancies on the lodgings space travelers would be likely to find on other planets, but his fancy produced only familiar earth environments transplanted. Nothing alien, nothing reversed, could ever enter his imagination. Thus Wilkins' cosmos remains uniform and unified throughout; it may be larger, but it remains Earth augmented, and the totalizing myth remains powerfully intact.[18]

Like Wilkins, Bishop Francis Godwin, in *The Man in the Moone* (1638), was responding to the new science of the day and to the mythic patterns that structured his world. Godwin's moon people know Eliza-beth to be a great queen; thus the moon is simply a far province of empire, and the cosmos is still small, still unified, and still closed. The moon seems "a very *Paradise*" to Domingo Gonsales; there is a popelike religious leader, Imozes, whom he cannot see; and the people speak a single language, as if they have remained in a state of pre-Babel purity.[19] The moon people are obviously believers, living in a more innocent, even prelapsarian state of goodness. When Domingo utters the words "Iesus Maria" inadvertently, all the moon inhabitants fall down and repeat it, praying. Miracles are ordinary—even severed heads can be reattached.[20] The strange sights do not bother Domingo, rather they succor him. "For by this voyage am I sufficiently assured," he writes, "that ere long the race of my mortall life being run, I shall attaine a greater happinesse elsewhere, and that everlasting."[21] On his return to earth, Domingo hopes to publish an account of his travels, but he intends first to get state approval, to be assured that his story "may not prove prejudiciall to the affaires of the Catholique faith and Religion, which I am taught (by those wonders I have seen above any mortall man that hath lived in many ages past) with all my best endeavours to advance."[22] *The Man in the Moone* is nothing more than a medieval dream-allegory modernized. The metaphor has been changed by the discoveries of science, but the myth remains unchallenged.

Cyrano's voyages to the moon and sun are the most interesting of the pre-Romantic travel tales, the most imaginative, the most iconoclastic, the most critical of the Church—but the myth remains intact. The voyage to the sun was simply the next logical step in the exploration of the cosmic landscape, as Lovell, Cyrano's English translator, wrote in 1687: "the Moon having been discovered, though imperfectly, by others, but the Sun owing its Discovery wholly to our Author."[23] Lovell so valued the insights Cyrano gained from the celestial philosophers that he recommended immediate mounting of further expeditions to avoid the loss of such wisdom, a loss, he writes, "so great, that one would think, none but the declared Enemy of Mankind, would have had the Malice, to purloyn and stiffle those rare Discoveries . . . which undoubtedly would have gone far, as to the settleing our Sublunary Philosophy, which, as well as Religion, is lamentably rent by Sects and Whimseys."[24] In Cyrano, we see not only the doctrine of plurality of worlds but also the continuation of the old idea of the individual human as microcosm.

> For tell me, pray, [writes Cyrano] is it a hard thing to be believed, that a Louse takes your Body for a World; and that when any one of them, travels from one of your Ears to the other, his Companions say, that he hath travelled the Earth, from end to end, or that he hath run from one Pole to the other? Yes, without doubt, those little People, take your Hair for the Forests of their Country; the Pores full of Liquor, for Fountains; Buboes and Pimples, for Lakes and Ponds; Boils, for Seas; and Defluxions, for Deluges: And when you Comb your self, forwards, and backwards, they take that Agitation, for the Flowing and Ebbing of the Ocean. Doth not Itching make good what I say? What is the little Worm that causes it, but one of these little Animals, which hath broken off from civil Society, that it may set up for a Tyrant in its Country?[25]

Satire may signal the last stages in the decline of a system, but it is usually not designed to *replace* the system. Neither telescope nor microscope was able to shake the foundations of the myth; each merely served to expand the scope of the landscape and heighten humanity's sense of magnitude. Cyrano's "tyrant Louse," like Rabelais' Gargantua and Voltaire's Micromegas, was simply an expansion of the metaphor inspired by scientific discovery, but the cosmic hierarchy remains. Cyrano's voyages manipulate the metaphor but maintain the myth.

The real theme of these pre-Romantic voyages, or so-called works of proto-science fiction, was epitomized admirably in 1605 in the title of Bishop Joseph Hall's bizarre burlesque of travel tales, *Mundus Alter et Idem—Another World and Yet the Same*. Like the century-old *Utopia* of More and the later *New Atlantis* of Bacon and *The Antipodes* of Richard Brome, Hall's hyperbolic satire uses the remote and mysterious landscape of a far land, Terra Australis (or Antarctica), to express moral and philosophical ideas. His geography is more up to date, for he, like Wilkins and Godwin, responded to new discoveries and exploration, but his Antarctica, like the moon of Wilkins and Godwin, was simply a late medieval English landscape extended—another world, yet the same. Another metaphor, but the same myth. The original Latin preface, by one William Knight, and apparently approved by Hall himself, is more significant. Of the mock voyage he is introducing, Knight writes: "The new shall show forth the shape of the old, and you will think that the two are all one. . . . And truly for myself I do believe this world that you are about to discover as if it were new, was the very same that the Platonists dreamed of, that one which they did name, after the ancients, the World Invisible or Idea of the World."[26] In this remarkable passage, Knight is going beyond the metaphor to the very myth itself. To him, the landscape of Antarctica is the world beyond the frame, the world of myth that validates the living power of the metaphor.

The doctrine of plurality of worlds thus provided the landscapes for new voyages of the imagination, but it was not seen therefore as a breakdown of the great Christian world view, rather as an opportunity to confirm it. Many of these pre-Romantic voyages were written by clerics; it would indeed have been strange had they been the vanguards of fragmentation. In fact, their new landscapes were glimpses of paradise, confirmations of faith and prior experience, the unfolding of new chapters in God's eternal plan. New worlds—yet the same.

I have no quarrel with those who wish to label these works "science fiction." But superficial similarities of landscape provide only a superficial concept of science fiction. A voyage to the moon does not make science fiction any more than a voyage to Hell makes Christian allegory. Voyages to the moon and into space have been written throughout recorded history, but only since the Romantic revolution have such voyages reflected the distinct mythic patterns of reversal that created modern science fiction. Science fiction has not yet been born in these pre-Romantic voyages, as wonderful as they are, for the dilemma born of fragmentation lies still in the future.

It is in the shattered landscapes of early nineteenth-century Romantic narratives that science fiction does, in my judgment, appear for the first time. The patterns of reversal that signal the final rejection of the Christian myth, thereby creating a new genre, appear, I think, most clearly and dramatically in Mary Shelley's third novel, *The Last Man*, published in 1826.[27]

The novel begins with the discovery by the "author" in 1818 of the scattered pages of a manuscript in the famous Sibylline Cave in Naples. They are the pages written by Verney, the Last Man. When assembled, they tell the tragic tale of the extinction of the human race by plague. By placing Verney's completed story in the "timeless" Sibylline Cave in the form of an oracular prophecy, making it possible for a manuscript written in the year 2100 to be found in 1818, Shelley shatters the linear flow of time, which in Christian teleology *must* have a stop, and replaces it with a spiraling, indeterminate sequence that turns back upon itself and never ends—for if it did, why would Verney, the Last Man, bother to write a book? The "author" tells us that the chaotic order of the story is explained by the disorder of the "leaves" in the cave—yet the story is, in fact, linear, rigorously ordered, complete, and logical—but in reverse. By metaphorically reversing the flow of time, Shelley destroys generic expectations conditioned by conventional biblical narrative, and produces, literally, a new genre that uses traditional narrative form to destroy traditional narrative form, thereby subverting the Christian *telos* and philosophical world system.

Shelley accomplishes this simply by reversing the Christian narrative of creation, "de-creating" the human race by telling the story of human history in reverse. From the opening page, it is as if the clock of human experience had suddenly begun to run backward, and the characters, although they appear on the surface to live according to the normal forward linearity of time, actually relive in a matter of a quarter century of "real" time the complete history of human life on earth from the nineteenth century *backward* to the creation of Adam.

The England of 2092 is a republic, but politically and socially, it is England of the Regency. With the deadly rise of the plague, contemporary manners and civilized living gradually retrogress. Ordered society collapses, and social entropy increases. At this point, Shelley begins to pepper the text with biblical allusions in reverse historical order. Like an

Old Testament prophet, Verney has visions of plague and death. As the remnant of survivors leave England to seek a better place, Adrian becomes a Moses leading an Exodus to a Promised Land. The vast abandoned resources of civilization, like manna from heaven, provide the wanderers with food and necessities. In France, Adrian has to deal with a false prophet who lures his followers into idolatry, but Adrian destroys him, and leads his flock onward. Later, after wandering through the wilderness of France, Adrian finally mounts the pass through the Jura and beholds the Promised Land, but he drowns a short time later in the Adriatic before reaching it. As the survivors dwindle, Flood imagery increases. In desolated England, Windsor Castle had been an Ark, a "haven and retreat for the wrecked bark of human society."[28] Verney later compares the destruction of humankind by plague to the Flood, and the "perennial flood" of ocean eventually takes his last companions from him. As the four remaining survivors reach Milan, Verney writes that "we made laws for ourselves, dividing our day,"[29] as Adam, in Eden, had ordered his world by fiat. Earlier in the novel, Verney had referred to himself as the "father of all mankind,"[30] and as the Last Man, he ultimately tries to return the cosmos to chaos so he can re-create it in narrative.

> It is all over now—a step or two over those new made graves, and the wearisome way is done. Can I accomplish my task? Can I streak my paper with words capacious of the grand conclusion? Arise, black Melancholy! quit thy Cimmerian solitude! Bring with thee murky fogs from hell, which may drink up the day; bring blight and pestiferous exhalations, which, entering the hollow caverns and breathing places of earth, may fill her stony veins with corruption, so that not only herbage may no longer flourish, the trees may rot, and the rivers run with gall—but the everlasting mountains be decomposed, and the mighty deep putrify, and the genial atmosphere which clips the globe, lose all powers of generation and sustenance. Do this, sad visaged power, while I write, while eyes read these pages.[31]

In an ironic echo of Genesis, the plague takes seven years to destroy humanity and then rests.[32]

Two primary patterns in this audacious work of fiction clearly express the change that produced science fiction. The first is the sense of a future; the second is the fragmentation of the landscape. The two are inextricably related. Any established mythological structure always and necessarily looks to the past. It is, after all, an established system. Its continued vitality relies upon maintenance of the status quo, and the artistic metaphors that give it expression always look—even if the landscape is altered in time or space—to the past, to the epic archetypal events that established and secured the system. In the Christian system especially, there was no future because it was a closed temporal system. From the time of Christ himself, Christians, like Domingo Gonsales, have looked forward to the imminent end of time and the transfiguration of this life into eternity. The Renaissance landscape commemorated the past, and William Knight saw only an ancient Platonic world in Antarctica. In Christianity, there was no future. But in science fiction there is nothing but a future. The ruined temples that often appeared in pre-Romantic landscapes were noble reminders of origin, nostalgic images of the mythic past on which the present is built, but the ruins in science-fiction landscapes are the shattered remnants of a *dead* past, the fragmented strata on which a new future *must* be built. In *The Last Man,* the past is both literally and figuratively destroyed. Verney is not only the Last Man, he is also the First Man, for by recording his chronicle and leaving it in the Cave of Cumaean Sibyl, where it is found *in the past,* he has succeeded in establishing *in narrative* a new myth. Thus, Shelley's novel suggests that it is in narrative, in fiction, that a rebirth, a new totalizing system may emerge. *The Last Man* is the chronicle of the death of the Christian world view, but it is also the Book of Genesis for a new world view—and this was the Genesis of science fiction. It is the old myth reversed, torn down, and then rebuilt in a fictional text.

Mary Shelley has thus established the mythopoeic foundation of science fiction. But note that, as a reversal of time and a reversal of myth, the narrative merely establishes the *conditions* for mythmaking; it does not create literally a new myth. Verney's epic adventure has succeeded only in figuratively destroying the old myth; Verney has not yet established himself as a new mythic archetype—that yet remains in his future, a future that, by Shelley's clever manipulation of the Sibyl's Cave, automatically becomes *our* future as well by means of fictional narrative. This circular process symbolizes the Romantic dilemma. *The Last Man* announces the death of the old myth, but it only dramatizes the need for the new and sets the stage for the acting out of the new. It does not actually create the new. The landscape of the year 2100 is a ruined landscape, a dead landscape, and Verney surveys the remains and ponders his future. With "wild dreams"[33] he stocks a small boat and pushes off into the future, and we know that the greatest adventure is yet to come. It is the archetypal tableau of science fiction, for it symbolizes the future creation of myth, thus implying the present need for myth. It is the present that lives on the shattered landscapes of the old myth and that therefore looks to the future for the reconstruction of myth.

This is the role of landscape in modern science fiction—to dramatize the need for a new totalizing myth in a world fragmented by the loss of the old. Landscapes dominate science fiction, for they set the stage on which humanity is to act out the mythmaking process, and they confront people with the heroic challenges required of mythic transcendence. Science fiction, I repeat, does not create the myth; rather, it dramatizes the need for mythmaking in a world without a vital totalizing myth. Science fiction, then, is not simply mythopoeic—it is *metamythopoeic*. It is the modern world's metaphor for the loss of myth, just as the voyages of Godwin and Wilkins were the pre-Romantic world's metaphor for the expansion and validation of existing myth. "A given culture," writes Hayden White, "is only as strong as its power to convince its least dedicated member that its fictions are truths." We are no longer able to do this for ourselves, for, says White, our "sustaining cultural myths . . . have one by one passed into the category of the fictitious."[34] When we no longer believe in our myths, the only alternative is to create new myths, and it is this need that the landscapes of science fiction dramatize.

The metamythopoeic drama of modern science fiction is most apparent in the landscapes of postholocaust stories. The ruins that litter the postholocaust landscape are the remnants not of civilization but of civilization's myths. The buried Statue of Liberty in the final scene of the film *Planet of the Apes* drives the hero to despair, not because of what it is at that moment—a ruined masterpiece—but because of what it represents to him, a survivor from preholocaust America. Machinery, ruined cities, crumbled highways, the decaying towers of Oxford in Brian Aldiss' *Greybeard,* the buried cathedral in *Riddley Walker,* books, names, a postman's jeep, an unopened letter, even the grocery list in Miller's *A Canticle for Leibowitz*—these are the distillate that remains after our "sustaining cultural myths" have evaporated from the distorted memories of survivors. Like the landscape that Verney surveys, these landscapes are littered with dead myths, and on that same landscape we know that a new myth will be enacted.

Other science-fiction landscapes function in much the same way. The dystopian city, for example, is a representation of one of the

individual myths made possible by the "open" myth of Romanticism—
one of the many tyrannies engendered by the dilemma of Romanticism.
It invariably fails and is destroyed, littering the landscape with its ruins,
and the mythmaking process begins anew. *Logan's Run* is a characteristic example of this type of landscape. The alien planet is a new world, but
unlike Wilkins' new world in the moon, it is not a confirmation of the
existing, living myth, but yet another stage setting on which the process
of mythmaking may be acted out. I believe that nearly all science-fiction
landscapes may be analyzed in this manner, for the acting out of the
process of mythmaking is one of the defining characteristics of modern
science fiction, and the landscape, even if it does not exist in the literal
future, functions as the stage on which the living future grows from the
ruins of the dead past. Landscape is the metaphor that expresses the
"total mythological structure" that shapes it. In a world that has lost its
shaping structure and that, as a result, fragments its loyalties and its
beliefs among countless individual structures, science fiction reflects
the inevitable failure of fragmented existence and dramatizes the need
for a center, for a uniting myth that can reassemble the scattered limbs of
Osiris.

Notes

1. Mark Rose, *Alien Encounters: Anatomy of Science Fiction* (Cambridge:
Harvard Univ. Press, 1981), 36–37.

2. Northrop Frye, *A Study of English Romanticism* (Chicago: Univ. of
Chicago Press, 1982), 4.

3. Ibid., 4.

4. Ibid., 5.

5. Ibid., 5.

6. Morse Peckham, "Toward a Theory of Romanticism," *Romanticism:
Points of View,* ed. Robert F. Gleckner & Gerald E. Enscoe (Englewood Cliffs,
N.J.: Prentice-Hall, 1970), 231–57.

7. D. W. Robertson, Jr., *A Preface to Chaucer* (Princeton: Princeton Univ.
Press, 1963), 239.

8. A. Richard Turner, *The Vision of Landscape in Renaissance Italy*
(Princeton: Princeton Univ. Press, 1966), 33–34.

9. R. R. Haas, "Introduction to the Exhibition," *Landscapes from the
Golden Age* (Grand Rapids: Michigan Council for the Arts catalogue, 1972), 12.

10. Ibid., 16.

11. Luke Herrmann, *British Landscape Painting of the Eighteenth Century*

(New York: Oxford Univ. Press, 1974), 12–91 passim. In Constable, writes Kenneth Clark, "naturalism is raised to a higher mode by his belief that since nature was the clearest revelation of God's will, the painting of landscape, conceived in the spirit of humble truth, could be a means of conveying moral ideas." Both Constable and Wordsworth, Clark continues, "believed that there was something in trees, flowers, meadows and mountains which was so full of the divine that if it were contemplated with sufficient devotion it would reveal a moral and spiritual quality of its own." With the decline of faith, landscape itself has become a religion. (Kenneth Clark, *Landscape Into Art* [New York: Harper & Row, 1976], 151, 230.)

12. Barbara J. Shapiro, *John Wilkins, 1614–1672: An Intellectual Biography* (Berkeley: Univ. of California Press, 1969), 30.

13. Ibid., 30.

14. Ibid., 33.

15. Ibid., 34.

16. Ibid., 31. In "A Discourse Concerning the Beauty of Providence" (1649), a popular sermon delivered at the height of the Civil War, Wilkins offered comfort to those upset by events with his plea to accept things as they are, for they are ordained by God. Wilkins, too, was obviously unhappy with events, but he felt it necessary to accept patiently and submissively a "world gone awry," a doctrine that "led to an affirmation and acceptance of the status quo." (Ibid., 69–70.)

17. Ibid., 40.

18. Ibid., 264.

19. Bishop Francis Godwin, *The Man in the Moone and Nuncius Inanimatus,* ed. Grant McColley, *Smith College Studies in Modern Languages* 19, no. 1 (Oct. 1937): 32–35. Wilkins also earnestly promoted the creation of a single universal language.

20. Ibid., 39.

21. Ibid., 41–42.

22. Ibid., 7.

23. Cyrano de Bergerac, *The Comical History of the States and Empire of the Worlds of the Moon and Sun,* (trans. A. Lovell, A.M. (London, 1687), [2].

24. Ibid., [3–4].

25. Ibid., 101.

26. Bishop Joseph Hall, *The Discovery of a New World,* trans. John Healey, ed. Huntington Brown (Cambridge: Harvard Univ. Press, 1937), 141–42. Wands translates the phrase "Idea of the World" as "archetype of the world." See Bishop Joseph Hall, *Another World and Yet the Same,* trans. & ed. John Millar Wands (New Haven: Yale Univ. Press, 1981), 4.

27. References are to Mary Shelley, *The Last Man,* ed. Hugh J. Luke, Jr. (Lincoln: Univ. of Nebraska Press, 1965).

28. Ibid., 189.

29. Ibid., 313.

30. Ibid., 113.

31. Ibid., 318.

32. Ibid., 310.

33. Ibid., 342.

34. Hayden White, "The Forms of Wildness: Archaeology of an Idea," in *The Wild Man Within,* ed. Edward Dudley & Maximillian E. Novak (Pittsburgh: Univ. of Pittsburgh Press, 1972), 6.

18

"The Adjutant":
Suggestions for Maps in Time and Space
from Greene to Johnson to Lem
Donald M. Hassler

> Extravagant theories . . . in those parts of philosophy where our knowl-
> edge is yet imperfect, are not without their use. . . . since natural objects
> are allied to each other by many affinities, every kind of theoretic
> distribution of them adds to our knowledge by developing some of their
> analogies.
>
> —Erasmus Darwin, *The Botanic Garden*, 1789

As I ponder the topic of "mindscapes," one set of images pointing toward a cluster of questions suggested by the images comes to mind in what some may consider too self-conscious an indulgence of my own mind. Furthermore, a remark by David Samuelson caused me to have more thoughts, or doubts, about what I have written as a response to this question of mindscapes. He said that the question includes *everything* in its answer and so is meaningless. I generally find those sorts of questions the most interesting, and so am always coming up with meaningless answers—that my colleagues point out to me. Specifically, though, Samuelson's problems about "meaning," which is really a problem about defining standards and even rank-ordering evaluations (some writing is true genre science fiction and therefore good; other writing is bad), was also a large problem with the Enlightenment men of the eighteenth century and with critics of literature and art of that time. My essay is about that problem of definitions, of genre, of evaluation—and about some extensions of the problem into modern writing. In fact, the epigraph above taken from one of the notoriously "bad" writers of the eighteenth century anticipates what I will have to say about a small piece of writing that even its author, a modern critic of both distinction and

257

firm distinctions, has himself relegated to the scrap heap of the "bad." But like the picturesque of the eighteenth century, my notion of mindscapes toys with the "bad"—despite, or maybe because of, David Samuelson.

Moreover, if metageneric discussions such as these are to mean anything, they must go beyond the narrow periodization and rigid genre consistencies that usually police literary studies. I am grateful for such an open topic. It promises to help me open up recesses in my own work and my own reading that the decorums and conventions of scholarship may have kept hidden. And as I have had the hunch for some time now that the two categories of reading and scholarship I am most drawn to (eighteenth-century literature and modern science fiction) are close kindred in some way, this topic allows further speculative mapping of my hunch. As an aside, I might say that I am grateful, also, for precedents set at the Eaton Conference by scholars such as Paul Alkon and George Guffey for talking about these links across time between the eighteenth century and modern science fiction. Finally, the three writers I will be talking most about are not themselves limited just to imaginative writing or "high art" but are also scholars with a serious self-conscious interest in mapping the mind. Hence the results of this tentative investigation have less to do with artistic and final effects of taste or aesthetics in discrete works of literature than with the methodological bases of the investigation itself. Like all maps, I suppose, this essay then is intended to be a miniature, small-scale approximation of the vast spaces, or "mindscapes," it means to chart.

The three writers I will discuss and place, perhaps, at three compass points on my crude map though, significantly, all on the same map (the fourth point on my speculative compass will be mentioned in a moment) are Samuel Johnson from the eighteenth century and Stanislaw Lem and Donald Greene from our time. The last name is the least recognizable because he has chosen to identify himself primarily as a scholar—though the other two are by no means mere artists in their self-conceptions of their work and in our understandings of these works. But I am indebted to Professor Greene for bringing this essay into focus for me, and it is his work that is the most problematic for discussion in a chapter like this. So I introduce the image set and cluster of questions first in the context of his work as a rigorous scholar and as a writer. And the questions are fundamental questions of methodology that have concerned us since the eighteenth century.

Is the mind best imaged as a Gothic building with mysterious recesses? (Here I have in mind my fourth compass point, Horace Walpole, so close to Johnson in the eighteenth century yet so far that I cannot integrate *The Castle of Otranto* fully into this discussion though it remains as a haunting presence.) Or are we better served to image the mind as a cut-and-dried barracks that must continually be policed? Moving from Walpole to a modern Gothic, I might illustrate the opposition implied by my two questions with the familiar contrast in *The Left Hand of Darkness* between the Gothic mysteries of buildings in Karhide and the rigid discipline of Orgoreyn barracks; and certainly the proliferation of the architectural metaphor from Pope's grottos to the latest "city" in science fiction is widespread. Clearly in our time, however, and in the study of eighteenth-century literature in particular, Donald Greene would police the barracks. Here is what a colleague says about Greene, who sounds to me now like David Samuelson, in the recent *Festschrift*[1] done in his honor:

> It was once said of Donald Greene that he thinks if he could correct eighteenth-century studies, he could save the world . . . . that intellectual rigor which denounces abstract speculation . . . describes Greene's technique in eighteenth-century studies, and indeed, as Johnson himself would point out, indicates the way of honesty, evidence, and caution without which the world would in fact be lost. (xvii)

Yet I find in this very *Festschrift* that characterizes so clearly the policing, scholarly rationality of Greene that there are maps, in fact, to the mysterious recesses of his own mind. The scholar who would not now condone speculation was a poet in his early years, and I think it is significant that he chooses both to mention this and not to authorize the inclusion of his poems in the list of his writings. He writes, "The location of this last, in particular, I have no intention of disclosing" (471). He does have listed, however, a short story that he published in the November 1951 issue of the *Atlantic Monthly*.[2]

Such discoveries in a *Festschrift* for a distinguished contemporary scholar may have little significance except for the fact that Greene's presence and his firm strictures against just the sort of readings I find most provocative have haunted both my rational working methods and my own recessed impulses for some time. In fact, the careful editing, or "policing," that Greene manages in this list of his writings may be the nudge that started me in this current investigation of hidden rooms because he chose not to list a small controversy that he and I and Walter Jackson Bate carried on in the pages of *Studies in Burke and His Time* in 1972–73. I think the neglect of Bate here (never mind the exclusion of my short piece), which is centered on Greene's harsh review of Bate's book on the burden of the past, seems to be consistent with Greene's continual attempt to clarify, or more accurately to deny, exactly the mysterious maps that are my topic in this essay. These, ultimately, must be deeply psychological or Freudian maps that chart the twisting and turnings under the pressures of precursors—or the burden of the past. In any case, I searched out Greene's nearly hidden *Atlantic* "first" story in the dark recesses of our library (the poems may come later) in order to discover what he wanted to police from his own work.

The protagonist in "The Adjutant" is a scholarly and morally well-tuned office manager at a training camp for "paratroops"; and the action turns smoothly, reminding me of a Lionel Trilling fiction, on nice moral distinctions in the mind of this adjutant over the delicate question of why he admires so deeply the man of action that he himself cannot be. He is a frail man with weak eyes. As I read Greene's story of the Second World War buried in the stacks of late-century Kent State University, I got the image clearly that just as the character in the story feels inferior to men of action so the scholar in us stands in awe of the artist. And, in part, it is because we know the artist so well through our scholarly maps that the sense of awe as well as the mixture of repressing and revealing are so strong. Speculating about why the scholarly adjutant had requested assignment to the paratroops, Greene writes:

> He did not tell them that it was because he was a student of literature. He had been with these fine men before, many times, on the plains of Troy. [Then a long heroic catalog follows.] He loved their courage, their aliveness; he was glad to be near them, if only as a humble camp follower. (68)[3]

I have little doubt that my act here of ferreting "The Adjutant" from its hiding place in the stacks in order to place it near the work of one of Greene's greatest heroes and then to place Johnson himself next to Lem will arouse Greene's more characteristic desire to police or correct. But I do mean to persist, if I may, with the notion that there are maps of mental geography in our scholarly libraries, perhaps the best maps for such psychic territory, that are at least comparable to the speculative maps of a Mesklin or an Arrakis. And as with most speculations, these mental maps of scholars cross over time boundaries. In fact, these are always metageneric maps in which the scholar and the artist, the mapper and the mapped, or the text itself and commentary on the text intermingle; and I think it is no violation of sense to search across time periods for examples of such self-referencing texts, or maps of mind. Here is the well-known architecture image that Johnson places at the start of his description of "The Happy Valley" in *Rasselas*[4] and that B. H. Bronson in the Rinehart teaching edition notes must have been " 'planted' for future narrative development":

> [It] was so large as to be fully known to none but some ancient officers who successively inherited the secrets of the place, was built as if suspicion herself had dictated the plan. To every room there was an open and secret passage. . . . They then closed up the opening with marble, which was never to be removed but in the utmost exigencies of the kingdom. (609)

Even though we must notice with Greene and others that Johnson would police matters for both logical clarity and moral niceness as rigorously as any scholar-writer in modern times (the rooms are closed up), nevertheless he clearly makes room for the hidden recesses and mysterious chambers. Moreover, Walter Jackson Bate, in particular among recent critics, has pointed out how reluctant and even uncertain Johnson is when he writes what he knows he is going to sign, when he himself approaches closest to the mysterious recesses of artistic creation. Like the adjutant, Johnson wants to be near what he cannot totally become himself; and so his continual maps of *terra incognita* are always maps that are self-conscious and self-referencing.

In modern science fiction, Stanislaw Lem is one of the most interesting examples of the scholar-artist; and though many texts of his with their didactic, intricate, and wry effects might remind us of both Johnson and Greene (Greene and Lem both had significant involvements with the Second World War and are about the same age), I find images in as well as commentary about his 1971 text translated as *The Futurological Congress*[5] particularly suggestive for the ideas in this essay. Not only is the protagonist, Ijon Tichy, both a man of action and a scholar attending the Congress but also the initial setting for the Congress is a building and a sewer system immensely equipped with mysterious recesses and hidden areas. Later in the story, the time confusions and manipulations of the body itself of Tichy leave little doubt that "correct" and well-policed readings of the text would probably be wrong readings. In other words, both the promise of clear maps (no one tries to be clearer than Johnson and his followers led now by Greene) and the denial of clarity in favor of mysterious recesses or *terra incognita* lie side by side in the Lem text—just as in the Johnson text and in the Greene *Festschrift*. A very recent reading of *The Futurological Congress* by Robert M. Philmus[6] helps makes this point because it emphasizes the metageneric and self-referencing qualities in the text: "The coherence of *Futurological Congress* [like a good scholarly mapper, Philmus makes clear and detailed points about the use of articles in Polish and so uses an English title different from the Kandel translation] resides in its *being* [italics his] what it is significantly about" (315).

Hence I conclude by suggesting again that some of the better maps for mental geography, that is images that touch on some of the speculative concerns of modern science fiction, come from the act of scholarship itself and that scholarship, in spite of what it may say about itself, is more accurately mapped as a large, even fantastically enormous and intricate building such as both the Johnson palace and the Lem hotel rather than as a well-policed barracks. Even the most pedantic adjutant, dedicated to keeping all his papers in order, knows this at heart and he himself often may provide a good map of the *terra incognita*. Thus with such maps in hand we may look for science-fictional effects in the strangest places and in distant time periods while, also, working at clear definitions and descriptions of the genre.

Notes

1. Paul J. Korshin & Robert R. Allen, eds., *Greene Centennial Studies: Essays Presented to Donald Greene in the Centennial Year of the University of Southern California* (Charlottesville: Univ. Press of Virginia, 1984).

2. Donald Greene, "The Adjutant," *Atlantic Monthly* 188 (Nov. 1951): 67–72.

3. In addition to some comments on his role as a scholar, Greene himself has written the following on the background to his story and on the "mystery" of how he narrowly avoided a military rather than an academic career. I cite a letter to Paul Alkon, dated May 9, 1987, from which Greene has given permission to quote:

> There are not really too many "mysterious recesses" of my mind disclosed in the story. As in most fiction my protagonist owes some details to myself—notably the "weak eyes" (fully correctable by glasses, but army medics were always changing the required standards). But I was never "frail," nor I think was my protagonist. I was quite a good technical gunner, and loved the complex intellectual theory

involved in maneuvering the big coastal and anti-aircraft guns. But thanks to my academic background and experience, I kept finding myself assigned to administrative chores. For nearly a year I was acting commander of an AA battery, when my boss was ill. Obviously with a view to preparing me for higher things, I was sent to the Canadian equivalent of a "staff college," and given the rare grade of D (distinguished).

I should have foreseen it, but idiotically I didn't. One day without warning I was called before a board of senior officers and quizzed about administrative matters. My answers were apparently accurate but not enthusiastic. As a matter of fact, I was somewhat resentful about having been called away from a long-anticipated battery exercise, with real live ammunition. At last the chairman sensed that something was wrong, and asked, "Are you really interested in being promoted to an appointment as a staff officer?" I said as politely as I could, "Not in the least." I preferred to stay with the guns and the gunners. That ended the interview, rather acrimoniously. I suppose, if I had acquiesced, I might have ended the war a colonel, instead of a mere captain, and goodness knows that might have happened after that.

I think my repulsion by the idea of a staff appointment may have owed a good deal to my reading of memoirs and novels of WW I, where staff officers play a poor role by comparison with line officers. (Well, they go back at least to the "popinjay" in *1 Henry IV,* 1:iii). When the war was nearing its end, and the authorities came to the conclusion that the Japs were no longer interested in the Pacific Coast of North America, I was offered the adjutant's job at the paratrooper training center, which appealed to me for essentially romantic reasons. Paratrooping was something new and exotic. The rank and file were all carefully selected volunteers, and a bright and attractive lot of kids they were. But disillusionment set in, and that of course is the "theme" of the story.

4. Samuel Johnson, *"Rasselas," Poems, and Selected Prose,* ed. B. H. Bronson, 3rd ed. (San Francisco: Rinehart, 1971).

5. Stanislaw Lem, *The Futurological Congress,* trans. Michael Kandel (New York: Harcourt Brace Jovanovich, 1985).

6. Robert M. Philmus, *"Futurological Congress* as Metageneric Text," *Science-Fiction Studies* 40 (Nov. 1986): 313–28.

Examples: A Forum

I

The Ultimate Mindscape: Dante's *Paradiso*

Jean-Pierre Barricelli

> *O voi che siete in piccioletta barca,*
> *desiderosi d'ascoltar, seguiti*
> *dietro al mio legno che cantando varca,*
> *tornate a riveder li vostri liti:*
> *non vi mettete in pelago, chè, forse,*
> *perdendo me, rimarreste smarriti.*
> *L'acqua ch'io prendo già mai non si corse.*
>
> (*Par.* 2.1–7)
>
> *[O ye who in a little bark, eager*
> *to listen, have followed behind my ship*
> *that singing makes her way,*
> *turn back to see your shores again;*
> *do not put forth on the deep, for, perhaps*
> *losing me, you would be left bewildered.*
> *The waters I take were never sailed before.]*

This epigraph is Dante's way of telling us that, if we have had trouble understanding the poem to this point, from the *Inferno* through the *Purgatorio,* we had better put down the book because the final third of the journey through the hereafter will present insurmountable conceptual problems.

The bark, we know, stands for human intelligence, which now must be nourished and furbished entirely differently from the accustomed manner of ordinary mortals. Dante's word for it is "transhumanize" *(transumanar)*:

> *Transumanar significar*
> *per verba*

267

> *non si porìa*
> (Par. *1.70–71*)
> *[To transhumanize with words cannot be defined.]*

It suggests a passing beyond humanity that defies verbalization. Given the identify of *seeing* and *knowing* that the poet develops throughout the *Paradiso,* the spiritual landscape becomes the ultimate mindscape. As the pilgrim begins his ascent through the heavenly spheres, he questions the ratio of God's love that reaches the souls assigned to a lower sphere, like that of the Moon or of Mercury, as compared with those assigned to an upper sphere, like that of Saturn or the Fixed Stars, and is informed that where perfect bliss exists everywhere, no soul can yearn for a higher location. Where harmony and fulfillment prevail, there is no lower class of the blessed, for so God has established,

> ". . . *come noi sem di soglia in soglia*
> *per questo regno, a tutto il regno piace*
> *com'allo re ch'a suo voler ne invoglia.*
> *E in la sua volontade è nostra pace:*
> *ell'è quel mare al qual tutto si move*
> *ciò ch'ella cria e cha natura face."*
> *Chiaro mi fu allor come ogni dove*
> *in cielo è paradiso . . .*
> (Par. *3.82–89*)

> [". . . *our rank from height to height*
> *through this kingdom pleases the whole kingdom*
> *as it does the king who wills us his will.*
> *And in his will is our peace:*
> *it is that sea to which all things move,*
> *both what it creates and what nature makes."*
> *Then it becomes clear to me that everywhere*
> *in heaven is paradise . . .]*

Perfection is the balance between desire and satisfaction, and this is the condition of the blessed.

The "untranshumanized" mind, however, that grapples with human logic, reason, and the senses, including that of sight, still perceives geographically, fashioning the distances of sightscapes from the Earth-hugging Circle of Fire to the remote Empyrean of the Godhead into landscapes. The puzzle of seeming geographical disparity—that is, of distance physically sensed but metaphysically denied—is finally solved for Dante by stereopsis, or a flexible three-dimensional vision that can move variously leveled objects onto the same plane, the way the bottom drain of a swimming pool seems from the surface much closer than it is. This stereoscopic experience Dante gains toward the end of the *Paradiso* as his vision is about to achieve perfection: the Mystic Rose, in which the blessed are ranked tier on tier as if in a stadium, scintillatingly white and basking in God's eternal radiance. Even so, the pilgrim sees not the Rose directly but a vision of it reflected in the sea of that radiance.

> *E come clivo in acqua di suo imo*
> *si specchia, quai per vedersi adorno,*
> *quando è nel verde e nei fioretti opimo,*
> *sì, soprastando al lume intorno intorno,*
> *vidi specchiarsi in più di mille soglie*
> *quanto di noi là su fatto ha ritorno.*
> *E se l'infimo grado in sè raccoglie*
> *sì grande lume, quanta è la larghezza*
> *di questa rosa nell'estreme foglie!*
> *La vista mia nell'ampio e nell'altezza*
> *non si smarriva, ma tutto prendeva*
> *il quanto e il quale di quella allegrezza.*
> *Presso e lontano, lì, nè pon nè leva;*
> *chè dove Dio sanza mezzo governa,*
> *la legge natural nulla rileva.*
>
> (Par. 30.109–123)

> [And as a hillside is mirrored at its foot
> in water, as if to see itself adorned
> when it is decked with grass and flowers,
> so I saw, rising above the light all around
> in more than a thousand tiers,
> as many of us who have won return above.
> And if the lowest rank gathers in
> so much light, then what must be the size
> of this rose in its highest leaves!
> In that breadth and height my vision
> did not go astray, for it absorbed
> the extent and quality of that rejoicing.
> There, near and far do not add or subtract;
> for where God governs directly,
> natural law is of no effect.]

Thus is "his will our peace." Dante's paradisal mindscape blends the

Circle of Fire and the Moon with the Fixed Stars and the Empyrean and all spheres in between. He is now beyond hindrance from distance, beyond the limiting conditions of time and space. In a way, the poet transhumanizes *himself,* setting for himself a superverbal challenge: that of rising through nine spheres in thirty-three cantos and producing for the reader ever brighter, ever more luminous, ever more refulgent impressions, beginning with the first which is *already* totally resplendent.

And one of the many miracles of the miraculous poem is that the poet succeeds. Apart from the entrancing atmosphere provided by the music of the spheres, Dante relies on a noncontrastive array of colors: white, yellow, silver, gold, and a sprinkling of pastels; on constantly reshaped images of diaphanous water (in Scripture, after all, a river symbolizes divine grace); on recurring and intensifying references to even greater light, sharpened with neologisms to abet the mystification (*circunfulgere* [*Par.* 30.49], for instance, meaning literally "to circumshine"); and on linguistic devices, primarily the use of the vowel *i,* the highest-sounding phoneme, which builds like a crescendo from canto I to canto 33, wonderfully aligned with the verb *to see* and its many *i* sounds in Italian (see, for example, the triple rhyme on *vidi* [*Par.* 30.95–97–99], meaning "I saw"—a verbal insistence reminiscent of I *John* 1.1–3, or the rhymes on double *i*s like *invii/disii/finii* relating to "penetration/desire/end" [*Par.* 33.44–46–48]). Indeed, the 145 verses of the final canto contain 422 *i* sounds, or otherwise put, only 6 verses are abandoned without such a sound. The effect is one of uplifting musical resonances that shape as otherworldly a geography as only a mind that has passed beyond humanity can fathom.

Only by creating such a mindscape of sounds and visions, in which the key concept (imitating metaphorically the action of divine grace) is *penetration* or *interpenetration,* can the three concentric yet equal circles of the Godhead-Trinity on the final page make sense—transhumanized sense. Totally intangible, as this ultralogical mindscape must be especially when his sight reels blinded by the culminating view of God, Dante thinks he has a memory of a vision that is the sense of a feeling that shapes a flashing intuition. His journey is the longest on record, not because it went *outward,* scientifically, like that of Ulysses (*Inferno* 25), but *inward,* humanistically—a journey into the mind.

2

Pascal's Terror

Gregory Benford

The silence of those infinite spaces terrifies me.

—Blaise Pascal, 1623–1662

Jean Cocteau, in the first volume of his diaries, remarked that André Gide "has never experienced the discomfort of infinity." To the reserved French mind of that time perhaps infinity was simply too messy, too unconstrained, to be admitted into experience.

But an earlier Frenchman had seen that the problem of infinity opened by modern science was basic. Most awful in the perspectives opening to the seventeenth-century mind was that *silence*.

To Pascal, a man in love with the absolute, whether in the calculus of probabilities or in his acute theology, that refusal of the universe to tip its hand, to lend purpose to human action, was terrifying. Though Aristotle had said "either an outright denial or an outright acknowledgment of the being of the infinite leads to many impossibilities," Pascal had to struggle with a genuinely infinite real universe, and not merely the mathematical infinities of Greek mathematics.

Enumerating the Abyss

Astronomy had thrown open the window and it could not be shut again. Distances beyond human ken seemed to rob our lives of purpose. On so vast a stage, who could plausibly believe that we were at stage center?

The Greeks had an uncanny knack for catching the scent of problems long before they were truly understood. Infinity was no exception. Their word for it was *apeiron,* which meant unbounded—but also indefinite, chaotic, totally disordered. Aristotle said, "being infinite is a privation, not prefection but the absence of limit."

The desire for a limit is basic in us. I can well remember the first time I felt a creeping fear at the idea of a quicksand universe that went on and on, into which I sank.

The problem has not gone away. John Updike keeps wrestling with it, particularly in his overtly theological novels such as *A Month of Sundays*. His *Roger's Version* is expressly about the argument from design, which Hume supposedly disposed of long ago but which keeps cropping up in such newfangled guises as the astrophysicists' Anthropic Principle. (This hotly debated thesis holds that we can "predict" many of the properties of the universe because if matters were different, we would not exist.)

Saul Bellow keeps nibbling at the vacancy of "realistic" life (and literature) beside the universe's yawning gulf. Less intellectual authors ruminate less acutely. Normal Mailer tries to punch it in the jaw, but his reach seldom makes contact unless he slides into fantasy, as in *Ancient Evenings*.

Some have noticed that you can go the other way, approaching the infinite through the infinitesimal. Physics abounds with quantities that become infinite as dimensions become tiny. The force between electrons does this as they approach each other. Black holes pack infinite mass into infinitesimal space. A singularity is an infinity you can hold in the palm of your hand. This development in modern science led to infinities that are whole entities with definite boundaries, rather than as an ever-expanding frontier without definite boundaries.

William Blake saw a world in a grain of sand. This image reverberates through the miniature worlds of Jorge Luis Borges, often with an air of seeking to purge immensity by retreating into the labyrinthine minute. His most anxious works, though, prefer the denumerably infinite. His garden of forking paths reduces the infinities of time to an enclosed area, framing the paradox. His library of Babel opens endlessly and meaninglessly, since it contains all truths and all lies, with no way to tell the difference.

Some of these literary methods of grappling with infinity seem to come from a kind of cultural agoraphobia. In a way this is easy to understand. Consider the Hilbert Hotel, named for the German mathematician David Hilbert. A customer comes, only to find that, though the hotel is infinitely large, it is filled. So he proposes that the room clerk simply move the person in room 1 to 2, and the occupant of 2 to 3, and so on. Presto!—a new room is available. The point is that common sense is useless here. One plus one equals two, but one plus infinity always equals infinity.

The nineteenth-century discoveries in the mathematics of infinity have led to a cool knowledge of analytical properties, but no deeper gut feeling. Physicists subtract away infinities in their calculations, arranging cancellations so that the masses of observed particles come out right—but they do not fathom what is going on any more than Pascal did.

Some authors seem to deny that infinity is interesting, since, finally, it is all the same. Alas, no. There are clear distinctions between the kinds of infinitely large collections of things (sets). This was proved by Cantor in the nineteenth century, who showed that infinities can have different sizes. The set of irrational numbers, for example, is bigger than the set of whole numbers; they are called *trans*finite. In principle one can count the rationals; the irrationals, never.

Infinity thus confounds common sense. To underline this, consider a one-dimensional universe. Cantor showed that such a world (a line, really) has just as many mathematical points in it as a two-dimensional world—for example, the plane of this page of paper. There are as many points on this page as there are in the whole book—indeed, in all books! Or in our entire three-dimensional world, or a hypothetical four-dimensional universe.

This astonishing fact, flatly noncommonsensical, mingles with our knowledge that the physical universe may indeed be infinite. Our imaginations cannot avoid infinite classes of things, and our telescopes report equally terrifying vistas.

Averting Our Eyes

Italo Calvino's science-fictional works, such as *Cosmicomics,* often reflect a way of joking away the immensities, a common response. In "The Denial of Death," Ernest Becker suggests that humans strike dramatic attitudes when they encounter reminders of "the suction of infinity." Partly this fear lies in the incomprehensible nature of matters infinite, or as one schoolboy put it, "Infinity is where things happen that don't." Euclidean space lets straight lines meet at infinity, but nobody goes there, so it does not matter. Or does it?

People *care* about infinity—vaguely, perhaps, but feelingly. Giordano Bruno, a sixteenth-century cosmologist who announced the infinite plurality of worlds, died at the stake for his troubles. The universe we know today is about a hundred billion light years across, a distance that tumbles into the pit of meaninglessness number.

I think science fiction should address the problem of infinity more clearly than conventional fiction, which often merely broods about it. In fact, many modern Anglo Saxon texts evade the promise of the strangeness and immensity of, for example, other cultures (the infinity of human facets). "The Jewel in the Crown," to pick a recent novel series turned into upscale TV drama, promises to confront India in its richness, but ends up being about (surprise, surprise) the English class system. Science fiction may have inherited some of these reflexes.

After all, how otherwise to account for the pervasive use of faster-than-light travel? Of course one can cite Aristotle's unities of time and place, which heighten dramatic power. Going to the stars becomes very much like taking the stellar subway; you do not even get to look at the view. Collapsing the true scale of the universe this way robs it of significance and power.

Notice that swearing off the faster-than-light drug can have grand effects. Poul Anderson's *Tau Zero* takes a frail crew at speeds razor-close to light speed, employing the relativistic time-stretching physics allows. Their payoff, as they lose all contact with humanity, is a vast view of the evolution of a (closed!) universe as it swells, pauses, and then squeezes back down into an again-primordial fireball. Refusing to subvert the size of those vast spaces lifts the novel above the myriad dull quickie galactic empire stories.

The urge to diminish nature's scale runs deep. Two centuries after Pascal, another Frenchman sent an artillery shell to a fictional moon and began in earnest another subverting strategy: filling the infinities with people. Pascal thought of the heavens as forever serene and outside the human realm; Verne made it a subway stop. Of course, this savvy move made human adventure narratives possible, and all the attendant analogies with the West's frontiers. This persists; Heinlein especially depicts the stars as frontier, raw and waiting to be tamed, rather than as a wilderness immense in mystery—the unknowable, the huge, the nonhuman.

To map is to claim. And once the galaxy was partitioned, weighed, its gravid pulses known, to some extent science itself had domesticated the infinite. The process proceeds eternally, as we now peer back at distant quasars, seeking to see the core fires of the first birthing galaxies.

Very few science-fiction narratives occupy this grand scale—largely because it is fearsomely hard to populate it plausibly with people, but also, I suspect, because of that persistent terror.

Cosmological measurements of the mass density in the universe imply that the governing geometry of space-time is indeed open, which means the universe will continue to evolve to larger scales and flatter local space-time—forever. Unless there is about ten times as much mass around than we can detect (which means it must be in the form of either dead black holes or energetic, superlight particles), our prospects are indeed infinite, cold, and slow.

Consider, too, the beginning. Immensities lurk there, as well.

In the 1970s Roger Penrose and Stephen Hawking showed that Einstein's gravitational equations inevitably implied a true singularity as the origin of our universe. Penrose proclaimed his "cosmic censorship hypothesis," which holds that God abhors a "naked" singularity—that is, one we can actually see. No one knows if this hypothesis is right. It is imposed by fit to banish the enormous mathematical obstacles a naked singularity would present to theorists.

Now Hawking seeks a way to dethrone that primordial singularity by finding a probability function that describes the various states the universe could be in—a "wave function" of the universe. Though some physical effects would remain singular, the wave function would be continuous through the very birth of everything—indeed, would describe how God made choices in creating the universe.

So it goes in science, then—the desire to find a deeper essence, a truer key that persists smoothly, that banishes the reality of infinity. This desire is a common thread in all human activities.

Portentous Silence

But at least the universe is filled with *some*thing.

Emptiness itself signals infinity, too, and our defense against that is to either fill it (perhaps with ourselves) or wall it off. This has the quality of making a deal with infinity, allowing it limited expression. (Pascal himself had the impulse to bargain, even with God. His famous wager holds that skeptics might as well believe in God, since there is no loss if He does not exist after all.)

Thus another strategy for avoiding the implications of true infinities lies in the constructions of great artifacts. I remember seeing my first skyscraper when I was ten (and thinking what an ugly name that was). My mother pointed to it outside the train station in Chicago and said, "Gosh, doesn't it make you feel insignificant?"

I remember frowning up at the great stack of stones and thinking, "Why should it? *We* made *it,* not the other way around."

I suspect something like this animates Larry Niven's *Ringworld,* Asimov's Trantor, Bob Shaw's *Orbitsville.* The striking facet of the Ringworld is that it is indeed so vast that you cannot plausibly explore it in a human lifetime—but you can *see* it all in one glance, hanging in the sky. This sense of locality promises closure, relief from true immensity rather than embracing it.

Perhaps humanity equally cannot stand emptiness, the flip side of infinity. For Pascal feared the meaningless of it, the absence of any hint that human effort had pith and substance. Nearly all science fiction attempts to answer this supreme agoraphobia by populating the yawning abyss. The longing for alien contact seems to fulfill a parallel need.

Yet this is a curious reassurance, since on the face of it such a discovery will deprive us of what many still believe to be a true uniqueness. So I think the clue behind the longings of UFO fans and "Star Trek" episodes and endless science-fiction texts is that aliens give us companionship, making the infinities comfy.

A truly strange and unknowable alien undercuts this comfortable feeling, and thus is quite rare in science fiction. Similarly, the use of time in science fiction so often veers away from truly labyrinthine implications. The infinities of causal loops in Robert Heinlein's "By His Bootstraps" and onward are often seen as horrifying. A standard cliché of such loop stories is that the narrator ends trapped in one, feeling himself or herself tiring, filling with angst and ennui.

But this betrays and denies the nature of a truly fixed causal loop, for the victim caught in one cannot experience loss of energy or accumulation of knowledge—everything really *will* be the same each cycle. The infinity of time becomes a cage that implicitly denies the premise—but even that seems preferable to the abyss of meaningless repetition.

So what interests me most is science fiction that does not subvert the infinite. I prefer Olaf Stapledon's *Star Maker,* which many find hard to read. Their difficulty probably stems from the novel's resolute refusal to ground its vision in concrete detail, to give the feeling of a mapped territory. Instead, immensity is seen abstractly, its ponderous forces unrolling through measureless time.

By contrast, the novel *2001* made its approach to the infinite clearly symbolic. Taking another tack, the film *2001* grounded the implied infinity in hard surfaces, such as the eighteenth-century bedroom wherein human mortality plays itself out.

Like the alien, the infinite is a subject best crept up on. Much must be implied, the reader must be caught by sudden visions. I attempted something like this in a novel, *Against Infinity*, only to find much later that an entire symbolic undercurrent seemed to be working to other purposes. The enormous is sometimes a legitimate metaphor for the infinite, but the core of the mystery lies in the difference.

So in the end, our ceaseless grappling with infinity demands art of a peculiarly intellectual kind. Yet it should carry the exhilaration of throwing open the windows onto uncountable vistas.

Should we feel dwarfed by infinity? Physically, perhaps. But our imaginations, both in mathematics and physics, have transcended our bodily limitations. Cantor discovered the species of the infinite. Hawking may find a way to introduce new physics into that primordial singularity, perhaps plumping it forth with the yeasty forth of quantum processes.

And in literature? The essence of enormity must be attacked indirectly—by leaving in the narrative a feeling for the noncentrality of humans themselves. And by finding fresh expressions for the prospect that unlimited space and time promises more, finally, than our ultimately futile attempts at closure and domestication.

3
The Revolutionary Mindscape
Gary Kern

Everyone is a realist. Just as, according to Socrates, every man chooses what he believes to be good, so, according to Roman Jakobson, every writer—or at least every "realistic" writer—writes what he believes to be real. With Socrates, good and bad are absolutes; with Jakobson, reality, or rather its reflection in literary realism, is historically mutable.[1] The realistic writer seeks to reproduce the reality he experiences as faithfully as possible—to write "realistically." After he has written, another writer agrees with him and writes in the same manner; a school is founded. Whatever its name, it claims to have a firm grip on reality. A newcomer disagrees. No longer excited by the devices of the realistic school, which have become conventional, he alters them, changes their emphases, deforms them, in his own attempt to capture the reality he experiences. Others agree with him. Thus we have a series of moments in the literary reproduction of reality, which build a school, tear it down, and build another. Realism, symbolism, expressionism, futurism—all claim greater insight, understanding, and reproduction of reality than their predecessor.

Of this process we may say that each school creates a "mindscape," a literary construction of a time and place that is meant to match the reality in the nonliterary world. And each individual writer, of course, creates his own personal mindscape within the general school. All these mindscapes may be compared among themselves and with that already constructed by the reader. They are fixed in time and transitory. Just as realistic painting is subject to conventions, changes in perception, and the rise and fall of schools, so no art form, not even photography, can lay hold of the world's physical and mental landscape and keep it for all time.

Where then is fantasy? It distinguishes itself from all would-be realistic schools by creating a mindscape fundamentally different from the observable external world. It would not call itself realistic, in the sense of reproducing reality, yet would claim a special reality for its creations. As a product of imagination, it lays claim to the remoter reality—the future, the rare occurrence, the transcendent reality of the mind.

To illustrate these matters, we could make a scheme in which ongoing reality is given the capital letter R1, R2, R3; each successive school claiming to grasp reality—the small letter r1, r2, r3; and each school of fantasy literature—the letters f1, f2, f3, as follows:

$$R1: r1 - f1$$
$$R2: r2 - f2$$
$$R3: r3 - f3$$

Here R changes in time, but does not nullify itself. It remains eternally real and forces fresh interpretations. The schools r1, r2, r3 each cancel out the predecessor. When a whole string of them has been canceled out, each may be read with historical awareness and accorded a greater or lesser degree of reality as we know it. In the string f1, f2, f3, each does not refute the predecessor, since f1 may contain unicorns and f2 androids: both are departures from realism, but in singular directions. They may draw upon their predecessors, as if upon real happenings (e.g., the utopian tradition of Plato, More, Skinner; the robot tradition). Yet they are not immune to the ravages of time, as clearly one may appear more modern than another. Also, insofar as reality supersedes any of their predictions or exceeds any of their inventions, they are made obsolete, mere literary monuments within the continuing tradition.

Fantasy must distinguish itself from all other literature, in effect treat all the other schools as if they were a single school of realism. It is this squeezed-down realism, this commonplace way of describing things, that fantasy seeks to blow up, to make four-dimensional, unusual, and surprising. This is not always an easy task. Against a slowly unfolding tradition of realistic literature, or a steady trade in standardized pulp novels, it is always possible to think up new tricks, some unpredictable turns in the depiction of reality. But prolonged periods of calm suddenly explode in change: the evolution of forms is punctuated with radical transformations, new relationships to reality.[2] In terms of literature, the big R presents dramatic problems to all the little r's, and so the little f's have a difficult time distinguishing themselves. This is a period of revolution.

After October 1917, all Russian writers were pressed to discover new ways to depict reality, because the world known to them had suddenly changed. The old little r—symbolism—was out of date: it quickly transformed itself, went into hiding, and exerted its influence surreptitiously. By whatever name—neorealism, proletarianism, futurism—each new writer and group of writers made a claim to capture the new reality. However, the big R now seemed fantastic by comparison with its predecessor; the little r's of necessity became fantastic by comparison with theirs, and the little f's experienced an identity crisis. A fantastic realism appeared, well before the magical realism of Latin American literature. It was one that gave birth to a literature of revolutionary mindscapes.

Famous examples come to mind: Evgeny Zamyatin, who extended contemporary reality to its fantastical logical conclusion. Mikhail Bulgakov, who inserted the fantastic world of the Devil into modern materialistic Soviet reality. Boris Pilnyak, who strung together fragments of events that reproduced revolutionary reality and simultaneously obliterated realistic literature. Andrei Platonov, who described the word as operating by abstract Marxist concepts, as conceived by the uneducated revolutionaries of his day. Should we call these revolutionary mindscapes "realistic literature"? How much more fantastic they are than the traditional sort of fantasy, which became old-fashioned and escapist. For example, Aleksandr Grin, who wrote of quirky hobgoblins and demons. Or Aleksei Tolstoy, whose Red spaceship to Mars could have been launched in the nineteenth century.

Realism and fantasy stand opposed to each other, yet intermix. In revolutionary periods a crisis occurs in the relationship. Fantasy invades the realistic mindscape. Or the realistic mindscape fills with fantastic objects. The latter is what we observe in our own, technological revolution, where the speed of change has led to incredible transformations. Standard artistic modes, in seeking to incorporate the new realities of their day, must deal with a host of things that seem fantastical if measured by conventional standards—test-tube babies, surrogate mothers, transsexual operations, mechanical prolongation of life, genetic engineering, and so on. In contrast, the forms we designate as "fantasy" appear routine and dull—pulp "romances," sword and sorcery epics, the all-too-predictable "other worlds" of much science fiction.

Notes

1. The discussion draws on the article of Roman Jakobson, "O khudoz-hestvom realizme" ("On Artistic Realism," 1921), *Selected Writings,* vol. 3 (New York: Mouton, 1981), 722–31.

2. It is actually Leon Trotsky who deserves credit for the "punctuational-ist" theory of evolution. In his article, "Karl Kautsky" (1919), he distinguishes between the long periods of equilibrium, when the laws of natural selection appear imperceptible and the species appear as stable as Platonic ideas, and "epochs of biological crises" when the same laws assert themselves "over the corpses of vegetable and animal species." (Leon Trotsky, *Political Profiles,* trans. by R. Chappell [London: New Park, 1972], 65–66.)

4

Suggestions for a
Typology of Mindscapes
David N. Samuelson

At first glance, "Mindscapes" as a critical concept appears so all-encompassing as to allow few distinctions. All landscapes in verbal or visual art are mental images, selecting and distorting experience, as with Tolkien's "green sun." Landscapes typically are foregrounded for strangeness or mimesis, backgrounded for characterization and symbolism of Higher Truths. Before I seem to be giving in entirely to the argument often made by Frank McConnell that genre distinctions in fiction are largely irrelevant, let me say that I find them inescapable, even within the range of science-fiction prose and film narratives.

Most landscapes in science fiction do not challenge McConnell's thesis; they hardly pretend to be different. Even far off in time, Earth continues to look much the same. Variant plant species may prove time travelers went to Bradbury's past or Wells' future. But each sees land, sky and water, mountains, jungles and deserts, much as they now exist somewhere on this planet (like the settings of the *Star Wars* films). Cityscapes more obviously differ, leaving ruins, reaching new heights of architectural engineering, or doing both side by side (as in *Brazil* and *Bladerunner*), but yesterday's ruins and marvels are also visible today.

At the other extreme in a quasi-Fryean schematic should lie theoretically pure products of imagination, but typical landscapes of fantasy are tamely mimetic, though they may be said to be charged with magic. Visual exceptions come to mind—*Yellow Submarine, Fantastic Planet, The Neverending Story* (originally a novel)—with surrealistic effects denying any reality beyond the artist's imagination.

Landscapes actively employed in that variant of fantasy we call science fiction occupy in-between status, exploiting tensions between the known and the unknown, or between the empirically verifiable and the psychologically projected. The mental construction of literary landscapes is overtly laid out by J. G. Ballard, who clearly leans toward the archetypal. Seeing Earth as an alien planet, he subjects it in his novels to great stresses, both natural and man-made, never letting us escape the perception of landscape by a fallible observer. Because of his ambivalent or ambiguous observers, Ballard's landscapes, though precisely detailed, are nonetheless murky. Murkier still are those of writers proffering landscapes within the mind, usually aided by new technologies. Zelazny's "Dream Master" exploits patients' conventional associations; William Gibson's "cyberspace" has little visual dimension.

Unearthly settings in hard science fiction also tend to resemble Earth, at least enough for us to interact with an alien biosphere. Extreme extensions of familiar forms yield world-girdling cities (Asimov's Trantor) or life forms (vegetable for LeGuin, oceanic for Lem). From astronomy or planetology, writers like Benford, Clement, and Forward derive a base on which to construct alien appearances, both physical and perceptual. However imperfectly known, physics and chemistry also continue to apply, and part of the fun lies in calculating what they allow or require. As for artificial landscapes, man is unquestionably the measure of ships, stations, colonies, even spacefaring civilizations made to order (Zebrowski). Humans may not have made these artifacts within the fictions, but the fictions themselves were made by humans; sun-surrounding rings (Niven), Dyson spheres (Shaw), and endless tubes (Bear) further test the known/unknown iconic border detailed by Gary Wolfe.

Acceptable mindscapes vary with time in hard science fiction, relying as it does on science for local color. As scientists map the brain, we may obtain better fictional approximations from inside of what it looks like and does. Yet the inner space of the body was already familiar enough for Isaac Asimov's novelization to "improve on" the film *Fantastic Voyage*. Mapping the real estate of our solar system affects science-fiction landscapes much more obviously and frequently.

The fictional lunar topography explored by Marjorie Hope Nicholson has been significantly updated. The Venus of John Varley and the later Frederik Pohl is much less habitable than that of earlier stories by Pohl, Heinlein, Anderson, or Weinbaum. Wish-fulfillment obviously permeates Mars in Heinlein as well as in Burroughs and Bradbury. Zelazny may deliberately replay outmoded visions of both worlds, but hard science fiction gravitates toward recent data. Indeed, the growth of information often reduces the scope of speculation, though it may expand its intensity.

Arthur C. Clarke, science fiction's foremost real estate promoter, does not neglect Earth's past, present, or future, but he seems more at home in extraterrestrial settings. His early novels soberly describe Mars, the moon, and space stations, later ones appropriating Titan and the alien vessel Rama. Whereas Ballard uses landscape primarily to characterize observers, however, Clarke uses it to characterize the universe, revealing the sensibility of his narrator (himself?) more indirectly. Landscapes progressively approximating to consensus views of science are especially obvious in the two Space Odyssey books/films (*2061* is not in the same direct line).

2001 goes outward as well as forward in time from veldt to space station to Moon to Saturn (Jupiter in the film), through a "star gate" to a world so alien it can only be suggested symbolically. Bringing the alien closer to home, *2010* updates the appearance of Jupiter's moons, comparing and contrasting underwater life and death on Earth and on Europa. The face of Jupiter is even changed by the distant aliens of the first story as they elevate it from its proto-star status, in order to cultivate and protect the nearby aliens of the sequel. As they grow increasingly mimetic, however, Clarke's landscapes continue to symbolize Higher Truth, suggesting simultaneously the strangeness of the universe and the ability of human beings to incorporate it into their framework of significance.

Biographical Notes
Index

Biographical Notes

POUL ANDERSON is a Hugo- and Nebula-winning author and one of the great creators of mindscapes in science fiction.

JEAN-PIERRE BARRICELLI is Professor of Comparative Literature at the University of California, Riverside. His most recent book, *Melopoesis,* is about music and literature, and was published by New York University Press.

MAX P. BELIN is a freelance writer currently living in Los Angeles.

GREGORY BENFORD is Professor of Physics at the University of California, Irvine, and the author of *Against Infinty* and *Artifact.*

DAVID BRIN is an astrophysicist and award-winning author of *The Postman* and *The Uplift War.*

MICHAEL R. COLLINGS is Professor of English at Pepperdine University and has published widely on Stephen King and science fiction.

PETER FITTING is Professor of French at the University of Toronto and writes on fiction and film.

DONALD M. HASSLER is Professor of English at Kent State University and an eighteenth-century scholar.

RONALD J. HECKELMAN teaches English and rhetoric at Rice University.

GARY KERN is a Soviet scholar and noted translator. His most recent book is *Zamyatin's "We": A Collection of Critical Essays* and he is currently working on a study of defectors.

BILL LEE is Professor of English at Sonoma State University.

WILLIAM LOMAX is completing his Ph.D. degree work at the University of California, Los Angeles.

REINHART LUTZ is a Ph.D. candidate in English at the University of California, Santa Barbara.

FRANK MCCONNELL is Professor of English at the University of California, Santa Barbara. He had a Fulbright grant for East Germany in 1988.

JOSEPH D. MILLER is a senior research scientist in the Department of Biology at Stanford University.

WENDY DONIGER O'FLAHERTY is Mircea Eliade Professor of the History of Religions at the University of Chicago. Her latest book is *Other Peoples' Myths,* published by Macmillan in 1988.

ERIC S. RABKIN is Professor of English at the University of Michigan. He is the author of *The Fantastic in Literature.*

JAMES ROMM is Assistant Professor of Classics at Cornell University and is working on a book on fantasy and travel narratives.

DAVID N. SAMUELSON is Professor of English at California State University, Long Beach.

GEORGE E. SLUSSER is Curator of the J. Lloyd Eaton Collection and Adjunct Professor at the University of California, Riverside. He is currently working on a study of new French science fiction to be published by Southern Illinois University Press.

PASCAL J. THOMAS graduated from the Ecole Normale Supérieure, has a Ph.D. degree in mathematics from the University of California, Los Angeles, and teaches at the Université de Toulouse.

JACK G. VOLLER teaches English at Southern Illinois University at Edwardsville.

GARY WESTFAHL teaches Reading at the University of California, Riverside.

Index